The
BOOK
WORM
CRUSH

LISA
BROWN
ROBERTS

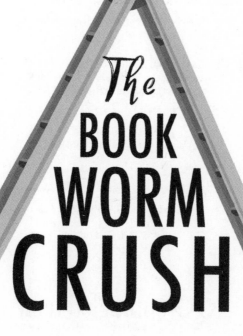

The
BOOK
WORM
CRUSH

Entangled Publishing, LLC
2614 South Timberline Road
Suite 105, PMB 159
Fort Collins, CO 80525
rights@entangledpublishing.com

Entangled Teen is an imprint of Entangled Publishing, LLC.

Visit our website at www.entangledpublishing.com.

Edited by Liz Pelletier, Heather Howland, and Lydia Sharp
Cover Illustrated by Elizabeth Turner Stokes
Interior design by Toni Kerr

ISBN 978-1-64063-707-8
Ebook ISBN 978-1-64063-646-0

Manufactured in the United States of America
First Edition October 2019

10 9 8 7 6 5 4 3 2 1

entangled teen
an imprint of Entangled Publishing LLC

To *The Replacement Crush* readers who
asked for Toff and Amy's story
—and waited so patiently—
this one's for you!

CHAPTER ONE

*A*my McIntyre darted anxious glances up and down Shady Cove's Main Street to make sure she was alone. On any other night, she'd bask in the cozy glow cast by the old-fashioned streetlamps. Tonight, however, she wished for Professor McGonagall's magic wand to douse the lights.

Amy wasn't a troublemaker or a rule breaker, yet here she was, creeping around in the dark after curfew, defiling public property. She swallowed a nervous giggle. Not defiling, more like…enhancing.

Wait.

What was that sound?

Footsteps?

Or her hyped-up imagination?

Kneeling on the ground next to one of the repurposed surfboard benches that dotted Main Street, Amy worked quickly to ensure her secret project wouldn't blow away, her fingers fumbling as she struggled to tighten the final knot.

Done.

She jumped up and slung her backpack over her shoulders, anxious to escape before someone caught her.

Crash!

An explosion froze her in place. Was that glass? A burglar

breaking into a shop? Adrenaline crackling through her veins like lightning, she told herself to breathe. It was probably nothing, but she needed to *move*. She took a shaky step backward out of the streetlamp's glow.

A police siren wailed much too close for comfort.

She'd snuck out of her house to make secret preparations for tomorrow's Instagram post for a contest she was entering. The last thing she'd expected was to encounter actual danger — or the cops. Her anxiety skyrocketed. Was the cop after the glass breaker? Or had someone seen her skulking around and called 911?

Unlike Cammie Morgan, the heroine of the Gallagher Girls, her favorite spy book series, Amy had not planned an escape route. She had no plan A, let alone a plan B. Why hadn't she thought this through better? This was why her best friend, Viv, always did the planning.

Heart pounding, she scanned the street for bad guys or, better yet, Jason Bourne squealing up to the curb in a vintage MINI Cooper to rescue her.

Hold up.

She didn't need a hero to swoop in to save the day. Escape plan or not, she could save herself. She hoped.

After taking a deep, calming breath, she dashed down the street, hoping whoever broke the glass wasn't chasing her.

Thankfully, she'd dressed in all black. She tried to keep to the shadows as her feet pounded the pavement like empire-crushing Katniss Everdeen from *The Hunger Games* and Cammie Morgan combined into one fierce warrior. Or so she imagined…until she tripped over an abandoned skateboard and it sent her sprawling. Her backpack flew off her shoulder, spewing its contents all over the ground.

Crappity crap.

She scrambled to gather the yarn scraps, loose sketch

papers, and colored pencils scattered across the sidewalk. The siren wailed louder, closing in.

Ugh. What had she been thinking, sneaking out after curfew on her secret mission? She should've known it wouldn't end well. She was a bookworm, not a daredevil.

A bookworm about to be busted by the law.

Double crap.

*T*off Nichols was bored. Check that — he was restless. Antsy. Confused. That's what happened when your forever-single dad announced he was getting married. To your childhood best friend's mom.

"Weird," Toff muttered to no one. "It's too freaking weird."

He sat in his old VW van, parked on a quiet, dark corner at the far end of Shady Cove's Main Street. It was after midnight, and not much was happening in the sleepy beach town. He cranked up the volume on his speakers, the pounding beat of his favorite surfing playlist filling the van. He took a swig of his energy drink, even though he didn't need any extra adrenaline — his natural energy level was high enough.

What he needed was to think. To wrap his head around the idea that his dad was getting hitched. And not to just anyone — to Viv's mom.

"I know you understand, Toff," his dad had said. They'd sat in rickety deck chairs, watching the sun set over the sliver of ocean they could see from their house. "You'll be a senior this fall, then leaving for college in a year. It's time for me to take the next step in my life, and that's to marry Rose."

He sighed. His mom had died nine years ago; it wasn't like his dad was cheating. Toff flipped down the visor where he'd pinned an old photo of his mom and him. He was about six years old, building a sandcastle on the beach, his mom kneeling with him in the sand, laughing, her blond hair blowing in the wind. She looked so happy. So healthy.

He flipped up the visor, his chest squeezing like an invisible hand had grabbed ahold of his heart.

It wasn't that he didn't like Rose. He did—a lot. Her daughter, Viv, was already like his sister. They'd bonded in kindergarten and stayed close through high school, even though he was all about surfing and Viv was a super nerd and obsessed with books. Plus she was dating Dallas, one of his best friends, so he got to torture her even more, which he enjoyed.

"Whatever," he muttered. "It's cool. It's fine." But the idea of his dad remarrying didn't *feel* fine, for reasons he couldn't nail down.

A sudden flash of movement caught his eye. A silhouetted figure darted in and out of the streetlights. As the person came closer, he could tell it was a girl, long hair streaming behind her as she ran. His muscles tensed. This wasn't a late-night jog. She was running like she was being chased.

And then she tripped, and Toff's stomach bottomed out. *Shit.*

He started the engine and hit the gas.

𝒯ires squealed at the curb, and bright headlights exposed Amy like she was under a spotlight. Her stomach pitched as she scrabbled on the ground, stuffing the last of her scattered items into her backpack.

Yep. She was doomed.

She squinted in the headlights' glare. This was it—her ride to the slammer. Should she put her hands up like they did in the movies? How much did handcuffs hurt, anyway? Her parents were going to freak when they were called down to the police station.

"Amy! Get up!"

Whoa. How did the cop know her name? Slowly, she staggered to her feet, commanding her brain to kick into gear. She blinked away the headlights' glare and focused on the vehicle. No flashing blue and red lights. The siren wail was closer, but it wasn't coming from this car.

This *van*, she corrected herself. This one-of-a-kind Scooby-Doo-style surf van that anyone in town would recognize.

Holy crapoli. It wasn't Jason Bourne to the rescue—it was Toff Nichols, the surf god of Shady Cove and the lustful object of her 100-percent-unrequited crush.

Toff jumped out of the van and ran toward her like he was an action-movie hero, then skidded to a stop and grasped her shoulders, his sky-blue eyes blazing with intensity.

"Are you okay?" His gaze darted up and down the street, then back to her.

Crash!

They both jumped as the sound ricocheted off the storefronts.

"Come on!" Toff grabbed her backpack from the ground, and they ran to the van. He yanked the passenger door open and practically shoved her inside, then ran around to the driver's side and hopped in, brushing his messy, sun-streaked hair out of his face.

Amy struggled to breathe. If she had to be rescued, he was the perfect guy to do it, even if it was embarrassing.

Unlike her, Toff wasn't afraid of anything.

...

"Talk to me, Ames. Are you okay?"

Toff stared into the wide, panicked eyes of Amy McIntyre, Viv's book-nerd friend. Amy stared back, her amber gaze locked on his, but she didn't speak. His gut clenched at the thought of anything bad happening to her. A siren wailed, sounding like it was headed straight for them. He glanced out the windshield, scanning the street for trouble, but he didn't see anything.

Amy blinked up at him like a robot that had just powered on. "I, um, I'm not hurt. I'm okay." Her voice wobbled. "I heard a crash and...panicked." She sucked in a breath like she couldn't get enough air. "Did you hear it?"

"No." His music had been cranked too loud to hear anything else. "Was someone chasing you?"

He fixated on her pale face framed by that wild red hair that had always caught his attention. Even though they were safe in his van, his body was taut, muscles coiled and ready to spring into action. Thank God he'd gotten to her before some jackass did. Not that he wouldn't have happily kicked the guy's ass.

"I don't know. Like I said, I panicked." She glanced away, her cheeks turning pink.

The siren's whine pierced the air, making him wince.

"You were smart to run," Toff said. "The cops are after somebody."

"I know," she said, her voice barely above a whisper. She met his gaze. "I think they're after me."

Toff blinked. Did he have swimmer's ear? No way did she say what he thought he heard.

Suddenly the spinning red and blue lights of a cop car lit

up the inside of Toff's van from behind. The siren whooped twice, then went silent.

Amy clutched his forearm. "Will you help me out, Toff? Please? Just, um, pretend you've been with me tonight or something. Okay?" She glanced down at her hand on his arm and yanked it away like he'd burned her.

He had no trouble understanding her this time. "The cops are really after *you*?" That didn't make sense. She was the most straight-and-narrow girl he knew next to Viv.

"I think so." She bit her lip, glancing over her shoulder and out the back windows. Toff checked the rearview mirror. The cop was still in his car, probably running the plates.

"Please, Toff? I'll owe you for the rest of my life." Amy gave him a pleading look that punched him in the gut.

What had she been up to? Whatever it was, he wasn't about to turn her over to the po-po. Amy was one of Viv's best friends, automatically putting her into his sphere of protection. Not to mention she'd probably never even jaywalked, let alone done anything that would get her arrested.

She'd never survive a good cop/bad cop interrogation. She'd break like a cheap boogie board, confessing to something she didn't even do. She'd end up in jail, which she was way too sweet to handle. She'd turn into a hardened, angry shell of her former self, covered in ugly face tats, trading cigarettes for ink. Yeah, she might be released early for good behavior, but she'd never be the same.

And it would be all his fault.

Okay, so *maaaybe* he'd binged too many episodes of that show about innocent people sent to prison. And maybe the show had freaked him out.

Whatever.

He locked eyes with her, willing her to trust him. "Don't worry, Ames. I've got this."

As he turned to face the sheriff approaching his side of the van, a welcome surge of adrenaline shot through him. He lived for the rush, and this was going to be a good one.

The sheriff, a lean, fit guy who looked like he could easily chase down criminals, peered inside Toff's window, doing a sweep of the van with his flashlight. "What are you two up to this fine summer evening? You realize curfew was two hours ago, right? Unless you're both eighteen." He cocked a skeptical eyebrow, then pointed the flashlight at Toff's face, making Toff squint and shield his eyes with his hand.

California curfews suck. He'd be eighteen in three months, but it wasn't worth arguing with the sheriff. He'd already had to do community service once after being busted. He wasn't doing that again, and neither was Amy.

"Good evening, Officer Hernandez," Toff said, reading the embroidered name on the sheriff's uniform. He reached out to give Amy's knee a reassuring squeeze. "My girl and I were just, you know, enjoying some quality time together." He lowered his voice to a confidential whisper. "Just the two of us, if you get my drift. Guess we lost track of time."

The sheriff trained his flashlight on Amy. Toff could hear her breathing fast and shallow. *Chill, Ames*, he wanted to say, *I've got this.* Instead, he squeezed her knee again, hoping she'd get the message to play along.

"Young lady, I notice you're wearing all black." The sheriff lowered his flashlight and peered at her. "Any particular reason?"

"Uh, n-not really."

Wincing at the uncertain wobble in her voice, Toff upped his game. "It's okay, babe." He winked at her. "We can tell him." When he saw panic flare in her eyes, he turned back to the sheriff. He'd have to handle this solo. Amy had obviously never faked her way out of trouble before, unlike him.

"See, her dad's not exactly a fan of mine, so she had to sneak out of the house to meet me. I told her to wear black so she wouldn't get busted." Toff flashed his most charming grin. "You know what it's like when you want to be with your girl, but her parents don't approve, right, Officer Hernandez? Like Romeo and Juliet."

Next to him, Amy coughed. Was she choking? Alarmed, he glanced at her. She waved one hand frantically in front of her face, coughing into her other hand. He grabbed his energy drink from the cupholder and handed it to her. If she *had* done something crazy enough to get the cops' attention, she needed to work on her game face.

"We'll leave now, sir," Toff said. "I'll take her straight home."

Officer Hernandez clicked off his flashlight and crossed his arms over his chest, studying them through narrowed eyes. Toff moved his hand up Amy's leg, searching for her hand so he could squeeze it to reassure her and to convince the cop they were a couple. Her whole body stiffened under his touch, and he immediately felt like a jerk. He dropped his hand to the gearshift knob.

"Young lady, is this young man your boyfriend or do you need a ride home?"

Wait, what? Toff tensed, struggling to keep his face a neutral mask instead of a glare. This was BS. He'd swooped in to save Amy, not hurt her.

"Yes, sir," Amy whispered. "I mean, I'm here because, um, he's my, uh…" She darted him a nervous glance. Her face transformed from ghost white to tomato red.

Why was she acting so freaky? He totally had her back.

"H-He's my… We're…um…together." Her voice faded away on the last word.

"We're sorry, Officer," Toff said in his best suck-up-to-authority voice.

The sheriff hitched his holster belt higher on his hips. "Okay, then. Let's see some identification from both of you. Insurance and car registration, too."

Toff popped open the glove box for the registration and insurance card, handing them over, then grabbed his wallet from his shorts' pocket. He glanced at her. "Is your wallet in your backpack, babe?"

She shook her head. "I, um, didn't bring it. I just sort of… ran out…when you, um, picked me up."

"What's your name, young lady?" asked the sheriff.

"A-Amy. Amy McIntyre."

"Spell it for me, and tell me your address."

She stuttered out the information while the cop slashed his pen across a notepad. He muttered something under his breath, then headed back to his car.

Toff blew out a breath as soon as he was out of earshot. "Ames, you've gotta work with me. It's okay." He smiled, hoping to reassure her. "He's gonna let us go. Just be cool."

She nodded, her gaze locked on his like she was drowning and he was her life preserver. If they were a real couple, he'd pull her into a hug. But they weren't.

A twinge of guilt poked at his gut.

"Sorry about the PDA," he said. "Just trying to convince the cop. I promise I won't do it again."

"It's okay. I know you were pretending." A flicker of emotion flashed in her eyes, but it was gone before he could identify it.

He glanced in the rearview mirror and saw the sheriff talking into his radio. What the heck had Amy done? "You've gotta tell me what you were up to, Ames." He stared deep into her eyes, determined to make her spill her secret.

She shrugged, her pale skin lit up by the red and blue

lights flashing through the van's back windows. "Later." Her voice was barely a whisper. "After he leaves."

Toff scrutinized her, searching for evidence of criminal activity, starting with her feet. Black Chucks instead of boots that could hide knives or throwing stars. She looked like normal Amy, except for the all-black yoga pants and sweatshirt instead of her usual colorful outfits. His inspection moved to her hair and lingered. Red curls tumbled messily over her shoulders. Something was different tonight. What was it?

"No sparkles!" He grinned, proud of his excellent observation skills.

Amy's forehead pinched like he'd said something stupid, but he knew he was right. She always wore sparkly stuff in her hair. One time she'd done this Princess Leia cinnamon-roll hairdo and stuck chopsticks in her hair, with fake jewels dangling from them. He'd joked about borrowing them for sushi. She hadn't laughed.

"Smart move." He tilted his chin in approval. "You would've been spotted in the dark if your hair lit up like bicycle reflectors."

She scowled. "I don't wear bike reflectors in my *hair*, Toff." She touched her hair self-consciously.

"Mr. Nichols."

Toff jumped, startled by the sheriff's voice at his window.

"This isn't your first curfew violation." Officer Hernandez raised an eyebrow. "Technically, I should ticket you." He glanced at Amy. "Both of you."

• • •

*A*my's night was spiraling out of control.

Of course Toff had prior curfew violations.

Who would've thought prepping for a bookworm social media contest would spin off the rails? Running from the cops—and maybe a burglar—and being rescued by her secret crush was stressful enough, but now she was getting busted *because* of him?

She never should have left the cozy comfort of her bedroom and bookshelves, but she'd wanted to surprise Viv with a cool project for their first-round contest entry.

Next to her, Toff squirmed restlessly as the sheriff stared him down. Could she get them out of this somehow? Maybe up her fake girlfriend game? Pull a Lara Jean from *To All the Boys I've Loved Before* and kiss him?

Um, no.

But maybe a little more PDA would convince the sheriff they weren't criminals. Sucking in a deep breath, she scooted closer to Toff on the bench seat. He glanced down, clearly surprised.

"Put your arm around me," she whispered, ignoring her internal rule follower, who was having a meltdown.

"You sure?"

She nodded and Toff complied, draping an arm around her shoulder and pulling her in close. *Whoa.* Toff was holding her. For real. She swore she could feel sunshine on his skin, dissipating her goose bumps.

"Teenagers," the sheriff grumbled.

Toff casually wound one of her curls around his finger like they did this all the time. Omigod. Was this how Lara Jean felt when Peter Kavinsky stuck his hand in her back pocket? Taking another deep breath, she tentatively placed her hand on Toff's chest and smiled up at him. *Thump. Thump.* His heartbeat was slow and steady, unlike hers, which was banging around in her chest like a wild monkey.

Officer Hernandez pinned them with a fierce bad-cop stare. "I'll let you go with a warning. Believe it or not, I remember what it's like to be young and in love." He cocked a bushy warning eyebrow. "But if I catch you after curfew again, Mr. Nichols, it's a ticket. I won't care how *distracted* you were."

The sheriff's radio squawked, most of it in coded numbers and words Amy didn't understand, but she froze when she heard "Code 594." Officer Hernandez stepped away from the van, spouting back his own secret code response.

"Way to fake it, Ames," Toff said, admiration threading his voice. "I didn't think you had it in you." He extricated his finger from her hair and loosened his grip, but he kept his arm around her shoulders. "We can leave as soon as he gives me back my papers."

She said nothing, her gaze tracking the sheriff. Her heart was still doing a drum solo, but not just because of Toff.

"Amy? You okay?"

"What if he arrests me?" she whispered, turning to face him. "He said code 594. That's the code for vandalism. What if there was a witness?"

Toff blinked at her, then swallowed, his Adam's apple sliding up and down.

"You've gotta tell me what you did." He glanced at the sheriff, who was pacing, still on his radio. "It's the only way I can help you." He flashed her a quick grin. "Whatever you did, I've probably done worse."

"I… It's ridiculous. You'll laugh when I tell you."

"I won't, I swear. Shredder's honor." He flipped her an exaggerated shaka wave. "I'm an expert at this stuff. Let me help."

Amy sighed. Despite the near disaster with his prior curfew violation, if anyone could get her out of this, it was

Toff. He'd pulled off tons of pranks and stunts over the years with hardly any consequences, because almost everyone fell under his blue-eyed, sweet-talking spell.

She steeled herself for his reaction. "I was…yarn bombing."

He gaped at her. "Did you say…bomb?" His voice rose an octave on the last word.

"Shh! It wasn't a *bomb* bomb," she hissed, darting a glance at Officer Hernandez. "It was a yarn bomb. I knitted a bunch of flowers and tied them to a bench on Main Street—"

"Whoa." He put up a hand. *"Knitted?"*

She nodded, eyeing him warily. This was the part where he laughed hysterically at her nerdy granny hobby. "You promised you wouldn't laugh."

He ran a hand through his messy hair and grinned, his eyes flickering with amusement. "So you're a threat to national security? I'm harboring a fugitive in my van?" He tilted his head toward the back seat. "Are there weapons in your backpack? Knitting sticks that explode?"

She huffed with indignation. "*Needles.* They're called needles, not sticks." There were legit reasons she preferred book boyfriends over real-life boys, even this boy. "And it was for a contest."

Toff grinned down at her. "You need to chill, Ames. No way is yarn bombing a crime."

"Technically it is. Kniffiti, sort of like graffiti."

"Kniff-*what*-i?"

She could sense the laughter building inside him like a teakettle about to whistle. She peeked out the window. Officer Hernandez scribbled on his ticket pad. *Crud.* This was no time for joking.

"He's writing me up!" Amy clutched Toff's arm. "I'm going to jail like Jean Valjean in *Les Mis*!"

He darted a quick glance at the sheriff, then faced her,

his expression determined. "I don't know who this John dude is, but you're *not* going to jail." Curiosity flickered in his eyes. "What kind of contest turns sweet, innocent Amy into a fugitive on the run from the cops?"

Sweet, innocent Amy? That didn't sound like a compliment, coming from him. "You wouldn't understand."

"Try me."

She shook her head, eyes widening in panic as the sheriff strode quickly to the van. Toff followed her gaze, then pulled her in close, back to fake boyfriend mode. Officer Hernandez tore a piece of paper off his ticket pad and handed it to Toff, who took it reluctantly. Amy stifled a whimper, keenly aware that Toff's arm had tightened protectively around her shoulders.

"Official warning, Mr. Nichols. Remember what I said. Next time it's a ticket."

Relief for Toff washed over Amy, but when the sheriff focused his dark, criminal-detecting eyes on her, relief was replaced by terror.

This was it. She was headed straight for the slammer.

"We had a report of someone dressed in black causing trouble earlier tonight," Officer Hernandez said. "Knocking over trash cans, breaking glass." His penetrating gaze swept over her, then Toff. Panic skittered up Amy's spine.

Officer Hernandez shrugged. "Turns out it was just a couple of rampaging raccoons."

Wait, *what*? Her body was so jacked up on adrenaline, she struggled to process his words.

"Wow," said Toff, his voice choking slightly on the word. "We'll be careful. Those little bastards are mean."

Was he…trembling? Shivering? Amy snuck a peek. He was laughing, the jerk. Silently, yeah, but definitely laughing, holding a closed fist to his mouth.

"Time for you two to skedaddle." Officer Hernandez pointed at Toff. "No stops along the way."

Toff nodded, apparently unable to speak. After the sheriff headed back to his car, Toff rolled up his window and let loose, laughter gusting out of him in waves.

A cascade of emotions swirled through Amy like a tornado—relief, embarrassment, surprise—none of which compared to the overwhelming mortification of sharing the scariest, weirdest night of her life...with Toff.

CHAPTER TWO

"**I** saw who dropped you off last night."

Amy froze mid-step in the hallway outside her bedroom. Slowly, she lowered her phone, pausing her attempt to formulate a coherent text to Viv about last night that wouldn't lead to a tornado of text replies. Reluctantly, she turned to face Brayden, her eleven-year-old brother, who grinned like he'd just found out he never had to go to school again.

"You were dreaming," she whispered as they hovered in the hallway. Toff had dropped her off, but the house had been dark and she'd assumed everyone was asleep when she snuck in and tiptoed to her bedroom.

She'd assumed wrong.

The tantalizing aroma of coffee wafted from the kitchen. She'd had a tough time falling asleep last night and needed caffeine. Her brain kept replaying the night's events over and over like a song stuck on repeat, her stomach twisting with anxiety when she imagined the sheriff dragging her off to jail.

Amy needed to suck down a vat of coffee, then get to Murder by the Sea, the bookstore Viv's mom owned. She had to get to Viv before Toff did and tell the story her way, downplaying the crazy stuff. Toff and Viv were as tight as sibs, and he wouldn't hold back any gory details about raccoons or the sheriff…or pretending to be her boyfriend.

"I wasn't dreaming." Brayden took a step closer. "If you want me to keep quiet about Toff, we need to negotiate."

"Toff?" She blinked innocently, hoping she could fake out her brother like she had the sheriff. "I don't know what you're talking about. I was in bed by ten o'clock last night."

She wished it were true. After Toff finally stopped laughing about the raccoons, the ride home had been painfully awkward. She'd tried to act normal but failed, babbling about books while Toff listened—or tuned her out. It was hard to tell with him. She wasn't sure who was more relieved when they reached her house, Toff or her.

"Liar." Brayden's gaze narrowed suspiciously, even as the hint of a grin formed at the corner of his mouth. "What were you doing in his van? Past midnight? You know Mom and Dad will freak if they find out."

She tensed. He was right. Their parents were pretty chill, but she was supposed to introduce them to guys she dated. Last night wasn't a date—far from it—but Brayden didn't know that. If he told her parents that Toff had brought her home, they wouldn't be happy.

"Kids? Come in here and eat!" Mom's voice rang out from the kitchen, startling them both.

Amy grabbed Brayden's arm, dragged him into her bedroom, and closed the door. "Okay, what do you want, Artemis Fowl?"

"Were you and Toff kissing in his van?" Brayden put a closed fist to his mouth and made obnoxious, wet smooching sounds.

"No!" she whisper-yelled. "He just gave me a ride home. As a friend. That's it."

"*After* curfew." Brayden crossed his arms over his chest, his expression smug.

She glanced in the mirror hanging over her dresser to see if she looked as flustered as she felt. She'd styled her hair in a loose twist, accented with sparkly butterfly pins. She'd been surprised when Toff had joked about her "hair reflectors." He didn't seem like the type of guy to notice details like that.

"Mom and Dad will be 'so disappointed' if they find out about Toff." Brayden met her gaze in the mirror, making air quotes around Mom's favorite you're-in-trouble expression.

The top of his head reached her chin. Before she knew it, he'd be towering over her, but she was still the big sister and she needed to rein him in.

"What do you want, Brayden? Money? I'll go as high as ten bucks, but that's my final offer."

"Nope." Brayden shook his head, his grin widening as they stared each other down in the mirror. "Since you're *friends* with Toff, I want you to hook me up with a private surf lesson. He's the best."

"What?" She jerked away from Brayden's reflection to gape at him in 3-D. "I can't… He won't…" No way was she asking Toff a favor for her annoying little brother. That was the type of request only close friends could make. Or a girlfriend.

"I bet he will if you ask him," he persisted. "Sometimes he demos tricks for my posse and me and gives us tips."

She didn't spend nearly as much time at the beach as Brayden did, but she'd witnessed Toff in his Pied Piper role. The kids worshipped him, and he was patient and funny with them, adding more fuel to her fiery crush.

"Your *posse*?" Amy cocked an eyebrow.

"Yeah, my bros. My homies. My peeps. Toff's down with my boys."

She snort-laughed. Her brother was ridiculous.

"He is!" Brayden insisted. "He's cool, when there aren't

any *girls* around." He narrowed his eyes as if this was all her fault. "It stinks when girls show up because he, like, forgets all about us."

Amy didn't doubt that, but Brayden was delirious if he thought she had enough clout with Toff to sweet-talk him into one-on-one surf lessons.

"Maybe he's just tired of you little grommets pestering him."

"I'm not a *grom*," Brayden protested. "I'm almost eleven, and I know how to surf—"

The door flew open. Mom scowled at them, spatula in hand like a palace guard brandishing a weapon, wearing a T-shirt and shorts instead of armor. "What's going on in here?"

United in the face of danger, Amy and Brayden moved to stand shoulder to shoulder. "Nothing," they said in unison.

Mom cocked a warning eyebrow.

"Amy was giving me tips about styling my hair."

Amy coughed, stifling a laugh at his flimsy alibi. Brayden's choppy, short hair was the same red as hers, but that was where the similarity ended. Mom usually had to beg him to wash it, let alone comb it.

"*Riiight,*" Mom said. "And skin-care tips, too, I hope." She pointed her spatula at Brayden. "Like the importance of sunscreen, especially for redheads."

"Exactly." Amy nodded, widening her eyes innocently. Brayden groaned. Not a week went by that their mom didn't trot out what she and Brayden called The Ginger Lecture.

Mom regarded them suspiciously. "I don't know what you two are up to, but I don't have the energy to interrogate you. I'm covering for Natasha in the herbal store today." She pointed her spatula toward the kitchen. "You know we only do fancy breakfast once a week. Time to eat."

Crud. She had forgotten what day it was. She *really* needed to get to the bookstore, but Saturday breakfast was mandatory.

Brayden wiggled around Mom and raced down the hall.

"Where's Dad?" Amy asked. Usually he did the cooking. He was a pastry chef, but he'd lost his job a few months ago.

"He went geocaching with Dallas's parents." Mom tucked a loose hair behind her ear and forced a wan smile. "I gave him a kitchen pass from breakfast today. He needed fresh air, and I needed him to stop baking. I've eaten more desserts these past couple of months than in my whole life."

Dad was passionate about food and had focused all his energy in their kitchen since he'd been laid off. He'd told Amy it was his way of fending off depression, which worried her. She hoped he found a new job soon.

"You feeling okay, sweetie?" Mom lowered her spatula, her brow wrinkling in concern. "You went to bed early last night, especially for a summer Friday night."

"I'm fine," she squeaked, then cleared her throat. "I was just tired."

She didn't like telling lies, but she'd missed curfew only once before—99 percent of the time she was a trouble-free daughter. Though if her mom knew about the trouble she almost got into with Toff last night, she'd probably lock her up like Rapunzel.

And her hair wasn't long enough to make an escape ladder.

"What are you two up to today?" Mom asked as Amy quickly rinsed the breakfast plates in the sink, almost dropping one in her hurry as she moved to stack them in the dishwasher. She needed to blast out of here.

She'd managed to fire off a "be there soon" text to Viv in response to Viv's text of a string of emojis and questions marks, along with a photo of the yarn-bombed bench.

"You need to finish your chores before you go anywhere," Mom said to Brayden.

"Ugh," Brayden groaned. "I have more chores than any of my friends. Trash, recycling, *and* litter box? It's…it's… inhuman."

"True." Amy side-eyed Brayden. "You're much more animal than human. Lazy like a sloth."

He pointed his butter knife at her. "And you're like a cat, creeping around in the middle of the *night*—"

"Just once, I'd like to enjoy a Saturday morning breakfast with my sweet and loving children," Mom interrupted. "Children who happily contribute to the family by doing a few chores."

Brayden clutched his throat and made a gagging noise. Mom winked at Amy. Even though Mom was stressed about Dad being out of work, she liked teasing Brayden, who overreacted to everything.

"I'm hanging out at the bookstore with Viv," Amy said, closing the dishwasher and wiping her hands on a dish towel.

"Great! You can drop me off at the *beach*." Brayden's eyebrows lifted meaningfully. "So I can *surf*."

"No way." The last thing she needed was to delay her arrival to the bookstore and risk encountering Toff at the beach.

"Not so fast, Bray," Mom said. "Chores first. And you need to walk Goldilocks."

Their sleepy golden retriever thumped her tail on the floor under the kitchen table.

"B-But that's not—"

"Don't you dare say the F-word, Brayden," Mom warned.

Amy giggled, because in their house the F-word was "fair."

"What about Amy's chores?" Brayden protested.

"I'm done." She grabbed her backpack from the coatrack. If her brother would just *do* stuff instead of whining, his life would be so much easier.

"See you later," she said, backing out of the kitchen.

"Honey, can you pick up Brayden at the beach later today?" Mom asked. "I'll drop him off on my way to the herbal store."

Amy frowned. She wasn't in the mood to be Brayden's Uber driver.

Mom unleashed her guilt-inducing sigh, and Amy gave in easily, like she always did.

"Fine." She pointed at Brayden. "But you have to leave when I say so. And no harassing other surfers for lessons." She couldn't handle any more embarrassment when it came to Toff.

Her brother rolled his eyes. "Whatever."

"Tell Natasha hi for me," Amy said, grabbing the car keys from the hook.

Brayden squished his lips into another exaggerated kiss as she left the kitchen, but she ignored him.

As she drove away, she cringed, mentally reliving her pathetic attempt at fake PDA with Toff. She pressed on the gas, hoping Toff was still out surfing with the dawn patrol instead of swinging by the bookstore to entertain Viv with his version of kniffiti gone bad. If she was lucky, she could completely avoid him for the rest of the summer and pretend kniffiti night never happened.

CHAPTER THREE

*A*my flushed with pride when she saw people taking photos of her yarn-bombed bench on Main Street. In the light of day, the multicolored knitted squares glowed, along with the bright-orange crocheted poppies wrapped around the bench arms. She wanted to take her Instagram photos, but talking to Viv was her first priority.

She wasn't surprised to see Dallas's Vespa scooter parked in front of the bookstore. Until he left for college in August, he and Amy had to share custody of Viv. Luckily, Viv never played favorites between her best friend and her boyfriend.

Amy entered the store, the bells strung on the door announcing her arrival.

"Hey, girl!" Viv's deep brown eyes sparkled with excitement as she came out from behind the counter. She wore a *Major League Reading* T-shirt and jeans that fit her curvy figure perfectly. "Looks like you did something sneaky in the middle of the night," Viv said. "Something you forgot to tell me about, involving needles and yarn."

She glanced around the store, worried about eavesdroppers, but no one was there except Dallas, who emerged from the sci-fi and fantasy aisle, smiling at Amy from behind his hipster black-framed glasses. He wore his usual outfit—shorts and a nerdy T-shirt. Today's shirt said, *Never trust an atom. They make up everything.*

"I didn't forget," Amy said to Viv. "I knew you'd see the bench this morning, and I wanted to surprise you." *And impress you*, she thought, crossing her fingers in hopes Toff would stay far, far away from the bookstore today.

"It was a great surprise," Viv said, grinning broadly. "Nice homage to Lucinda, by the way. Those poppies match her new book cover exactly. It's perfect for the first contest challenge."

Amy flushed with pride and relief. Maybe she could salvage last night after all. Maybe Toff would keep his mouth shut. Maybe he wanted to pretend it never happened, too.

Viv's grin turned devious. "I'm glad you survived your yarn-bombing adventure." She twisted a glossy brown curl around her finger, blinking innocently. "Police, bomb threats. Sharp weapons."

"And a rescue by some dude in a van." Dallas drummed his fingers on the counter and smirked. "From rabid raccoons."

Ugh. Air whooshed out of her as she deflated like a popped balloon. Toff had gotten to Viv first after all. And he'd blabbed to Dallas, too.

"Why didn't you text me? Or call me?" Viv demanded.

"I didn't want to interrupt your date night with a bunch of freak-out texts." Besides, deconstructing last night was an in-person, full-bowl-of-M&M's conversation. "I hoped Toff wouldn't be a blabbermouth," Amy grumbled. She sank into an overstuffed chair in the cozy reading circle and dug her yarn and needles out of her backpack. Knitting was her stress relief.

"He only told me," Dallas said, still smirking. "And I told Viv. Accidentally. I assumed you'd already told her."

"Flipper can't keep a secret to save his life," Viv said with a shrug.

Dallas nodded. "He's worse than any girl I know."

"Hey! Don't be sexist." Viv smacked Dallas playfully on his shoulder. He didn't flinch, looking at her like she was the sun and he was Icarus, though Amy knew Dallas was smart enough to swerve before his wings burst into flames.

"Does the whole town know?" she asked Dallas.

"No one else knows you two pulled a Bonnie and Clyde." He grinned. "That's what Toff called your escape from the cops."

Amy blinked, pausing her knitting. "He did?"

"Honestly, I'm shocked he even knows who they are," Viv said.

"Hey, no smack talk," Dallas protested. "He's smarter than he lets on."

Amy and Viv shared a look. It was cute to watch Dallas defend the other half of his bromance. They'd secretly dubbed Toff and Dallas their favorite BROTP, followed closely by all of Chris Hemsworth's bromances, which were legion.

The bell on the door jingled, and the topic of conversation walked in, making Amy's pulse stutter.

So much for avoiding him the rest of the summer.

Toff flashed a grin. "Oh, hey, Ames. I didn't know you'd be here." He juggled three plastic cups. "You can have my smoothie if you want. I can grab another one."

"No thanks. I already had breakfast." She was proud of herself for sounding casual. Even though she was annoyed with Toff for blabbing, her heart had melted into a puddle of sparkles when he offered her his smoothie.

That was the problem with crushes—they weren't rational. Rational was Dallas's forte, not hers. She was a romantic, through and through.

Toff handed a smoothie to Viv and another to Dallas, then parked himself in the chair next to Amy. If she wanted to reach out and touch him, she could. Which she would *not*.

He gestured to her knitting project and slanted her a wicked grin. "You getting ready for another brush with the law, Bonnie? I don't know about you, but I had freaky nightmares about gangster raccoons coming at me with knitting sticks." His grin deepened, showcasing his dimples. "I Googled 'kniffiti.' You can get twenty years to life for that shit." He tilted his cup toward her in a mock salute. "Hard-core, Ames. *Hard. Core.*"

So much for her sparkly puddle of crush goo. Right now she wanted to stab him with her knitting needles.

"Shut up, Flipper," Viv snapped. "Amy's bench is awesome. All you did was drive the getaway van. She's the artist."

Toff rolled his eyes at Viv, then aimed his full-power wattage at Amy again. "The bench looks great. I already selfied with it." He made exaggerated air quotes. "Hashtag Raccoon Rebel. Hashtag Bonnie and Clyde."

Was he mocking her or just having fun? Amy's cheeks burned, but she stiffened her spine, determined not to be rendered mute by a pair of sky-blue eyes and dimples so deep she could stash an M&M in each one. "You forgot Hashtag Curfews Are for Losers. *Clyde.*"

Everyone laughed, Toff the loudest of all.

"You never told me what type of contest you almost went to jail for," he said, a challenging smirk quirking his lips. "If you win, you should split the cash with me, since I saved you from the slammer."

"It's not that type of contest," Amy said, frustration and embarrassment battling for top position. "No cash prize."

Toff tilted his head, frowning slightly. "What's the prize, then? A trophy? Like gold knitting sticks or whatever?"

Amy shot him an eye roll. She wasn't used to this much attention from Toff, especially in a twelve-hour span, but right now she was more annoyed than twitterpated. "The prize is an interview with my favorite author, Lucinda Amorrato."

Toff blinked. "What?"

She bit her lip, reluctant to go into details he'd just tease her about. "Lucinda's publisher is having a social media contest. There are three challenges, and anyone can enter. Lucinda picks the winner, who gets to meet her. I'm posting a photo of the bench for the first one."

Assuming she went through with entering the contest. She was starting to doubt herself. If she couldn't pull off preparations for challenge one without a rescue, how could she possibly complete the other challenges? Thankfully, she had Viv. Amy would gladly let her take over the planning.

Toff chewed on his smoothie straw, then spoke around it. "So Lucinda's, what? An extreme knitter? And that's why you yarn bombed the bench? The best knitter wins?"

Amy gaped at him, and Viv heaved an extra-loud sigh. "Don't strain your brain, Flipper. It's a bookworm thing. You wouldn't understand."

Toff shot Viv a stink eye.

"What's everyone doing today?" Dallas asked. He tossed a hacky sack at Toff, who broke his stare down with Viv to catch it. Amy smiled at Dallas, grateful for his obvious attempt to change the subject.

"Working," Viv said with a resigned sigh as Hiddles, her cranky cat named after Tom Hiddleston, snaked around Dallas's ankles. Hiddles hated everyone except Dallas.

"Surfing." Toff stretched out his muscled, tanned legs, and Amy tried not to stare. "I hit the waves early this morning, but I'll go back out again soon. I need to train for the Summer Spectacular if I want to win."

Dallas snorted. "Didn't you already win it three times?"

Toff shrugged. "Why stop at three?"

"We need a box to stuff your ego in." Viv shook her head in fake disgust. "Now that I'm about to become your sister, I'm allowed to harass you even more."

The grin disappeared from Toff's face.

Amy's hands froze mid–purl stitch. "Wait, what?"

"What Viv said," Toff said flatly.

Viv frowned at him. "Hey. You okay, Flipper?" She sank onto the cozy, worn love seat across from Toff, and Dallas joined her.

Toff blinked and cleared his throat. "I'm good. Just, you know, adjusting to the idea of having to actually be related to you, Wordworm." He smiled, but it was forced.

Amy could tell, since she'd spent a lot of time analyzing his smiles over the years.

"I think it's awesome," Dallas said. "Your dad and Viv's mom are great together."

Amy gaped at Viv. "Wait. Your mom's getting married?" She glanced at Toff. "To your dad?"

"Yep. I'm stuck with Wordworm forever."

She took a minute to process this news. She knew about their parents dating, but marriage? *Wow.* "When did this happen?"

"I just found out last night." Viv glanced at Toff. "Apparently they decided to tell us at the same time. Separately."

Toff nodded. "My dad bribed me with a grilled steak."

Dallas laughed, but his eyebrows knotted when Toff didn't join in.

"You're okay with this, right?" Viv asked Toff. "You ignored my royal wedding meme texts this morning. I mean, it's obvious they're gaga over each other. It's kind of embarrassing, really."

Toff shrugged. "Yeah. It just surprised me."

Amy could tell he was hiding something. "When's the wedding?" she asked.

"They're waiting until next fall," Toff said.

"My mom said they wanted to give us time to get used to the idea." Viv shrugged. "They spend every weekend together, so it won't be much different." She shot Toff a grin. "And this way we don't have to live together senior year and fight over chores."

Toff smirked at Viv. "That would've sucked, especially because I'm never touching a litter box."

"Don't listen to him, Hiddles," Dallas stage-whispered to Viv's cat curled on his lap. "He's a monster."

Amy studied Toff. He was saying the right things and the sexy grin was back in place, but she sensed an unspoken tension. Not toward Viv—she knew he already thought of her as a sister. No, it had to be about the marriage.

Well, she *was* a champion of romance and the official co-leader of the Lonely Hearts Book Club. Maybe she should use her expertise to help.

"I'll be right back." She jumped up and headed for the romance section, which she knew like the back of her hand.

She glanced at the fun romance display shelf she and Viv changed regularly. The current display was summer vacation romance. They'd featured a couple of road trip books and several books with surfer heroes. Amy had picked those and Viv had teased her mercilessly. *Whatever.* They were awesome books.

Amy perused the shelves with books organized by subgenre and author name. She grabbed one of her favorites, a *Sound of Music* retelling featuring a widower hero and the governess who wins his heart. Amy sighed happily. She'd read that book at least three times.

Viv's mom wasn't a governess and they didn't live in the

1820s, but still. The book was amazing, showing the emotional journey of a man who thought he'd never love again. Toff's dad was a widower, so it wasn't totally off base.

She plucked another book off the shelf—*Redo in the Rockies*, a modern story about two people who reconnected at a high school reunion. That might work better, since it was set in a small town like Shady Cove. The hero was a billionaire who'd come home to take care of his sick mom. Toff's dad was a retired pro surfer who made custom surfboards. Amy shrugged. Close enough.

A burst of laughter from the front of the store caught her attention. Dallas was demonstrating martial arts moves with Toff as his victim, trapping him in a headlock.

"Hey, guys, knock it off," Viv said through her laughter. "Customers about to beam aboard."

The guys stopped attacking each other, still laughing. Viv was a *Star Trek* nerd, as was Dallas. Amy smiled, remembering how Viv had won over Dallas in the most adorable, geeky way ever, captured on YouTube for eternity. Three hundred thousand thumbs-up votes didn't lie.

Toff plopped back into his chair as a family with two small children entered the store and Viv hurried to greet them. He grinned at Amy. "I would've beat him if Viv hadn't stopped us."

"In your dreams, dude," Dallas scoffed. Outmaneuvering Dallas was one skill Amy knew Toff didn't have. The two of them had a running bet about who had more trophies: Toff for surfing or Dallas for martial arts.

Amy took a breath, then held out the books. "Here. You should read these."

Toff's eyes widened as he stared at the covers, but he made no move to take the books. He glanced at Dallas, panic flashing across his face.

"If Amy's recommending them, they must be good." Dallas

pushed his glasses up the bridge of his nose. "She and Viv are experts. I would know."

She beamed. Last fall, Dallas had spent weeks designing inventory software for the bookstore and become familiar with the stock, whether he wanted to or not. He'd also accidentally crashed a Lonely Hearts Book Club meeting and gotten a sneak peek into the rabid intensity of romance readers.

"Um, thanks, Ames." Toff blinked at Amy and cleared his throat. "But I don't read novels."

It was true she'd never seen him with a book, and it was also true this was his greatest flaw, as far as she could tell. Well, that and his cockiness, though that was understandable, given his talent. Not reading novels? She'd never get that.

Unfortunately, a lot of the guys she knew didn't read fiction, which bothered her, but if she made that a deal breaker, she'd never date anyone. She took another deep breath and called upon her bookish strength.

"I know you don't read much, but these books are relevant to your situation."

Toff side-eyed the book covers. "I, uh, don't think —" He held a fist to his mouth, just like last night when he'd tried to stuff his laughter.

"Keep selling it, Amy." Dallas sucked through his smoothie straw, then pointed his cup at Toff. "Books save lives."

Amy loved Dallas. Not the way Viv did, of course, but as a friend. He was funny and sweet and smart. Best of all, he read novels—fantasy and sci-fi mostly. A hot nerd, for sure, but nerdy enough Viv had nicknamed him McNerd, which had stuck.

"Dude." Toff rolled his baby blues at Dallas. "Books do not save lives. You might save them with your Jackie Chan moves, but not a book." He glanced at her and shrugged apologetically. "Sorry, Ames, I just don't—"

"I dare you to read one," Amy blurted. Adrenaline spiked her pulse rate. Had she said that out loud? Based on Toff's shocked expression, she had.

Dallas laughed. "I second the dare. Do it, Flipper."

"Please," she said, hoping she didn't sound pathetic. "Just try a few chapters. I promise you'll be hooked."

Toff stared at her, and for once she couldn't decipher his expression.

"Yeah, uh, thanks, but I'll pass." He stood up abruptly. "I've gotta split."

Embarrassed, Amy set the books aside. So much for her first attempt at book pushing. So much for helping out her secret crush. *Stupid, stupid idea*, she berated herself as Toff called out a goodbye to Viv and did the bro-dude handshake/hug thing with Dallas.

Toff paused when he was halfway out the door, turning back to Amy with a crooked smile. "Stay out of trouble, Bonnie." The door slammed shut behind him, the tinkling bells echoing in the store.

Through the window, Amy watched Toff emerge from the bookstore into the sunlight. Within seconds, a group of girls surrounded him like they'd followed a homing beacon. He threw back his head and laughed at something one of them said, then slung his arms around two of the girls as they wandered off.

Amy's heart sank all the way down to her toes. Yeah, they'd fake relationshipped their way out of trouble, but Toff would never see her as more than Viv's weird book-nerd friend with a yarn-bombing side hustle. With a sigh, she resumed knitting as Viv rang up the two picture books the parents had picked out for their kids.

Viv said goodbye to the customers, then joined Amy,

sitting across from her. She cleared her throat and focused on her with big brown eyes full of sympathy. "Toff's the Jerry Maguire of Shady Cove, Amy. You know that. Great at friendship, bad at romance."

Ouch. She knew exactly what Viv meant. She loved that movie, even though it was old-school.

"I know how impossible it is to turn off a crush," Viv said sympathetically. "I love Toff, and I wish he were right for you, but he's not. You deserve a prince, not a court jester."

Amy appreciated her concern, but part of her rebelled at the assessment. Shouldn't *she* be the one to decide who was right for her? She started to say just that, but Viv was frowning at her phone. She looked up, pinning Amy with a determined stare.

"A lot of people already posted for the first challenge. You need to post yours ASAP."

She swallowed. Viv was right, but…

"Maybe I shouldn't bother. Look how last night turned out. It was a disaster."

"What are you talking about?" Viv protested. "That bench is amazing. People have been taking pictures of it all morning." She tapped her phone screen. "And it's perfect for the first challenge. Total cover love."

"Yeah, but…" Amy chewed her bottom lip. "I don't think it was worth the stress. I'm not cut out for competition. I'd rather read about it than do it."

Viv didn't say anything, but Amy could tell she was processing what she had said and didn't like it. Viv had a horrible poker face.

"Listen to this," Viv said, scowling at her phone. "This is today's HeartRacer tweet. 'Are you a fierce and fanatical reviewer? Strut your stuff on social media and tag us. If we like your posts, we'll retweet and regram. You get new followers and a shot at meeting Lucinda. Three challenges. Three chances.'"

Viv set her phone aside, laser focusing on her. "That's *you*. A fierce and fanatical reviewer."

Amy squirmed at Viv's intensity. "That's *us*. If I do this, it's with you. That's the plan, right?" That's how they'd always done everything.

Ever since they'd met, Viv had been in command and Amy had been the copilot. When Viv started her book review blog, she'd had to convince her that readers wanted her book opinions, too, insisting on posting Amy's reviews, which had morphed into Redhead Recs, and readers loved her book recs.

Same with their Lonely Hearts Book Club. Viv got the club up and running, and Amy eventually became the co-leader, after more coercing from Viv. Now she loved running the meetings, but that was because she felt safe with the small group of readers who loved romance as much as she did.

Viv went quiet again, her attention shifting to the framed library READ posters on the walls. Amy loved those posters. Her favorite was the one with Gal Gadot, star of the *Wonder Woman* movie. If she could be a superhero, she'd choose Wonder Woman, hands down.

"I love books as much as you do," Viv finally said, "but Lucinda's *your* unicorn author. You have to meet her. She hasn't given an interview or done a book signing for almost twenty years." Her eyes went wide. "Since before we were *born*."

"But you want to meet her, too, right?" Amy asked, trying to tamp down the panic rising in her chest. She couldn't do this contest by herself. No. Way.

Viv shrugged. "I get to meet a lot of authors when my mom's friends come here to do book signings."

"But they're mystery authors," Amy protested, "not

romance authors." She inhaled sharply. "I'm sorry. You know I love your mom's mystery series."

"It's okay," Viv said. "I know what you meant."

She didn't understand Viv's sudden lack of enthusiasm for the contest. She and Viv considered themselves ambassadors of a maligned genre, raving about romance on their review blog. True, Viv wasn't as big of a Lucinda fan as she was, but Lucinda was an icon.

Meeting her would be like Charlie winning the golden ticket and visiting the chocolate factory.

"Look," Viv said, "I know you wanted us to do this together, but I really need to spend time with Dallas before he leaves for school. It's already going to be tough, since I'm working in the store so much." She smiled reassuringly. "You can win this without me, I promise."

Amy gaped at her. "The odds of me winning are a zillion to one."

"No problem," Viv said. "*You're* one in a zillion." She leaned in, determination tightening her features. "You have just as many opinions as I do. Your reviews are fantastic." She tugged at her necklace and grinned. "Honestly, you should be in the spotlight, not me."

Wow. Amy didn't know what to say.

She chewed her lip. Maybe it was time to stop playing it safe.

"You *really* think I can pull it off?" Amy asked, but deep in her heart, a dream was burrowing in and taking root. "Even after how I messed up last night?"

"You didn't mess up." Viv's eyes sparkled with excitement. "And really. If you can fake out a cop with Flipper, you can *definitely* win a social media contest."

. . .

*A*my squinted in the bright sunlight, adjusting her phone's camera filter. She snapped one last photo of Lucinda's new book perched on the bench, making sure to include in the frame the poppies she'd knitted.

After talking with Viv, she had a lot to think about. She still didn't believe she could win, but she also didn't want to look back with regret, knowing she hadn't even *tried* to meet the person who'd inspired her love of reading.

Taking a fortifying breath, she uploaded her photos to Instagram, tagged HeartRacer Publishing, then entered her usual bookworm and bookstagram hashtags, along with a few customized ones.

#PoppiesArePopping #UnicornAuthor #NoRegrets

She hesitated, recalling Toff's comment about posting his own bench selfie. What the heck. If she was posting this, she might as well go all in. Besides, he had way more followers than she did. She could use more eyeballs on her account. Maybe they'd like what they saw.

Amy's fingers flew across the screen as she canceled her original post, screenshotted from his page the selfie he'd taken, then created a new post—a collage with her photo and Toff's selfie photo. She tagged *@SurferGodCA*, then added all the hashtags again, plus a new one, *#BonnieandClyde*.

She squeezed her eyes shut, wished on her bench for luck, then opened her eyes and posted the photos. Grinning, she realized she'd forgotten one more hashtag: *#HereGoesNothing*.

CHAPTER FOUR

*A*fter leaving the bookstore, Toff returned to the beach, taking occasional breaks from surfing to flirt with girls chilling on the beach and on their boards challenging him for waves. Girls liked him—a lot—and he returned the favor.

He wasn't a total player—he stuck with one girl at a time—but just for a short time. Usually three weeks max. Almost six weeks with that Swedish foreign exchange student his sophomore year, but that had been his patriotic duty.

"Hey, Toff! Come hang out with us!"

A bunch of younger kids swarmed him as he kicked back on his towel, taking a rare solo break.

He shaded his eyes to check out his fan club. He recognized the groms as beach regulars. His dad had always taken time to teach other kids when Toff was a little grom.

Some families went to church together. Toff and his dad surfed. Dad believed in karma and paying it forward, and so did he. Plus, the kids made him laugh, especially the redhead with the smart mouth who pushed his way to the front. He definitely remembered him.

"Can you help me with my nose riding?" The redhead squinted down at him. "Um, please?"

Toff grinned up at the kid. He'd helped him out before,

but he couldn't remember his name. Something about him was familiar, though, like a shadow of someone he knew.

"Have you tried it?" he asked, standing up and brushing sand off his arms.

"Yeah, but I'm not very good." The kid shuffled his feet in the sand while his friends laughed and poked at one another.

"So you're a longboard fan?" That was Toff's ride of choice. As much as he liked competing as a short boarder, he loved long, chill rides on his log with his friends or by himself.

"I like both." The redhead shrugged. "You make everything look easy. How do you do it?"

Toff grinned and ruffled the kid's hair. "Come on." He headed toward the water, his own board in tow, the kids trailing him like puppies chasing a big dog.

"What's your name?" he asked as the redhead staked pole position right next to him, motioning his friends to step back.

"I'm Brayden." He eyed Toff with a sly grin. "You're dating my sister."

"Wh-What?" Toff gaped at the kid, who might as well have sucker punched him.

Brayden must have confused him with someone else. The D word made him twitchy. Dating meant commitment. Restaurants and movies and…and…presents and other stuff he'd never done with a girl. That was Dallas's style, not his.

"Amy," Brayden prompted. "You dropped her off last night. Way after curfew." The kid waggled his eyebrows.

So that's why he looked familiar—the red hair. Something about the smile, too.

"Smooth move." Brayden pantomimed driving a car. "Rolling in with no headlights and the engine off."

Toff smirked. "You always spy on your sister?"

"Nah." Brayden shrugged. "She doesn't do anything

interesting. Usually." He side-eyed Toff. "She *never* misses her curfew."

Toff appraised Brayden through narrowed eyes. Had Amy told him they were dating as a cover story? That made sense. Being out with a guy was better than confessing she'd been out breaking the law, not that it was much of a law. He still laughed whenever he said the word "kniffiti" out loud, which he had, more than once.

"How come you two are sneaking around, anyway?" Brayden puffed himself up like he was ready to throw down. Toff swallowed a laugh.

He'd never dealt with a girl's protective brother before. Facing down one half his size was funny as hell. Toff grinned at his inquisitor. He'd already pretended to be Amy's boyfriend once to keep her out of trouble. Might as well do it again.

"We're keeping things on the down low." Toff glanced around, pretending to be worried about eavesdroppers, then leaned over to whisper in Brayden's ear, following a hunch. "Since your parents are strict about her dating."

"*Oooh*. I get it." Brayden's shoulders relaxed. "That makes sense, especially since you're, you know, *you*."

Toff straightened. "What's that supposed to mean?"

"Well, you're not exactly…" Brayden waved his hand around like Toff had flies circling him. "I mean, the last guy she dated showed up in a *tie*." He clutched his neck like he was strangling himself. "He was boring, but my parents liked him. 'Official seal of approval.'" He made air quotes, and Toff laughed.

Two girls strolled by, slowing down to check him out. Instinctively, Toff flashed his sexiest grin.

"Hey!" Brayden yelled at the girls. "Keep moving!" He turned his fiery glare on Toff.

Toff's mouth dropped open; then he shrugged an apology

at the girls. "Sorry, ladies." The girls exchanged confused looks and walked off.

"You shouldn't be flirting, since you have a girlfriend," Brayden accused. "It's one of the dating rules."

"Rules?" This was worse than faking it for the cop.

Brayden's face blotched the same red as Amy's had when he'd teased her about kniffiti. "Yeah. She says she doesn't want me to be a Wickham," he said. "She says his name like he's a serial killer." He crossed his eyes and stuck out his tongue, then pantomimed stabbing someone with a knife.

Toff laughed. This kid was a crack-up. "Who's Wickham?"

"Knowing her, some guy from a book." Brayden rolled his eyes. "She acts like people in books are real, dude. It's so weird."

Toff could easily picture Amy lecturing her brother and Brayden balking. Two battling redheads. After what he'd seen last night, though, he'd put his money on Amy. There was a spark inside her just waiting to be lit.

"You don't need to worry," Toff said. "I don't know who Wickham is, but I'm sure you're not a serial killer." He tousled Brayden's hair again. "Ready to work?"

"Yeah."

As Toff directed Brayden and his friends to set up their boards on the sand to practice cross-stepping, Toff thought about Amy.

How she'd curled up against him in his van, her hand on his chest, blinking at him with those pretty eyes he hadn't appreciated until that moment. The way she'd looked at him… For a few seconds, he'd believed her act. He'd forgotten he was faking, too. His body had lit up, firing on all cylinders, and if the sheriff hadn't been there, he would have kissed her.

But talking to her in the bookstore this morning had reminded him why she belonged in his friend zone. Amy was smart. Bookish. Sweet but kind of clueless about real life, believing that reading a book would somehow make him feel better about his dad's wedding. Plus, she was one of Viv's best friends, so if he screwed things up, Viv would bust his balls. So would Dallas. Literally.

"Hey, Toff! Am I doing this right?"

He watched Brayden, who wasn't doing it right but looked up at him with a hopeful expression.

Toff grinned. "Let me show you."

*A*my wasn't thrilled about tracking down Brayden on the beach, mostly because she knew exactly where to look — wherever Toff was. She was already regretting tagging him in her Instagram post and regramming his selfie. Had he even seen it yet? Even if he hadn't, when he finally did, she didn't want him to think she was turning into a creepy stalker because of last night.

Shading her eyes, she scanned the beach…and there they were, the blond Pied Piper and the children he'd lured with his surfboard.

Great.

She made her way slowly across the sand, stopping to say hi to a few friends — aka stalling — but she couldn't avoid him forever. Once she reached them, she hung back, hoping to make eye contact with Brayden while not attracting Toff's attention.

Unfortunately, her brother spotted her instantly, waving his hands in the air. "Hey, Amy! I was right! I told you your boyfriend would hook me up with a lesson!"

Toff turned around, shooting her a sexy, knowing smile.

She froze. Icicles filled her veins instead of blood. She couldn't have moved even if she'd wanted to. Unfortunately, Toff moved, heading straight for her after saying something to the kids.

He stopped in front of her, staring down at her with laughing eyes. "Hey, girlfriend," he singsonged. "What's up?"

"I'm not— I didn't tell him— He's just—" God, she hated how much Toff rattled her, standing there all buffed and tanned in his swim trunks. With any other guy, she'd laugh this off. But not with him.

Toff grinned, tossing his hair out of his eyes. "You don't have to explain, Ames." He gestured back and forth between them, shaking his head. "Definitely not happening."

Her mouth fell open. He didn't have to make it sound like a joke, let alone a horrible idea. Where was a stabby knitting "stick" when she needed one? Was this what dating Toff would be like? A constant barrage of cocky attitude?

She narrowed her eyes, annoyed. "I know *this* isn't happening." She mimicked his hand gesture. "My brother got the wrong idea when he saw you drop me off last night."

"We'll have to crush his dream," Toff said, smirking. "But we should let him down slowly."

Her heart pounded against her rib cage, demanding to know what was going on, but she didn't have any answers. Desperate to escape whatever game Toff was playing, she turned her back on him and waved at Brayden.

"Brayden! Time to go!"

Her brother ran up to them, red-faced and grinning. "Can I stay longer? Please?" He whined the last word, grating on her nerves, which were already shot. "Toff's teaching me some cool tricks and—"

"No," Amy cut in. "We need to go *now*."

Brayden's face fell. He mumbled something under his

breath that sounded like "prisoner," but Amy ignored him.

"Let him stay. I can give him a ride home," Toff said, surprising her—and her brother, based on his awed face.

"Cool! Thanks, bro!" Brayden fist-bumped him.

"I didn't say that was okay," she protested, but Brayden ignored her and sprinted back to his friends.

"Why'd you offer him a ride?" She slanted a suspicious look at Toff, which wasn't easy, since he stood so close that their shoulders touched.

He shrugged. "I guess I like rescuing redheads."

"He doesn't need rescuing from his *sister*." Amy put her hands on her hips, annoyance overtaking her stomach flutters.

Toff's gaze swept her up and down. "You're a criminal, Ames. It's my duty as a law-abiding citizen to step in." His annoyingly pretty eyes locked on hers. "Tell you what. I'll make his day by giving him a lift; then you can break the bad news that we're not really dating." He cocked an eyebrow. "Since you're the one who told him I'm your boyfriend, you get to break his heart. Deal?"

"But you're *not* law-abiding." Amy narrowed her gaze. "And I don't make deals with the devil."

He laughed, his eyes sparking. "I'm only part devil. The rest of me is pure angel."

She would not be swayed by his flirting, or whatever this was. She put her hands on her hips. "One, I never told him you were my boyfriend." She swallowed, hardly believing they were having this conversation, then plunged ahead. "In fact, I told him we were just friends."

Toff cocked a disbelieving eyebrow, amping up her indignation.

"And two," she ground out, "his heart won't be broken when he realizes you aren't my boyfriend."

He tilted his head, lips quirking. "What about your heart?

I didn't break that, did I? Faking it for the sheriff last night?"

Amy's mouth opened and closed like a fish as she struggled for a reply. He didn't know about her crush, did he? She'd worked so hard to keep it a secret.

"You can just drop Brayden off. You don't need to, um, stick around." She took a step back, her feet sinking into the damp sand. "I've gotta go."

"Sure. See you later, *girlfriend*." Toff grinned, then sauntered toward Brayden and his friends.

She blushed. Hearing him teasingly call her his girlfriend threw her emotional Geiger counter completely out of whack, even though she knew he was joking.

She turned her back on the surf god and fled.

CHAPTER FIVE

*A*my pinned the list of the HeartRacer publishing contest challenges to her bulletin board and stepped back to study it. She had it memorized, but seeing it in black and white somehow made it more real. She was still apprehensive about tackling this solo, but she'd taken Viv's words to heart.

HEARTRACER PUBLISHING SOCIAL MEDIA CONTEST
Want to meet Lucinda Amorrato, America's Favorite Romance Author? Need to Expand Your Social Media Reach? Here's Your Chance!
CHALLENGE ONE: *Cover Love! Wow us with a creative post featuring your favorite book cover.*
CHALLENGE TWO: *OTP! Who are your favorite fictional One True Pairings? Show us your 'ships!*
CHALLENGE THREE: *Win over a reluctant romance reader—our toughest challenge!*
June 9th: *Challenge One Deadline*
June 16th: *Challenge Two Deadline*
June 26th: *Challenge Three Deadline*
July 5th: *Winner Meets Lucinda Amorrato! Event hosted by HeartRacer Publishing and The Sunset Bookstore in LA! Details to follow...*

Amy skimmed the challenges again. She already knew her topic for her OTP, but the third challenge would be hard. The easiest approach would be to pick someone who already loved to read another genre and convince them to read a romance. She tapped a pencil against her lips. Maybe Dallas? No, he'd already done that when he was trying to win over Viv. Maybe Rose? No, she read the occasional romance, so she technically didn't count as a "reluctant romance reader."

Amy sighed, sitting down at her desk and twirling her calligraphy pen on her homemade Thor desk blotter, featuring twelve of his bromance memes, one for each month. She'd figure out challenge three somehow.

Maybe she could get Brayden to read a YA romance. *Ha.* She snorted at the thought. He'd be as resistant as the boy in *The Princess Bride* was to "kissing books" when his grandpa started reading to him. Though supposedly that kid grew up to be the author of *The Princess Bride*, so he'd definitely been converted to the swoony side.

Bzzz. Her phone vibrated with a text.

Viv: Your IG post is adorable! Flipper's a hit. As usual. I texted him not to let it go to his head.

Uh-oh. Amy's stomach tumbled over as she opened the app on her phone. Whoa. More than two hundred likes in the past three hours, way more than she'd ever had before. She scanned the comments. A lot of people complimented her yarn bombing, but even more people, um…"complimented" @SurferGodCA. One comment jumped out at her: "*Adorbs! Are you 2 cuties 2gether? You should be!*" Followed by a bunch of heart emojis.

Crap. She'd never considered anyone would look at her post and go *there*.

"*Nope!*" she typed. *See that, heart?* She thought of Toff's skeptical face on the beach when she'd told him Brayden had jumped to the wrong conclusion. Scowling, she typed, "*JUST FRIENDS*," hoping the all-caps and tongue-out emoji face made her point. She thought of how he'd laughed his butt off about the raccoons and added the green puking emoji face for emphasis. Her heart raised a feeble protest, reminding her of how he'd swooped in to save her, how worried he'd been that someone was after her. And how determined he'd been to save her from a ticket.

Be quiet, heart. We're competing, not swooning.

Next to the HeartRacer list was a poster featuring the cover from Lucinda's bestselling book that kicked off her most famous series. A gorgeous illustration of the heroine holding a sword to the hero's neck, it was included in her favorite book subscription box, along with a scented candle that was supposed to smell like the hero. The woodsy candle smelled great…though not as good as the whiff of up-close-and-personal Toff scent she'd inhaled when he'd wrapped his arm around her in his van.

Ugh. Stop. Keep your mind on what you should *be on.*

Amy blinked, refocusing on the HeartRacer list and the contest. She could only imagine what it would be like to meet Lucinda in person. If—by some miracle—she won the contest, she'd have to write a script of exactly what to say. Even then, she'd most likely mess up.

She wished she had the confident swagger of the U.S. women's soccer team winning it all or the courage of the Notorious RBG pumping iron and throwing down Supreme Court decisions in her eighties, but she didn't.

It wasn't like she could sign up for classes in swaggery bad-assery or hire a competition coach for her bookworm contest.

Her scalp tingled, and goose bumps pricked her arms as an idea bubbled from her heart to her brain, or was it the other way around? *No*, she warned herself, *bad idea.* But her brain ignored her command, taunting her with images of Toff—vivid memories of him hoisting trophies overhead when he won surf comps, pushing his teammates in pop-up drills on the beach in his role as surf captain, and teaching younger kids like her brother, who shadowed him everywhere.

He'd be a great coach, whispered a voice in her mind. *If you really want to win that contest.*

"It's not a surf contest," she said aloud.

So what? argued the voice. *It's all about confidence. Believing you can win. Bringing the swagger.*

"He doesn't know anything about books."

But he knows how to win, the internal voice persisted. Not just any voice—her voice.

Argh.

Amy shoved her chair away from her desk, crossed to her bed, and sank into her pillows. She closed her eyes. This time her heart served up a memory instead of her brain—Toff strutting across the stage at last year's Surfer Ball, wearing a crown and waving a trident scepter when he'd been crowned King of the Sea.

He'd pulled off something incredibly brave and heroic that night, way bigger than the yarn-bomber rescue. He and Dallas both had. She still remembered the hint of awe in Toff's eyes when he credited Dallas and his martial arts skills for saving the day. That night had definitely cemented their bromance.

She opened one eye and waved her giant size-fifty knitting needle in the air. If she squinted, she could pretend it was a sword. She'd only used these needles once; they were so unwieldy. Brayden called them her vampire-killing stakes.

Could she be as bold as Toff and Dallas?

With a thunderous crash of her door against the wall, her

brother burst into her bedroom and launched himself onto her bed. "Guess what!"

Speak of the devil. The *other* devil had obviously given him a ride home, like he'd promised.

Amy scowled at Brayden. "You're supposed to knock." She wanted to put a lock on her door, but her parents refused on the grounds of safety. She'd rather have privacy than safety.

"You don't have to pretend anymore." He grabbed her other giant knitting needle, jumped off her bed, and danced around the room, practicing sword moves. "Toff told me you guys are keeping things on the down low so Mom and Dad don't freak."

What. The. Heck. Hadn't Toff asked her to "crush Brayden's dreams" and tell him they weren't dating?

"There's no secret," Amy snapped. "We aren't dating."

Brayden side-eyed her like she was jabbering in an alien language. "If you want to keep your boyfriend a secret from the 'rents, we need to make a deal."

He wandered to her desk and picked up her Harry Potter Funko Pop, then shot Amy a menacing look. "If you want this guy to live." He grabbed the Wonder Woman figure off her bookshelf. "Or this one." He smashed the characters' faces together and made kissing sounds.

"Brayden." Her voice was a growl. Nobody messed with her Pops. "Put them back."

"You do the litter box and I'll keep my mouth shut," he said through the side of his mouth, sounding like a character from a 1940s gangster movie.

She bit back a laugh. This was ridiculous. She was bargaining with her brother to keep a secret that wasn't even real.

"Trash? Recycling? You do those and I'll do the litter box." Brayden gripped the figurines tightly in one hand, looking hopeful.

She shook her head.

"You're willing to risk me ratting you out?" He grabbed a knitting needle and held it to Harry's throat.

"Yep." She pointed to her door. "Now put them back and leave." If Brayden outed her, she'd tell her parents the truth—she'd been out late and Toff gave her a ride home. As a friend.

A ruckus sounded down the hall, distracting Amy. Goldi's paws skittered on the floor, and she yapped her excited, new-person bark. A deep laugh sounded from the foyer. A deep, *familiar* laugh.

Brayden tossed the Funko Pops onto her bed and raced down the hall.

Amy's skin prickled with goose bumps.

No. Way.

Why hadn't Brayden warned her?

"Hey, Amy!" Brayden yelled. "Toff's here!"

"Maybe you could yell louder, Brayden," she whispered sarcastically. "I don't think everyone in California heard you."

"You have to come out here!" her brother hollered. "You know guys aren't allowed in your bedroom."

Goldi barked in agreement.

Amy cringed, mortified. Did winners ever stab their siblings? Of course they did. Just look at *Game of Thrones*.

Toff's deep laughter echoed down the hallway, into her bedroom, and danced up her spine. At least her parents weren't home. She'd have to get rid of him before they came back from running errands.

She slid off her bed and checked the mirror over her dresser. After the beach, she'd changed into one of her favorite T-shirts: *I Like to Party (and by party I mean read.)* Perfect. One more thing for Toff to tease her about.

"Here goes nothing," she muttered. She stuck a glittery

butterfly clip in her hair for luck.

If the universe had just sent the perfect competition coach right to her door, who was she to refuse?

Toff waited for Amy in the McIntyres' kitchen, where Brayden had dragged him. He hadn't planned to come inside, but curiosity had won out. He'd had fun with Amy last night—and today—especially when she teased him, and he wondered how long she'd been hiding that feisty side. Plus, he felt kind of bad about how hurt she'd looked when he'd rejected her book recommendations.

Not that he'd ever read one of *those* books.

His stomach growled. The kitchen smelled great, like bacon and coffee and something sweet and delicious. He was always hungry, especially after surfing.

"Amy's doing weird book stuff. She'll be out in a minute." Brayden handed him a cookie from a Tupperware container. "*You* know how she is." He shot him an exasperated look, like he and Toff shared a burden.

Toff grinned and took a bite of the cookie. *Whoa.* This was one seriously tasty pastry.

"How many burpees can you do in a row? Do you swim a lot of laps? What's your favorite Sharknado movie?" Brayden fired questions like a machine gun while their dog, a bouncy golden retriever, danced around Toff, licking his bare legs. He leaned down to pet her, and she flopped onto her back, offering her belly.

"Brayden, leave Toff alone. Go take out the trash. Goldi, go to your bed."

Toff straightened to face Amy, who stood with her arms

crossed over her chest, scowling. Usually girls were happy to see him. He wasn't sure if she was annoyed because of her brother or because he'd decided to come inside instead of dropping Brayden off like she'd said.

He couldn't put a finger on why he was standing in her kitchen. All he knew for sure was he'd needed to come inside and just...see her or whatever. Make sure she hadn't accidentally stabbed herself with a knitting stick.

"Hi." She barely glanced at Toff, then nudged the dog, who was still lying belly up, with her bare foot. "Brayden, take Goldi outside."

"But you just told me to take out the trash." Brayden shot Toff a dude-back-me-up look.

Toff shook his head. No way was he getting in the middle of these two.

Amy huffed in frustration. "So do both. And poop scoop while you're at it."

Brayden glared at his sister. "You're doing the litter box." He pointed at her, then Toff, then back to her. "You scoop the cat poop, or I spill the boyfriend scoop." He snorted. "You lied, Amy. Toff's your boyfriend. Why else would he be here?"

Toff smashed his lips together, holding in a laugh. Amy's pretty eyes widened, and she blushed as red as her hair.

"If you want any more surfing tips from me, you'll stop spying on your sister."

Brayden looked more stunned than his sister did, which was saying a lot.

Toff leaned against the kitchen counter, warming up to his role. "Nobody threatens my girlfriend, not even her brother. Get going, kid. You've got chores to do." He pointed to the door leading outside, then pinned Brayden with his toughest don't-eff-with-the-team-captain glare.

Brayden stared up at him, mouth half open. He didn't

look scared so much as impressed. Toff held in his grin until the kid and the dog left the kitchen; then he turned to Amy, blasting her with his flirtiest grin.

"I've got this fake boyfriend act down. First I fake out the sheriff; then I scare off your brother."

Amy blinked, then reached up to twist her hair into some sort of bun shape. Something small and sparkly fell out and landed on the floor. She bent down to grab it. When she stood up, he read her T-shirt and laughed.

"Nice shirt. You and Dallas should start a nerd shirt store."

Her eyes flickered, reminding him of when he'd called her knitting needle a stick and teased her on the beach. He liked sparky Amy.

"What are you—" She took a breath and tugged self-consciously at her T-shirt. "What are you doing here, Toff? You could've just dropped off Brayden."

"Is that any way to talk to your boyfriend? Especially after last night?" He put as much innuendo as he could into those last two words, hoping she'd play along.

She didn't.

"I don't like being mocked. Besides, you're the one who told me to crush Brayden's dream and tell him that *this*"—she mimicked his gesture from the beach—"isn't happening."

A jolt of surprise shot through him. "Hey, I didn't mean— That's not what—" Frustrated, he ran a hand through his hair, still damp from surfing. He hadn't meant to upset her, but somehow he had.

"Did you come inside to make fun of my yarn bombing?" Amy brushed past him, opening the fridge and pulling out sandwich makings. His stomach growled again.

"What? No, I just…" Where was his flirt game?

Amy grabbed plates from a cupboard and started slapping bread, cheese, and ham together. She opened a jar of mustard and glanced at him. "Mustard? Mayonnaise?"

"Uh…both? Thanks." Was she still upset? Did mad girls typically make sandwiches for the object of their anger?

"Thanks for scaring Brayden. That was awesome." She glanced over her shoulder, setting him off balance with a mischievous smile.

"Is that why you're feeding me?" He pulled out a stool and sat at the counter, figuring her smile meant he could make himself comfortable.

"No. I'm feeding you because the whole neighborhood heard your stomach growling."

His neck burned, and it wasn't from sunburn. Amy opened another cupboard, pulled out a bag of potato chips, and tossed it to him. He caught the bag one-handed and opened it, pulling out a handful. As he crunched his chips, he scanned her from head to toe.

Sparkly stuff in her hair, like always. Were those butterflies? Weird but sort of cool.

Nerdy book T-shirt. No surprise there.

Jeans that fit her…just right. He coughed, chip dust clogging his throat. Amy filled a glass of water and brought it to him.

"You okay?" she asked when the choking finally stopped.

He nodded, slugging down water.

"Good. Brayden would never forgive me if you died in our kitchen."

He laughed, almost starting another choking attack. She was funnier than he would've guessed.

Toff cleared his throat and focused on checking out the kitchen, since it was safer than checking out Amy. It was one of those homey kitchens, like Dallas's. A room where people actually cooked, with spice racks, jars full of stuff he didn't recognize, cookbooks, and a couple of well-used aprons hanging on a hook. He and his dad mostly grilled outside or ordered takeout.

The fridge was covered with magnets and photos, including one of Amy and Brayden sitting on Santa's lap with their dog. From last year.

"What'd Santa bring you? A book about living the crime life?"

Amy cut him a look that was mostly annoyed, partly embarrassed, and a little bit of something he couldn't read.

"It's this silly ritual my mom makes us do every year." She opened the fridge and put away the sandwich makings. "She swears she's going to do it until Brayden turns twenty-one." She closed the fridge door and faced him, hands on her hips. "It's child abuse, if you ask me."

"Maybe you should call Officer Hernandez and turn her in."

She rolled her eyes, but her lips quirked up as she joined him at the counter with their plates.

"Thanks," Toff said, his stomach rumbling with appreciation.

She definitely made a guy work for a smile. Usually it didn't take any effort for him to earn a girl's smile. A rush of adrenaline fizzed in his veins. He was always up for a challenge.

He allowed himself one long, slow, appreciative perusal of all he could see of her above the countertop and gave her a lazy grin. Spending more time with the yarn bomber was definitely worth pursuing.

"You know, Ames, before kniffiti night, I would've guessed you were on Santa's nice list. Now I'm not so sure." He picked up his sandwich and eyed her. "Just how naughty *are* you?"

CHAPTER SIX

*W*hat was happening? Why was Toff Nichols sitting in her kitchen, eating a sandwich like he belonged there, and flirting with her?

Until this moment, Amy had been proud of herself. She'd somehow managed to act cool and composed from the minute she saw him standing in her kitchen looking all suntanned and windblown and—and—*whatever*, in those board shorts riding low on his hips and his *Surf Naked* T-shirt.

God, he was a cliché. So was she, with her ridiculous crush on him. Maybe they belonged together after all, like the Instagram commenter suggested.

Yeah, right.

Toff took a big bite of his sandwich and chewed, his pretty-boy eyes with the overkill eyelashes fixed on her, waiting for a response to his come-on line.

Well, she wasn't going to flirt back. No matter how much she'd dreamed of this, it was just like kniffiti night—an act. A game. She didn't know why he was playing it, but she could bring her own game and act like she was immune to his flirting.

Besides, they had business to discuss. The worst that could happen was… Well, she wasn't sure which would be worse—him saying no or him saying yes.

"Guess you'll have to ask Santa," she said briskly. "So, listen, before my annoying brother comes back in here, I need to ask you a favor."

"Another one?" He popped a potato chip into his mouth, keeping his eyes on hers. "It's like you think I'm your real boyfriend or something."

"I'm well aware that you're my *fake* boyfriend," she said primly as heat flooded her cheeks. "I mean, you *were*, with the sheriff. But not anymore."

"So what's the favor, *babe*? Need a hot date to a party? Want a private surf lesson? Or some other type of private tutoring?" He shot her an over-the-top leer, which she did her best to ignore.

Focus, she told herself. *Meeting your unicorn author is the prize, and he can help you win.*

"I need a coach for a contest I'm entering, not a hot date." She made herself lock eyes with him. "I want to win. And you know how to win."

Toff tilted his head, reminding her a little bit of Goldi, all blond and beautiful and...confused. "It's not a surfing contest, is it?"

"It's the publisher contest. The one I mentioned earlier. The reason I yarn bombed the bench."

"You skipped the important part." Toff sized her up, no longer in flirtastic fake boyfriend mode. "What exactly do you have to *do* to win?"

Amy bit her lip, hoping she could explain why she wanted his help without embarrassing herself. "I...I need to, um, go big or go home, I guess," she said as heat suffused her body.

He crossed his arms over his chest and leaned back on the counter stool, his lips quirking up. Did he flex his biceps or was she hallucinating?

"I need specifics, Ames. Just how big are we talking?"

He was definitely flexing, damn him. She should have written a script for this conversation.

"I have to share my book love on social media. Bring my best book nerd game, but I need help."

Confusion clouded Toff's eyes. "You don't need a coach for that. You love books. That's all you and Viv talk about."

"It's not *all* we talk about." Amy scowled. "It's like a popularity contest. My social media posts need to get a lot of likes, retweets, regrams. A lot of 'buzz.'" To her dismay, she made air quotes. She swallowed, forcing herself to ask for what she really needed. "I need a…a…swagger mentor." She cringed. The dorkiness was strong with her today.

Toff grinned, the confusion in his eyes replaced by speculation. "I get it. You've got stage fright, basically. Performance anxiety." He shot her a suggestive wink, which she pretended was a tic in his eye.

"So will you help me?" She was half hoping he'd turn her down.

"Depends. Tell me more about being a 'swagger mentor.'" This time he made mocking air quotes; then he leaned forward, resting his elbows on the counter and blasting her with so much…*swagger*…she wanted to smack him. Or kiss him.

There will be no kissing, she scolded herself.

"You know what I mean." She waved her hands in his general direction, cheeks on fire. "This…this…*thing* you do."

His grin deepened, showcasing both dimples. "Which thing? Flirting? Winning? *Swaggering?*"

Argh. Amy covered her face with her hands, not caring what he thought. This was, hands down, the worst idea she'd ever had.

His deep laughter curled around her, and she jumped when his hands touched hers, gently pulling them from her face. He held onto her hands, cupping them with his own on the counter between them.

Amy's heart banged around in her chest. *Say no*, she willed him. *Say yes!* she thought, just as quickly.

"I think I know what you're asking," he said, toning the swagger way down. "But I'm not sure I know how to teach it to you."

She bit her lip, glancing away. "I understand. It was a dumb—"

"But maybe I could, uh, role model or something."

Her eyes flew to his face. For once, he wasn't teasing.

"I've worked with surfers who don't have much confidence." This time he winced. "Sorry. No offense, it's just—"

"No, you're right. You saw me in action last night. I almost blew it with the cop." She tucked a loose hair behind her ear, and he tracked her movements with his bright-blue gaze. Was he noticing her sparkles? "Good thing you had enough swagger for the both of us."

His attention flicked back to her face. "You brought your game when it counted." He released her hands and leaned back. "Your fake girlfriend game was pretty good when we needed it to be, so we know you've got swagger potential."

He drummed his fingers on the countertop, pursing his lips like he was making a tough decision. "How much can you pay me?"

"P-pay?" she sputtered. What was his damage?

"Winning doesn't come cheap, Ames."

She glared. There was a big difference between funny and cocky—which he usually was—and jackassery. He'd just crossed the line.

"I'm *kidding*." Toff leaned across the counter, blasting her with another dimpled smile that froze her brain and heated up her body. "How about we do a trial run? I'm up for one coaching session." He took a bite of his sandwich and gave her a thumbs-up as he chewed and swallowed. "You can pay me in food."

The romance was strong with this one. *Not*. Why was she crushing on him? Like Viv always said, hormones had a mind of their own.

Anyway, he'd said he'd help—that was the important part.

"Awesome." She blew out a breath and flattened her palms on the counter. The worst part was over with. Now it was time to set some boundaries, for both their sakes. "We need to set a few coaching rules."

"What is it with girls and rules?" Toff scoffed.

"Maybe the reason girls need rules is because guys are so…so…" She flung her hand up, flustered. "You know how you are. How a lot of guys are, at least. That Y chromosome unleashed a pox upon humanity."

His lips quirked, but he didn't say a word, which surprised her. Maybe she'd used too many syllables.

"Anyway." She blew out a breath. She was veering off track. "My coaching rules are simple. One, you can't go too easy on me. I can handle the pressure." She wasn't sure about that, but she had to develop a thicker social media skin than the tissue-thin one she had. Online trolls freaked her out.

"Push you to the max. Got it." He resumed devouring his lunch.

"Two." She had to ask this, even though it was going to be super awkward. "You have this, um… You're just… I mean… How you are with girls…is very…distracting."

He stopped eating and gave off that teakettle-about-to-whistle vibe again, his eyes crinkling at the corners, mouth twitching.

"I thought you *wanted* my swagger."

She wanted to tear her gaze from his, but it was like he'd hypnotized her. "I…do…but, um, for professional reasons.

Not personal." The air between them snapped, crackled, and popped, like that old cereal commercial.

"So, uh"—she paused, breathed—"if you could just rein in all *that*"—she waved her hand in his general direction—"when you're coaching me."

And the Academy Award goes to…Amy McIntyre, for best performance while slowly dying inside.

Toff smashed his lips together, but his eyes were laughing. "Rein in all *this*?" He pointed to himself with both hands in a cocky check-this-out gesture.

"Omigod. See what I mean? You can't do it." She wanted to laugh. To scream. To undo her request for a coach.

"Want me to wear a bag over my head? Or a mask?" He reached for more chips.

She narrowed her eyes at him, which made him grin.

"How have I been missing out on all *this*?" he said, imitating her and fluttering his hand at her the way she'd done to him. "We could have a lot of fun together. Running from cops and raccoons, tying up the town with yarn—"

"This was a bad idea," she interrupted, pushing away her plate. "This is important, not a joke."

"If you want serious coaching from me, you'll get it." His jaw went tight, his eyes glinting like blue steel. Teasing Toff was gone, just like that, replaced by competitive Toff.

"Um, well, I…" Amy reached up to tighten her hair twist, Toff's eyes tracking her movements like a hunter stalking his prey.

"How about this?" He steepled his fingers, elbows resting on the counter. "You want to make the coaching rules, that's fine by me. You tell me if you want a hard-ass coach or a cheerleader. Whichever will help you win."

Before she could respond, the kitchen door flew open and Goldi skittered across the tile floor with Brayden close behind.

"Hey! You guys are eating!" Brayden accused, looking put out. Goldi barked in solidarity.

She pointed to the sandwich on the counter. Brayden ran to grab it, then climbed onto the stool next to Toff, his hero. She rolled her eyes. Toff caught her reaction, shooting her a sideways smirk that somehow communicated amusement and commiseration, dissolving the tension between them. How did he do that with just a smile?

Brayden grabbed a few potato chips and tossed them to Goldi, who attacked them like they were delicious prey.

"No people food for the dog!" Amy scolded, earning an exaggerated, full-body *whatever* reaction from Brayden.

"She's so bossy," Brayden said to Toff. "I don't know how you stand it."

Toff's eyes danced with laughter. "I like bossy." He stole the potato chip bag from Brayden and moved it out of reach. "No feeding the dog."

Instead of arguing or grabbing for the chip bag, Brayden nodded. "Okay."

Amy's mouth dropped open. *Holy shitoli.* Toff was the Brayden Whisperer.

"Excellent sandwich, Ames. Thanks," Toff said, toasting her with his glass of water before he took his last bite. "Right, Brayden?" He gave Brayden that killer stare again, the one that had sent her brother scurrying outside to do his chores.

Brayden almost choked but recovered fast. "Yeah, it's great." He copied Toff's toasting gesture, holding up his sandwich. "Thanks, Amy."

"You're welcome, *boys*." She had to regain the upper hand somehow.

Toff pushed his plate aside and propped his elbows on the counter, resting his chin on his folded hands. "I'd say one of us is more of a *man* than a boy."

"You're right," she said, smiling sweetly. "Sorry, Brayden. You're definitely a young *man*." A tremor of giddiness shot through her. This was fun, turning the tables on the flirting pro.

He didn't move a muscle…except for his tongue, which he ran slowly over his lips, licking off chip salt. Her face burned. So much for taking on the champion.

"You should go on tour," he said. "Amy the bookworm comedian."

"Yeah, it's true." Brayden nodded vigorously. "She's funny but, like, weird funny. You ever watch her vlog?"

Omigod. He'd say anything to get Toff's attention. Thank goodness her feeble attempts at recording video book reviews were locked down on a private channel.

"Not yet," Toff said, leaning back and stretching his arms over his head. His T-shirt rode up, providing a glimpse of his tanned and toned six-pack. He gave her a lazy grin. "Maybe I will."

She wasn't sure how much longer she could pretend to be immune to Toff—fake, real, and everything in between. Her resolve was fading, which was no surprise.

To her relief, Brayden's phone vibrated on the counter, emitting the *Star Trek* Intruder Alert warning.

"Uh-oh! Mom and Dad will be here in two minutes!" Brayden's anxious gaze bounced between Amy and Toff. "Toff can hide in my bedroom and sneak out the window."

Toff sat up straight, snapping out of flirt mode. "No kidding? Are your parents that strict? They'll freak out if I'm just eating lunch with you?"

As usual, Brayden was being dramatic, but Toff didn't know that. This was her opportunity to get rid of him and his distracting six-pack. She opened her mouth to tell him *Yes, they are and you should leave now*, but his expression took her aback. He looked so concerned, like he really didn't want her to get in trouble with her parents.

She heaved a resigned sigh. Their conversation had completely depleted her willpower reserves.

"Um, no, you don't have to go. It's fine." She turned to Brayden. "You're overreacting, Bray. How do you know they're almost home anyway?"

"I set it up on the Family Finder app." He waved his phone in the air. "I get a notification when they turn onto Monarch Lane." He grinned at Toff. "Gives me time to hide the evidence."

Toff laughed. "Wow, Ames. You didn't tell me your whole family are criminals."

"They're not," she said, glaring at her brother. "I don't know what he's talking about."

"And you never will," Brayden said ominously. Toff laughed again and reached over to muss Brayden's hair, who stared up at him with worshipful eyes.

Amy jumped off her stool and grabbed their empty plates. Goldi ran to the front door, whining with excitement, like Mom and Dad had been gone for months instead of a couple of hours.

There's no reason to panic, she told herself. So what if there was a boy in the kitchen? She didn't have anything to hide, unlike her brother, who was hiding who knew what? As if he'd read her mind, Brayden bolted from the kitchen, tearing down the hallway to his bedroom, slamming his door behind him.

"When's the last time anybody inspected that kid's bedroom for contraband?" Toff asked, baffled amusement threading his voice.

"Months," Amy said as she rinsed their plates in the sink. "Nobody wants to go in there. It's a hazmat zone."

Toff's laughter filled the kitchen again, followed by the

crinkling sound of the potato chip bag. Maybe she should've made him two sandwiches.

The front door opened, and her parents' chatter floated down the hall. Amy told herself to breathe. Her parents knew who Toff was—everyone did because of his local surfing fame, even though her parents usually skipped the competitions. Plus, they'd gone to school together forever.

To her surprise, he stood up from his stool, smoothing his hair and brushing crumbs off his shirt. Did he actually care about making a good impression on her parents? She found that hard to believe.

"That traffic was ridiculous!" Mom exclaimed. "It's not worth driving all the way to—" Her voice broke off when she spotted Toff. Dad was close behind her, carrying a box. Amy opened her mouth to introduce Toff, but he beat her to it.

"Hi, Mrs. McIntyre," Toff said, stepping forward to take the canvas grocery bags from her mom. "I'm Toff. Let me help you with those."

Mom slowly handed them over, shooting Amy a "what's-going-on?" look. Dad set his box on the kitchen table and studied Toff like he was trying to place him. At least he didn't look upset that she had a guy in the house while they were gone.

"Mom, Dad, you remember Toff Nichols from, uh, school and stuff. He came over for lunch because I, uh, needed to… um—"

"Wait a sec," her dad said, running his hand over his scruffy red beard. "You're the Cupcake Kid! I remember you."

Oh no. No, no, *no.* Dad couldn't tell that story. He *couldn't.* Amy wished she could transform into The Wasp like in Brayden's favorite movie. She'd fly across the room and sting her dad. So what if he was allergic?

Mom shared a laugh with Dad, while Toff turned to Amy, bewildered.

She'd been so close—so freaking *close* to surviving Toff's unexpected visit without major mortification, except for Brayden. And asking for a swagger coach. But now her parents had shown up and were about to ruin everything.

"Um, it was a long time ago," she said, focusing on Toff's T-shirt instead of his face. "I'm sure you don't remember."

"Remember what?" He sounded anxious.

Would it be rude to ask him to leave? Immediately? To save both of them from humiliation? She bit her lip and glanced at him. Nope, he definitely had no memory of attending her tenth birthday party, the one and only time she'd invited him to an event.

"Amy's birthday party," Dad said, grinning at Toff like *Of course you remember that, right, kid?* "Ninth? Or was it your tenth?"

"Tenth. When you ate all the cupcakes," Mom added helpfully, making Amy groan out loud.

"I...did?" Toff looked baffled and slightly embarrassed. That was a new look for him. Amy kind of liked it.

"Oh yeah. It was a minor catastrophe," Dad said, on a roll now. "When it was time for the 'Happy Birthday' song, Emily—"

"That's me, Mrs. McIntyre," Mom said, shooting Dad a reproving look.

Amy rolled her eyes. Her parents were so old-fashioned about that stuff. Well, her mom was. Her dad wasn't as bad.

"Right, right," Dad said, waving off Mom's correction. "So my wife found you in the kitchen—with Brayden, I think— eating all the cupcakes." He cracked up again, and Mom smiled at Toff like he was still ten years old. And busted.

"He didn't eat *all* of them," Amy piped up, mortified for Toff—and herself. She stole another peek at him. Holy wow. She'd definitely never seen *that* face, and she'd mentally cataloged all his expressions for years. He was definitely wishing he'd escaped when he had the chance.

"So, um, then what happened?" Toff asked, sounding almost shell-shocked.

Dad shrugged. "Fortunately we had a bunch of candy for the rest of the kids."

"There were two cupcakes left," Mom added. "Thank goodness, because Amy bawled her head off when she saw what you'd done. We put a candle in one cupcake and sang 'Happy Birthday' to distract her."

"And I ate the last cupcake," Dad chimed in, "since I was the one who made them." He grinned at Toff. "I figured I deserved it."

"Amy didn't invite you to any more of her parties," Mom said, shooting her a not-so-subtle wink. "But I guess she's finally forgiven you if she fed you lunch today."

"I…I… Wow. Shi— I mean, um—" Toff ducked his head and tugged at his hair, his neck blotching red. "I'm sorry. I don't remember that at all."

"What are you two up to today?" Dad asked. His expression was way too interested. She cringed, dreading where this was going. She shouldn't be surprised, though, considering Dad's guilty pleasure was watching *The Bachelor*.

Amy squeezed her eyes shut and willed her brother to set off the burglar alarm, or the fire alarm, or *something* to save Toff from further humiliation.

Wait a minute.

She could end this. She didn't need a Brayden disaster distraction. She could rescue Toff instead of letting him circle the drain of desperation while her parents watched.

"Toff needs to leave," Amy said, gathering her courage and taking his hand in hers. "He's already running late for a—a—somewhere he has to be."

She tugged at his hand. He blinked at her, then at their joined hands.

"Uh, yeah, I... Right." He cleared his throat and glanced at her dad. "It was nice to meet—I mean—see you again." His smile was crooked with embarrassment. "Sorry about the cupcakes. I promise it won't happen again."

She squeezed his hand and dragged him past her parents toward the front door, ignoring their wide-eyed gawking. Her heart clanged around her chest, and her palm was sweaty in his, but she didn't care. She needed to escape as much as he did.

Once outside, she released his hand and hurried toward his van parked on the shoulder of the road.

"I am *so* sorry," she mumbled, not looking at him when he joined her at the van. "I had no idea they'd bring that up."

Her gaze roved over the van while she waited for him to speak. It was straight out of a surf movie, a classic seventies Volkswagen van, icy blue with white trim. A couple of surfboards were strapped to the roof rack. Stickers from surf competitions and beaches up and down the coast dotted the side panels.

Toff opened the sliding side door. He leaned in, and she heard cans rattling. He emerged holding an energy drink. "Want one?"

She shook her head, nervously chewing her bottom lip. Was he still embarrassed? Mad? His blush had faded, but he wasn't smiling. He snapped open the can and chugged, his Adam's apple bobbing up and down.

This was her cue to leave. She turned away, ready to flee to her house, which she would never leave again, for real this time.

"Ames, wait."

Slowly, she turned back to him, surprised at how deflated

he looked. He leaned against his van, brushing hair out of his eyes, scowling.

"A heads-up would've been nice. That I, like, *ruined* your birthday. Made you cry." He shot her a frustrated look. The realest one she'd seen from him, ever. She took a tentative step forward, then another. Of all the things he'd said to her during their brief, bizarre, fake-not-fake relationship, this was by far the sweetest.

"I was ten years old. It's no big deal." She took another step closer, smiling with encouragement like he was a skittish dog—a gorgeous skittish show dog with trust issues. "It's a funny story." They stood toe to toe. She tilted her head back to look him in the eye. He met her gaze, still frustrated. Still embarrassed. "I wish I had a picture from that day. You had chocolate frosting all over your face. So did Brayden."

A ghost of a smile crossed his face.

"I bet it was Brayden's idea," she said. "He probably conned you into it, even though he was only three and you were ten."

His ghost of a smile took solid shape, filling in. Lighting up.

"I can't believe I don't remember your party," he said, shaking his head in disbelief.

"Well, you *were* Mr. Popular, even back then. It was probably one of many parties you went to that weekend. I'm sure it's all a blur of pin the tail on the donkey and cupcakes."

His grin blasted her at full wattage. He straightened, stepping away from the van, their bodies separated by centimeters. Or was that a millimeter? Amy couldn't breathe, and she was out of funny comebacks.

"I have a lot to make up for," Toff said, his voice low and rumbly. "I'll text you tomorrow, and we'll figure out a game plan for your coaching lesson."

She nodded, sneaking a peek at him. He didn't look

deflated anymore. Or embarrassed.

"Thanks for the escape from your parents," he said. "Make sure they know Brayden ate the rest of those cookies today, not me." He chuckled as he got into his van and slowly pulled away, flipping her a peace sign.

Amy watched his van disappear down the hill. That had felt like actual flirting when they ate lunch. Had he meant it, or was that his default setting?

She turned back to the house. She needed a major de-stress knitting session to recover from her time with the Cupcake Kid, aka Clyde, aka Coach.

What had she gotten herself into?

Toff: Hey, Wordworm—did I really eat all the cupcakes at Amy's bday party when we were kids? And make her cry?

Viv: You did, dork. We need to talk more about THE WEDDING! Are you sure you aren't freaking out that you're going to be related to me?

Viv: Flipper?

Viv: Flipper?? Why'd you ask about the cupcakes??

Viv: You can't ignore your future sister forever. You know where to find me, and McNerd knows where to find you, too.

CHAPTER SEVEN

Show us your #OTP, your favorite #SHIP, and tell us WHY! Make sure to tag @HeartRacerChallenge2 if you want eyeballs on your entries! Post by June 16!

*A*my sat at an outside table at The Bean, drinking a melty mocha that was no longer iced, rereading her One True Pair post for the big contest. She chewed her thumbnail, worried her idea was cliché. Everyone loved *Pride and Prejudice*. She had nothing new to say about her beloved Lizzie Bennet and Mr. Darcy.

Why even try?

Viv had read her piece and said it was good, which was code for "it could be better." She knew Viv had suggestions for improvement, but she didn't ask for them, since Viv and Dallas were driving up the coast for some fancy anniversary dinner tonight. *Must be nice,* Amy thought, *having a modern-day Mr. Darcy plan a perfect date night.*

She gave herself a mental shake. That wasn't fair. She was thrilled for Viv and Dallas. She was just…lonely. And suffering from a creative block.

Exhaling a defeated sigh, her attention wandered to the busy street. The tourists were out in force today, meandering in and out of Main Street's shops and cafés. Lots of people stopped to photograph her yarn-bombed bench. Amy stood and stretched. She could use a distraction.

"Hi." She approached a family of four snapping bench photos with the mom's cell phone. "Want me to take a picture of all of you?"

The mom beamed. "Thank you! This bench is so adorable! We have to get photos."

Amy tingled with pride as she took photos of the laughing family.

"Do you know who did this?" asked the mom. "Was it someone local?"

"Yes," Amy said, blushing.

"Oh, wonderful! Please tell them what a wonderful job they did. I hope the police don't remove it."

Amy bit her lip to keep from laughing. "I'll pass along your compliment. I think the sheriff's office is okay with it."

She'd called them yesterday, disguising her voice to ask about the bench, and had been told the artwork would stay because it didn't damage anything and got so much positive feedback from the community.

All that panic with Toff had been for nothing. Well... not *nothing*. It had led to him being her contest coach. And unrealistic daydreams about spending more time with him... in his van.

The bench-loving family waved goodbye, and Amy noticed how the dad held the mom's hand, even though they were sort of old. She let out a happy sigh. She was a Romantic with a capital R, which was ironic considering she hadn't had a boyfriend since sophomore year, and that guy had been sorely lacking in the romance department.

She returned to her bistro table and flipped through her sketchbook. She always handwrote her book reviews before typing them up for Viv's blog. She liked experimenting with different lettering styles and doodling in the margins. Today she'd drawn Mr. Darcy's haughty face at the country ball where he first meets Lizzie and Lizzie gives him the stink eye. Much as she liked her drawings, she still felt stuck, unable to adequately express her love for P&P, her forever OTP.

"Just do it," she muttered out loud. Isn't that what the sports commercials said? It was probably exactly what her *coach* would tell her. Reluctantly, she pulled up the contacts on her phone, typed in "Thor," and opened a text window.

It was a dumb nickname for Toff, but she'd chosen it after watching the first Thor movie when she was only twelve because of Chris Hemsworth's hair, which was sort of like Toff's.

Unlike her text window with Viv, which had years of texting history, the Thor window was blank. But that was about to change.

"No time like the present."

Hey, Coach. I need your advice.

She waited for the reply dots. Nothing. He was probably still asleep. Or surfing. Maybe he'd changed his mind—

Her phone rang, and she stared at it in shock. Who called instead of texted? Coach Thor, apparently.

"Hello?" she said tentatively.

"What's up, grommet?" She heard the teasing grin in his voice and reminded herself to be chill—to try out Swagger Amy.

"If you're going to call me grommet," she said, "this isn't going to work."

"How about Li'l G?"

She rolled her eyes. "I'm going to ignore that. Why'd you call instead of text?"

"Your text sounded like an emergency."

"Did you see a 911? 'I need your advice' does not equal an emergency."

Wow. Swagger Amy was a badass. Too bad she only showed up for texts and calls but not in person.

"Want me to hang up and text you now?" His grin was at maximum wattage—she could hear it in his voice. She also heard lots of background noise.

"Are you at the beach?"

"Yeah, but I'm done for the day." He hesitated. "I'm starving. Wanna make me a sandwich? You can have all the advice you want if you feed me."

"I'm at The Bean."

"Cool. You can buy me a sandwich instead."

She puffed up with annoyance. Why did he—?

"I can see your angry eyes from two miles away. I was kidding, Ames. I'll buy my own lunch." He paused, and she heard a glugging sound, like he was chugging water. "We need to work on your sense of humor."

That was a low blow. "I am a very funny person!"

He laughed again, making her want to throttle him.

"See you in ten, *grommet*."

He disconnected before she could clap back.

"Thanks, Lynette. See you around."

"I hope so. You know where to find me."

Toff took the foot-long sub sandwich from the girl who'd added extra cheese and meat at no charge. He got that type of special treatment a lot. He knew why it happened, but sometimes he felt guilty. Guilty but not too guilty.

When Amy had texted him, he hadn't realized at first that

it was her, because there was no name attached to the number. He was surprised he'd never texted her, since she was part of Viv's posse. He'd added her as a contact after ending the call, except he wasn't sure how to spell her last name so he'd used Amy MacAttack.

Toff joined Amy outside, sliding an iced mocha across the table.

"For me?"

He nodded toward her empty glass. "Gotta have fuel to work with your coach."

"Oh. Thanks."

Why did she look surprised? Was it so unbelievable he'd do something nice? He still felt weirdly awkward about their ate-all-the-cupcakes-and-ruined-your-party history, but he was also the guy who'd saved her from the clinker.

Frowning, he tore open the sandwich wrapper and dug in. He needed fuel, too, after ripping it all morning. The waves were choppy, scaring away some of the tourists, which made him happy. He tried not to lash out at newbies, but it got old, having to watch out for kooks who didn't know what they were doing. He and his friends had their favorite hidden surf spots, but people kept finding them.

The sun was finally shining after a typical morning of coastal fog. Toff scooted his chair outside of the sun umbrella's shade and unzipped his hoodie, exposing his bare chest. He tilted his chair back, closed his eyes, and let the sun warm him.

At the sound of choking, his eyes flew open. Across the table, Amy coughed and wheezed, waving her hand in front of her face, which was tomato-red.

"Wrong pipe?" he asked, and she nodded, her eyes teary. "Water?"

She shook her head.

He resumed devouring his sandwich, keeping an eye on

her in case he had to do the Heimlich. Eventually she stopped, wiping her eyes and clearing her throat. She drank from her iced mocha and gave him a wobbly smile.

"You okay?"

"Yeah." Her voice sounded froggy.

"You sure?"

Amy nodded and sipped from her mocha again. "I'm fine."

"Good." He swallowed the last bite of his sandwich, crumpled up the wrapper and napkins, and tossed them into a nearby trash can. He leaned forward, resting his arms on the table. "Ready to be coached by the best?"

She glanced around, her forehead pinched like she was confused. "Sure, but I thought I was being coached by *you*."

When her jab registered, Toff acknowledged it with an appreciative grin. He was right about spending more time with sparky Amy—this was gonna be fun.

Sweet with a side of smartass was proving to be his kryptonite.

*W*ould it be weird to ask Toff to zip up his hoodie? Yes. Definitely weird. She would just have to handle him, pecs and all, even though his proud peacock display had made her choke.

"Tell me about the contest." Toff gestured to her sketchbook. "Can I have a piece of paper? And a pen?"

Reluctantly, Amy tore a page from her pricey Moleskine sketchbook, then slid the pencil box toward him. Toff chose a purple pencil and scrawled *Amy's Contest* across the top of the page.

"Give me the basics."

"Okay." She tucked a strand of hair behind her ear, focusing on the pencil in his hand instead of the unzipped hoodie. "HeartRacer—that's the publisher—announced three social media challenges, three themes. I have to post something for each challenge on social media. The more, um, buzz I generate, the more likely HeartRacer is to regram my stuff. I've already done the first challenge, as you know."

"Yep. Cool." Toff listed *1*, *2*, and *3* down the side of the page, adding "kniffiti" after the number 1. He glanced up. "Then what? How do you win this thing?"

Amy cleared her throat. "Well, assuming my posts get enough attention—"

"Which they will, because of your coach." His jaw tightened, steely eyes fixed on hers.

Was that face supposed to pump her up? He looked like he wanted to punch somebody.

"Do you have any coach faces that aren't so…scary?"

His blue eyes widened, then he laughed. "That wasn't a scary one. *This* is a scary one." He made the don't-eff-with-me face that had sent Brayden scurrying off to do chores.

Amy smirked. "How about you let me finish explaining before you try out any motivational strategies?"

Toff wiped his hand down his face. "Coach face, *off*."

"Thank you." She would not reward him with a laugh, no matter how much she wanted to. "The best part is the winner gets to meet my favorite author."

"Who's your favorite author?" His pencil hovered over the page.

"Lucinda Amorrato."

"Spell it for me."

Amy did, and Toff scribbled *Eyes on the Prize* and the author's name diagonally on the bottom corner of the page. His note-taking method was completely random—a sacrilegious waste of Moleskine—but she'd have to let that go.

"And then what?" He tapped the pencil on the paper, his legs bouncing up and down under the table.

Amy glanced away. Would Toff make fun of her answer? If he did, she'd fire him on the spot. She took a breath, then let loose, hoping he'd get how important this was to her.

"Okay, so meeting Lucinda would be like you meeting…I don't know, Kelly Slater?" An expression of appreciative surprise crossed his face when she mentioned the surfer most people deemed the best in the world. She kept going. "Lucinda's my idol. She's the reason I'm a bookworm. The worlds she creates are just…just…"

She made a small explosion noise and swept her hands up and out, like her fingers were fireworks. "Way better than real life. Someday I want to… I hope I can…do something that impacts people like she does." She shrugged. "Maybe writing. Maybe illustrating. Something to do with books."

She exhaled and sucked down a big slurp of her iced mocha, already regretting how she'd just bared her soul to the person most likely to laugh at her.

He nodded slowly, his gaze trained on her face. She waited for him to make fun of her, or say something coach-y, but he took his sweet time.

"So ten years from now," he drawled, sticking his compostable straw in his mouth like a cowboy in an old Western movie, "when you make your acceptance speech for the Book Grammies—or whatever the biggest award is book people have, because you'll win that, too—don't forget to thank Toff Nichols, the World Surf League champion who taught you how to bring the heat, and the *swagger*, back in the day."

"Right," Amy said, smiling as relief swept through her that he wasn't laughing, that he got how much she wanted to win. "Exactly."

Toff scribbled WINNER! on the page and circled it, then tossed the pencil on the table. "So how'd the kniffiti post work out? Did you get a lot of 'buzz'?" He grinned, flashing air quotes.

He didn't know? When he hadn't mentioned it, she'd assumed—or hoped—it hadn't blipped his radar. She'd estimate 90 percent of his posts were surfing-related, with the other 10 percent food-focused.

"Umm…okay, I guess." She picked up her pencil and started doodling. She'd checked her account before he got here—her bench post was up to almost four hundred likes and about thirty regrams. Though most of the comments were about Lucinda or Amy's kniffiti, there were also more questions about Toff and her.

Unfortunately, HeartRacer still hadn't liked or regrammed her post, which didn't bode well. But that was why she had a coach, right? She looked up from her doodle, meeting Toff's steady gaze.

Was this another coach face? It must be. Cryptic. Assessing. Determined.

He picked up his phone from the table. Amy held her breath as he swiped the screen. Watching him was like watching an old-fashioned silent movie, when actors made over-the-top faces to convey their emotions.

It was easy to read his the emotions flitting across Toff's face—surprise, amusement…swagger. Amy took a sip of her melting drink, pulse thrumming in her ears, wishing he'd get it over with already and say something.

He finally looked up, rocking his trademark cocky smirk. "So we're not '2 cuties 2gether'? That hurts, Ames." He pounded his chest with a closed fist. "Right here."

She huffed in exasperation, hoping it hid her embarrassment. "That's not the point."

"It's not?" He blinked innocently.

"No." She shifted in her chair and gestured to his phone. "What my *coach* needs to know is that HeartRacer Publishing hasn't liked my post, let alone regrammed it. That's a problem."

Toff's smirk faded. "Not enough buzz?"

She shook her head.

He glanced at his phone again, swiping the screen. Frowning, he set the phone aside. "It's a good post—"

"Thanks."

"—but it's not enough." His eyes narrowed. "We need to up your game big-time. You ready?"

This was it. She felt like she'd just discovered the secret door in the closet that led to Narnia. Should she cross the threshold?

"Yes."

Toff gave a curt nod. "Tell me about the second challenge." He picked up the purple pencil, poised to resume taking notes.

"I have to post my favorite OTP and why I love them."

"What's an OTP?"

She needed to remember he was new to her book world. Time to coach her coach. "It means One True Pairing, a couple you ''ship'—"

"Ship?" His eyebrows bunched over his nose.

"It's when you want a couple to be together or love a couple who is already together."

"Are we talking real life or books?"

"Both, but I'm mostly into fiction 'ships." She chugged her iced mocha. "The first famous 'ship was Spock and Kirk from *Star Trek*, from the original series."

She held out her hand for Toff's pencil, then wrote on his paper while she explained. "People used to call that 'ship Kirk/Spock and then just K/S, which turned into just 'slash,' for slash fiction. Romances between two guys." She drew a big purple slash and set down the pencil.

Toff glanced up, eyes wide. "Does Dallas know about this?"

"I'm sure he does. He's a huge Trekkie." Amy studied Toff's expression, trying to gauge the meaning behind his question. He wasn't homophobic, was he? That would crush her crush faster than just about anything.

"Huh. Cool." Toff resumed chewing on his straw. "This book stuff is more complicated than I realized. So who's your OTP?"

She would not 'ship herself and Toff. Would *not*.

"I have several, but my top two are Harry Potter and Hermione Granger and Mr. Darcy and Elizabeth Bennet from *Pride and Prejudice.*" She was 99 percent certain Toff knew HP but not P&P.

He frowned. "But Hermione ended up with the redheaded dude, not Harry. Hey, did you ever notice your brother looks a lot like that guy? Ron, right?"

Brayden had only heard that a million times. He hated Ron Weasley for that very reason, which was a shame, since they shared a lot of qualities.

"'Ships can be canon or not," she explained patiently, "like Harry and Hermione."

"What?" Toff took the straw out of his mouth. "Are you even speaking English right now? Because I know all those words"—his lips quirked up—"but I don't think they belong in a sentence together."

She let out a long, exasperated sigh. "Maybe it would help if you read what I've written so far for my OTP entry."

As soon as she said the words, she wanted to take them back. This wasn't just any book review—this was her OTP. It was almost like letting him read her diary. She was nervous about anyone reading it, let alone Toff.

"Great idea." He stuck his hand out, palm up. "Fork it over."

Instinctively she leaned back, clutching her journal to her chest. "Toff, this is hard for me. I'm not like you, able to flaunt my stuff for the whole world to see."

He cocked an eyebrow. "Isn't that why I'm here? To help you learn how to flaunt it?"

She swallowed. Unfortunately, he was right. "Please don't make fun of it." She hated how her voice came out as a whisper.

"I'd never do that."

"You like to tease. It's what you do."

He looked away from her, frowning, still chewing on his straw. She hoped she hadn't insulted him, but she had to protect herself. This was a trial coach run for both of them.

When he faced her again, the intensity of his expression took her breath away.

"I might not get all the book stuff and the OTP whatever, but I get how important this is to you." His gaze locked onto hers. "You can trust me. I promise."

Wordlessly, she slid her book across the table to him, heart pounding. He was a very persuasive coach.

"Thanks." He shoved up the arms of his hoodie, frowned, then shrugged out of it altogether. From across the street, someone whistled. Toff didn't seem to notice, his attention already focused on reading her contest entry.

Amy's mouth went dry as her gaze skimmed over him. His torso belonged on a steamy book cover. Not like she hadn't seen it a thousand times before at the beach, but he was just so…close. Why weren't these tables bigger?

She blew out a breath. This scenario was…not okay, but what could she say, *Please cover up so my virgin eyes don't bleed with want?*

"I'll be back in a minute." Amy jumped up and grabbed her mocha glass. She needed a refill. Better yet, she'd crawl into the ice machine and cool herself off.

She didn't know what was making her hotter—half-naked Toff or the fact that he was, at this very moment, reading her treatise on true love.

*T*off basked in the sun as he read Amy's OTP thing. He should've asked her to grab him a soda refill, but she'd disappeared into The Bean before he could, like the rabid, vandalizing raccoons were after her. He grinned, shoving his hair out of his face, and read.

Elizabeth Bennet and Mr. Fitzwilliam Darcy
My OTP, Now and Forever
by Amy McIntyre

So that was how she spelled her name. Eh, he liked MacAttack better.

I was first introduced to the perfection that is *Pride and Prejudice* by my mom when I was thirteen years old. We spent two nights bingeing her favorite series of all time, the BBC version of *P&P* starring Colin Firth and Jennifer Ehle, who are brilliantly cast in their roles as Mr. Darcy and Elizabeth (Lizzie) Bennet. Watching that series and then reading Jane Austen's incredible novel changed my life. *P&P* turned me into a hopeless romantic, which is a curse and a blessing.

A blessing, because now I'm a huge fangirl of fictional romance and have read so many fantastic books that I'm a reader for life.

A curse, because I know deep in my 'shipping heart that I will never experience in real life the type of love Lizzie Bennet does with Mr. Darcy in Pride and Prejudice.

Toff gnawed on his straw. *Damn.* She was hardcore obsessed with imaginary people. And "true love." He shifted on his chair.

Why are Lizzie and Mr. Darcy my OTP? So many reasons. I'll try to summarize, but it feels like cheating—like watching a movie based on a book but never reading the book.

Toff snorted. "Okay, McJudgey McIntyre."

He never read the books that went with movies. Why bother? It was the same story, or close enough. His mom had read him the first two Harry Potter books aloud, but then… well, he hadn't wanted to read the rest of the series after she died. He'd watched the movies, though, pretending she was with him.

A wave of memories slammed into him, of curling up with Mom as she read out loud, acting out all the Harry Potter characters, using different voices. Her Snape voice was the best, making him scared and excited all at once. He blinked away the memory and resumed reading.

Why Lizzie Is Perfection:
Smart, funny, and sarcastic.
Calls out Mr. Darcy when he's a jerk.

Defends those she loves, even her sister Lydia, who's a train wreck.

Admits when she makes mistakes, like completely misjudging Mr. Darcy.

Says "no" when the wrong guy proposes, paving the way for the right guy.

Not intimidated by people who think they're superior to her, like Caroline Bingley, who tries to ruin Jane Bennet's love life and steal Mr. Darcy from Lizzie.

Refuses to conform to society's expectations by settling for just any marriage instead of the perfect marriage.

Toff grinned as he read. He had no idea who these people were. The story sounded like a soap opera, but it was obviously Amy's jam. Whoever judged this contest should be impressed by her passion for this book.

Why Mr. Darcy Is Perfection:

Loyal, especially to those he loves, like his sister, Georgiana; his best friend, Charles Bingley; and Lizzie...eventually.

Proud of his heritage and family.

Nice to his servants.

Toff snort-laughed. How big of the guy to treat his servants like human beings. He crunched an ice cube in his mouth and kept reading.

Will do anything for Lizzie, even chase down the evil Wickham.

Toff frowned. He'd heard that name Wickham before but couldn't remember where. He shrugged. Probably Amy and Viv book-babbling. A shadow fell over him, pulling him out of his thoughts, and he glanced up. It was Lynette, the sandwich maker. She handed him an energy drink. "On the house. You look…hot."

"Thanks." He took the ice-cold can and snapped it open. He guzzled a long swig, while her heated gaze checked him out like *he* was a sandwich and she was ravenous.

"I'm off work in an hour." She ran her tongue over her lips, dropping her gaze to his lap, just in case he didn't catch her meaning. Toff darted a glance at The Bean's door.

"She's still inside," Lynette said, tilting her head toward the café.

Toff arched an eyebrow. "So you thought you'd swoop in?"

"I'd hate to see a delicious treat like you go to waste."

Toff's jaw clenched. She'd just pissed him off in at least three different ways. He tilted his chin toward the café. "You've got customers waiting. And I'm not one of them."

Lynette blinked in surprise, then spun around and stalked off. Toff guzzled more of his free drink—which he now planned to pay for once he and Amy were done—and resumed reading about why Amy thought this Darcy dude was so effing perfect.

Messes up his first marriage proposal to Lizzie horribly but learns from his mistake.
Dances at a country ball even though he hates them. Because Lizzie.

Toff rolled his eyes. What was it with girls and dances? Prom, the Valentine's dance, the Surfer Ball his school did instead of Homecoming. They were fun but not a big deal.

Pulls off the most romantic, heroic grand gesture of all time, against which all grand gestures will be measured forever. And does it anonymously.

A grand what?

"Are you finished?"

Toff jumped at the sound of Amy's voice. She sat down across from him, giving off a skittish vibe, just like on kniffiti night.

"You okay?"

"Yeah, fine. Just, um…wondering." She pointed at the page. "What do you think?" She twisted her hands together, her gaze darting around like a squirrel.

Why was she staring above his head? Off to his side? Everywhere but at him. He glanced down to make sure he hadn't spilled ketchup on himself or something else gross. Nope.

Wait a minute. Was *he* grossing her out? That would be a first.

He knew he wasn't ugly. Okay, he knew he was easy on the eyes. He had a mirror. And plenty of feedback like he'd just had from Lynette. It wasn't like he hadn't been…appreciated by plenty of girls.

He thought back to the night in the van with Amy. She'd put on a good act for the sheriff, and at one point he'd thought maybe she wasn't faking. He'd forgotten that he was faking, too, for a few seconds. A few minutes, if he was honest.

Across the table, her hands fluttered around her hair, adjusting the sparkly clips, still looking everywhere but at him.

"Amy."

He willed her to look at him. He was gonna figure this out right now. As her coach, he needed to know if he repulsed her. Or the opposite. Or if she was completely neutral. It was a professional assessment, not personal.

"One, two, three. Eyes on me."

She didn't laugh when he tossed out the kindergarten pay-attention command, but her gaze zinged right to him, bouncing down to his chest, then back up. Her face pinched like she was disgusted by what she saw. Not at all like the sandwich chick. *Damn*. This was embarrassing. He shoved his arms back into his hoodie and zipped it up to his neck, even though he was burning up.

Across from him, Amy breathed a sigh of relief and relaxed into her chair, her skittishness gone.

So much for their coaching gig turning into something more interesting.

Whatever. It wasn't like he had time or energy for any type of relationship, and she was definitely a girl with high expectations. Her bar was set so high by this *P&P* book and probably every other romance she'd read, no real guy would ever meet her standards.

She wasn't great for his ego, that was for sure. He rubbed his forehead, trying to get his head back in the coaching game.

"Great writing." He tapped on the sketchbook. "Drawings, too. Is this the Darcy dude?" He pointed at the snooty-looking guy she'd sketched. "And Lizzie?" He pointed to the girl with the smirk.

She nodded. "You liked it?"

"As much as I can like anything about a boring book." He grinned. Maybe if he kept his repulsive self covered up, they could get back to joking around.

"High praise indeed." She smiled, then glanced at his empty glass. "Oh! I should've grabbed yours when I got mine. Sorry. Want me to refill your soda?"

She was all sweetness and light, now that he was zipped up like a mummy.

"No thanks." He tapped the can Lynette had brought out, scowling.

"So what's your plan for this challenge?" he asked, shifting back into coach mode. "What will get you maximum exposure for the contest?"

Her smile faded. "I'm not sure. I could put a review on Viv's blog—"

"The Hunkalicious Heroes one?" Toff fake shuddered. Viv should be ashamed of herself for that blog name. It was so…objectifying. He fiddled with the zipper on his hoodie. Maybe he was feeling sensitive because the sandwich chick had objectified him, and Amy had un-objectified him. He wasn't sure which was worse.

Was this how girls felt with guys constantly checking them out?

"Maybe try Instagram again?" Amy suggested.

Toff bounced his thumbs on the table. "Tell me more about your planet."

She blinked. "My planet?"

"Where the book people live."

She rolled her eyes, but he pulled another smile out of her, which felt like a win. Weird. She was the one trying to win something, not him. He took a swig of energy drink.

"What do you want to know?"

"Is Instagram the best place to drum up buzz?" Like he'd told her, her first post was…cute, or whatever, but it hadn't gotten the results she needed.

She reached up to mess with one of her sparkle thingamajigs. He didn't know why they always caught his attention, along with her wild red hair.

"You know how people just check out what they're into, right?" she asked.

He nodded. His entire feed was about surfing.

"Well, there's this thing called bookstagram."

He raised an eyebrow.

"It's a hashtag, but it's also…a community. For my planet." She smiled again, a big one. A real one.

"So what's most popular? Stuff like your first post? Do people really get that excited about book covers?"

She stared at him like he'd just asked if the sky was blue. He laughed, putting up his hands like he was fending off an attack. "Okay, okay. But your first post didn't do as great as you wanted, and it was a picture of a book. What else gets a lot of likes?"

Amy pursed her lips, considering his question. Her lips sparkled, too, with gloss. He knew all about lip gloss. He'd done enough kissing to taste every flavor.

"Bookface."

He blinked, refocusing. "What face?"

She grinned, her whole face lighting up. "It's easier to explain if I show you photos." She grabbed her phone, fingers flying, wild red hair falling around her face.

"Here." She held out her phone.

Toff checked out the #BookFaceFriday Instagram feed. It wasn't what he expected, but he had to admit the photos were cool—snaps of people posing holding books over their faces, wearing clothes that matched the book covers, or showing partial faces that looked almost exactly like the faces on the book covers.

"So this is what book nerds do for fun?" He returned her phone and grinned. Her reaction didn't disappoint, eyes flashing, her cheeks turning pink, highlighting her freckles.

"Are you going to help me or not, Toff?"

That got his full attention. "When I say I'll do something, I do it." She wanted a coach? She'd get one.

"Um, okay. Good." She smiled, but it wasn't the big one

he liked. "So if I do Instagram for my OTP, I can post photos for all my copies of *Pride and Prejudice*—"

"You have more than one copy of the book?"

"You have more than one surfboard." Amy crossed her arms over her chest, her sparky indignation back. "I don't get that, either, but I know you have your reasons."

He shoved his hand through his hair. "*Good* reasons. Competition blades, different-size boards, cruiser logs, custom boards I made with my dad—"

"See? Same thing." Amy twirled a strand of hair around her finger, distracting him.

"But the book is identical, right? The exact same words, only with a different cover?" This made no sense. "My boards aren't identical."

Amy shrugged, her cheeks flushing. "Let's just agree to disagree on this, okay?"

He could do that. He needed to stop staring at her hair anyway and focus on something else. "How about a video? Show off all your different book containers that way."

"I'm not ready for that yet." She ducked her head, running her fingernail along a rusted seam in the table. "I, um, have a fear of public speaking." She peeked at him. "I'm sure that sounds dumb to you. You have no trouble performing in front of an audience."

That didn't make sense. "But I thought you'd already recorded videos with Viv. The ones Brayden talked about."

Her cheeks went even pinker. "Yeah, but..." She bit her bottom lip, distracting him again. "You'd have to watch one to understand." She squeezed her eyes shut. "I was hoping we could avoid this."

"Avoid what? Me watching your videos?"

She nodded, looking like she wanted to bolt.

"Ames, they can't be any worse than the hundreds of crazy

meme videos I've watched."

He grabbed his phone and opened his YouTube app. He typed in "Hunka—" and boom. The channel popped up before he even had to ask her how to spell Hunkalicious, right under "Hunka Hunka Burning Love" by Elvis Presley. He clicked on the first video thumbnail, which was frozen on an open-mouthed Viv.

Amy sank lower and lower in her chair while Toff watched two minutes of Viv blabbing about books. In the video, Viv did all the talking while Amy sat next to her, holding up books and ping-pong paddles with thumbs-ups and thumbs-down images, smiling like that chick on TV who spun the letters on that game show his grandma loved.

Amy didn't say a word, on screen or sitting across from him.

Toff paused the video. He couldn't take anymore. It was too painful. He scanned the comments, expecting them to tear into Amy. Instead, they were mostly about the books, either arguing with Viv or telling her how smart she was. But the few comments about Amy called her "the redhead" and talked about her clothes or her hair, like she was some mannequin or whatever, which she was not.

This was…awful. How could she go along with this? Was this Viv's dumb idea? He scowled at Viv's frozen image on his phone screen. He'd tell her exactly what he thought the next time he saw her. He sucked in a breath, composing himself before he looked Amy in the eye. He was about to close the app when one comment caught his attention.

"Hey, Red, I love your recs on the blog. Why don't you ever do them here? Put Viv in time-out and you talk for once."

Toff couldn't agree more. His fingers drummed restlessly on the table as he debated what to say and how. Now he realized why she'd asked him for help. *Legit* help. She had to come out of her shell to win this contest. She didn't belong on the sidelines holding up stupid signs while other people hogged the spotlight. Yeah, he loved Viv, but she had to get out of Amy's way.

"I know I'm pathetic in those videos," Amy said softly. "I'm a joke. No one takes me seriously, if they even notice me at all." Her voice wobbled. "Thanks for not laughing."

Toff's head jerked up. "You're not a joke, Ames."

She shrugged, glancing away from him.

"I mean it."

He willed her to look him in the eye, hoping she could tell he was serious for once. She took a breath and met his gaze. The energy between them shifted, like an electrical storm descended right over their table, crackling with lightning bolts.

A bead of sweat trickled from the nape of his neck down his spine. Burning up, he unzipped his hoodie, but this time, instead of looking away, Amy's gaze tracked the zipper, her cheeks going pink when the jacket fell open. Slowly, she raised her eyes back to his.

Aha. Not repulsed after all.

Their gazes locked and held. She broke the stare first, glancing down to doodle, drawing hearts. Determination tightened his muscles. If that author's books meant so much to her, he had to help her pull this off.

Maybe she wasn't ready to jump straight to a video, but they had to do better than her first post. He grabbed his phone and scanned the #bookface posts again, adding an OTP hashtag. After a few minutes, he knew what they had to do.

"Okay. I've got a plan."

Amy glanced up, startled. "Already?"

He nodded. "Do you trust me, Ames?"

"Um, maybe?" She bit her lip.

Maybe? "You have to trust your coach, or this won't work."

"Oh." She broke eye contact, glancing down at her notebook again. "Yes, I trust you for that."

"Good. Can you meet me tomorrow at the bookstore?"

"Sure. Why?"

"I'll explain tomorrow. I'll be there by eleven. You need to get there first, though, and grab a bunch of books with, uh, couples on the covers."

"Couples?"

He grinned. "Romances. Like the ones you tried to force on me. And bring one of your OTP books, too, about these two." He pointed to her doodles of the snooty guy and the smirking girl. "But just one."

"Uh…why?"

"You're supposed to trust me, remember?"

"Okay, Coach." She blushed, but he didn't know why.

"Good." He crushed his empty can. He was *not* going to eff this up. "I won't let you down."

CHAPTER EIGHT

*T*off was already fifteen minutes late. Amy hovered in the romance section of Murder by the Sea. She'd already selected most of the books for whatever Toff's plan was, but she hadn't chosen any with couples on the cover. No way was she doing a couple-y bookface pose with him.

Five more minutes. If he didn't show, she'd leave. Maybe it was for the best if he bailed. Yesterday's lunch had been awkward and nerve-racking, especially the way it ended with Toff promising to help her, looking all intense like he'd sworn a vow to be her knight going into battle.

Her phone buzzed in her hand.

Toff: Be there in a flash

Amy bit her lip, her pulse rate revving up. She moved down the aisle to her favorite shelf—Redhead Recs—featuring her must-reads. Viv's mom had suggested that she and Viv create a shelf dedicated to their favorite books, and they'd jumped on the idea.

Amy grabbed one of her latest favorites, a gay romance about the prince of England falling in love with the son of the United States president. She'd shipped them so hard, even recording a secret video review that she'd never make public because of how embarrassing all her gushing had been.

"Ready to bookface, Bonnie?"

At the sound of Toff's voice, Amy yelped and jumped, dropping her stack of books. Toff grinned as he stepped closer, his dimples and sky-blue eyes freezing her in place.

"Chill, Ames. It's just me." He squatted down to grab the books, a whiff of his soap filling her nose. Like a junkie, she inhaled deeply.

Stop it, she scolded herself.

He stood and handed her the stack of books.

"You're late," she said, instead of *thank you*, hoping to prevent herself from being sucked into his flirty whirlpool.

Toff chuckled and glanced at the REDHEAD RECS shelf. His eyes widened. "Whoa. You have your own shelf? Impressive." He picked up one of her handwritten shelf talker cards, and her stomach clenched with panic. "'All the feels,'" he read aloud. "'Superhot alpha hero who's not an alphahole!'"

Amy prayed to Saint Jane Austen for an invisibility cloak or an instant coma. *Wake me up ten years from now*, she begged Saint Jane, *or beam Toff to the other side of the planet.*

Unfortunately, Saint Jane was off duty.

Slowly, Toff turned to face her, lips smashed together. Amy tensed like she was standing next to a volcano, just waiting for it to explode—with laughter.

"What's an alpha hero?"

"Navy SEALs," she said, tossing her hair over her shoulder in a feeble attempt at swagger. "Fighter pilots. Spies like James Bond."

"Got it." Toff leaned against the bookshelf, smirking down at her. "Kickass dudes like me."

"N-No. You're not...like that." He wasn't a superhero alpha like Thor wielding a hammer. Maybe he pulled off unbelievable surfing maneuvers that made his fans go crazy. And maybe he had sponsors knocking down his door encouraging him to go pro. That didn't make him…

Okay, it made him a low-key alpha.

Toff grinned like he'd read her mind. "So what's an alphahole?"

"The worst kind of guy. Controlling. Using his hotness for evil."

"Evil?"

"Never mind." She pointed to her recs shelf. "This guy's an old-school alpha hero."

Toff grabbed the Regency romance off the shelf. "He's wearing a top hat. And a weird scarf. What's that gold stuff on his boots?" Toff glanced up, lips quirking. "I don't think a real alpha hero would dress like this."

Amy snatched the book from his hands and put it back on display. "They're called Hessian boots. The gold 'thingy' is a tassel. Regency heroes wore—" She broke off. Why were they even having this conversation? Desperate for a Viv rescue, Amy glanced down the aisle, but her friend was nowhere in sight. She squared her shoulders and faced Toff head-on. "So what's the plan?"

"It's not a *plan* plan," he said with a nonchalant shrug. "I'm going for more of a vibe. I'll know it when we do it."

That sounded alarmingly…laid-back. Weren't winners more go-getter than that? Trying not to worry, Amy turned and headed for the front of the store.

"Also, I'm *late* because I swung by my house after surfing," Toff said, catching up with her as they rounded the corner into the reading nook. "I showered just for you, Ames."

Amy stopped short, nearly crashing into Viv and Dallas.

"You showered for Amy?" Dallas's green eyes glinted with laughter behind his glasses. "TMI, dude."

Viv's gaze darted suspiciously between Amy and Toff. "What's going on?"

"Photo shoot." Dallas adjusted his backpack covered with *Star Trek* patches. "Wish us luck."

"Wait, what?" Viv put her hands on her hips, staring them all down. "Why don't I know what's happening?"

"Do you ever, Wordworm?" Toff teased.

"You're not helping, *Clyde*," Amy muttered, then smiled at Viv. "We're doing Bookface Friday photos for the contest," she said. "Flipper has some brilliant plan that's not a plan that'll get more buzz, or so he claims." She shot him a dubious glance, then looked at Dallas. "So you're our photographer?"

"Yep."

"Why didn't I get invited?" Viv demanded, looking more hurt than angry. A twinge of guilt twisted in Amy's stomach. She hadn't told Viv about Coach Toff yet. She didn't want her getting the wrong idea or any lectures about the dangers of spending time with him.

This was about winning, nothing else.

"I'll show you the pictures when we're finished," Amy said, hoping to assuage her. "You can help me decide which ones to post."

"*I'm* helping you decide," Toff said, his voice deepening with bossiness. "I'm your coach."

Spoken like a true alphahole.

"This is *my* contest entry, Toff," she snapped. Yeah, he was helping her improve her swagger game, but she wasn't going to let him take over everything. "I decide what we post."

He didn't blink, her words bouncing off him like bullets off Superman's chest.

"Ack!" Viv sputtered, throwing her hands in the air. "What the heck is going on?"

"I'm coaching Amy so she wins the publisher contest," Toff said. "Dallas is my assistant today."

"More like his wrangler," Dallas joked. He pulled Viv into

a hug and kissed her on the cheek. "We'll be back before your shift's over."

"Wait a minute," Viv said to Toff. "What do you mean you're *coaching* Amy?"

"I'm showing her how to bring the heat," Toff said, flexing his biceps. "Prepare to be amazed, Wordworm."

An hour later, Amy's stomach hurt from laughing. Posing for Bookface Friday photos with Toff was shaping up to be a great idea—awkward, embarrassing, and wreaking havoc on her nerves but also fun.

After the first attempt, directed by Toff, she protested. "If I'm not taking the photos, I need to stage them," she'd told him. "Otherwise, I feel like it's cheating. The photos have to be what I want, since I chose the books." She was proud of herself for standing up to him. "Besides, bookface is my area of expertise, not yours."

Toff and Dallas shared a cryptic look. "Okay," Toff agreed, "but how about if Dallas takes behind-the-scenes shots, too?"

She frowned. "What? Why?"

"For fun." Toff grinned. "We're allowed to have fun, right? That's *my* area of expertise."

"Okay...I guess."

She could enjoy those photos later, in the privacy of her bedroom, after the contest, when she fell off Toff's radar and their friendship—or whatever this was—went back to normal.

Under her direction, they posed for three more photos, two featuring her and one featuring Toff, posing up and down Main Street and drawing a lot of attention, which Toff loved but she didn't.

"Can I stage the next one?" Toff asked when they took a snack break. "Please?"

"I don't know…" Amy loved book number four and had no idea what he had in mind. "I guess so, but if I don't like it, we're reshooting it the way I want to."

Toff's grin lit up his whole face. Totally unfair coaching maneuver. She ripped open her package of peanut M&M's and poured a few into her hand. M&M's made everything better.

"What's your plan?" Amy handed him book number four, which featured an out-of-focus photo of a girl with her back to the camera, looking up at the sky, dark hair streaming down her back.

He set the book aside. "I'm not doing that one." He nodded at Dallas, who pawed through his backpack and pulled out one of Amy's favorite 'ships of all time.

What the…? Amy gulped. She hadn't brought this book, *Summer Sweethearts*, for a very specific reason—the cover. A cover that just so happened to feature a blond guy and a redheaded girl, which wasn't the reason she'd bought it. Or 'shipped it. Not at all.

Who am I kidding?

"I didn't pick that one," she protested weakly.

"I know," Toff said. "Dallas did."

"But…how did you know I like this book?" She stared at Dallas, confused.

Dallas crumpled his bag of chips. "I read your book reviews, too, Amy, not just Viv's." He leaned across the café table and spoke in a stage whisper. "Don't tell Viv, but some of your reviews are even funnier than hers, including this one."

"I asked him to pick a book that you 'shipped' or whatever, with a couple on the cover."

Amy ran her palms along her jeans. *Do not panic. Find your swagger.* Flustered, she turned to Dallas. "Uh…thanks."

She appreciated his compliment, but that didn't change the fact that Toff had a speculative, dangerous gleam in his eye as he studied the cover.

"It was my backup plan," he said, "in case you chickened out and didn't pick any books with hot couple covers." He flashed her a steamy look. "Which you didn't."

So maybe he did have a plan. Amy bit her lip. It was definitely a hot cover, or maybe sweet-hot. The couple rested their foreheads against each other, the tips of their noses touching, their lips almost touching, mouths curved in matching I'm-about-to-kiss-you smiles.

"But why do we need a couples cover?" Her voice was weak. No swagger at all.

"Because you want buzz," Toff said, pinning her with a laser-focused coach stare. "Because challenge number two is supposed to be about 'ships.'" He made air quotes. "And 'ships' are about couples."

"And because you love this book," Dallas chimed in. "Don't deny it. I read all about it."

"But i-if we do this…" She swallowed, unwilling to state the obvious.

"*When* we do this," Toff said, "you just have to pretend we're faking out the sheriff again. It's easy. Just act like you want to kiss me, like you did before." His gaze dropped to her mouth. "Just…you know…fake it." He continued staring at her mouth, which did nothing to ease her anxiety.

"It won't be easy," Dallas said, elbowing Toff, "since you're a pain in the ass, Flipper." He turned to Amy. "I'll make sure you don't have to suffer too long." He pantomimed snapping a photo, moving his index finger up and down quickly.

"Whoa." Toff sat up straight, his attention caught by something down the street. His face split into a grin. "This is perfect!" He jumped up from his chair. "Come on, Ames."

He grabbed her hand, and they jogged down the street, Dallas behind them, until Toff skidded to a stop in front of a patrol car.

Oh no. No, no, no. "Bad idea, Clyde," Amy hissed.

Toff ignored her. "Get this car in the background," he ordered Dallas, who gave him a thumbs-up. He put his hands on her shoulders, leveling her with an intense coach glare, followed quickly by his flirtiest smile. "Trust me."

The deadly combo did her in.

"Fine. Whatever." The sooner they got this over with, the sooner she could leave.

"Stand right there." Dallas pointed to the sidewalk in front of the sheriff's car. Toff tugged her to the spot. "Who's holding the book?"

"I am." He glanced at her. "I mean, is it okay with you if I hold the cover?"

She nodded.

Toff stepped closer to her. Maybe she could still make a break for it.

"Kick off your shoes," Dallas said, and they both turned to stare at him. "Just do it." Shrugging, Toff kicked off his flip-flops. Amy did the same, wondering why. "Step in close, until your toes are touching."

Amy blinked up at Toff, who rolled his eyes at Dallas, then focused back on her, his face crinkling in a funny smile. "Don't worry. I showered *and* cut my toenails."

"Ugh," she said, temporarily grossed out enough to struggle to regain her composure. "TMI, Clyde."

Toff laughed, and the next thing she knew, their big toes were touching, which meant she was eye level with his neck. She sucked in a breath, trying to avoid touching him anywhere but his toes. Or huffing him like a junkie.

This photo better get liked and regrammed by HeartRacer

and a million other people.

"Hold up the book," Dallas ordered. Toff held it up in front of their faces. "Crap."

Toff lowered the book. "What's wrong?"

"You're too tall, or Amy's too short." Dallas scratched his spiky black hair, looking around. "We need a stool or something."

"On it." Toff dashed into the herbal store, returning with a plastic footstool.

Natasha, owner of the herbal store, followed him outside, smiling when she saw Amy. Amy gave her a half-hearted wave. Natasha was a longtime member of the Lonely Hearts Book Club, even though she nitpicked every book they read.

"What's going on?" Natasha asked.

"It's a publisher contest," Amy said. Toff plunked the stool down in front of her. "I'll tell you about it at book club."

Toff held out his hand, but she ignored his offer, stepping onto the stool unaided.

"Now try it." Dallas gestured for Toff to move in close again.

A small crowd had gathered to watch, taking photos with their cells. Amy squeezed her eyes shut. This was her worst nightmare and biggest fantasy all rolled into one tangled mess.

Toff didn't hesitate, closing the gap between them. They stood eye to eye now. "Welcome to my ozone layer."

"You're a dork," Amy said, struggling to resist his dangerous, flirty superpowers. Toff moved in closer and rested his forehead against hers, just like the book cover. Now they were nose to nose. Mouth to…mouth. _Almost._ She estimated their lips were about a fingertip apart.

She was terrified to breathe. What if she had bad breath? What if he did?

What if…what if…they accidentally kissed? All it would

take was a strong breeze to push them close enough to touch lips. Her stomach dropped to her toes.

"Perfect!" Dallas called out. "Hold up the book."

Toff did, and someone in the crowd whistled. "Told you," he whispered. "We're hot, babe."

He didn't have bad breath. Not at all.

Amy's pulse pounded in her ears. If she survived this photo shoot, she could do anything. Climb a mountain. Hang glide. Talk to Lucinda Amorrato without forgetting her words.

"Lower it a bit," Dallas said, "so I can see the tops of your heads."

Toff lowered the book a smidge. He moved even closer, his mouth just centimeters from hers. His teeth grazed his bottom lip and she felt the ground shake. Was that an earthquake? Or her imagination?

"Just kiss her, already!" someone called out—was that *Natasha*?—and the crowd laughed.

Amy swallowed. She hoped Toff couldn't tell she was trembling. "W-We don't have to actually kiss for the photo," she whispered. "Only our hair is in the picture."

"A kiss would get a lot of buzz, Bonnie." His mouth curved wickedly.

She inhaled sharply and took a step back, almost falling off the footstool.

Toff caught her and resumed their bookface position, his lips nearly grazing hers. "Just think of all the likes you'll get."

In her peripheral vision, Amy saw Officer Hernandez emerge from Natasha's herbal store clutching a paper bag, doing a double take when he saw them. "You two again."

"Nothing to see here, Officer Hernandez," Toff said, standing up straight. "Bookfacing isn't a crime. We're just a couple of lovebirds *not* breaking curfew."

Dallas zoomed in on the sheriff, then her and Toff,

snapping away with his camera as Officer Hernandez squinted suspiciously.

Amy swallowed a laugh as Toff touched his nose to hers again. His lips were definitely grazing hers. Her skin felt like it was crackling with anticipation. And panic.

"Lower the book," Dallas ordered. Toff complied.

Wait? Why was he taking photos of their faces without the book cover? That wasn't how bookface worked.

"I bet he's got herbal Viagra in that bag," Toff whispered against her lips. "Go-go for the po-po."

Amy snort-laughed, uncontrollable giggles overtaking her, Toff's joke triggering her stress release valve. This must be what hysteria felt like.

Still laughing, Amy whacked Toff on the chest and he staggered backward, pretending to be hurt. All the while, Dallas kept snapping photos. Scattered applause rang out, and the crowd slowly disbursed. To her surprise, Natasha shot her a wink and disappeared back into her store.

Officer Hernandez's face pinched, and he did the two-fingered warning gesture, pointing to his eyes, then to Toff. "Eyes on you, Nichols. Eyes. On. You." He frowned at Amy. "Watch out for this one, young lady. He almost got you into trouble once before."

"She likes trouble," Toff called after the sheriff, who unlocked his patrol car, shaking his head.

"She does *not*," Amy protested, jumping off the footstool.

"Sure you do. I'm just being an alpha. I thought you liked that." Toff's dimples bookended his mischievous grin.

"Time for one last outtake." To her surprise, Toff pulled her backward against his chest, resting his chin on top of her head. "We did it, by the way."

"D-Did what?" Amy was so stunned by the feel of Toff's body pressed up against hers, she could barely speak.

"Hit the vibe I was going for." His hands cupped her waist, and her heart stuttered to a stop. "Say cheese, Bonnie."

Dallas grinned as he snapped more photos.

Just a coach, just a coach, just a coach, Amy chanted in her head while her stomach did somersaults.

"Amy, you look like you're about to pass out. I thought you took a shower, dude," Dallas joked, looking up from his camera. "Hold your breath if he smells that bad."

Amy almost smiled. *Almost.*

"I don't stink, McNerd," Toff argued, still holding her. He bent down to whisper in her ear. "Um, I don't, right?"

Omigod.

"Uh…you smell like soap." *And sunshine and unicorns and starlight and—*

"Ha!" Toff straightened. "Amy says I smell awesome."

"I didn't say that!" He couldn't read her mind, could he?

Time to get her head back in the game, because that's definitely what he was playing—a game. *Eyes on the prize*, she told herself. *The prize is Lucinda Amorrato, not Toff.*

Dallas smirked. "Last one. Say cheese!"

"Cheese!" Amy forced a wide smile.

"Rabid raccoons!" Toff yelled as the sheriff drove off.

"Got it!" Dallas grinned as his fingers scrolled across his viewfinder. "Wow. Um…yeah. We got a lot of…good ones."

"Of course we did." Toff released his grip on Amy's waist and grinned like he'd just smoked another comp.

Amy took a breath and stepped back. "Okay, I think we're done for today," she said briskly, her heart still pounding. "All that's left is the *Pride and Prejudice* cover. I can do that one by myself."

Toff's face fell, disappointment clouding his eyes.

Huh. She hadn't expected that reaction.

"You sure?" Dallas asked, stowing the troublemaking

book in his backpack. "I'll take the photos if you want." He side-eyed Toff. "I won't tell you how to set up your shot."

Amy smiled gratefully at Dallas. He was the best, the pinnacle of boyfriend perfection. Lucky Viv. "That's okay. I'm sure Viv's waiting for you. My phone takes decent photos."

Dallas shrugged. "Okay, cool."

The three of them walked back to the bookstore together, but for once Toff was quiet. She hoped he wasn't scheming.

Dallas flipped her a mock salute as he opened the door to the bookstore. "I'll tweak these photos tonight and send you a link to download them tomorrow."

"Thanks!" Amy returned his salute, then turned to Toff. "You can go now."

His eyebrows shot up. "Usually the coach decides when a session is over, not the other way around." He crossed his arms over his chest, frowning down at her. "Is this a temporary thing, or are you firing your coach?"

A bolt of panic shot through her at the thought. It was more that she was still freaked out about his fake flirting, not that she could tell him that. Calling on all her swagger, she lifted her chin. "Not yet, but I might."

Toff's eyes narrowed. "What if I refuse to be fired?"

Amy puffed up. She felt like a general drawing her line in the sand. "That's my call. I don't need your help with this last one, so go torture Viv or Dallas."

They locked gazes for a long moment, currents of… of *something* arcing between them. Finally Toff nodded, a satisfied smile curving his mouth.

"Now, that's more like it," he said. "You keep bringing that kind of heat, Ames, and you're gonna win this thing."

CHAPTER NINE

*L*ater that night, Amy lay in bed doodling in her notebook. She still hadn't recovered from the bookface photo shoot, and drawing was her way of journaling.

She didn't know if she'd ever recover.

After standing up to Toff, she'd bolted like Cinderella rushing to get home before the magic faded. She hadn't even said goodbye to Viv, though they'd made up for that with a long string of text messages, mostly reassuring Viv that things weren't, in fact, a disaster.

She hoped.

Her phone buzzed.

Toff: I want you to know I'm about to watch the P&P movie. The one with hottie Keira Knightley. I can't watch the series. Too long.

Whoa. Amy read his text again, then typed a reply. **How about you read the book before you watch the movie?**

Toff: Not gonna happen

The winking-face emoji popped up on her screen, followed by alternating book emojis and sleeping face emojis.

She returned fire with a volley of eye-roll and thumbs-down emojis.

His reply was fast. **I'm trying to show some OTP R-E-S-P-**

E-C-T Bonnie. There was a pause, then, **I'm sorry about earlier. Didn't mean to make you feel uncomfortable**

If only he knew why I was uncomfortable. She was grateful this was a text convo so he couldn't see her blushing.

Amy: I hope you like the movie. Don't tell me if you don't.

His response didn't pop up right away. When it finally did, the butterflies in her stomach twirled and swirled just like the ladies of Beauxbatons in their pretty blue dresses, making Ron Weasley blush.

Toff: Come over and watch it with me.

Amy clutched her size-fifty knitting needle, which she'd found in Brayden's disaster-zone bedroom. Watch a movie with Toff? At his house? Just the two of them? Not just any movie, but one of the most romantic ones ever made?

Watch the part where Mr. Darcy helps Lizzie into the carriage, his hand grazing hers in slow motion…with Toff? That scene slayed her every single time. She sucked in a breath and typed, **I've already watched it a million times.**

Toff: Great. You can fill me in on the parts I sleep through. Followed by the silly tongue-out emoji. **You know where I live, right?**

Of course she knew.

Amy: Yes.

Toff: Excellent. Bring Whoppers. Red Vines. Junior Mints

Amy sighed. Mr. Darcy he was not. Time to snap out of her fantasy.

A knock sounded on her door. "Come in."

The door opened, and her dad peeked in.

"Hi, honey. Mom and I are headed out to see Natasha's play at the community center." He stepped into her room and grimaced. "Pray for a fire alarm or an earthquake."

Amy laughed. "You're terrible, Dad. The play isn't that bad."

"Are you kidding?" Dad's eyebrows shot up. "It's about a group of women who kill all the men in their village, then go on a—"

"Patriarchy-smashing rampage. I know. I read the script." Amy pointed her knitting needle at her dad. "Women are feeling a lot of rage these days, Dad. You can handle ninety minutes of fake rage."

"What if it's not fake?" Dad put his hand on his heart. "What if they drag me from the audience as their sacrifice?"

Amy's phone buzzed on her lap, but she ignored it. "Dad, get a grip. You're a cinnamon roll. Those theater women love you."

"You sure you don't want to go instead of me?" he asked hopefully.

"No. I, um, might have plans."

"Doing what?" Dad frowned. "I thought you were staying home with Brayden."

"What? Why?" Amy wasn't letting Brayden ruin her night before it even began. "He's almost eleven years old, Dad. He doesn't need a babysitter."

"Mom's worried about leaving him unattended. Remember what happened last time?"

Amy threw her head back against her pillows and groaned. Brayden had tested out their burglar alarm, locking himself out of the house, then breaking back in. The police had not been amused.

"Please, sweetie? I'll bake you whatever you want tomorrow."

Amy's fantasy of watching a movie with Toff crumbled like dust. "Okay." She sighed. "But you have to make *macarons*."

"Deal. Thanks, honey." Dad backed out of the room and closed the door behind him.

With a sigh, Amy fired off a text to Toff. **Sorry. Can't make** it. **Have to babysit your biggest fan.**

He responded quickly. **Bring him with you.**

No way. She'd rather reread that awful fan fiction Viv wrote about Prince Harry and Daniel Radcliffe than have her brother mock her favorite movie.

Amy: I can't. Sorry.

Toff didn't reply. Amy set her phone aside, cursing her brother. She grabbed the old-school gothic romance she was making the Lonely Hearts Book Club read for their next meeting. Maybe she could lose herself in a romance without annoying siblings.

Bzzz. Amy glanced at her phone.

Toff: Can you stream it?

Amy: Yes. Why?

Toff: Let's watch P&P online together. 30 minutes? I need to make a candy run, since you're not coming over

Watch the movie together but not in the same room? She'd never phone-watched a movie with a guy before. At least it wouldn't be as awkward as watching it sitting next to him. It might even be fun, right?

Deal, she texted. **See you in 30.**

"Ready?" Toff said into his phone thirty minutes later. He'd made sure not to be late this time.

"Ready," Amy said. "Go."

He pressed play on his laptop. He was bummed Amy couldn't come over. He'd had a lot of fun with her today, way more than he expected…and he'd come *this close* to kissing her, for bookface reasons.

He tore open a package of Red Vines and put his phone

on speaker. "You promise I'm not going to fall asleep?"

Amy huffed. "If you do, it's because you have a heart of stone."

Toff chuckled and took a bite of licorice. "Who says I have a heart?"

"Well, something must be in there," Amy said after a beat. "You did save me from the raccoons."

Toff grinned. "Maybe I was saving the raccoons from you."

On his laptop screen, fancy piano music played while the sun rose over a field. Keira Knightley walked across a meadow, reading a book. That looked like something Amy would do. Toff was 90 percent sure he was going to fall asleep in this movie, but he'd try his best to stay awake.

Coaches didn't fall asleep on duty.

"Why are all these girls so stoked about a dance?" he asked a few minutes later. He felt sorry for the dad, who was stuck in a den of estrogen, with a wife and five daughters. "Who's the poor guy they all want to marry?"

"Shhh," Amy said. "Watch."

And so he watched, for two hours and forty-eight seconds, and didn't fall asleep.

He ate the entire package of red licorice and two boxes of Whoppers. Fifteen minutes in, he put his phone on do not disturb so he could ignore texts from his friends and focus on the movie.

He had a lot of questions about all the weird rules, like who could marry who and why Lizzie supposedly wasn't good enough for the Darcy dude just because her family was poor. When he watched the Wickham drama go down, he remembered Brayden's comment on the beach.

No wonder Amy told Brayden she didn't want him to "be a Wickham." That guy was a jerk, convincing Lizzie's flaky sister to run off with him after he'd acted like he was all into Lizzie.

By the time they got to the scene where Darcy did that slo-mo walk across the field to Lizzie, after his aunt reamed her out, with all that piano music building up, Toff was fully invested in these two hooking up. He took his phone off speaker and held it up to his ear.

"You must know," Amy whispered along with Darcy on the screen. "Surely you must know it was all for you."

Of course she had the movie memorized. Dorky but cute, just like her. He didn't tease her about it, though. He needed to see how this thing ended…which was happily ever after, of course, with kissing in front of a fire pyre, and Amy going almost completely quiet.

Almost but not quite.

As the closing piano music played, and he listened to Amy sighing happily in his ear, he had to admit, at least to himself…the movie didn't suck.

"So, did you like it?" Amy asked.

Toff made a fake snoring sound, then pretended she'd jarred him awake. "Sorry, what? I fell asleep."

Amy huffed. "I'm having second thoughts about our coaching deal." He heard a rustling sound in the background. "I need to go."

"No, don't." Toff sat up quickly, accidentally knocking empty candy wrappers off his bed. "The movie was good, Ames." He ran a hand through his tangled hair. Coaching her was tricky, not at all like coaching a surfer. "I get the OTP thing now that I know the story." It was true, even though he thought Darcy had a stick up his butt.

He didn't want to piss her off, but he had one more piece of coaching advice, an idea he'd had while watching the movie. "What about drawing your own P&P cover as part of your OTP post?"

She was quiet, too quiet. Had he just undone their movie truce? *Crap*.

"Why would I do that?"

He was relieved she sounded confused, instead of like she wanted to throttle him.

"Those drawings you showed me in your notebook were great. If you drew your own P&P cover and posted your cover with our shots, it would…uh…bring more *you* into the post."

"More me?"

He liked that smile he heard in her voice. "Yeah." She went quiet again, and his own smile drooped. "What's going on in that bookworm brain?"

"I'm thinking my drawings are okay but not great."

He scowled at his laptop as the credits for the movie rolled. "You sell yourself short, Ames. You're talented. Strut your stuff."

"You really think drawing my own cover is a good idea?"

The uneven mix of hope and uncertainty in her voice did something to his gut—something new and unnamable. He wished Amy could siphon off just 5 percent of his swagger. He wouldn't miss it, and she needed it way more than he did.

"I do," he said firmly. "You've got this, Bonnie." He hesitated. "Trust your coach."

She was quiet for so long, he checked his phone to make sure the connection hadn't dropped.

"Okay," she said as he put the phone back to his ear. "I'll do it."

CHAPTER TEN

Viv: We need to talk about THE WEDDING! And the COACHING! Text or come see me TODAY!

Toff: Too busy, Wordworm.

Viv: I know Dallas is surfing with you later. You can't hide.

Toff: Dallas who?

*T*off waited his turn in the lineup, sitting on his board, the waves rocking him up and down. So far, he'd managed to avoid talking to Viv about the wedding, She was stoked about it, and he knew he should be, too, but whenever he pictured it, his stomach knotted.

He loved his dad and wanted him to be happy. He loved Viv's mom, too. She'd been a part of his life for as long as he could remember. He'd always been cool with their parents dating, but he'd never imagined they'd take it to the next level and make their relationship permanent. Move in together.

Swear those vows before God and everybody about "till death do they part." A shiver racked his body as the vow echoed in his mind.

He'd have to talk to Viv eventually but not today. And never about coaching. He felt…protective of what he was doing with Amy. Whatever it was. So today was just him and the waves, and later, reviewing OTP/#BookFaceFriday photos with Amy.

The sun peeked through the fog as he waited for a rideable wave. He'd been surfing all morning in the typical June Gloom weather. Dallas had been bitching about it for days, joking that it was sunnier in Wisconsin, where he used to live, than in Southern California.

"Yeah, but you don't have an ocean in Wisconsin, dude," Toff had said. "It'll burn off. It always does."

He didn't mind the gray skies or the cold. He needed to be in the water, the only place he felt he was his true self, or whatever. The best part of surfing was how he blocked out everything else. He focused on melding with it, not conquering it. Usually his worries disappeared like mist in the sunshine, but today they kept poking at him.

This morning Dad had dropped another bomb—he and Rose were having an "impromptu" engagement party next Friday, and Toff's attendance was mandatory.

He tilted his head up, soaking in the sun. His friends in the lineup laughed and joked with one another, but he tuned them out, his thoughts bouncing from his dad, to Rose, to Viv, to Amy—who was taking up a lot of headspace—then back to his dad...to his mom.

Last night, he'd dreamed about Mom, which hadn't happened for a long time. Dream Mom was perfect. She hadn't lost her hair to chemo or lost so much weight he worried she'd wither away. Dream Mom was strong and healthy, and he'd buried his nose in her thick hair, inhaling her perfume while she hugged him tight. For a few seconds, in that real-not-real space between asleep and awake, he'd thought she was still alive.

Then reality crashed down like a monster wave smashing him underwater.

Sometimes, out of nowhere, the scent of her perfume overwhelmed him, usually in the kitchen. One time, about a year after she died, the overpowering aroma had been so strong, he'd frozen in his tracks, unable to move. He'd searched the house, certain a bottle must be hidden somewhere, leaking the familiar flowery scent, but he'd never found it.

He still remembered riding his bike into town that day to the herbal store, the smell of Mom's perfume lodged in his nose. He'd asked Natasha, the herbalist, about the perfume. He figured she'd know, since her store was full of weird-smelling stuff. She'd taken him seriously, not laughing at his question. Like most of Dad's friends, she'd paid him a lot of extra attention after Mom died.

"Toff! Yours!"

The sharp voice startled him out of his thoughts. It was Murph, one of his friends from the school surf team, bobbing up and down on his board, pointing to the incoming wave. Shading his eyes, Toff watched a decent-size wave form in the distance. He waited patiently as it undulated toward the crowded lineup. Timing was everything.

Now.

He spun his board around and faced the shore, then paddled fast to catch the breaking wave as it lifted him up. He popped up on his board, balancing and leaning into the rail, taking the drop onto the face of the wave. He carved perfect turns, like the champion he was, completely in the zone.

Until some asshole dropped in, slicing across the wave, heading right while Toff rode left. Their boards collided, Toff's board flying out from underneath him, the wave knocking him underwater. *Shit.* He struggled to reorient himself, then resurfaced, spitting out water, and grabbed onto his board, glad for the ankle leash. A hot streak of fiery pain tore through his stomach. *Son of a bitch.* Dropping in like that was a bullshit move.

He scanned the water, not surprised to see his friends already on it, yelling at the guy and chasing him off like a pack of sharks. Sometimes his friends were chill when kooks did dumb stuff, but that guy was good enough to know the rules. Unlike Toff, the snake didn't look like he was hurt.

"You okay?" Murph yelled, paddling toward him on his board. "Need me to tow you in?"

Toff gave him a thumbs-up, but he wasn't okay. He heaved himself onto his board, pain shooting through his torso. He looked down to see a gash in his wet suit, blood seeping through the fabric. *Dammit.*

Murph waved his hands in the air to signal for the lifeguards.

"Don't do it," Toff snapped. "I can get myself back to shore."

"Too late," Murph said.

"Screw you," Toff said, but his heart wasn't in it. He lay on his board, paddling half-heartedly with one hand, clutching his stomach with the other. He wondered if he'd busted a rib in addition to the cut. "Who was that asshole?"

"Don't know," Murph said, paddling next to him and breathing hard as he towed Toff on his board, "but he won't be back."

Kendra reached them first, running fast with her lifeguard's first aid kit. Toff stumbled when his feet hit the sand. A few people ran down to meet him, their expressions wide-eyed and worried.

"Back off!" Kendra yelled, and everyone did except Murph. Kendra was fierce, reminding Toff of Nakia in *Black Panther.*

Toff sank onto the sand, wincing in pain as sharp spasms racked his torso. He stretched out his legs, pressing his hand on the wound. The last thing he wanted was a scene.

"Hey, Kendra, how's life?" Toff said casually, trying to sound like he had a paper cut instead of a bleeding gash. He knew all the lifeguards who patrolled the beach, but he'd never been on the receiving end of their help before.

"Did you hit your head on your board?" Kendra asked, all business. "That was a hell of a crash. Follow my finger with your eyes."

"Nah," Toff said, his gaze tracking her finger. "Just this stupid cut. You looked bored, so I thought I'd give you something to do."

Kendra ignored his joke as she unzipped his wet suit, slowly pulling it down to his waist, exposing the gash in all its ugly glory. *Shit.* That sucker was deep.

"Lie down," she ordered, so he did. She tore open a packet from her first aid kit and applied gauze to the wound, then grabbed his hand, placing it firmly over the bandage. "You need to apply pressure to stop the bleeding."

Toff winced, struggling to maintain his chill. "Guess it's couch time. I was ready to call it a day anyway."

Kendra shot him a withering look and grabbed her radio from her lifeguard belt.

"Hey, man." Murph crouched next to him, grinning. "You'll do anything for attention, huh?" He tilted his head toward the clump of anxious girls hovering several yards behind Kendra. "You're gonna have a badass scar. Chicks love scars."

Toff tried to laugh, but doing so hurt.

Kendra's radio squawked and crackled, and Toff heard the words "ambulance" and "contusions" and "heavy bleeding."

"No ambulance." Toff struggled to sit up, but Murph pushed him back down.

"Chill, dude. They've gotta follow procedure. You know that." Murph glanced at the girls, then waggled his eyebrows at Toff. "Just think of all the action this is gonna buy you."

Toff closed his eyes and groaned. "Not worth it," he muttered. He knew what was coming next. A stretcher ride to the parking lot, where he'd be loaded into the ambulance. X-rays. Stitches. His dad putting him on lockdown. Coach Diggs freaking the fuck out.

"Want me to call your dad?" Murph asked.

"We already did," Kendra said, holstering her radio. "He's meeting you at the hospital."

That didn't surprise Toff. Like him, his dad knew all the lifeguards. Once upon a time, Dad had surfed the pro circuit. Now he made custom boards for pros and anyone else who could afford to pony up major cash. His dad always cut the lifeguards a good deal, calling it *mahalo* karma.

"Can you text Dallas?" Toff asked Murph. "He's supposed to meet me here." After a few rides, they were going to grab food and then meet up with Amy.

"The McNerd? Sure." Murph nodded and stood up, moving out of the way as two more lifeguards parked the red lifeguard truck at the berm and ran toward them, carrying a stretcher.

"Crap," Toff muttered. He glanced at the crowd surrounding them, which was now at least twenty gawkers, most of them holding up their phones and recording. Wasn't there a law against that? Invasion of privacy or something?

"Yo, Nichols."

"What's up, Esparza?" Toff forced a grin as the guys set the stretcher in the sand. "You do delivery service now? Where's my lunch?"

"At least your pretty face is still intact. Ready for a stretcher ride?"

"I can walk." Toff pushed himself up on his elbows, but Esparza put a restraining hand on his chest. Frustrated, Toff shot a glare at the crowd of gawkers. "Can you get rid of my fan club? I don't wanna be a meme."

Esparza tilted his chin at Kendra, who blew her whistle and hollered at the crowd to disperse.

"Call me! I'll visit you in the hospital!" "Snapchat me! I'll bring you cookies!" Voices floated toward him, and Toff gritted his teeth.

Esparza grinned down at him. "Sucks to be you, huh?"

"It does right now," Toff muttered.

He closed his eyes and braced himself for the upcoming humiliation. He'd keep his eyes shut until he was in the ambulance and pretend this was all a bad dream. As the lifeguards lifted him onto the stretcher, he winced. He hated being a wimp, but damn, this hurt.

Suck it up, he told himself. *You'll be back in the water in a couple of days.*

*B*rayden crashed into the kitchen, panting like he'd just run a marathon, Goldilocks at his heels. "Amy! Amy! Toff's hurt!"

Amy froze in place, clutching the salad bowl with both hands.

"He was attacked by a shark!" Brayden exclaimed, clutching his stomach, still out of breath. "There was a lot of blood."

The wooden salad bowl clattered to the floor, lettuce and chopped veggies flying everywhere. Goldi ran to the food, unfazed by Brayden's announcement.

"Slow down, Brayden," Dad said sharply, rushing into the kitchen from the family room, followed by Mom. "Start over."

"Amy? Sweetie?" Mom sat at the table, her worried gaze bouncing between Amy and Brayden. "Come sit down."

Amy shuffled to the table and collapsed into a chair. *Toff hurt, Toff hurt, Toff hurt.* The words clanged in her ears like angry, dissonant chimes.

"There was an ambulance and blood and lifeguards and..." Brayden's words jumbled together. A head-to-toe shiver rocked her to the core. She grabbed a paper napkin, tearing it to shreds.

Shark. Blood. Ambulance. *Omigod omigod omigod.*

Where was her phone? She needed to call Viv. Dallas. *Somebody.* Her mom put a stilling hand on Amy's trembling fingers.

"We'll find out what happened," Mom said, tilting her chin at Dad, who nodded and left the room, phone to his ear. How did she stay so calm? Mom never panicked, no matter what.

Brayden flopped into a kitchen chair, finally out of words. His face was ghost white, his freckles popping out like ink on paper.

"D-did you see it happen?" Amy stuttered.

Brayden shook his head. "There's a bunch of videos on Snapchat."

Videos? *Omigod.*

"Brayden, give me your phone right now," Mom demanded. "I don't want you watching—"

Dad poked his head around the doorframe, still on the phone. "He's okay," Dad whispered. "Already home from the hospital."

Home? How could that be?

"No shark." Dad glared at Brayden. "Surfing accident."

"He's home?" Amy asked, her voice sounding far away. "Are you sure?"

Dad nodded, and relief slid over Amy like a warm blanket chasing away the shivers. Brayden darted anxious looks between her and Mom.

"Come here, Bray," Amy demanded. Brayden dragged

his feet, head down like he was in trouble. She didn't know whether to yell at him or hug him. He deserved both. Amy pulled him into a hug. A really tight hug with an extra squish of you-make-me-crazy.

"You almost gave me a heart attack," she said, squeezing him tight. "You can't go around spreading crazy rumors—"

Mom put a hand on Amy's shoulder. "Thank God Toff's okay. That's what matters."

Amy released her hold on Brayden. Mom was right.

"I should call Viv," Amy said, jumping up from her chair. "Toff's practically her brother."

Mom made a shooing motion, and Amy sprinted down the hall to her bedroom where she'd left her phone. Viv answered on the first ring.

"He's okay," Viv said, out of breath. "My mom's at his house now."

"Why aren't you there?"

"I told Mom I'd woman the store. She wanted to be with Toff and his dad." Viv gulped for air. "I guess Paul was freaked out at the hospital."

"I'll bet," Amy said. She was going to be freaked out for hours, and she and Toff weren't even related. "Have you talked to him?"

Viv snorted. "I tried, but he's all doped up on painkillers. He kept asking for Oreos and beer; then Paul took his phone away."

Relieved, Amy collapsed onto her bed. That sounded like normal Toff. "How bad is the injury? What happened?"

"I'm not sure how it happened. A crash, I guess, and his board fin sliced his stomach."

Amy cringed, trying not to picture it.

"My mom says the cut's all stitched up, and he doesn't have a concussion. He'll recover."

"Thank God," Amy breathed.

"He can't surf until he gets his stitches out, though." Viv sighed. "He's going to be a giant pain in the butt if he can't get in the water."

Amy considered that, trying to imagine not being able to do her favorite hobby. "Like if someone told us we couldn't read for two weeks," she said. "We'd go crazy."

Brayden peeked around the bedroom door. "Is Toff okay?"

Amy nodded and gave him a thumbs-up. Brayden headed for her bookshelves and grabbed her beloved Yara Greyjoy Funko Pop and her Spider-Man. Amy gave him a thumbs-down, but he ignored her.

"Are you going to visit him tomorrow?" Amy asked Viv. Brayden nodded enthusiastically, pointing to himself.

Oh no. Brayden was *not* visiting Toff, not on her watch. She shook her head, scowling. Brayden pretended to rip off Spider-Man's head.

"Maybe," Viv said. "His dad wants him to rest, so he's banning visitors for a few days, but Mom said I was 'an exception to the rule' because they're about to *Brady Bunch* us."

"You should make Toff cookies!" Brayden said way too loudly. "He's your *boyfriend*!"

Amy threw a skein of yarn at his head. *Shut up!* she mouthed.

"What did Brayden say?" Viv asked, her voice sharp. "Did he just say Toff was your boyfriend?"

"Uh, no." Amy chucked another skein of yarn at her brother and motioned for him to leave. He stuck out his tongue, tossed the Pops on her bed, and left, slamming the door behind him.

"Amy? It sounded like he said—"

"He did." Amy groaned, flopping back on her pillows. "I

was going to tell you—"

"That Toff's your *boyfriend*? I thought that was fake!" Viv huffed into the phone. "Is this why he's coaching you?"

"No. He's my coach, that's all." Why were they even having this conversation? Because of her stupid brother. *Argh.*

"Then why did Brayden call him your boyfriend?" Viv demanded.

"I was going to tell you, but—"

"You were going to tell me that he *is* your boyfriend?" Viv sounded like she wanted to climb through Amy's phone and shake her.

"No! That he's not. But he pretended he was with Brayden."

"Why did he do that?" Viv sounded suspicious.

"I don't know. Just messing around, I guess. You know how he is." She sighed. Now that he was hurt, Amy wondered if she should let him off the hook with the coaching deal. Probably. He'd need to focus on recovering, not helping her win a contest.

In the background, Amy heard laughter and voices. "I've gotta go," Viv said. "Customers."

"Okay."

"We're not finished, you and me." By the tone of her voice, Amy knew Viv was in sassy mode, with her hand on her hip. "There's more to this. I can tell. You need to tell me exactly what's going on."

The call disconnected, and Amy yelled into her pillow. She was going to kill Brayden.

She squeezed her eyes shut, imagining Toff bleeding on the beach. Riding in an ambulance. Getting stitches. Banned from the water. She thought about the fun they'd had with the bookface photos—their "vibe."

How he'd apologized by watching her favorite movie with her. How she was starting to develop her own tiny bit of swagger. How good it felt to stand up to him and see that spark of admiration in his eyes.

Amy swallowed, staring at the ceiling. She was so relieved he'd be okay. She wondered what she could do for him, if anything.

He'd been there for her, with the kniffiti rescue, agreeing to coach her, and their silly bookface photos. She wondered how she could be there for him or if he'd even want her to be.

Because suddenly, she really wanted to be.

"What happened out there?" Dad demanded. "You've been dropped in on plenty of times."

Lying on the couch, Toff met his dad's eyes, which were the same blue as his but with crinkles around the corners from years of sunshine and laughter. That's what Viv's mom had said after a couple of glasses of wine at dinner a few weeks ago. Toff had taken one look at her and Dad making goo-goo eyes and fled the scene.

Right now, he was just relieved to be out of the hospital. He hated them, since they brought back bad memories of his mom. At least he didn't have a concussion, and his ribs were bruised, not cracked. He had fifteen stitches covered by a large bandage. Nasty black bruises ringed the bandage like an ugly picture frame.

"Come on, Dad," Toff protested. "I'm not perfect. That jackass dropped in out of the sky. I tried to avoid him, but it happened too fast." He shrugged. "Maybe I got distracted." That part was the truth, at least. Yeah, he'd been in the zone, but he'd been thinking about Mom right before he charged the wave.

Dad frowned, and Toff read his expression easily. Getting distracted was an amateur move, and Toff was no amateur.

"Shit happens out there," Toff said defensively.

"Right. But not to you."

Why was his dad acting like this? He was usually the most chill guy around. He knew that accidents could happen to anyone. He hardly ever got upset with Toff, laughing off most of his "antics," as he called them.

"I'll be fine." Toff shrugged. "Back in the water in a few days."

"Didn't you hear what the ER doc said? Two weeks on land, buddy." Dad's forehead wrinkles deepened. "You have to rest, especially if you want to seal the deal on a scholarship for college."

College was the last thing he wanted to talk about, since it would just lead to more arguing about whether or not he'd go pro or go to college after he graduated next year.

Toff had been scouted by most of the SoCal colleges with surf teams, and he knew he'd have multiple offers as long as he slayed this fall's school comp season. To do that, he needed to be in top form, which he was. Or had been until now.

"I called Grant," Dad said. "He and the Ace crew send their best. He doesn't want you to worry about missing the Surf for Sea Life event next Saturday."

Damn. Toff had been so distracted by his injury, he hadn't thought about AceWare, his local sponsor, and next week's fund-raising comp. Grant and AceWare had sponsored him, hoping Toff would hit the pro circuit after he graduated high school instead of going to college.

He knew surfers aiming to qualify for the pro tour who'd dropped out of high school. They took online classes or did independent study while they traveled the world, surfing in qualifying events to rack up points toward earning a spot on the pro tour for the following year.

That's what he wanted to do, but unfortunately, Dad had been adamantly opposed ever since Coach Diggs first proposed the pro idea when Toff turned fifteen and big sponsors started contacting them. It killed Toff to watch some of his friends already on the circuit, where he wanted to be.

"My son's going to college," Dad had told Coach Diggs. "I'm not letting him make the same mistakes I did."

Toff didn't think Dad had made a mistake by going pro when he was seventeen. He'd traveled the world for years, winning big, partying with friends he still saw when they came through town to surf. He'd met Mom in Australia while competing. How could that be a mistake?

Dad had pulled out all the stops in the middle of their fiercest argument, the summer between freshman and sophomore year.

"Your mom and I promised each other that if you turned out to be a surfing rock star, which you are, dammit, you'd at least finish high school."

Dad had gone straight for Toff's gut and his heart, busting out Mom's scrapbook. She'd updated it until the year she got sick. It was packed full of photos of the three of them. Most of the photos were taken on beaches, like the one framed on their coffee table, of four-year-old Toff and his first boogie board, clutching his favorite stuffie, a penguin.

Toff closed his eyes, the throb of a killer headache nudging at his skull. He hated that he was letting down his sponsor and missing out on a fund-raiser he cared about.

"So now what?" He opened one eye, dreading the answer.

"Rest, especially this first week. Not much activity at all until your stitches are removed." Dad reached behind his neck to tighten his long gray-blond ponytail. "Depending on how long it takes your ribs to heal, you can probably surf again in July."

"July?" Toff sat up abruptly, sucking in a breath at the sharp pain, but his dad gently pushed him back down. "I can't wait that long. I'll die."

Dad rolled his eyes. "You might die if you're dumb enough to get on your board while you're still hurt." He gave Toff his harshest look, the one he used for giant screwups. "I mean it, kid. You've gotta take it easy."

Toff grumbled. "That's code for 'have no life.'"

"You *do* have a life, thank God." Dad scowled down at him. "This could've been a lot worse."

Toff closed his eyes. He didn't want a lecture. He wanted to sleep.

"You hungry?" Dad asked, his voice gruff. "Thirsty?"

Toff shook his head. "Sleepy. Go away."

"Fine," Dad grumbled, "I'll leave." But he grabbed a worn blanket from the footstool and draped it over Toff, tucking it around him like Toff was five years old. Toff pressed his face into the pillow so his dad wouldn't see his smile. Dad flicked off the lamp, leaving the room with a heavy sigh.

Toff blew out a breath and flopped onto his back, staring up at the ceiling in the darkened room. What a crappy day. At the hospital, Dad had gone into freak-out mode, which had freaked out Toff. Dad never overreacted.

Fortunately, Rose had shown up and calmed Dad down, staying with them through the X-rays, sutures, and doctor lectures. Toff wished Rose had stuck around after they got home to distract his dad, but she'd said they needed space.

Space was the last thing they needed.

He'd been lucky, surfing as long as he had with only minor injuries. He'd had a few small gashes, cuts from rocks and coral, lots of bumps and bruises, and a sprained wrist.

Today's was the worst so far. Maybe that was why Dad

freaked. That, and the doc saying the fin had almost sliced his liver.

Toff didn't want to think about that. He needed a distraction. He let his thoughts wander back to Amy, since that's where they wanted to go. Was it the pain meds? Or was it just because of her?

His head felt fuzzy, floaty. Must be the meds. The pain in his torso had subsided to a dull throb. He closed his eyes, letting himself float. His thoughts blurred and tilted, a kaleidoscope of images swirling in his mind. Images and other sensory input, too—like a girl's soft hand tugging at his, dragging him across the beach, then letting go. In his dream, he chased the laughing girl, whose red curls bounced as she ran just out of reach of his grasping hands.

Right before sleep overtook him, he caught up to the mystery girl, grasping her hand and spinning her around. His chest flared with heat, with recognition. Before he could say her name out loud, she wiggled out of his grip and ran off, laughing.

His last thought before drifting into oblivion was that he needed to catch her before she disappeared forever.

CHAPTER ELEVEN

Viv: 911! 911!

Amy: Are you okay? I'm still asleep. It's 5:30 a.m.!

Viv: Wake up!! HeartRacer loves your OTP post! They're shipping you and Toff!

Amy: What??

Viv: Check your IG!!

Amy: Oooomiiiiiigoooooodddd

Check out @RedheadRecs' adorable Insta feed! Super swoony shout-out to this second challenge contest entry! Can you say chemistry? Now that's an #OTP! We hope this relationship is fact, not fiction! #BookFaceFriday #BonnieandClyde

P.S. We love that original P&P cover!

. . .

*A*my lay in her bed staring at her phone, still not believing what she saw. After Viv's emergency text woke her up way too early, she'd filled a plate with macarons, then crawled back into bed. Dad had made good on his babysitting bribe, thank goodness, because she needed major sugar to process what was happening.

Overnight, she'd gained more than five hundred new Instagram followers, which was amazing by her standards. Her account was small, nothing like the big-time bookstagrammers she admired, whose posts easily garnered thousands of likes.

Amy took another bite of macaron. *Yum.* She hoped Dad had hidden a stash of these where Brayden couldn't find them. Savoring the pastry, she scrolled through the photos. Coach Toff had been right. She wanted buzz? Thanks to his "outtake" photos, she had it and then some.

The day after his accident, she'd decided to trust her gut and choose the photos without him, since he was mostly sleeping and in a lot of pain, according to Viv. Besides, this was her contest entry, not Toff's.

She and Viv had reviewed the photos together, impressed at what a great job Dallas had done. He'd captured her and Toff laughing, arguing, and doing a whole lot of side-eyeing and smirking. No surprise, Toff was, um, exceptionally photogenic. More important, the photos were funny and flirty but harmless.

Or so she'd thought, until they came to the last batch of photos—the couple of poses for the *Summer Sweethearts* book.

"If I didn't know better," Viv had said, gaping at the photos, "I'd think you two were…together. Like, really together." She'd waggled her eyebrows, and Amy had blushed, unable to tear her gaze from the photos.

Dallas had captured the few seconds when they were nose to nose and Toff was biting his lower lip, looking like…like…

kissing was definitely about to happen. Until she almost fell off the stool.

"I'm not going to post this one. I can't." She'd secretly save it for the rest of her life, but no one else could see it. *Ever.*

"You have to," Viv had said vehemently. "I hate to say it, but you do. People will love it, especially HeartRacer, since they published *Summer Sweethearts*."

After a futile argument with Viv, Amy had decided to go for it, hearing Toff's voice in her head telling her to "bring the swagger."

"It'll cheer him up to get a bunch of Insta love," Viv had said. "Take his mind off the pain from his injury."

"Like he needs more admirers."

"Why do you care about that?" Viv had asked. "Since this is a strictly coaching relationship."

"I don't care. At all."

Eyes on the prize, she'd told herself as she uploaded the photo that almost tricked her into believing a connection had flashed between them, if only for a few seconds.

Now, with the reaction to her contest entry blowing up and her followers increasing, she wasn't sure how to deal with the attention. Toff might be used to being a star, but she wasn't. She blew out a shaky breath, reached for a second macaron to calm her nerves, and scanned more of the comments.

"Darcy and Lizzie Forevah. Great cover drawing!"

"I love Summer Sweethearts, too! You two are hotter than the real book cover!"

"Surfers are sexy trouble!"

"Just read some of your reviews—love them!"

"I am here for this ship. Are you 2 together? Please say yes.

#BonnieandClyde"

"OMG! You're living my trope dream! Booknerd + hot jock!"

"Your book reviews are so funny! I love your Redhead Recs!"

"That bench is so cute. I love to knit, too."

Amy set aside her phone, her stomach tumbling and twisting. She was dreading Toff's reaction to finding out they were a 'ship. Hopefully he'd just laugh it off.

The question was, how long could she pretend she wasn't secretly 'shipping herself and Toff?

CHAPTER TWELVE

*T*off sat up in his bed, the effort making him grunt. He hurt more today than he had yesterday, which had passed in a blur of pain meds, sleeping, and mindless YouTubing. He staggered into the living room and collapsed onto the couch with a groan. Dad emerged from the kitchen, coffee cup in hand. "How's the patient?"

"Lousy." Toff stretched out on the couch, his long legs taking up all the available space. "You can't keep me prisoner forever, Dad. I'm not staying locked up until I get my stitches out."

"You survived so far."

Toff snorted. "Barely. You could've let my fans in to visit."

Dad rolled his eyes. "Don't be obnoxious. I don't even know what those girls see in you."

They stared each other down, glowering, then their scowls morphed into matching grins. Dad had had his own groupies back in the day. Still, he was always warning Toff not to objectify girls.

"I don't," Toff always said. "They're the ones who objectify *me*."

It was true. Girls mostly wanted him for his looks, for his body, which wasn't a bad deal most of the time. But sometimes he got tired of everyone seeing him as a mimbo. That was another reason Amy intrigued him. She seemed interested in his brain and his body. At least, he hoped she liked his body. He knew she wanted his coaching brain for sure.

"Can I have my phone back?" he asked. "It's like you time warped me back to the Dark Ages."

Dad rolled his eyes, then pulled the phone from his back pocket and handed it over. "I've never seen so many text notifications in my life."

Toff grinned. "Like you said, Dad. Fans."

A knock sounded on the open front door.

"Come on in, Dallas," Dad called out. "You can help me tie down my idiot son."

Toff made a move to sit up again, wincing. His dad raised a warning hand. Frustrated, Toff flopped his head back on the couch cushion.

This. Sucked.

Dallas strode into the room looking purposeful, which annoyed Toff. No one should look like that during summer break, especially not wearing that stupid *Trek Yourself Before You Wreck Yourself* T-shirt.

"Hey, dumb-ass." Dallas grinned, plopping onto the footstool next to the couch. "You're not going anywhere on my watch."

"Did you coordinate or what?" Toff glared at Dallas, then his dad.

Dad smiled approvingly at Dallas. "He's just smarter than you, Toff."

"Bruised or cracked ribs?" Dallas glanced up at his dad.

"I'm right here," Toff said, annoyed, but Dallas ignored him.

"Bruised pretty bad," Dad said. "Stitches. No concussion, thank God."

Dallas nodded, turning his attention back to Toff. "I've

cracked ribs before, sparring in tournaments. Bruised them a few times, too. I know how much it hurts, dude." His gaze held sympathy behind the dork glasses, then it turned hard. "You have to chill out. You can't do anything stupid, which will be hard for you."

"Shut it, McNerd." Toff shifted on the couch, grimacing as pain squeezed his midsection, radiating from his stomach to his back.

Dad squeezed Dallas's shoulder. "I knew you were his smartest friend. Maybe he'll listen to you."

"I'm not a moron," Toff grumbled. "I don't want to make things worse. I just don't know what I'm gonna do trapped on the couch."

"ESPN," Dallas said. "YouTube. Netflix. PlayStation."

"There are these inventions called books." Dad gestured to the overflowing bookcase on the far wall. "I've heard they're even better than TV."

Toff closed his eyes, huffing with exasperation. Second only to the ongoing "go pro or go to college" battle between him and Dad was the "why don't you read a book" battle. It had intensified when Dad and Rose started dating. Occasionally, Dad came home with books Rose thought Toff might like — the dorky stuff Dallas read, with trolls and wizards or whatever. The occasional biography. None of which interested him beyond a few pages.

"Yeah, great idea," said Dallas. "Maybe try one of the books Amy picked out for you. She's a pro at book recs."

Toff shot Dallas a warning glare.

"Amy? Viv's book club friend?" Dad asked. "She recommended books for *you*?"

Toff nodded reluctantly, not liking the way Dad's eyes sparked with interest at the idea of him reading.

"Excellent. Amy gets a visitor pass, too," Dad told Dallas,

like Toff was in a coma instead of just bandaged up.

Toff growled. "*I* decide who gets a visitor pass, Dad, not you." He frowned as he remembered something. "Hey, I thought you told Rose that she and Viv could come over anytime."

"I did. Rose came by yesterday, but you were asleep. Viv wasn't with her."

So much for his almost-sister bothering to check up on him. He glowered at Dad like it was his fault. "You know what? Maybe I don't want you giving out any visitor passes."

"So you *don't* want to see Amy?" Dad shrugged, but he flashed that shit-eating smirk Toff hated. "Okay, take her off the list, Dallas."

"No! That's not what I meant." Toff threw his head back against the pillows in frustration.

From his chair, Dallas choke-laughed. "So...yes or no to Amy visiting?" he asked innocently.

Toff stared him down. Of course he wanted to see Amy. They had to figure out which bookface photos to post before the deadline. Plus, he just...wanted to see her.

"Visitor pass for the book lover," Dad announced, grinning and raising his arm with a flourish. He disappeared into the kitchen, and Dallas turned his attention back to Toff.

"Viv wants to see you," Dallas said. "She's hoping you bruised your tongue instead of your ribs so you can't talk."

Toff flipped Dallas the bird.

Dallas laughed. "Listen, I know this sucks, but you'll survive."

"Says you," Toff grumbled.

"Surfers are such babies. You wouldn't last two minutes on a Tae Kwon Do sparring mat, especially not with me." Dallas stretched out his legs. "You check out social media lately?"

"No, I just got my phone back." Toff frowned. "Why? Are

people talking about my accident?"

Dallas shook his head, but Toff could tell he was holding in a laugh.

He pointed to his bandage, irritated with his friend. "This isn't funny, dude."

"It's not," Dallas agreed, "but *this* sure is." He tapped his phone. "Check out Amy's OTP Instagram post."

"She did it without me?" A stab of disappointment twisted his gut. He'd been looking forward to choosing photos together.

"You were out of commission yesterday. She had a #BookFaceFriday deadline." Dallas's grin was stupidly big and smug. "Besides, I took great photos. She didn't need you, *Coach*."

Toff narrowed his eyes at his supposed friend, then unlocked his phone.

"Check out her feed," Dallas said. "Somehow I managed to make even you look good."

Toff ignored the jab, scanning Amy's Instagram. She'd posted a couple of times. The first being the shot she did without him and then the one with the book Dallas picked.

A surge of self-satisfaction shot through him when he saw how many likes her posts had. He scanned the comments. The kudos for Amy's book reviews jumped out, making him happy. That's what he'd hoped would happen—for people who liked her photos to go check out her reviews on that Hunkalicious blog she and Viv did.

This was exactly what she needed—people other than her friends to see how smart she was. To compliment her. To boost her swagger.

"The Bonnie and Clyde comments are funny," Dallas said, "but I don't know why everyone's shipping *you*. I get why people like Amy, but you? Eh." Dallas shrugged, his shit-eating grin worse than Dad's. "What's so great about another hot surfer who can't even stay on his board?"

"Shipping us?" Toff looked up, ignoring Dallas's smack talk. "What are you talking about?"

"Look again." Dallas smirked.

Toff wondered if he had a painkiller hangover, because he wasn't following. He checked Amy's feed again. The post with him and Amy had two shots: the #BookFaceFriday photo, with only his hair and Amy's hair visible, matching the cover models, and then an outtake photo from when they'd been laughing and joking around.

Whoa. Hold up. In the outtake photo, they were face-to-face and…damn, they looked *hot* together. It was obvious he'd been about to kiss her—until she'd panicked and almost fallen off the stool.

Toff couldn't take his eyes off her expression. And his. "Wow. I'm surprised she posted this one."

"It was a tough sell. Viv was the one who convinced her to do it, believe it or not." Dallas kicked back in his chair. "And now the online bookworm contingent wants you two to hook up. You're officially part of an OTP, dude."

Toff blinked, then scanned the photo's comments, surprised by all the #BonnieandClyde OTP shipping. Whoa. Toff wondered how Amy felt about being shipped with him. Probably not too happy.

Even so…he and Amy being shipped *because* of her OTP posts? That was awesome buzz for her challenge entry. He couldn't have planned that if he'd tried.

Dad walked back in with a plate full of toasted bagels with cream cheese and set it on the coffee table. "You're welcome," he said to Toff.

Toff grinned. "Thanks, Dad." He grabbed two bagel halves, slapped them together, and took a huge bite.

"So," Dad said, "Viv and Amy can come over today, but no one else except them and Dallas. I have to drive to San Diego for an appointment, so *somebody* needs to keep an eye on you. I know he'll keep you in line."

Toff rolled his eyes. Being landlocked and babysat for the next couple of weeks was going to suck.

"We can play Candy Land," Dallas said, "and paint each other's nails."

Dad smirked. "Make sure Amy brings books. Since you aren't concussed, you can read while your nail polish dries."

"You guys suck," Toff grumbled, even though they didn't. Even though he knew they were harassing him because they cared.

He glanced at the hot photo again, zeroing in on Amy's face. Was she faking for the camera like she did for the sheriff? Didn't look like it.

He grinned and set his phone aside. Why not mix in some kissing with the coaching? Kissing was harmless. Fun. Something he could do even with jacked-up ribs.

Maybe the next couple of weeks wouldn't completely suck after all.

"Why can't I come with you to see Toff?" Brayden whined over his bowl of Gorilla Munch cereal.

"Because he's in pain and you'll just make it worse."

Viv had texted her earlier with a message from Dallas. Toff wanted books and visitors. She didn't believe the books part, but she'd play along.

Brayden stuck his tongue out and kept eating.

"I assume you've talked to Toff." Mom sipped her tea.

"How's he doing?"

Amy shifted on her chair, not meeting Mom's eyes. What exactly did she think was going on between her and Toff anyway? She was surprised Mom hadn't given her the third degree yet, but the shark-not-shark scare must've thrown her off her usual Mom game.

Thank God her parents never looked at social media. As much as he loved *The Bachelor*, her dad would go crazy with all the shipping of her and the Cupcake Kid. *Ugh*. She couldn't think about that right now.

"I, um, haven't heard from him," Amy said. "But Viv says he's going to be fine." She shrugged and made eye contact with Mom. "He has stitches and bruised ribs but no concussion."

"Good." Mom nodded, looking thoughtful. "I heard through the grapevine that his dad and Rose are getting married. I'm so glad. They deserve to be happy."

Amy definitely agreed with that, being the champion of HEAs that she was. "Did you—" She hesitated, then plunged ahead. "Did you know Toff's mom? When we were kids?"

Mom set her teacup on the table. "Put your bowl in the dishwasher, Brayden, then take Goldi for a walk."

"What? Why?" He shot Amy a glare like this was her fault.

"Because I said so. Amy and I need to have a girl talk."

Uh-oh. Amy's stomach flip-flopped, and she barely noticed Brayden stomping around the kitchen, grumbling about child labor laws. He left the house with Goldi, slamming the front door behind him.

Mom laughed. "That boy is something else."

Amy didn't laugh. She was too worried about what Mom had to say.

"Don't look so panicked, sweetie. I just wanted us to talk in private without your snoopy brother around." Mom sipped more tea and shifted in her chair, turning to face Amy.

"Yes, I knew his mom. When you kids were very young, in kindergarten, some of the moms and dads would go out for coffee after dropping you off at school." The look in her eyes was distant, like she was searching for a memory. "Some of us had a harder time than others adjusting to our little babies going off to school."

"Mom. Kindergartners aren't 'little babies.'"

Mom blinked away the faraway look and smiled at Amy. "If you ever have kids—which you shouldn't until you're at least thirty—I'll remind you of this conversation."

Amy reached for the blackberry jam and smeared it on a piece of toast, not wanting to think about babies and Toff with the same brain waves.

"Anyway." Mom cleared her throat. "Deanna. Toff's mom. She was lovely, from Australia. She had that fabulous Aussie accent and was a natural surfer, just like Toff's dad. And she was funny. She always made me crack up."

"No wonder he's so good at surfing," Amy muttered. Some people won the DNA lottery: looks, athletic ability, charisma.

"Yes," Mom agreed. "They had Toff out on a boogie board when he was three years old."

Amy could picture it—an adorable little Toff, suntanned and hair bleached blond by the sun, king of the toddlers on the beach.

"We spent a lot of time together that kindergarten year, commiserating about our *babies* going out into the big world of school." Mom sighed. "Deanna got sick when you kids were in second grade. At first she thought it was fatigue from fighting off pneumonia—she had a bad go-round with it. But she didn't get better."

Mom stared out the sliding glass doors that opened onto the deck, her gaze distant. "It all happened so fast. From fatigue, to the cancer diagnosis, to hospice."

A tear trickled down Mom's cheek, making Amy's eyes burn as she imagined how it must have been. Poor Paul, losing his wife. Poor Deanna, to die so suddenly, when her son was so young. And poor Toff, losing his mom. He didn't have any brother or sisters to rely on, just his dad.

"Anyway." Mom grabbed a tissue and blew her nose. "It was so hard on Paul, but he did his best with Toff. They spent every spare minute at the beach. I think it was how they both healed and honored Deanna."

Amy wondered how it might've been if Toff's mom were still alive. Would Deanna and Mom be close friends? Would Amy have grown up with Toff always around, like Viv had?

"So…how did Toff end up spending so much time with Viv and her mom?"

Mom smiled. "Rose grew up in Shady Cove. So did Paul. Once upon a time they went to the same schools as you kids."

Amy blinked. "Really?" She never knew that, but then, she'd never asked. She wondered if Rose and Paul had dated back in high school.

"From what I know," Mom continued, "once upon a time Paul and Rose were friends the way Viv and Toff are now. It's sweet, when you think about it, everything coming full circle." Mom cupped her teacup with both hands. "Honestly, I wish they'd married years ago, but Paul took his time, letting Rose get over her divorce."

"I remember when that happened." Five years ago, seventh grade. That's when Rose's mystery writing career took off. Viv always joked that her mom was killing her dad over and over again in her books.

"Rose really stepped up when Deanna died," Mom said, "helping with birthday parties, Halloween costumes, that sort of thing. I think that's why Toff and Viv are so close, all that time they spent together as kids." Mom raised an eyebrow.

"I always wondered if Viv and Toff would date." Her smile turned mischievous again. "Guess I pegged that one wrong. Want to tell me what's going on with you and Toff?"

"Nothing," Amy said too quickly. Mom's other eyebrow shot up. "I asked him to help me with the publisher contest. That's all that's going on with us."

"How is he helping exactly? Does he like to read?"

"Um, no." Amy squirmed in her seat. "But he knows how to compete. How to win." He was great at pushing her outside her comfort zone, too, using his one-two punch of hard-ass coach mixed with flirting to motivate her.

Mom observed her intently, like a psychic trying to mind read. "So you asked Toff to help because he's competitive? Is that the only reason? Or do you have an ulterior motive?"

"Mom!" Amy blushed furiously, but she'd deny this all day long if she had to.

"You made him a special Valentine when you were in fourth grade, honey. And fifth grade. Sixth, too."

"Omigod, Mom! Do you keep a journal about every little thing I do?" How did she know about those anyway? Amy had hidden the valentines in her sock drawer, never daring to bring them to school.

"Maybe." Mom grinned. "Also, who do you think put away your laundry until you started doing it?"

Amy covered her face with her hands.

Mom laughed. "Honey, it's nothing to be embarrassed about. We all have crushes."

Easy for her to say. Amy let her hands drop from her face and took a deep breath.

"Okay, fine. To answer your question, I don't have an ulterior motive. I really am nervous about this contest. About the whole book world checking out my Instagram...checking out *me*." And now it was happening on a scale she wasn't sure she was ready for. "Anyway." Amy brushed her hair behind her ears. "I'm not sure he can still do it, with the injury and all."

Mom tilted her head, watching Amy like a cat watches a mouse. "You might be surprised. Toff seemed to be enjoying himself the other day. With you."

Dad wandered into the kitchen at the exact wrong time, overhearing Mom.

"I was just thinking about the Cupcake Kid! I hope he's doing okay." Dad shot her a grin. "How about you and I make him some cupcakes? Since you and Viv are going to see him."

"What a wonderful idea," Mom said, winking at Dad.

Oh. My. God. Was her dad playing matchmaker? Were both of her parents? This was worse than Mrs. Bennet fluttering around the house when Charles Bingley and Mr. Darcy arrived at Netherfield Park, desperate to marry off her daughters.

"Grab your apron," Dad ordered. "I know the perfect recipe."

With a resigned sigh, Amy rose from her chair and took an apron from the hook. When her parents were united in a mission, they were unstoppable.

CHAPTER THIRTEEN

"**H**ey! Took you long enough," Viv said as soon as Amy entered the bookstore.

Viv was right. Amy had spent too long deciding what to wear, which was silly, since this was just a get-well visit to her coach…whom all of #bookstagram was *shipping* her with.

Toff still hadn't texted her. She hoped it wasn't because he was upset about being a hashtag or, worse, being part of a ship—with her as the other half.

Viv's mom emerged from the mystery aisle, reading glasses perched on her nose, several pencils stuck in her messy bun, and cat slippers on her feet.

"Amy! Sweetheart, I haven't seen you in forever. How are you?"

Amy grinned as Rose enveloped her in a hug. She loved Viv's mom. Someday, if she was lucky enough to work in publishing, she hoped to work with quirky, talented authors like her.

"I'm great," Amy said. "How are you?"

Rose shrugged, looking slightly harried. "A bit stressed. I'm on deadline for my publisher, but Toff's accident had me so worried, I couldn't write a word for two days."

Viv sidled up next to her mom, giving her a sideways hug. "Flipper will be fine, Mom. He's got a thick skull, and the rest of him will bounce back fast, since he's in great shape." Viv pointed at Amy. "Don't tell him I said that or he'll gloat."

Amy nodded, her cheeks heating as she tried not to think about what great shape Toff was in. Viv slanted her a suspicious look, but Amy focused on Rose.

"We're bringing him cupcakes, and, um, books." Amy shrugged, not believing Toff would read a word.

"Oooh, cupcakes." Rose's dark eyes lit up. "Did your dad make them?"

"Yeah. I helped a little, but he was so into it, I mostly let him do his thing." Amy's chest pinched as she thought of her dad bouncing around the kitchen, singing along to the *Chef* movie soundtrack. He missed his job so much.

"He'll find a new gig soon, sweetie," Rose said, reading her mind. "Everyone in town loves his pastries. Not just in Shady Grove. He's a legend up and down this part of the coast."

Amy wasn't sure about her dad's "legend" status, but she hoped Rose was right about him finding work soon.

Viv shifted into bossy mode. "Go grab those books Toff refused to take earlier."

Right. Amy scurried off, grabbed the books, then rejoined Viv and her mom.

"Let's see what you picked," Rose said. Reluctantly, Amy showed her the books, feeling bad she hadn't selected any mysteries, but she had a good reason for her choices.

"Romances?" Rose looked doubtful, but then her expression softened. "I admire your passion for your genre, honey. It's worth a try." Rose smiled. "We'll make a reader out of that boy eventually." She squeezed Amy's shoulder and gave Viv's curls a gentle tweak. "Give Toff my love."

• • •

Viv opened the box of cupcakes as Amy drove to Toff's house. "These look awesome, and they smell great." Viv inhaled deeply, then sat bolt upright. "Wait a minute. Does this have something to do with Toff texting me about your birthday party? The one he almost ruined by eating all your cupcakes?"

Amy wished Viv's mom wasn't a mystery author, because when Viv caught the whiff of a secret, she was like a dog hunting a buried bone.

Amy glanced at Viv, whose eyes were bright with speculation. She gripped the steering wheel tight. "He texted you about that?"

"Yeah. I wondered why he asked."

Amy slanted Viv an apologetic look. "I was going to tell you—"

"Tell me what?"

"That Toff sort of, um, dropped by my house for lunch the other day."

Viv's dark-brown eyes narrowed suspiciously. "Since when does Toff just 'drop by' your house?"

"It wasn't a big deal." It was, but Viv didn't need fuel for her fire. "He gave Brayden a lift home from the beach and I made him a sandwich. That's when I asked him to be my coach."

Viv shook her head. "I still can't believe you asked *Flipper*."

"I know, I know." She slanted Viv a quick look. "But now that I've entered the contest, I really want to win. Toff knows how to."

"True, but…" Viv frowned. "I just don't want you getting your heart broken."

"That's not going to happen." Amy stiffened her spine. "There's nothing going on with us." No matter what HeartRacer tweeted, she and Toff would never be a real-life OTP.

"You sure about that? That photo of you two was—"

"I'm sure." Amy pulled away from the stop sign. "Besides, you won't have to worry about my imaginary heartbreak after today. I'm sure Toff's going to want out of the coaching deal now that he's laid up."

Which stunk, because she really wanted his advice about being thrust into the social media spotlight.

"I don't know. He's pretty stubborn once he decides to do something." Viv leaned back in her seat. "Not to mention, he's going to eat up all the social media attention. Have you two texted about the OTP stuff yet?"

Amy shook her head.

"Huh. I'm surprised." Viv shrugged, then tapped the lid of the cupcake box. "So is this because you teased him about ruining your birthday party?"

"My parents did the teasing. My mom told him the story, since he didn't remember it. Then Dad called him the 'Cupcake Kid.' Toff was mortified."

Viv snort-laughed. "I wish I'd seen that. I can't believe he didn't remember."

"I can." Amy sighed. "Anyway, that's why my dad made him cupcakes, because he knows Toff likes them."

"And because your dad's awesome."

Amy smiled. "That, too."

They turned onto the road that dead-ended at Toff's house. She'd been here a few times for parties with Viv—parties where she watched Toff from afar while girls and guys alike swarmed him, vying for his attention.

Amy steered her car down the gravel driveway and parked. The house was a small bungalow with a sun-faded exterior, the gardens a bit overgrown. Toff's van was parked in the driveway, and an assortment of surfboards rested against the house, along with a couple of wet suits drying on a clothesline.

Viv pointed to a workshop behind the house that looked

like a garden shed on steroids. "Have you ever been in Paul's workshop?"

Amy shook her head.

"It's cool. You wouldn't believe how much cash people shell out for a custom board." Viv opened the passenger door and climbed out. "Let's go, girl. I want to see Toff's face when you give him the books."

"I'm sure he'll be much happier with the cupcakes than the books."

Laughing, they climbed the porch steps together.

"Yo, Flipper!" Viv yelled through the screen door.

"Door's open!" Toff yelled back.

Amy hesitated in the entryway. She wanted to see him, but she was nervous. What if he really *was* mad? Viv had a point. He hadn't texted her. She didn't want him to feel obligated to keep coaching her if he didn't feel up to it or wanted out.

She squared her shoulders, hoping to fake a little swagger, then walked into the living room, where Toff kicked back on the couch, wearing nothing but a pair of board shorts, his hair bedhead messy. A video game played on the TV screen. Her gaze drifted to his bare stomach where a nasty bruise bloomed out from a bandage like a Rorschach inkblot.

Toff's face lit up when he saw them. "Finally, someone other than my dad or the McNerd." His gaze flicked to Amy, and his grin deepened. "Hi, Ames. How's my favorite bookworm?"

"Hey!" Viv sputtered.

"Man, your buttons are easy to push, Wordworm."

Favorite? Amy swallowed. "Um, I'm okay. Better than you." She motioned to his bandage. "I'm glad you're going to be okay." She tucked a strand of hair behind her ear and smiled hesitantly. "Brayden told me you were attacked by a shark."

Toff's eyes widened. "He did?"

Did his face go pale underneath his tan? She blinked. It must be the lighting.

"He's a drama king." Her smile came easier this time. "You know that."

"Right," Toff said, his easy smile returning to match hers. "He definitely is."

Dallas joined them from the kitchen, pausing to kiss Viv on the cheek. "Tag, you're it," he said. "I need to run an errand for my mom, but I'll be back later with pizza. Good luck. You'll need it."

"Extra pepperoni!" Toff hollered as Dallas left the room. The front door slammed shut, and he turned his full attention back to Amy, blasting her with a megawatt grin.

"I've been thinking…" He paused dramatically. "If we're gonna be a ship, Ames, we need a name, like J-Rod. How do you feel about Tamed?"

A tingle crept up the back of Amy's neck. Somewhere in the distance, she heard laughter. Was that Viv?

"What do you think?" Toff prompted, oblivious to her delusional bookworm panic attack. "You know, Tamed. 'T' for me plus 'Ame' for you, Ames." His grin veered from teasing to dangerous. "Not that you could ever tame me for real."

Amy's brain shorted out. He wanted to name them, like they were a real couple? She was still trying to figure out how to respond to them being shipped. His amping this up wasn't going to help. Plus, Tamed was a horrible ship name. There was alpha, and there was caveman. They weren't going to cross that line.

"What'd I tell you?" Viv said, her voice cutting through Amy's brain fog. "I knew he'd love the attention. Hashtag Giant Ego."

Laughing, Toff returned his attention to the TV. "Hang

on." His thumbs manipulated the game controller, his sky-blue eyes focused on the screen.

Viv pointed to a chair across from the couch. "Sit," she ordered Amy. Amy sat, struggling to find her composure, let alone any swagger. Viv set the cupcake box on the coffee table.

"What a big baby you are, Flipper," Viv teased, "letting a little injury put you on the couch." She winked at Amy, and Amy realized she was changing the subject away from ships for her sake. Amy sagged with relief. Viv was the best friend in the world.

Toff paused the video game and squinted at Viv. "Hilarious." He levered himself into a sitting position, leaning his back against the worn cushions, his tanned, muscled legs stretched out in front of him. He pointed to his bandage. "You still gonna pick on me?"

"Don't I always?" Viv flopped into the chair next to Amy.

"Whatever," Toff said, turning back to his video game. "I need to kill this wolf."

"You're killing a wolf? For fun?" Amy asked, appalled. At least she'd found her voice.

He darted her a quick smirk. "It's a game, Ames. No real animals were harmed in the making of this mindless entertainment. I need raw meat for health points so I don't die."

Amy stole another glance at the mottled black-and-blue bruises on Toff's torso. She tried not to ogle the rest of him, which was all lean, sun-kissed muscle. What was it with him going shirtless all the time? She turned away from his distracting…Toff-ness.

He made a grunting noise, and when Amy snuck a peak, he was tugging a T-shirt over his head, his face contorted in pain. Should she help? But that would mean getting close and, um, touching him. His head popped through the T-shirt, and he met her gaze.

"Sorry," he muttered. "I know I'm gross or whatever."

Gross? He was the farthest thing from gross she could imagine. His injury looked awful, yeah, but the rest of him, not so much.

"So gross," Viv muttered.

Amy frowned at Viv. "He's not gross. He can't help how… how…you know." Her hand fluttered in his direction. She blushed, wishing she'd kept her mouth shut. "How the injury looks."

"Thanks." Toff shot an I-win look at Viv, who rolled her eyes, then grinned at Amy. "Seriously. How about Tamed? I mean, Bonnie and Clyde is okay, but Tamed has more bite."

Amy sucked in a breath. Time to get this over with.

"I don't think so. I don't want to encourage the fake ship. Bonnie and Clyde is bad enough. The outtake photos were a great idea, though. They got me a lot of buzz and new followers on Instagram and Twitter."

He chugged from a bottle of Gatorade. She was glad his mouth was temporarily occupied. She needed to talk fast while she had the chance.

"But I didn't expect people to, um, ship *us*." She bit her lip. "It's weird." And amazing and terrible. "Also, I understand if you can't coach me anymore."

To her surprise, he plunked down the Gatorade and shot her a coach glare. "You're trying to fire me again? While I'm in pain? That's a low blow, Bonnie."

Startled, she sat up straight. "I just assumed that since you're laid up, you wouldn't want to—"

"You assumed wrong." He crossed his arms over his chest. "I'm not bailing on you because of a stupid cut."

Uh-oh. That was the most intimidating coach face she'd seen so far.

"I told you he was stubborn," Viv said.

"It's, um, more than a cut," Amy said, giving her coach one last chance to escape. Or maybe she was trying to give herself an escape route.

Toff's glare softened. "This isn't because of the ship stuff, is it?" His lips quirked. "I mean, I totally see why it happened. I'm very shippable."

"Ugh!" Viv exclaimed. "Can we change the subject before I puke?"

Toff tilted his chin toward Amy. "Only if Amy wants to stop talking about our ship."

God, yes. "No more ship talk," she said, relieved. She'd ask him about how to handle the social media attention later.

Viv jumped up. "I need a break from all the testosterone flying around. I'm getting a drink. You want anything?"

Toff and Amy shook their heads, and Viv disappeared into the kitchen.

"She's been bossing me around since preschool," Toff said with a sigh, resting his head back against the couch cushions.

"I know." Amy took a breath. "Are you sure about coaching—"

"Like I said, I don't quit. Just gimme a day or two of pain meds and I'll be back to coaching you."

Her heart fluttered in her chest. "Really?"

"Hell yeah. I need something to keep me busy while I can't surf."

Amy wasn't sure whether to be insulted or not. She held up the books she'd brought. "Since you survived watching the *P&P* movie, maybe you could try reading a romance. You're going to be lying around anyway, right?" She hoped her smile packed enough swagger to activate his competitive juices.

To her dismay, Toff winced, squeezing his eyes shut and clutching his midsection, gasping for breath.

Panicked, Amy jumped up from her chair, dropping the

books. "What do you need? Pain meds? 911?"

Eyes still closed, he held up his hand and shook his head. "I'll be okay," he gasped, "as long as I…don't"—he spoke haltingly, pausing to take deep breaths—"don't…have to… to…" He sucked in a huge breath, then squinted up at her like a one-eyed pirate. "As long as I don't have to read one of *those* books." He pointed to the books she'd dropped on the floor, letting loose a deep, rumbling laugh.

"You—you—jerk!" Amy squatted down to retrieve the books. She wanted to throw one at his head. "I thought you were in real pain, Toff."

The laughter faded from his eyes. "You were really worried about me?"

She stood up, fisting her hands on her hips. "Yes," she huffed, "but I don't know why. Everything's a joke to you." She gestured toward his midsection. "Even this."

"That's not true." He scrubbed a hand down his face. "I just… I don't know." He shrugged. "It's easier to laugh than, you know…think too much or whatever."

Amy rolled her eyes. He was the dudiest dude she knew. No wonder he'd never had an actual girlfriend. That would require feelings.

She glanced toward the kitchen. What was taking Viv so long? Turning her back on Toff, Amy headed into the kitchen.

Viv leaned against the counter, phone to her ear. *My mom,* she mouthed, *having a mini meltdown.* Viv rolled her eyes as she listened. "Right, Mom. But can't you find another way to kill him that looks like an accident?"

Amy smiled, her frustration with Toff ebbing slightly. Sometimes Viv talked her mom down from plotting panic attacks.

"Aren't you supposed to be helping customers?" Viv said. "Give your brain a break, Mom." She shrugged at Amy and kept talking. "Yeah, he seems okay. Still a pain in the butt.

Dallas went to get us pizza." Viv gave Amy an apologetic smile. *Five more minutes*, she mouthed.

Amy nodded and headed back to the living room. Toff looked up from the couch.

"Sorry. I didn't mean to upset you." He smiled sheepishly. "I'm just pissed off, you know? About not being able to surf. Summer just started, and I feel like it's over already for me."

She heaved a sigh. It was hard to stay mad at him. He'd had the rug ripped out from underneath him, which had to suck, and to his credit, he hadn't used his accident to bail on her.

"Can you give me a hand? I need another pillow behind my back." This time his smile was pitiful, making him look adorable and kissable and slightly pathetic.

She glanced around, grabbed a throw pillow from a chair, then approached Toff cautiously, like he was a lion and she was the tamer. #*Tamed*, she thought, but she wasn't going to say it.

Laughter sparked in his eyes. "I'm not gonna bite, Bonnie." He leaned forward, wincing again, and motioned for her to put the pillow behind him. She moved closer and shoved the pillow into the gap between him and the couch cushion.

"Thanks." He glanced up, giving her puppy-dog eyes. "One more favor. Can you scratch my back?"

"Wh-What?"

"I can't reach, and it itches like crazy. Please? I don't have cooties."

Cooties was the last thing she was worried about.

"I'm begging you. It feels like an army of ants is crawling up my back."

He was unbelievable, but she couldn't abandon him to his imaginary ant army, right? She took a breath and stepped even closer, her knees bumping the couch. "Where?" Her voice came out strangled, which was exactly how she felt.

"Smack in the middle, babe."

"Don't call me babe." *Not unless you mean it.*

"Oh, I see how it is." He batted his baby blues at her and flashed his dimples. "You only like it when there's an audience, like on kniffiti night."

Heat flooded her cheeks. "That's not— I don't—"

"Chill, Ames. I'm just teasing you."

Tentatively, she reached a hand underneath his shirt, and when her skin touched his, fireworks exploded in her fingertips. His skin was warm and taut over his muscles. He leaned forward to give her better access and made an inappropriate moaning sound—at least that was how she heard it, probably because her mind was in the gutter. That was a downside of reading so many romance novels.

"Harder," he said as her fingernails scraped his skin. "Lower. Oh yeah. That's it. Don't stop."

Holy Wet-Shirt-Colin-Firth-Darcy. He definitely wasn't helping her gutter mind.

"You're too good at this." Huskiness threaded his voice. "I'm putting you at the top of my contacts list for when I have an itch that needs scratching."

Amy froze, her hand hovering over him. He had to know how dirty that sounded, right? Heat emanated from his back to her fingers and straight to her chest.

He glanced over his shoulder, eyebrows bunching. "Why'd you stop?"

Because she wanted to throw herself at him? Because she was dying of awkward yet wanted to put her hands everywhere she shouldn't? *Because, Toff Nichols, I am a giant dork and you are a surfing god. And because I'm stupid enough to want you to call me babe and mean it.*

CHAPTER FOURTEEN

*A*my scampered away from back-scratching duty just as Viv rejoined them from the kitchen.

"Here." Amy grabbed the box of cupcakes from the coffee table and shoved it at Toff.

"For me?" His face lit up.

"Yes, from my dad."

"Y-your dad?" He swallowed, eyeing her anxiously.

Was he still worried about the birthday party incident? That was cute. Sweet. Her heart thudded faster than it should. She toyed with the fringe on her hand-knitted top. "I helped make them, but it was his idea, and he did most of the work."

"Open it," Viv said, sitting down and taking a sip of water. "We don't have all day, Flipper."

"Not until Amy sits," Toff said, shifting his legs and pointing to the edge of the couch. She eyed him warily. What was he angling for now? A foot rub?

His face was a mask of innocence, reminding her of the Puck character in one of her favorite fantasy series—a funny and charming troublemaker fairy. She'd always been on Team Puck for that series, but the heroine fell for the broody prince instead.

"C'mon. I need someone to protect me from *her*." Toff

tilted his chin at Viv.

"No you don't," Amy said, but she sat on the couch anyway, blaming his Puck magic.

Toff lifted the cupcake box lid halfway, then stopped, shooting Amy a smirk. "Is there a yarn bomb in here? A raccoon?"

"Very funny."

He raised the lid, then squeezed his eyes shut, reminding Amy of herself when she was too embarrassed to make eye contact. Wait, was he blushing?

"Cupcakes," Toff whispered. "Your dad made me... cupcakes."

Amy nodded, chewing her bottom lip, debating whether or not to laugh.

Toff opened his eyes and exhaled. "Your family is hard-core, Ames, punking me like this. I guess I deserve it."

"What? No, that's not what this is," she protested. "My dad made them because he loves to bake." She smashed her lips together to hide her smile. "And he, uh, knows you like cupcakes. Obviously."

"They aren't poisoned?" Toff eyed her warily. "Payback for making you cry?"

Viv chucked an empty Gatorade bottle at Toff's head. "Say thank you, moron. When's the last time someone baked for you besides my mom? And she only bakes from a box, not from scratch."

"These look awesome," Toff said, pulling a cupcake from the box. "Thank you, Amy. And thank your dad for me, too."

The cupcake was a piece of art in Amy's opinion, with perfectly swirled mocha icing sprinkled with sparkling sugar, espresso chips, and a tiny bit of lemon zest.

"He's a pastry chef," Amy said. "Or was. No, *is*." She twisted a loose curl around her finger, frustrated. "My parents are really sorry about your accident. They hope you recover fast."

"Your dad's a pastry chef?" Toff's eyes widened. "Damn, I sure know how to pick a fake 'ship partner." He shot her a grin before taking a huge bite, closing his eyes and moaning with pleasure as he chewed.

"Gross," Viv said. "Do that in your bedroom, dude."

Cheeks burning, Amy glared at Viv, who smirked.

Toff took another bite. "Oh yeah," he groaned. His tongue darted out to lick frosting off his lips. "So good." He closed his eyes again, chewing and moaning.

Amy squirmed on the couch. This was worse than his reaction to the back scratching.

"Should we give you and your cupcakes some privacy?" Viv asked, her tone snarky.

Toff's eyes were at half-mast as he let out a long, satisfied sigh. "You can leave," he said to Viv. "Amy can stay." His gaze skimmed her up and down with appreciation. "And I'm not just saying that because you have magic fingers and gave me a foodgasm."

"Toff!" Viv exploded.

Amy gaped, not believing her own ears.

"What?" He smiled lazily, his eyes glassy. "She did. Gimme another cupcake."

Viv made huge tell-me-now eyes at Amy.

"I-It's not what you think," Amy whispered. "I scratched his back when you were in the kitchen."

"It was hot," Toff mumbled, his eyes drifting back to half-mast.

Uh-oh. Was he doped up?

"When's the last time you took pain meds?" Amy asked. "Or ate anything?"

"Don't give him an excuse," Viv huffed.

"Cupcake." Toff reclined lower on the couch, stretching

out his legs and resting his bare feet on Amy's thighs. "You can feed it to me, Ames."

Amy gaped at Viv. This was over-the-top, even for him. It had to be the painkillers talking. "Toff, when did you take your medicine?"

He shrugged. "Dunno. Check the fridge." He yawned, stretching his arms over his head, then turned on his side and curled his hands underneath his chin, reminding Amy of a little boy.

Viv jumped up and ran into the kitchen, returning with a pad of paper. "Almost an hour ago, so it must be kicking in." She showed the paper to Amy. "His dad's tracking the times." Based on the notes, this was his fifth pain pill since the day of the accident. Mostly he'd been taking Advil.

"I'm calling Dallas." Viv whipped out her phone. "Toff's dad gave him specific instructions. Maybe you're right and Toff needs more food in his system." She left the room, leaving Amy alone with dopey Toff.

"Pizza!" Toff exclaimed, only it came out slurred, like "pzzzaa." He stared at Amy, his eyes hooded. "Youalmoskizzme," he said, his words sounding like a slowed-down recording. "Imyvan. Bookfazze." He yawned again, nestling into the couch pillows. "Izokay. I almost kissed you."

Amy's heart thudded. *That* sentence was clear as day.

He struggled to open his eyes, lids fluttering, then gave up with a sleepy sigh, letting them drift closed. Had the sugar combined with the meds sent him into a food coma? "Kissgood," he mumbled. "Me." He sighed again. "Yullseee."

Amy blinked in surprise. "You'll see?" Was that what he meant to say—that she'd see what a good kisser he was?

A soft snore blew from his lips.

Amy didn't know whether to laugh or scream. She was trapped. He'd scooted down the couch, and now his legs pinned her to the cushions. Viv laughed from the kitchen, on the phone with Dallas, the sudden sound startling Toff, whose legs twitched on her lap. His legs were strong. Toned. Tanned.

"Cuckakes," he slurred. "Sweet. Mmm. Wanmore."

Oh no. He was moaning again. He couldn't be... This wasn't... Didn't guys...when they were asleep?

She needed to get off this couch, stat. Maybe she could lift his legs and slide out. Carefully, she slid her hands underneath his calves. His muscles tensed, then relaxed in her grip. Another soft groan escaped his lips.

Dear God.

What was taking Viv so long? She heard the fridge open and close, then another laugh. Dallas must not be worried about Toff's condition, which reassured Amy. Dallas was the mature one in their BROTP, no question.

Amy exhaled deeply, allowing herself a leisurely perusal of the invalid. She'd never been this up close and personal with Toff, that was for sure—well, except for his back, but that had been quick. She focused on his face. Long golden eyelashes. Mostly straight nose. Full, pouty lips. Strong jaw with a dusting of blond stubble.

Should she shove his legs off her lap and escape? That seemed unnecessarily mean. Toff was in pain. Tired. It wasn't like she had anywhere else to be. And she wasn't uncomfortable. His weight on her was...warm. Heavy. Nice. And he'd stopped moaning, so they'd survived the danger zone of, um...whatever.

Amy glanced at the coffee table. Those cupcakes were calling her name. Slowly, she moved her hands out from underneath Toff's legs, intending to reach for the box. He frowned in his sleep, pinning her against the couch like he didn't want her to leave. Smothering a laugh, she rested her head against the back of the couch and closed her eyes, willing her heart rate to slow.

It didn't.

At the sound of Viv's approaching footsteps, Amy opened her eyes. Before Viv could make a fuss, Amy shook her head. Another soft snore escaped Toff.

"I'm trapped," Amy whispered.

Viv rolled her eyes, but at least she didn't look mad. "Dallas says not to worry," she whispered, plopping onto the floor on the other side of the coffee table. "He says it's normal with pain meds. He's on his way." Viv pointed to the cupcake box and grinned at Amy. "Want one?"

Amy nodded enthusiastically.

Viv handed her a cupcake, shooting Toff a frustrated look as she leaned over the table. "Everyone spoils him," she said, "including you."

Amy shrugged, her cheeks heating. Guilty as charged.

"Omigod," Viv said, biting into her cupcake. "So good."

"I know." Amy licked frosting off the top of the cupcake like a little kid.

Toff mumbled in his sleep. Amy and Viv paused to listen, but his voice was too slurred to make sense of his words. They ate in silence, devouring their cupcakes until a familiar buzzing noise sounded outside—Dallas's Vespa.

Amy breathed a sigh of relief. Now that he was here, she'd make her escape. She glanced at Toff's angelic face. He looked so innocent while he slept. Maybe she'd stay a little bit longer.

Viv stood up, brushing off cupcake crumbs. "I'll go help Dallas with the pizza," she said, then left the room.

"Dongobeebee," Toff murmured.

Don't go? Don't go, Bebe? Bonnie?

"Stayme."

Stay? Stay with me? Stay, Amy?

Dallas and Viv stumbled into the living room, whispering.

Dallas grinned when he took in the scene. He focused his sharp gaze on Amy, more specifically on Toff lying on top of her. Well, sort of lying on top of her. Dallas's eye twitched. *Wait*. Did he just wink at her?

"Mmm," Toff mumbled. "Prronii."

Viv, Amy, and Dallas shared an amused look.

"Pepperoni?" Amy asked, and Dallas nodded. He set the pizza box on the cluttered coffee table while Viv went into the kitchen for plates.

"You're sure he's okay?" Amy asked Dallas. "He didn't OD?"

Dallas laughed softly. "He's fine." He stared pointedly at Toff's legs draped over her. "You want to stay like that? Or do you want to escape?"

"Noscape." Toff burrowed deeper into the couch, his strong legs anchoring her in place. "Stayme."

"Percocet is like a truth serum," Dallas said with a wry grin. "What else has he said?"

"Kizzames," Toff said softly. "Kniffiti."

Well, *that* word was clear as day, too. Amy's eyes widened in surprise, and Dallas's shoulders shook with suppressed laughter.

"I'd love to see him hypnotized," Dallas said, sitting cross-legged on the floor. "He'd give away the nuclear codes."

"Gebackereames," Toff slurred, his feet twitching like he was running.

Dallas cocked a questioning eyebrow.

Get back here, Ames. For whatever reason, she understood him perfectly.

Dallas grinned, pulled his phone from his pocket, and snapped a bunch of photos of her and Toff.

"Dallas!" Amy whispered, embarrassed. "What are you doing?"

"Don't worry. It's not going online." He glanced at her. "For Toff's eyes only. To remind him to eat before taking pain pills."

"Oh."

"Hmm," Dallas said, thumbing through the photos. "If body language means anything, he's interested in being a lot more than your *coach*." He flashed her a sly grin, and heat flooded Amy's face.

"He's just doped up," Amy said.

Toff was a master flirt, a master game player. Talking in his sleep didn't mean anything. She needed to remember he really *was* like Puck, the prankster fairy flitting in and out of people's lives, bringing the fun, stirring up trouble, like the real Puck did in *A Midsummer Night's Dream* with his love potion. Fairies always moved on to the next shiny object that caught their attention...or the next innocent human they could seduce with their fae magic.

And so would Toff.

CHAPTER FIFTEEN

*N*o way was Amy texting Toff, and he hadn't texted her, either. It had been two days since that awkward night at his house, which still felt like a weird mash-up of nightmare and dream. Her strategy was to pretend it hadn't happened.

She'd taken a shelfie of all of Lucinda Amorrato's books for today's Instagram post and tagged HeartRacer. She figured she might as well keep herself out there with all the new eyeballs on her account, including HeartRacer's.

She owned all twenty-five of Lucinda's books in hardback, thirteen in softcover, and five foreign editions, even though she didn't read German or French. She could just imagine Toff's reaction to that: "What? You own books you can't even *read*?"

Dallas had posted a photo on Snapchat of snoozing Toff holding a penguin stuffie that Viv had found in his bedroom. He'd cropped Amy out, at her request.

"He can take a joke," Dallas said. "He's always the one pranking everyone else. Payback's good for him."

Viv had texted her that he was upset about the photos, though, so Amy felt bad. Even if she personally loved the close-up shot of sleeping Toff.

Amy blinked away the image of Toff lying on the couch

with her. She had just ten days before the final "reluctant romance reader" challenge deadline, and she still needed to find a reader.

Toff was the obvious choice—especially now that they were a ship and it would play well on social media—but based on his ridiculous reaction to her book offer last night, she'd have to find someone else. He was *too* reluctant.

It was a shame. She was a firm believer that books could change hearts, and she hoped he'd have a change of heart about his dad and Rose's wedding after reading what she'd picked for him. Viv had tried to talk to him about it again yesterday, which he was not having.

Not smart timing, Amy had texted Viv, who'd replied with any eye-roll emoticon.

Viv: I know, but Flipper makes me so mad sometimes. Those perc pics weren't a big deal. He's just pouting because he can't surf at the fund-raiser today.

Oh, right. Surf for Sea Life. His local sponsor, AceWare, had tweeted about Toff not being able to compete because of his injury.

Amy refocused on her shelfie. Lucinda had written six perfect series and seven amazing standalone novels. Amy had grown up with the books because the first two series were for middle readers, and then Lucinda had written three series for teens. Now she'd moved on to adult romance, which Viv and Amy were totally binge reading.

Amy would love the chance to sit down and talk with Lucinda—assuming she didn't completely freeze up. She wanted to thank her for the hours and hours of escape into other worlds, for characters who made her laugh, and cry, and almost throw the books at the wall.

To thank her for getting her through the sleepover in the fifth grade when no one talked to her because she was a "have-to-invite" guest. The horrible ten-hour layover in the Chicago airport when she'd flown by herself for the first time to visit her grandparents and had been terrified.

And all the nights she escaped her everyday worries about being a misfit, a weirdo, an outcast who'd never feel comfortable in her skin. She really wanted to thank Lucinda for that.

Amy grabbed the minivan keys off the kitchen hook. Normally she'd bike, but her dad had asked her to pick up more groceries than would fit in her bicycle basket.

"You can pick up Brayden while you're out," Mom said.

"Where is he?" She didn't want to go grocery shopping with her brother. He'd whine the whole time and fill the cart with junk food she'd have to put back on the shelves.

Mom glanced at her phone, stalking her child like every other parent Amy knew. Whoever invented those apps would pay someday, somehow—revenge of the helicoptered generation.

"Looks like he's at the beach."

"I don't want to chase him down. There's a big fund-raising surf event today." Amy wondered if Toff was there, too, as a spectator. He'd hate that. At least she assumed he would, like if she spent a day in a bookstore but couldn't take anything off the shelf.

"I'll tell Brayden to meet you at the market in half an hour," Mom said. "He can bike there, and you can toss his bike in the van."

"Why can't he just bike home?" Amy knew she was being difficult, but she wasn't in the mood to watch over her brother today.

Mom sighed and gave her the you-don't-even-know-how-tired-I-am face. "Just pick him up. I don't want him getting into trouble."

"What kind of trouble?"

Mom shrugged, frowning. "I'm not sure. You know your brother. He's always up to something. He keeps turning off the location app, and he has a guilty face when he thinks I'm not looking."

"He always has a guilty face." Amy sighed dramatically. "Fine. I'll be my brother's keeper. But just for today."

Mom smiled with relief. "Thanks, sweetie."

Forty-five minutes later, Amy stood in the cereal aisle, wondering where Brayden was. She'd texted him three times, but of course he hadn't replied.

"Amy! Look who I found! Your boyfriend!"

Amy dropped her box of Lucky Charms. She bent to retrieve it, in no hurry to stand up, but she couldn't stay down there forever. If Toff wanted to yell at her about the Perc photos, too, she could handle it.

Brayden beamed, all flushed and sweaty, while Toff hung back.

"Hi," Amy said. She handed the cereal box to Brayden. "Put this in the cart."

"I want something else," he complained.

"Fine, whatever. Pick what you want." She kept her eyes on Toff, who stared down at the floor. He looked like he always did—windswept, suntanned, like he belonged on a brochure for beach life. But also like he wanted to be anywhere but here.

"How are you feeling?" she asked, taking a step toward him. "Look, I'm sorry about those photos—"

"No, *I'm* sorry." He kicked at the floor with his flip-flops. "Dallas told me I had you trapped on the couch." He rubbed the back of his neck, not looking at her. "Sorry." He glanced up, his blue eyes dimmed instead of lit up. "I'm not taking meds on an empty stomach again, that's for sure."

She smiled. "It was fine. I survived."

"Yeah. I guess so." He glanced at Brayden, who was studying his cereal options. "I'm not stalking you. Your brother's bike had a flat so I gave him a ride; then he dragged me in here."

Ouch. So much for her coach wanting to see her. "Oh. Okay." She twirled her hair self-consciously. "Um. Thanks for dropping him off. You can go."

Toff's eyes went wide. "I didn't mean I don't want to see you. I do. I mean, not like…" He shoved his hands in his shorts pockets and stared up at the ceiling. "I'm effing everything up today." He shook his head, then gave her a crooked smile. "So far today I've yelled at Viv, cussed out Dallas, argued with my dad… I tried to watch Surf for Sea Life, but it was too hard to watch and not compete." He scrubbed a hand down his face. "It's been a shit day. A shit week."

Amy nodded. "I'm sure it sucked, not surfing for the fundraiser today." She gestured to his general midsection, covered up by a Billabong shirt. "How badly does it hurt? It's been five days, right?" Not like she was counting. Ugh. Her turn to be embarrassed.

"It's better, but I've got to wait to surf until my stitches come out this Friday." He sighed. "Hope I don't flip out on anyone between now and then." He glanced over her shoulder and frowned. "Uh, your brother took off. Want me to help you find him?"

Amy groaned and rolled her eyes. "He's such a pain in the—"

"Yeah, he is." Toff laughed. "But I like him." His smile reached his eyes, and her heart did a little shimmy in her chest.

"I'll just text him," she said, reaching for her phone, but Toff surprised her, grabbing the grocery cart and pushing off.

"Nah. It'll be more fun to sneak up on him. C'mon."

Surprised, she kept pace with him as he steered the cart. He paused in front of the Pop-Tarts. "Does your dad let you eat these? Since he's a real pastry chef and these are, like, total crap pastries but also totally delicious?"

Amy laughed and plucked two boxes of the strawberry ones from the shelf. "Yes. He likes them, too."

Toff grinned, and his arm brushed hers as they rounded the corner, scouting for Brayden.

"My mom's always worried about Bray," Amy said. "She thinks he's up to no good."

Toff laughed. "I'm sure he is. I was at his age." He leaned on the cart as they walked slowly around the store's perimeter, scanning the aisles.

"What do you mean, 'at his age'? You're still up to no good." She shoulder bumped him.

Toff returned her shoulder bump, grinning down at her. "I need to spend more time with you. I'm already in a better mood."

She didn't know what to say to that, but her heart twirled like the suncatcher hanging from their back deck.

"Clean-up on aisle seven! Clean-up on aisle seven!"

"He's definitely not in aisle seven," Toff deadpanned, and Amy dissolved into giggles.

Aisle seven was a mess.

No surprise to Amy, it was the candy aisle. What did surprise her were the hundreds of round candies bouncing on the floor. Were those gumballs? At the far end of the aisle, two little kids pelted each other with the candies, laughing hysterically. A furious store clerk glared at Brayden, who hung his head in front of an enormous gumball machine display made of cardboard that had toppled to the ground.

Toff squeezed her hand, sending sparks shooting up and down her arm. His grin nearly blinded her.

"Don't worry, Bonnie. I've got this."

An hour later, Toff and Brayden loaded the grocery bags into the McIntyre minivan while Amy texted her mom that, yes, they'd be home soon; shopping just took longer than expected.

"Put the cart back," Toff ordered Brayden, who obeyed.

Amy watched her brother ride the cart across the lot to the cart corral. If it hadn't been for Toff's magical sweet-talking of the store manager and making Brayden clean up all the gumballs, who knew what would've happened? Could a kid go to juvie for retail disruption?

"Why doesn't he listen to me the way he listens to you?" she groused.

"Because you're his sister. And I'm a god."

Amy's mouth dropped open, and Toff laughed. "Kidding." He watched Brayden run toward them. "But he thinks I am, so I've got an advantage. You're just a human."

"You're saying I'm a lesser deity in the panoply of overlords?"

Toff blinked at her. "Uh…yeah?"

"Are you coming over to our house?" Brayden demanded, skidding to a stop in front of Toff.

"No," Toff said. Brayden's face fell. Toff reached out to mess up Brayden's already messy hair. "Get inside, kid."

Toff opened the minivan's passenger door, and Brayden climbed in. Toff slammed the door closed and turned to Amy.

"You doing okay? You aren't going to lock Brayden in time-out for the rest of his life?"

Amy laughed. "I'll let him out when he turns twenty-one." She swallowed. "Thanks for everything."

"That's what coaches are for." He ran a hand through his hair and leaned against the van. "Remind me what the final challenge for your contest is. We need to get going on that, right?"

"Um…" Should she ask him to be her reluctant romance reader? "We still have time," she hedged.

No. Anyone who faked a can't-breathe attack rather than even *hold* a book was a bad choice. She'd ask someone from Rose's mystery book club, one of those snooty readers who looked down their nose at romances.

"What's the challenge?" he prompted. "Something about reading a book, right?"

Amy nodded. "I need to find someone who doesn't like romance novels and convince them to read one."

Toff's eyes narrowed, like he was about to launch into intense coach mode. Amy braced herself, but Brayden pounded on the car window, startling them both.

Brayden plastered his face against the window, pretending he was gagging. Toff laughed and opened the door. "Dude. Chill."

"Are we going or what?" Brayden demanded, glaring at Amy. "You're not supposed to leave kids locked in cars with the windows up."

Amy rolled her eyes. "It's been maybe sixty seconds."

"Seconds count," Brayden said darkly.

Toff shook his head, laughing. "I might borrow him for a day, just to keep me entertained."

Brayden's face lit up. "I can come over now!"

"No," Amy said sharply. "You are not going to bug Toff."

Toff smiled. "I don't mind hanging out with redheads." His gaze skimmed over Amy's hair. "Where are your sparkles today?"

Self-consciously, she reached up to touch her hair. "Guess I forgot."

"Ugh." Brayden flopped his head against the headrest and squeezed his eyes shut. "If you guys are gonna kiss goodbye, just get it over with already."

"Shut *up*, Brayden," Amy said through gritted teeth, her cheeks burning. She dared a glance at Toff, whose gaze was fixed on her, not Brayden. Were his eyes turning colors? From sky blue to denim?

"You know what else you have to do for the last challenge, right?"

Kiss you? Amy thought, then blinked away the ridiculous idea. "What?"

"You need to do a vlog. Record yourself. But you have to talk." He grinned. "No waving paddles around like you do for Viv. She's not even allowed to be on camera with you."

"Who put you in charge?"

"You did when you made me your coach. Look how great #BookFaceFriday turned out."

God, he drove her crazy. One minute he was sweet and funny, and the next he was bossy, poking at her, teasing. "I—I told you I'm not ready for that yet."

"You will be." His gaze roved her face, lingering on her mouth. He cleared his throat and met her eyes again, blinking like he'd just come out of a trance.

He tapped his phone and grinned. "Looks like our ship is still sailing. I tweeted one of our #BookFaceFriday outtake photos with our #BonnieandClyde hashtag today. Dallas sent me the photos."

Amy gaped up at him, all the air whooshing out of her lungs. "You *what*?"

"Just giving you a boost, bookworm." His lips quirked as he backstepped away from the van. "Hey, thanks for the back scratch. I don't remember much from that night, but I remember that."

He shot her a wink, then spun around to leave before she could come up with a reply.

*T*he next afternoon, Toff's surfer friends sprawled around the living room, some on the furniture, some on the floor. His dad had finally relented on the "preapproved visitors" rule, probably because of Toff's pissy mood about missing the Surf for Sea Life comp.

Today, his whole crew inhaled burritos, chips, and guac while replays of the highlights from the Ballito Pro surfing event in South Africa played on TV.

"Sick! Check out that air!"

"Man, he jammed off that lip!"

"Tight carves, bro!"

On the screen, Toff watched a guy he'd competed against from San Clemente kill it, carving sharp turns on the face of a huge wave, catching air at the end. *That should be me*, he thought, his gut churning.

One of these days—soon—he and his dad were gonna have it out again. Toff should've tried to go pro by now. Waiting another long year until he graduated from high school just put him that much further behind his peers already on tour. Waiting until he graduated from college would lose him four years of prime time, but he didn't want to think about that right now.

Toff picked up his phone to check on the contest. His latest post had stoked the OTP fire on Amy's book planet. Somebody'd even posted a fan art drawing of the two of them sitting on a surfboard together in the middle of the ocean, arms wrapped around each other and kissing.

"Yo, bro, you getting a booty call? Or asking for one?"

Toff glanced up.

"Shut it." Claire chucked a pillow at the guy who'd joked about the booty call. "You'll never get a booty call unless you pay for it."

She tossed her blond dreads over her shoulder and glanced at Toff from the pillow fort she'd built with her boyfriend, Murph. Toff grinned and gave her a thumbs-up. Claire was cool. She was one of the best surfers on the team, and she'd bonded with Viv after joining Viv's book club last year.

Viv and *Amy's* book club, Toff corrected himself, recalling that awful video he'd watched with Amy being Vanna White.

He hoped the #BookFaceFriday success had given her confidence a boost. Just in case it hadn't, he'd come up with a plan to help with Amy's public speaking phobia and to dial up her swagger. She might resist it at first, but he had a feeling it would work.

Murph kissed Claire's cheek, then turned it into a raspberry, making her swat him away, laughing. Murph jumped up, pausing on his way into the kitchen for more food. "Want anything?"

"Nah." Toff shook his head. For once, he wasn't hungry.

It was cool seeing his friends, but he was tired. His ribs ached, and he hadn't slept much. After the embarrassing Percocet incident—which Dallas was still giving him crap for—he was sticking with ibuprofen, so the pain still kept him awake. At three o'clock this morning, he'd queued up Amy's favorite movie and watched it again, not that he'd ever admit it.

Toff's phone buzzed, this time with a text from Dallas.

Dallas: We're on for Wednesday night

Cool, Toff thumbed back. **Can Viv keep it a secret from Amy?**

Not happily, Dallas replied, **but she will.**

"Sweet!" Toff's friends cheered as they watched a guy shoot through an epic barrel wave on the screen. The slow-motion replay might as well be porn for them. Toff missed surfing so much it physically hurt, even more than his injury.

Just a few more days stuck on land, he told himself. In the meantime, he'd focus his pent-up energy on Amy. He grabbed his phone and opened their message window, which was slowly filling up, unlike a week ago when it had been empty.

Toff: Weds night—you, me, McNerd, and Wordworm are going out to celebrate our awesome bookface results.

Toff hesitated after firing off the text, considering his next move.

He opened his YouTube app and found the *P&P* movie clip right away, the one with the broody Darcy dude helping Keira Knightly into the carriage. There were hundreds of comments about how intense and romantic those twenty-three seconds were. Toff rolled his eyes, but he played the clip, muting it so his bros wouldn't give him crap.

The camera moved in for a close-up on their clasped hands like it was a huge deal. Maybe holding hands was back then.

Toff watched the clip a few more times. He had to admit those looks they gave each other were hot. When Darcy walked away, flexing his hand like he'd been zapped by electricity, Toff could relate. He was starting to feel *zapped* every time he was around Amy.

He hesitated, thumb hovering over the send arrow, then texted her the movie clip.

Toff: Watched your movie again. It didn't suck.

CHAPTER SIXTEEN

*A*t the sound of Viv's car horn beeping in the driveway, Amy stuck a bookmark in her current read—an old-school gothic romance full of angst and misunderstandings, set in a creepy castle on a cliff. It was over-the-top dramatic, and she loved it.

"Bye!" Amy called out to her parents, who were in the family room bingeing *Stranger Things*, trying to one-up each other on eighties trivia and debating whose childhood house looked most like the show's sets.

"Bye!" called her mom. "Home by midnight!"

Amy stilled at the mention of her curfew. It had been almost two weeks since Toff had brought her home late, but she still didn't trust Brayden not to rat her out. Then again, Toff had saved his butt at the grocery store. Brayden wouldn't care if Amy got in trouble, but he'd duel to the death to save Toff.

"Hold on." Amy's dad paused the TV show and bustled into the kitchen. He handed her a plastic tub filled with lemon madeleine cookies. "These are for Toff." Dad grinned. "I told you I was making extras for the Cupcake Kid. I hid them from Brayden or else your *friend* would be out of luck."

Amy cringed at the emphasis he put on *friend*. "Please stop calling him that, Dad."

"Friend? Or Cupcake Kid?" Dad wiggled his eyebrows. "What's your Facebook status with this boy? Just friends? It's complicated? In a relationship?"

"Daaad. Stop!" Laughing, Amy reached for the cookie container, but Dad held it out of her reach. "Toff can come inside, you know. So can your other friends. What's the rush?"

"Stop it, Quinn," Mom scolded, carrying two wineglasses into the kitchen. "Let her be."

"Ooh." Dad eyed the wineglasses and relinquished the tub of cookies to Amy. "I forgot to get out the cheese and crackers." He opened the fridge and started digging through the cheese drawer.

Since Dad was distracted by food, Amy could escape. "No time for my friends to come inside," she said. "The movie starts at seven thirty."

"Be safe," her mom said, refilling the wineglasses. "Curfew's at—"

"Midnight," Amy muttered. "I know."

Do I ever.

*D*allas stepped out of the MINI Cooper that Viv and her mom shared so Amy could climb into the tiny back seat. Toff was already there. Amy met his blue gaze, which was, as always, full of mischief. She knew he was coming, of course, since he was the one who'd texted her about tonight. But she hadn't thought the transportation logistics through.

A sliver of panic sliced through her as she scoped out the tiny back seat. "I can drive," Amy said. "We can take our minivan."

Dallas glanced at his watch. He was the only person their

age who wore one. "We don't have time to switch," he said. "Sorry."

"Get in the car, yarn bomber," Toff said, patting the seat.

So he was in that kind of mood. He must be feeling better.

"Let's go, girl," Viv said, leaning across the passenger seat. "I don't want to miss the previews."

Amy glanced at Dallas, whose green eyes blinked innocently behind his glasses. "He's not doped up. Promise."

Her eyes cut to Toff again, who pounded on the back of Viv's seat like it was a bongo drum. He slanted Amy a grin, pausing his drum routine. "Come on, Ames. I'll behave."

Reluctantly, she maneuvered herself into the tight back seat. She tried to shrink her body into the corner, but her legs still brushed against Toff's. Tonight he wore a long-sleeve Henley shirt with an AceWare logo and board shorts, as always.

"Not enough room? You can sit on my lap."

His grin sent tingles shooting to all the wrong places. So much for him behaving.

"I wouldn't want to hurt you." She gestured vaguely toward his ribs. In the rearview mirror, Viv shot a warning look at Toff, but before she could say anything, Dallas piped up.

"Warp speed, Mr. Spock."

"Aye, aye, Captain." Viv gave Dallas a gooey smile and hit the gas.

Amy exhaled a deep sigh. They were disgustingly adorkable together.

Toff shook his head in mock disgust. "You two are so weird."

Viv stuck out her tongue in the mirror. "You're just jealous because you've never stayed in a relationship long enough to get to the celebrity role-playing stage."

Toff snorted. "That's not even a thing, Wordworm."

"It is," Viv argued. "You just don't know about it."

"What's in there?" Toff asked, pointing to the plastic tub Amy clutched on her lap.

"Oh, um, here." She handed it to him, cheeks heating. "My dad made them for you."

Toff blinked in surprise. "More cupcakes?"

"No. Lemon madeleines."

"What?" Viv yelped from the front seat. "Your dad made madeleines for *Toff*? I love those cookies!" She scowled at Toff in the rearview mirror.

Dallas turned around in his seat, reaching his hand out. "Fork 'em over, dude."

"Mine," Toff said, clutching the tub to his chest and making a little-kid face. Everyone laughed, and he relented, opening the tub and sharing his treats. "Wow," he said after taking his first bite. "These are great. Tell your dad thanks."

"Or you could tell him," Viv said from the front seat, "if you were civilized instead of a caveman."

"Caveman not share." Toff made a grunting sound. "Caveman eat all the cookies." He stopped grunting and held out the tub to Amy. "Caveman only share with sparkly redhead."

Amy laughed and took another cookie, wishing she didn't blush so easily.

As they drove up the coast toward the nearest town with a movie theater, the back seat of the MINI felt very…cozy. Viv and Dallas chattered in the front seat while Amy tried to not touch Toff, but he wasn't making it easy.

"I've been keeping an eye on your Instagram and Twitter," Toff said. "Our ship is still going strong." His thigh bounced against hers, sending tingles up her leg. "But I noticed something's missing."

"Is this going to be a coach lecture?" she asked, moving her leg away from his.

"Not a lecture, more like an observation." His lips tilted up as he stretched his arm across the back seat, his fingertips grazing her shoulder. His gaze moved to her hair. "Lots of sparkles tonight. Good."

"Let's hear it, Coach. What's missing?" She was proud of how unaffected she sounded by the streak of heat his fingertips sent shooting down her arm.

"A couple of things."

Her shoulders stiffened defensively, and his fingertips brushed over her shoulder again. Was he trying to distract her? Soften her up before the coaching kill?

"First, you're not using our awesome #BonnieandClyde hashtag. Second, you keep saying we're just friends in your replies to people shipping us."

Amy's stomach flip-flopped. Where was he going with this?

"You *are* just friends," Viv piped up from the front seat, shooting Toff a warning look over her shoulder.

"Back off, Wordworm. Keep your eyes on the road."

"But she's right," Amy said. "We aren't a…a…thing."

Toff shrugged, tossing hair out of his eyes. "So what? You want to win, right?" His lips quirked. "Bonnie and Clyde forevah."

Her mouth opened and closed like a fish. *Toff doesn't know he's your secret crush*, she told herself, praying it was true.

"He needs a 'mute' button," Viv said to Dallas. "You're a programming genius—can't you make one?"

Toff grinned, eyes sparking. "The more eyeballs on us, the better, babe."

Swagger. She needed it, right now.

"How many times do I have to tell you not to 'babe' me?" Flustered, Amy turned to look out the window, surprised to see they weren't anywhere near the movie theater.

"Viv, are you lost?" she asked. "Where are we?"

The air went very still inside the tiny car as Viv, Dallas, and Toff darted anxious glances at one another, all of them avoiding eye contact with her.

Dallas cleared his throat. "Actually...we're here."

Viv zipped into a parking space in front of a neon sign on the building that read KARAOKE! ALL AGES!

No. No, no, *no*.

"I'm not doing this," Amy whispered. "Please." She gave Viv a pleading look. "Let's go to a movie. Anything but this." She turned to Toff. "This was your idea, wasn't it?"

He nodded, looking as proud as the peacock on her favorite *Pride and Prejudice* book cover.

"Why?" She was ready to fire her coach, for real this time.

"To get over your fear of public speaking."

Omigod. "Singing isn't public speaking, Toff. It's a zillion times worse."

Toff's brow furrowed. "You knew winning wouldn't be easy, right? You're gonna have to up your game for the final challenge, Ames."

Great. He'd launched into coach mode. Anxiety and frustration simmered in Amy's chest. So much for tonight being a celebration. Her coach had tricked her. Not cool.

"This happens all the time in surfing," Toff continued, oblivious to her desire to throttle him. "Everybody pushes their hardest, and the bar is constantly getting raised in each heat. Like in your contest challenges."

Scowling, Amy crossed her arms over her chest. "And *you* always move up to the next heat."

He shrugged. "Almost always."

Dallas turned around in his seat and shot Toff a look that only an idiot would misread.

"What?"

"Maybe shut up for a minute, moron," Dallas snapped, darting Amy a sympathetic look. He shot another glare at Toff. "I think you forgot tonight is a celebration."

"Sorry, Ames." Toff ducked his head, looking chagrined. He offered an apologetic smile and lifted his hand for a high five. "You're doing great so far. Gimme some heat."

Flustered, she high-fived him, her hand slamming onto his with as much heat as she could bring. He interlaced his fingers with hers and squeezed her hand, sending a shimmer of sparks straight to her chest.

"You can do this," he said, his intense energy almost convincing her she could. "I know you can."

"You don't have to go first," Dallas said.

"You can watch other people," Viv chimed in. "Once you see how terrible they are, it won't be so scary." She grinned. "It'll be fun! And we're all here to support you."

"Especially your coach," Toff said, releasing her hand.

"A heads-up would've been nice, *Coach*," Amy said. She wished she'd never agreed to this "celebration," but it was too late. Coach Flipper had made his move, and she couldn't escape.

Toff studied Amy from across the table they shared with Dallas and Viv in the karaoke bar.

He'd messed up. Dallas had reamed his ass out in the parking lot while Amy and Viv went in and got a table, and now he felt like shit. He hadn't realized Amy would freak so hard. He'd figured she wouldn't be thrilled, but he thought if Dallas and Viv were there, she'd relax.

So far, she hadn't.

Not his greatest coaching move.

Amy's hands fluttered like bird wings, playing with her long red curls, rolling up a paper napkin on the table, her fingers drawing in the condensation on her soda glass.

Viv and Dallas watched a woman on stage belt out a kick-ass rendition of Stevie Wonder's "My Cherie Amour." It was an ancient song his dad liked, but this lady made it sound new.

Toff grabbed a handful of tortilla chips from the basket on the table, willing Amy to look at him, but she wouldn't. He struggled to reconcile the sweet, quiet bookworm who was Viv's shadow with the girl he'd rescued from the sheriff who'd fake-flirted like a champ, with the girl who got all up in his face, giving as good as she got.

When she got fired up, it was like a light bulb went off inside her. Her eyes got all shiny. Her cheeks turned pink and even her hair seemed to glow. It was impossible to look away when she was wound up, which was why he kept poking and teasing. Pushing. She just needed someone to ignite the spark, and she'd light up the whole room. Win the contest.

Amy's tongue swept over her lips, and a jolt of a different type of awareness kicked through him.

The audience cheered and clapped as the singer took a bow, and Dallas and Viv returned their attention to Amy.

"Are you ready?" Viv asked.

Amy shrugged and bit her lip. Toff told himself to stop staring at her mouth like a freak.

"I…" Her shoulders lifted, then sagged. "You guys, I can't do this." She glanced at Toff, and he forced himself to look at her eyes instead of her mouth.

"It wasn't a bad idea," she said, keeping her gaze on him. "For anyone else it would probably work. I mean, I sing in the car, right?" She forced a nervous laugh and glanced toward the stage. "But standing up there...I just can't."

"I'll do it with you," Toff blurted, surprising everyone at the table, including himself.

"What?" Amy blinked at him, and even in the darkened club, he could see her cheeks go pale. Uh-oh. She was flipping straight into panic mode like she had in his van that night.

He couldn't watch her backslide. She'd started to build up her confidence in the short time he'd been coaching her. He reached out and put his hand on top of hers.

"I'm your coach, remember?" He kept his voice steady, soothing, like it didn't bug him that she'd recoiled from his touch. "Also costar and backup singer."

"You—you'd sing with me?"

She sounded surprised, which pissed him off. Hadn't he proven how far he'd go to help her out? With the sheriff? With her brother? Posing for all those photos?

He quashed his frustration. She was nervous. Scared. He'd dealt with that plenty of times at surf comps, helping younger surfers relax. He needed to try a different strategy. She was the girl who hated his scary faces.

"You can do this, Ames. You're as good as anybody else in here." He had no idea if she could sing, but it didn't matter. What mattered was her believing in herself. Getting up on the stage and pushing through her fear. She needed this small taste of being in the spotlight.

"C'mon. I'll do it if you will," Toff said. He wasn't a rock star, but he sang in his van, in the shower, out on the water waiting for a wave to come in.

Toff glanced at Viv, who narrowed her eyes at him. Why did she always think he was up to no good?

"What?" he demanded. "You don't think I can do it?"

"I know you can," Dallas piped up. "A duet's a great idea. What do you think, Amy? Just keep your eyes on us the whole time, and you'll be fine."

Toff tilted his chin at Dallas. At least one of his friends thought he was a good coach. He stood and held out his hand.

"Let's do this." He grinned, keeping his gaze locked on hers. "It won't be as scary as outrunning a raccoon."

*A*my stood next to Toff as he flipped through the binder of song choices. This was crazy. Absurd. Terrifying. Why had she agreed to this? She knew exactly why—because Toff had hypnotized her with those big blue eyes, then tugged her by the hand, his fingers warm and strong around hers, and she'd lost the ability to be rational.

Crushes were a curse, shutting down brain cells, derailing plans. That's what Viv had said when she'd tried to pretend she wasn't crushing on Dallas…although that had turned out well. *Really* well.

"How about this one?" He pointed to a song title, and she squinted to read it in the dark. "I Got You Babe" by Sonny and Cher.

"They used to have some TV show years ago, right?"

Toff shrugged. "No clue."

"I don't know the song." Even if she did, no way was she singing anything that had "babe" in the lyrics.

"This one." He pointed at "You're the One That I Want" by John Travolta and Olivia Newton-John from *Grease*. Was he trying to embarrass her? It was like he could read her mind and knew exactly how she felt about him and was forcing her to sing her true feelings.

"No." Her voice came out sharper than she intended, and she winced.

Toff was trying to help, but he still had no idea of the effect he had on her. How could he, since she was hiding it so well? Amy scanned the list, her gaze stopping at "Ain't No Mountain High Enough." It sounded familiar, but she couldn't recall where she'd heard it. No doubt it was better if you knew the song you were singing, but she'd just read the lyrics and do her best.

"How about this one?"

Toff leaned over her shoulder to read, his solid chest pressed against her back. He didn't need to move in that close, did he? Did he...*want* to touch her? Like in the car when he'd touched her shoulder? And at the table? She blinked and told herself to breathe. She was being ridiculous.

"Whatever you want, Ames." His voice was close to her ear, and his breath tickled her neck. Goose bumps rose along her skin.

He straightened suddenly, and cool air swirled up her spine, making her shiver. Toff wrote their names and song choice on the clipboard, then handed it to the next person in line. She followed him down the stage steps onto the dance floor.

"Want some liquid courage?" he asked.

"What? We're underage. Nobody will serve us here. We don't have wristbands." She held out her arm, which didn't have the purple wristband that indicated they were over twenty-one. Neither did Toff. Wait...what was that? One wrist was encircled by a couple of beaded bracelets; the other had the purple wristband.

He grinned and reached out to tweak one of her curls. "You're in serious need of my skills. There's always a way to break the rules. Just stick with me."

Her pulse pounded in her ears. That cockiness of his should get him arrested. It probably would someday. Why was she such a sucker for it? Why couldn't she fall for someone quiet and nerdy like her? She was a walking cliché, lusting after the hot, cocky surfer everyone else wanted, too. If she were a character in a book, she'd yell at the pages.

Or maybe she wouldn't.

It was always fun to read about the quiet girl winning over the sexy player. What would it feel like in real life?

Amy slanted him a glance. He scanned the dance floor, where people shimmied and grinded to a mash-up of hip-hop and electronic dance music. Most of the crowd was of legal age, and the drinks were flowing. Amy wouldn't mind a sip of liquid courage, but no way was she going to encourage Toff.

The song faded, and the DJ's voice boomed into the mic. "We're back for the second half of karaoke! First up is a duet by Amy and Toff. Come on up, you two, wherever you are."

As the crowd left the dance floor, Toff smiled like he didn't have a care in the world. She, on the other hand, was dying inside. He must've read the fear on her face because he reached out and took her hand again.

"Come on, Bonnie. We've got this." He tugged her toward the stage, and she heard Viv's whoop clear across the room. After all of this was over, Amy was going to kill her for the "let's go to a movie to celebrate" charade.

Amy followed Toff across the stage. They stopped in front of a monitor that displayed the lyrics for Singer One and Singer Two. She took a deep breath and glanced around the club, relieved she couldn't see anyone because the bar was mostly dark, and the spotlight shining on her and Toff blinded her to pretty much everything else.

The DJ grinned at them, or at least she thought so. It was hard to tell with all the piercings. "You two lovebirds ready?" He handed each of them a cordless mic.

Wait, what? Why did he think— Oh, maybe because Toff

still held her hand in a firm grip. What was up with that? *Coach support*, she told herself. *Nothing more.*

"Ready." Toff squeezed her hand, and her stomach flipped over. Panic seized her as her throat went dry. What if she had one of those awful dry hacking fits? What if—

Music blared out of the speakers, and she swallowed, staring at the monitor. Which singer was she? One or Two?

Toff's deep voice rang out through the speakers singing about mountains and rivers.

So she was Singer Two. Wait—*baby*? Had he just called her baby? Stupid lyrics. He squeezed her hand and tilted his head toward the screen where her lyrics were highlighted.

Amy came in a beat late, missing the "If you need me" line but chiming in for the line about calling on someone no matter where they were.

Holy crapoli. This was a love song, after all—the grand finale song in the *Bridget Jones's Diary* movie, when Renée Zellweger ran out in the snow in just her sweater and underwear to chase down a modern-day Mr. Darcy. No wonder her subconscious had picked this one.

"Don't worry, baby." Toff's voice took over smoothly, not missing a beat.

She jumped in as her lyrics lit up, her voice clear and on key, asking Toff to call her name, saying she'd be there in a hurry.

Now both their lyrics lit up, flashing the word "together!" at the top of the screen. And so they sang, together, spontaneously harmonizing when they got to the chorus about mountains, valleys, and rivers, none of which would keep them apart.

Toff pulled her in close, grinning down at her. He fist-pumped the air as his deep voice filled the room, looking into her eyes, singing lyrics that vowed to always be there when she needed. The audience cheered.

Wow. He could really sing. Was there anything he sucked at?

"Together!" flashed on the screen again, and she joined in, feeling a smile pull at her lips. This was ridiculous. Terrifying.

But also fun.

She could see Viv and Dallas cheering them on. This time, she sang as loudly as Toff. His eyes sparked, telegraphing his approval of her performance, which made her sing even louder. He grinned when he sang the line about getting her out of trouble, and she laughed as she thought of the sheriff.

They were on a roll now, on fire, perfectly in sync, like they did this all the time.

The whole crowd joined in for the chorus, clapping and dancing, everyone singing about scaling mountains and rivers for the person they loved.

As the song faded, the room exploded into cheers and applause. Amy's heart raced and she felt light-headed. Had she really done that? Had *they* really done that? Together?

Amy stepped out of the spotlight, handing her mic to the DJ. She smiled into the dark room, knowing how proud Viv was of her. Dallas, too. A warm pressure squeezed her fingers, and she glanced down. Why was Toff still holding her hand?

"Let's hear it for the best duet of the night!" The DJ did one of those arm-twirling flourishes as the crowd continued to voice their approval. "All right, let's see who's next. Bao the Man, you're up!"

Still holding her hand, Toff pulled Amy across the stage and through the crowded bar, pausing to high-five and fist-bump strangers congratulating them on their performance. Amy slapped a few high fives, too, and her entire body suffused with heat when a woman reached out to grab her arm and drunkenly whispered, "That was hot. You're totally getting lucky tonight."

The thought of getting lucky with Toff sent a tidal wave of desire crashing over her. If she were a surfer, she'd wipe out, unable to maintain her balance.

Her secret fantasy popped to mind, the one that had been torturing her since they'd watched *P&P* together. She'd read enough romances to queue up all sorts of fantasies about getting lucky, but experiencing it for real? With Toff the sexpert?

That was as likely as a real-life Mr. Darcy arriving at her house in a phaeton.

When they returned to their table, Toff finally released her hand, and Amy collapsed into her chair, adrenaline still coursing through her body. Who knew karaoke could be terrifying *and* fun? She glanced at Toff as he sat down across from her. Was it because of him? Could she have done this on her own?

He met her gaze and a slow, sexy smile spread across his handsome face.

"See? I knew you could do it." He took a long drink of soda and tilted his head toward the bar. "I could use a beer."

"Toff, don't," Viv warned. "We don't want to get kicked out."

Dallas raised his eyebrows and shrugged, which was all the encouragement Toff needed. He stood up and headed for the bar. Dallas glanced at Viv and Amy, and because he was the perfect boyfriend and realized they needed to girl squee, he stood up, too. "Back in a few."

As soon as he was out of earshot, Viv jumped up and moved to the chair next to Amy, then unleashed the squee.

"Omigod! That was— You were— He was—" Viv's dark eyes flashed with excitement. She leaned in close to be heard over the current karaoke singer, who was horribly off-key.

"It was like you guys had practiced, or you'd been doing

it forever. How did you— I mean, wow! You were totally in sync." She took a breath and grabbed her soda glass, pausing to suck from the straw, then raised her eyebrow. "That was serious chemistry up there, Amy. Real, not fake."

Two mugs of beer slammed onto the table as Toff sat down across from them before Amy could respond. She couldn't tear her eyes away as he lifted a mug to his mouth and took a long drink, his Adam's apple bobbing up and down.

"You're crazy, Flipper," Viv whisper-yelled. "What if we get kicked out?"

Toff lowered the mug to the table. "I never get caught." He turned his attention to Amy, making her stomach swirl. "Right, Ames?"

She nodded, trying to think of a snappy comeback, but nothing came. Dallas sat down and reached for the other beer, but Toff put out a hand to stop him.

"That one's for my costar." Toff's eyes freaking twinkled. Dallas shrugged and started to push the mug toward Amy, but she pushed it back.

"No thanks." She glanced at Toff, who watched her intently. "I mean, thank you for getting it, but I don't want any."

"Not a drinker?" Toff shrugged. "That's cool."

"No, I just… I'd hate to get caught."

"Mind if I have it?" Dallas asked, reaching for the beer.

"Go ahead," Amy said.

"Dallas!" Viv exclaimed. "You're as bad as Toff."

Dallas and Toff exchanged wicked grins and clinked their glasses together.

"Here's to America's new idols," Dallas joked. Viv raised her soda glass, nudging Amy to do the same.

"Not America's new idols," Toff said, shooting her a sly wink. "To the bookworm world's newest OTP, who just knocked it out of the park."

Viv nudged her foot under the table.

"And here's to Redhead Recs kicking butt on her final challenge," Toff continued, "because I know she will."

They all clinked glasses and drank. As Amy watched the guys down their beers, she felt a rush of accomplishment. Despite her fears, tonight had been a huge step forward. She'd belted out that song like a rock star. She'd loved the rush. The applause. Was this what Toff felt every time he competed? No wonder he loved it so much.

Amy glanced at him, surprised by the intensity in his eyes. He was completely focused on her, his expression unreadable. Which was strange, because Amy was pretty sure she knew all of Toff's facial expressions.

But this one—this one was brand-new.

"Watch out for raccoons," Toff joked as he walked Amy up the driveway while Viv and Dallas waited in the car.

She rolled her eyes, then flashed him one of those rare, approving smiles that she made him work for. He was turning into an Amy-smile junkie, craving more and more.

He took her hand as they slowly approached her house, in no hurry to say goodbye. He wanted to know if he was reading her signals right, to find out if she wanted the same ending to their night as he did.

All he'd thought of since they left the karaoke bar was what her lips would taste like.

"Sorry about not warning you about karaoke," he said. "I should've asked if you wanted hard-ass coach or cheerleader coach before I made plans."

"Yeah, well…it worked out okay. Better than okay. I had

fun." She smiled up at him, then bit her lower lip, igniting his internal fuse.

"You were great." He tightened his grip on her hand and stepped closer, officially crossing the coach boundary line. "*We* were great."

"I thought so, too." She reached up, pulling one of her sparkly clips from her hair. He wanted to touch that wild red hair, to tangle his fingers in it, find out if it was as soft as it looked. He suddenly realized he'd wanted to for days. Maybe longer.

"This is for you." She held up the hair clip, her eyes locking on his. Her eyes were beautiful, coppery like a penny. Freckles dusted her nose. He had no clue why she'd flown under his radar for so long.

"I should've given this to you after the bookface photos," she said. She sounded as out of breath as he felt. "I officially pronounce you my contest coach for the rest of the summer."

"I'm honored." Toff grinned as he took his prize, randomly clipping it into his own messy hair. Amy laughed, taking a tiny step closer to him. And another.

Bingo. He matched her step for step. They stood as close together as two people could without actually touching.

"Remember when we talked about coaching rules?" Every part of him was aching to touch her, some parts more than others.

"Yeah," she whispered. Her gaze dropped to his mouth. *Hell.*

"You asked me to rein it in, Ames." He reached up, tucking a lock of hair behind her ear. It was soft, just like he'd imagined. "Any chance you've changed your mind?"

Her teeth grazed her bottom lip as she nodded.

Oh hell yeah. Signal received.

He exhaled roughly, bending down to rest his forehead

on hers, cupping her waist with his hands. They were nose to nose, mouth to mouth, just like the bookface photo. She smelled like cinnamon mixed with sugar, a little bit spicy and a lot sweet, just like her.

"We've been here before," he whispered, smiling against her lips.

"But this time I'm not chickening out," she whispered back.

That was all the incentive he needed.

He kissed her softly at first, testing out her reaction. The last thing he wanted was to scare her away. Amy's hands tentatively roved up his chest, her touch heating him through his shirt. She gripped his shoulders, like she wanted more. He deepened the kiss, running a hand through her hair. Damn. Kissing her was even better than he'd imagined—sweet but hot, too.

A kaleidoscope of images swirled through his mind, a highlight reel of their time together, fueling the fire building inside him. She wrapped her arms around his neck, melting against him. He groaned, his mouth and tongue hungry, greedy, like he couldn't get enough, and neither could she.

His hand moved from her waist, toying with the hem of her shirt, ready to give in to the desperate need to touch her skin, when a light flashed in their faces. Amy jumped, breaking the kiss, and whirled toward the light.

"Brayden!" She looked ready to kill her brother.

Toff raised a hand to block the light from his eyes, squinting at the smug-faced kid holding a flashlight who was never getting a private surf lesson again.

"It's past curfew!" Brayden whispered louder than most people talked. "I'm helping you out."

"Shut off that light and go inside, Brayden," Toff ordered, keeping his voice low. "Amy will be there in a minute."

Brayden flicked off his light, and Toff reached for Amy,

just as another light flashed on, illuminating half the driveway. Fortunately, they were still in the shadows.

Her dad stepped onto the porch. "Brayden? Is that you? Is Amy with you?"

"Omigod," Amy muttered under her breath. "I—I can't believe this." Her voice sounded shaky. She was still breathing hard, and so was he. "Just call me Cinderella. I'd better go inside before the clock chimes twelve and I turn into a mouse."

Toff chuckled. "Brayden's the rodent, not you. Got any mousetraps lying around?"

Brayden ran toward the porch, yelling at his dad. "Amy's inside! She already went to bed!"

"On second thought, we'll let him live." Toff grinned down at Amy, reaching out to tug her against him, running his hand through her hair one last time. So soft.

He glanced toward the porch, where Brayden waved his arms around, talking way too loudly, obviously buying his sister time to sneak in through the side door.

Reluctantly, he stepped back and gave her a gentle push toward the house. "Go inside, Cinderella."

She gave him a wobbly smile, then scurried off, sneaking through the bushes on the side of the house. He grinned as she disappeared into the darkness.

That was one hell of a first kiss. He hoped it wasn't their last.

CHAPTER SEVENTEEN

*T*off texted Amy as soon as he climbed into bed after Viv and Dallas dropped him off.

Toff: Did you make it inside without getting busted?

No reply. He stuffed another lemon madeleine into his mouth. He'd never had this type of cookie before, but they were awesome. He was stashing them in his bedroom so his dad didn't polish them off, like he had the cupcakes. Toff was still PO'd about that. Those cupcakes were epic.

Toff: So are you still scared of public speaking? Or did I cure you?

Maybe that wasn't the best way to say it.

Toff: I mean, did karaoke cure you?

He waited, but still nothing. He was effing this up big-time.

Toff: Tell your dad these cookies are awesome. The cupcakes were, too, except my dad ate most of them. Jerk.

Toff: I mean my dad's a jerk. Not you.

Toff scratched his stomach. The bruising was puke-yellow now, with hints of faded purple. The stitches would come out tomorrow, well, today, technically, in about twelve hours.

He couldn't wait to get back in the water. Maybe Amy would come hang out with him at the beach. He knew Brayden would. Heck, that kid would probably be lying in wait.

Why hadn't Amy replied yet? Was she asleep? Usually girls replied to him ASAP. Was she regretting their kiss? He hoped not, because he sure wasn't.

He stuffed another cookie in his mouth. And another. Still no reply. He decided to Google *Pride and Prejudice* memes. He debated which one to send, then chose the one with the Darcy dude looking all moody that said, "Hey, girl. I love how you've improved your mind by extensive reading."

Made me think of you. He'd never Hey-Girl-memed a girl before.

A few minutes later, his phone finally buzzed with a reply.

Amy: Are you coaching or flirting?

Toff stared at his phone. This was it. Time to find out how she wanted this to go.

Toff: Both?

When she still hadn't responded ten minutes later, he sent one final text before signing off for the night.

Toff: Both. Definitely both.

He set his phone aside and rolled over in bed, sleep overtaking him quickly.

Amy: Are you on Perc again? Empty stomach?
Amy: Toff?
Amy: I'm guessing you passed out. We'll pretend this convo never happened.

. . .

*T*he insistent ping of text messages woke Amy from a deep sleep, in which she'd been dreaming of kissing Toff in a field of flowers…wait, were those flowers or cupcakes? She blinked herself out of her dream haze, then jolted awake, heart pounding.

She really had kissed Toff last night, not in a dream but in her driveway.

Omigod.

Her phone *pinged* again. Who was texting her this early? She fumbled for her phone on her nightstand. *Toff.* She scanned the flurry of messages she'd slept through.

Toff: I was not on Perc. Convo was real.

Toff: This book is BS. What kind of guy doesn't stick around to fight for his own business?

Toff: And why doesn't this chick tell her nosy neighbor to back off?

Toff: Okay, I admit the kid is sort of cute. But he's also a butthead. Like your brother. Followed by three goofy face emojis.

Toff: Hey! The dog in this book is a black Lab. Why is a yellow Lab on the cover?

Toff: Whoa. You didn't tell me there was sex in this book. Damn, Ames. Is this what you and Viv talk about in your book club? No wonder Dallas kept sneaking in.

Toff: Amy? You there?

Toff: BONNIE?

Toff: Your coach needs fuel. Chocolate banana is my smoothie of choice. Wanna do a special delivery to my house?

Amy stared at her phone screen, her heart in her throat. After last night's kiss—which was the best kiss of her entire life until her stupid brother ruined it—and Toff's texts, in which he'd straight-up said he was flirting, she hadn't been able to fall asleep for at least an hour. And now this?

She fired off a text to Viv: **Mayday! Toff's reading book! Sex scenes! Help!**

Viv texted back within seconds.

Viv: Are you sure he's not cheating? Texting you stuff from online reviews?

Maybe, but she didn't think so. He sounded emotionally invested in the story, which thrilled her. That was the best part of hooking people on books, and why she loved matching readers to recs on the blog. She hoped he'd finish it and absorb the message about his dad and Viv's mom deserving their HEA.

I don't think he's cheating, she texted Viv. **He sounds into it.**

She hesitated. **He asked me to bring him a smoothie.**

Viv: He can get his own smoothie.

Amy hesitated. She hadn't told Viv about the kiss and didn't plan to. It was just a heat-of-the-moment thing. A kiss she'd been dreaming about for years, but still.

How awkward was this going to be? *Ugh.* What if she'd just destroyed their whole friend group because she didn't keep her hands—and mouth—to herself?

Toff: Smooothiieeeee. Please. Two of them. I'll pay you back. I'll pay you double. I'm starving. I ate all your dad's cookies. I need sustenance.

So much for him forgetting. Or avoiding him for the rest of her life, because *awkward.* Two seconds later, her phone buzzed again, this time with a Toff selfie—a tousle-haired, big-blue-eyed, please-bring-me-a-smoothie selfie. Shirtless, of course.

Did anyone say no to him? Ever?

She certainly hadn't.

Ugh.

Amy tried to even out her jittery breathing as she reread

his texts. And stared at his selfie. He had used "sustenance" correctly in a sentence—he deserved a smoothie just for that, right? And the *P&P* meme he'd sent her was perfect. She'd already saved it to her phone. She could handle seeing him, right? It wasn't like she could avoid her coach.

Get it together, girl. Where's your swagger?

She could always leave his drink on the porch. There was no shame in ding-dong-ditching the guy whose kiss blew your mind, right?

Right.

Amy: See you soon.

CHAPTER EIGHTEEN

*T*off stood at the kitchen counter, downing Advil, watching Amy creep across the driveway toward his dad's board shop. This was way better than the video game he'd been playing. What was she up to? Yarn bombing Dad's board workshop? And where the heck was his smoothie?

His dad had left for his morning jog and probably to swing by the bookstore to suck face with Viv's mom. "I'll be back by ten," he'd told Toff. "Don't do anything stupid between now and then."

Did watching the other half of his Bonnie and Clyde OTP sneak around count as stupid? Only if he didn't ask her to come inside, which he would, after he figured out what she was doing.

She wasn't subtle, more like a clueless burglar, not even trying to hide. A very pretty, clueless burglar. Her red hair blew in the breeze, sparkly hair thingies glinting in the sun. He wasn't sure how he'd overlooked her the past couple of years.

When she tried the locked workshop door, her shoulders drooped. She glanced at the house, and he jumped back from the window. She must be trying to avoid him and drop off his smoothie with his dad, but why?

"Nice try, Ames," he said softly. "But you're not ditching

me that easily."

Toff glanced out the window again, but she was gone. What the heck? A flash of red hair caught his eye, and he leaned over the sink to see out the window better. It was the McIntyre red, all right, except it wasn't Amy. It was Brayden. Toff laughed out loud. He hustled through the house, wincing in pain but determined to get his smoothie.

And to see Amy. Mostly to see Amy.

He yanked the front door open, coming face-to-face with the delivery girl herself. Well, technically, face-to-back. She'd just set down two smoothie cups on the porch and was halfway down the steps.

"Well, hello there, little lady," Toff drawled. She froze, then turned to face him.

Toff lounged against the doorframe. That little shirt of hers had a lot of holes in it. Her pale skin peeked through the random pattern. He wondered if she'd knitted it.

"This isn't what it looks like," she said, carefully avoiding looking below his neck. He grinned. She really hated it when he didn't wear a shirt. Now that he knew she didn't think he was gross, it gave him the upper hand.

"What do you think it looks like?" He stepped onto the porch, smiling down at her. "Because I think it looks like you were just about to ring the doorbell. To come inside and spend quality time with your bored, injured coach." He brushed his hair out of his eyes. "It definitely doesn't look like you chickened out and were about to lay rubber peeling out of here."

Amy's cheeks went pink.

Huh. She'd been sneaking around and now she was blushing? Had the kiss freaked her out? That would suck, because he was hoping for more.

He glanced toward the driveway. A redhead popped up

behind her car, then ducked back down. Toff ran a hand over his mouth, hiding a smirk. He'd bet money Amy didn't know her brother was there, but Toff wasn't ready to out him. He needed one-on-one time with Amy, without interruption this time.

"Come inside, Ames."

"I—I can't stay."

He raised an eyebrow. Okay. Something was definitely up. Maybe he should change the subject to books, something she always liked talking about. "But I have questions about the book I'm reading. The one *you* picked out for me. You're not going to turn down a chance to book talk me, are you?" Toff gestured to the open front door. "Ladies first."

As soon as she stepped inside, Toff turned around and sent Brayden a signal, flashing him ten fingers twice, then a palm-out "stay" signal. He hoped the kid knew that meant to give him at least twenty minutes until he crashed the party.

"*Y*ou want one of these?" Toff asked, extending a smoothie cup.

Amy shook her head, and he disappeared into the kitchen. She heard the fridge open and shut; then he returned with one smoothie. Her heart raced as he approached her chair, but all he did was hand her a twenty dollar bill.

"That's too much money," she said, but he ignored her, crossing the room to flop onto the couch.

His shoulders relaxed, and he propped his bare legs on the coffee table. "Now that you've knocked the public speaking fear out of the park, how do you feel about doing a vlog?"

So he wasn't going to bring up the kiss. That wasn't exactly a surprise, but what did she think he'd say—how ardently he admired her, like Darcy said to Lizzie Bennet? *Ha*. Toff was hardly a romantic.

"Well?" Toff prompted. "You feeling ready to be on camera?"

Amy toyed with the fringe decorating the hem of the top she'd knitted. "Not yet."

His eyebrows rose. "Why not?"

How many of her fears should she reveal?

"Just tell me," he said. "I won't judge you."

"I guess it's…" Amy began, then stopped. She'd given this a lot of thought since she'd entered the contest. Whether it was risking getting in trouble like yarn bombing or doing karaoke, it all came back to confidence. To taking the plunge when she'd rather hold back.

Like taking the plunge and kissing him last night.

Honestly, what did she have to lose? Besides the contest, of course, and her pride. But Toff had been right about everything else, so why not this? Maybe she should put everything out there and see what stuck.

"It's like I said before," she started, looking him in the eye, determined to be honest and not hold back. "I want to be fearless. Like you." She leaned forward in her chair, shoving down her anxiety. "I'm tired of being the girl in the shadows no one notices."

Toff tilted his head, assessing her silently. She felt like he was sizing her up like a lab specimen rather than a potential hookup, which was just as well. She'd probably regret this later, but for now, it felt…freeing.

"You want to be Lizzie Bennet," he said, like he'd just solved a riddle. "You don't want to be that uptight, quiet girl who married that loser church dude just so she'd have somewhere to live. But you don't want to be the blond sister, either, even though she's the popular, pretty girl everyone loves."

Worst *P&P* review ever. He had so much to learn. Amy arched a displeased eyebrow. She'd practiced that look in the mirror and used it on Brayden.

"Not that Lizzie isn't pretty," Toff backpedaled. "I mean, she's totally hot in the movie and… But…not that it matters what she looks like…" He stopped and took an extra-long drink of his smoothie. "I'm effing this up," he said sheepishly. "I can tell by your face. I'm just not sure how."

She tried to hide her smile. It was fun watching him struggle for once. "Give it your best guess."

"Um." He rubbed his forehead like he had a headache. "Is it because I said Jane was the pretty one?" He squinted one eye, like that would help him locate the answer to his screwup. "Wait—you *do* want to be like Lizzie, right? I mean, she's cool. She didn't take any crap from Darcy. And she's funny. Smart. Like you."

Comparing her to Lizzie Bennet was the best compliment he could give her. It almost made up for his idiocy about Charlotte and not understanding why she'd settled for marrying the simpering Mr. Collins. If Toff had read the book, maybe he'd understand. Even in the twenty-first century, some guys didn't get how limited women's options used to be.

"Thank you," she said, "for saying I'm like Lizzie."

He smiled, but it was cautious, like he was waiting for the other shoe to drop. She'd drop it, but gently.

"Charlotte didn't have any options other than to marry Mr. Collins," she explained. "She couldn't get a job and support herself. Women were property of their fathers and their husbands, which is why Lizzie and Darcy falling in love was such a big deal." She took a breath. "Love matches were rare back then."

Toff drained his smoothie and grinned. "So if Lizzie B. could time-warp to today, she'd be shocked?"

"Yes, shocked and thrilled. She'd probably be president, I mean, prime minister, since she's British." This wasn't how she'd thought their convo would go, but hey, she was doing some literacy training on the side, so props to her.

Toff stood up. "I need my other smoothie. You want anything?"

"I'd like one of my dad's cookies," she said sweetly, taking a poke at him, "but you ate them all."

"Yeah, uh, sorry." He ducked his head, reminding her of ten-year-old Toff who'd devoured her party cupcakes.

"That's okay. I know where to get more."

Amy followed Toff into the kitchen, curious to check out the rest of his house. When she'd been here for parties, the house had been packed, with people spilling out onto the deck, and she couldn't do much snooping.

Unlike her kitchen, Toff's was sparse. Clean—too clean—like no one cooked. The fridge was covered with photos, including some of Toff when he was little, with his mom. Toff grabbed his cup from the fridge and levered himself onto the counter, dangling his long legs. She tried not to ogle. Other than the faded bruising around the bandage, he was… perfection.

"When do you get your stitches out?"

"Today." He sucked down at least half of his smoothie in one long gulp. Those legs of his must be hollow. "Wanna hang out at the beach with me later?"

Amy blinked at him, surprised. "Um…I don't know. I'm picking up some hours in the bookstore so Viv can spend more time with Dallas."

"Oh." Toff shrugged, glancing away. "No big deal. It's cool if you don't want to."

Had she hurt his feelings by not saying yes? *Crap.* Time to change the subject.

"You book-cheated," she blurted. "You read chapters out of order."

He raised his cup to take another long drink, his eyes never leaving hers. She swallowed, waiting for his rebuttal. When he turned his full attention on a person, it was almost too much. Usually his energy was diffused—joking and teasing with everyone in his vicinity, but lately she'd been the focus of maximum-wattage Toff.

"I didn't cheat." He lowered his cup to the counter. "I read four freaking chapters. Every word." He crossed his arms over his chest. He didn't look mad. Instead, he looked like he was enjoying himself.

"But you skipped ahead," Amy argued, wondering who exactly was in control of her mouth. "You had to, if you read one of the, um…those, uh, other scenes."

Toff braced himself on the counter, leaning forward. "Those 'other scenes' are the best part of the book. I'm still in shock that's what you like to read."

He licked his extremely kissable lips, which she now had firsthand experience with, and she squeezed her thighs together.

"You're just full of surprises, aren't you?" He studied her, his gaze roving over her face, dipping below her neck, and back up again.

Silence lay heavy between them. Silence and something else. Maybe it was her imagination again, wishfully conjuring a slow-building heat between them as she stared at his mouth like an idiot.

Then realization hit, and it set her off.

"Wait a minute." Frustration quickly replaced her squishy, crushy feelings. "Just because I read books that happen to have"—she swallowed but pushed forward—"sex in them doesn't mean that's the only reason I read them. And not all romances have sex scenes."

She and Viv had written a blog post about this. They'd tackled the sexist attitude from men, and some women, that romance books were "lady porn" and poorly written and formulaic. Righteous fire ignited inside her, and she unleashed her favorite tirade.

"These books are about relationships, Toff. About people overcoming obstacles and figuring out how to be their best selves. They have to earn the love." She narrowed her eyes. "And those *other* scenes aren't gratuitous. If you actually read the book in order, you'd realize those scenes deepen the relationship."

Toff blinked at her, his eyes wide, and she willed herself to calm down. Viv always said Amy was the mellowest person she knew, except when it came to defending books.

A knock sounded on the door, breaking the tension.

"I'll get it." Toff slid off the counter. "You really need to do a vlog, Ames. Just unleash that bookworm fire, and people won't be able to stop watching." His gaze went to her hair, and he reached out, fingers tangling briefly in the strands, his touch making her stomach dip. He held out a sparkly ladybug clip. "Almost lost this little bugger." He quirked a smile, then went to answer the door, which someone was pounding on insistently.

She slumped against the counter, her knees a little weak. He was a very *hands-on* coach. Not that she was complaining.

Pulling herself together, she headed for the living room, then hesitated. If she turned right instead of left, she could peek into his bedroom, which was all kinds of tempting.

You really shouldn't, she told herself. She cocked an ear toward the living room but heard nothing. Maybe it was safe to take a quick peek. Just one, to satisfy her curiosity.

. . .

*T*off stood on the porch, staring down Brayden. "That was about ten minutes, little dude, not twenty."

His conversation with Amy had swerved all over the place. Brayden's timing had sucked, interrupting them right when Toff was trying to figure out how to apologize for accidentally insulting her.

"I'm not an old man," Brayden said. "I don't wear a watch."

"You have a phone."

"I was playing *Cranky Cows*. I don't pay attention to time, dude."

Toff snorted. "Come inside. Let's see if I can sweet-talk your sister out of busting your butt for stowing away in the car."

"You said you wanted to borrow me for a day." Brayden's shoulders slumped. "I just wanted to see how you were doing." He glanced up. "When do you get to surf again?"

"Today, I hope. Have to see what the doc says."

"Cool." Brayden side-eyed him. "Were you and my sister making out? Is that why you wanted twenty minutes?"

I wish, thought Toff. He smirked down at the little spy. "Like I'd tell you if we were."

Brayden shrugged. "Maybe if you made out, she'd forget to get mad at me for sneaking over here."

Toff grinned as he ushered Brayden into the house. Getting to kiss Amy again was already high on his agenda. He'd have to find out if she was okay with it first, but if she was, he might as well do it for a good cause.

"I'll give it my best shot, kid."

...

*A*my drank in the details of Toff's bedroom like a parched nomad who'd discovered water in the desert. Okay, so maybe she exaggerated, but when you'd obsessed over someone for years, entering his secret lair was a dream come true. What hidden secrets did it hold?

Toff's bedroom walls were covered with posters of famous surfers and lots of blown-up photos of him and his friends surfing and hanging out on the beach. Plenty of pics of him posing with trophies. A photo of Toff, Dallas, and Viv laughing together at Slices Pizza mixed in with all the surf team pictures. Amy scanned the walls for girlfriend photos. There were tons of photos of him with girls but nothing that looked like an actual couple photo. Hmm...

His bookcase was full of trophies, not books. *Shocker*. Tons of ribbons with medals dangled from a row of coat hooks screwed into the wall. A vintage surfboard was mounted over his bed, which was a mess of tangled sheets and... *Wow*, her mind went straight to Toff's favorite chapters.

His desk was cluttered with empty glasses and stacks of paper. The computer monitor was covered in dust. Perched next to it was the cute, bedraggled penguin stuffie Dallas had used for the Percocet photo. She smiled. She had her own stash of childhood stuffies, too.

So much for finding any revealing secrets— *Wait*. What was that?

Redo in the Rockies was facedown on the nightstand, because of course Toff didn't understand the importance of using a bookmark so as not to crack the spine. She picked up the book and flipped through the pages. The first bedroom scene happened in chapter thirteen, and he said he'd read four chapters. She smirked. She knew he'd skipped ahead.

Okay, time to get out of here before she got busted. She spun around, ready to bolt, but instead came face-to-face with…Brayden? *Oh no.*

Toff stood behind him, looming over Brayden like a protector who knew she was about to flip out. Toff's gaze swept over her, darted around the room, then landed back on her. He leaned against the doorframe and smiled, a dangerous smile full of heat.

Whoa.

"Hey, Ames," Toff said casually, sounding like he found random girls snooping in his bedroom every day. "Find what you were looking for?"

Her anxious gaze darted between Toff and Brayden. Why was Brayden here? And why did he look so smug? He should be in panic mode, knowing she'd make him pay for this impromptu visit.

"I…um…was…um…" She had nothing. Zilch.

"Spying," Brayden announced, glancing up at Toff for approval. Toff grinned down at him, and Amy swore she saw Brayden sprout up three inches in height.

Her best option was to flee the scene immediately. "We need to go, Brayden. Toff has a doctor's appointment—"

"Not so fast." Toff stepped away from the doorframe, pushing Brayden into the room ahead of him.

Brayden beelined to the trophy shelf. "Wow! These are awesome! How many do you have?" He reached out, and instinctively Amy told him not to touch.

"It's fine. He can't hurt anything," Toff said, keeping his eyes on Amy, not Brayden. She crossed her arms over her chest, wishing she'd worn a hoodie instead of knitted top with a bunch of holes in it. She felt like he was staring into her soul. And the way he kept looking at her mouth? Her entire body was on fire.

"I…um…" Amy squeezed her eyes shut, then stared at her feet. "I'm sorry. I shouldn't have come in here. I was looking for the bathroom." *Liar, liar, pants on fire.* She glanced up, chewing on her bottom lip.

Toff cocked a disbelieving eyebrow. His eyes went to her mouth again, and his smile notched up a level from dangerous to Mayday. Brayden lifted a winners' ribbon off a display hook and draped it around his neck, fingering the medal.

"Brayden! Put that back!" If Amy didn't die of mortification from her own snooping, she would from her brother's stupidity.

"I'm going to win a bunch of trophies someday," Brayden said, ignoring Amy. He stared at Toff the way their dog moony-eyed the treat jar. "Just like you."

Amy hoped she never looked at Toff the same way her brother did, but she probably did. *Ugh.*

"If you work your butt off, you can do it," Toff said. He glanced at Amy and gave her that smile she was starting to think of as the Brayden Smile, the one that told her he knew Brayden was embarrassing her but not to worry about it. That smile was almost as dangerous as the new, steamy Mayday smile.

"Come on, Bray," Amy said. "We need to go."

Brayden turned from the trophies to Toff. "Want us to stay?"

"Sure, but I think your sister's had enough of me." He sent her a sly smirk that said exactly the opposite. Her body flushed with heat. He was the *worst.*

Except he wasn't.

Toff grabbed a small tube from the top of his dresser and tossed it to Brayden. "Wear that on the beach, buddy. It's the best waterproof sunblock there is, especially for gingers."

"Thanks!" Brayden held the tube like it was liquid gold.

"Let's *go*, Brayden," Amy said, pushing her brother out of Toff's bedroom, which she would never, ever step foot in again. Toff followed them to the front door, making Amy want to break into a sprint.

"I'm heading to the beach as soon as I leave the doc's," Toff said. "If anyone wants to join me."

"I do! I do!" Brayden turned pleading eyes on Amy. "We're going, right? You can just read on the beach or whatever while Toff and I surf." He flicked a hand at her dismissively.

Amy narrowed her eyes at Toff, who did his lean-on-the-door pose again, smirking down at her. He knew exactly what he was doing, using Brayden to get her to the beach.

"I don't know—" Amy began.

"I'll text you when I'm done at the doc's," Toff said. He spun Brayden around by the shoulders and pretended to kick him in the butt. "Get outta here, grom. I'll see you later." Laughing, Brayden took off running. Amy was poised to run, too, but Toff stopped her, putting a hand on her shoulder.

"Don't be too hard on him," Toff said, tilting his head toward Brayden, who disappeared around the side of the house. "He just wanted to check up on his idol."

Amy rolled her eyes, trying to pretend his warm hand on her bare shoulder wasn't interfering with her breathing.

Toff released her shoulder and flexed his fingers. He glanced at his hand and quirked a cryptic smile.

"Before you go, we have some unfinished business." His gaze dropped to her mouth, then back up to her eyes. "And I'm not talking about the vlog."

Her pulse stutter-stepped. "We do?"

He nodded, moving in close, the heat from his body radiating around her like a human sun. His expression was serious for once, instead of teasing.

"Your text asked if I was coaching or flirting. Do you want

to change back to our original coach rules? Where I 'rein it in' and we keep things all business? It's up to you."

Amy swallowed, blushing furiously. What should she say? *Bring all the kissing, please and thank you*?

If there was a time for swagger, this was it.

"Um…I'm…fine with changing the rules. I mean, uh, the kissing is okay." *Whew*. That was far from swagger-y, but she deserved a medal for saying that to his face. And naked chest.

"The kiss was 'okay'?" He faked a wounded look. "Ouch. I thought it was way better than okay, Bonnie." His wounded expression quickly shifted to off-the-charts flirty. "But I'm glad you're cool with changing the rules because I have a favor to ask."

"A favor?"

He nodded. "So usually before a doc appointment, I'd shower, but I can't with the stitches. I could really use a hand with a sponge bath." He slanted her a mischievous grin. "Two hands would be even better."

Her brain shorted out, unleashing a flurry of panicked messages, but her body was immobile and on fire, not sure whether to fight or flight. Or go find a sponge.

"Think of it like back scratching," he added, "only more fun."

She sucked in a breath, digging deep for composure, but she floundered. He was swimming in the deep end of the flirting pool, and she still needed water wings.

"Y-you're…crazy," she sputtered. "That's not what I meant by changing the rules."

He took a step closer, laughing. "You know I'm teasing, right?"

"When *aren't* you teasing?"

"Right now," he said, and the humor vanished from his eyes. "I'm one hundred percent serious about kissing you. If you're still okay with that." A hint of a smile tugged at his lips. "Just erase all the dumb stuff I said."

She swallowed, feeling the fizzy, crackly energy building between them. "I'll need a really big eraser," she whispered, taking a step toward him. She could do this. She wanted to do this. "I am...one hundred percent okay with kissing you. Even though you're an idiot."

"I'll find you that eraser," he whispered. "Later." He hooked his thumbs through the belt loops of her jeans, tugging her toward him.

She tilted her head back like a sunflower, drinking in his heat and warmth. The light around them shimmered, making everything brighter—his sun-kissed golden skin, those iridescent blue eyes, the flash of white teeth as he smiled, right before he pulled her in close.

He cupped her face, and this time when his lips touched hers, it wasn't a soft kiss that built slowly. This was a fast and furious kiss, a starter gun igniting them the moment their mouths touched.

Toff's fingers tangled in her windblown curls, massaging her scalp while his lips worked a different kind of magic on her mouth.

Fireworks exploded inside her chest, and behind her eyelids, and everywhere his hands touched her.

She slid her hands up and down the warm skin of his back, enjoying how his muscles flexed underneath her touch.

Total romance novel material.

And so much better than last night.

A car horn sounded from the driveway. *Brayden.* She was going to kill him. She'd ask Viv's mom for a slow, torturous method.

Toff released his grip on her, stepping back. They were both breathing hard.

"You'd better go before he tries to drive himself." Toff flashed a quick grin. "I'll see you later, Bonnie."

Still in a kissing daze, Amy nodded, turning toward the car. Her thoughts were scrambled, her body still trembling from the kiss. What were they doing?

The car horn sounded again, and she snapped out of her daze.

It's just kissing, she told herself as she headed down the driveway, *no big deal.*

Even though it was.

CHAPTER NINETEEN

*T*off kicked back in the doctor's exam room, naked from the waist up. It was time to get his stitches out. Time to be released from his prison sentence.

He felt like that mermaid in the cartoon movie who grew legs and hated living on land. Bored with waiting on the exam table, he took a picture of himself making a goofy face and Snapchatted it to Amy.

After she and Brayden had left, he'd resumed skimming the *Redo* book, hoping for more "non-gratuitous" scenes, especially after that hot kiss with his bookworm.

Plus that dog was awesome, always getting in trouble, but no one got mad at him because he was so lovable. Dad had mentioned getting a dog to keep him company after Toff left for college, but maybe he wouldn't now, since he was getting married. Toff frowned as anxiety streaked through him at the thought of the upcoming wedding.

Right on cue, the door opened, and his dad walked in with a bottle of water. "Want some?"

Toff shook his head and glanced at his phone. Amy still hadn't opened his Snap. He took another one and sent it to Dallas, who immediately sent a reply: a picture of him and Viv lying on the beach, grinning. That was where he should be, not cooped up in this chemical-smelling room.

Another knock on the door sounded. "Come in," his dad said, "we're decent."

Toff rolled his eyes at his dad, who shrugged and grinned. Viv's mom said that he and his dad had the same smile. He wondered if his smile was as smug as his dad's and if that was why Amy got so frustrated with him sometimes.

The door opened. He hadn't seen his pediatrician, Dr. Brooks, in ages, since he'd switched to a dude doc when he was fifteen, but Dr. Dave was on vacation. Dr. Brooks looked mostly the same, with her beaded black dreadlocks and purple eyeglasses.

"Well, if it isn't the Nichols men." She beamed at them. "Who's hurt this time?" She reached out to shake Dad's hand and then his. A prickle of panic streaked up his spine as he recalled the tetanus shot he'd had to get in the ER, just in case. He wouldn't need another shot today, right?

He was not a fan of needles. When he was a kid, his mom had taken him for ice cream after every shot. He'd cried the whole way to the ice-cream shop, and Mom always let him get the biggest cone they had. Clearing his throat, he blinked away the memory and watched Dr. Brooks as she pulled on examining gloves.

"You're lucky you didn't break any ribs. No concussion, either." She set her iPad on the small desk and studied Toff, her expression serious. "Have you been cleaning your cut regularly and putting on fresh bandages?"

Toff nodded.

"Excellent. Lie back on the table, Christopher."

He smirked at the use of his full name. She'd always called him that. He obeyed, stretching out on the scratchy tissue paper covering the padded table.

His dad moved in, standing at the foot of the table and

watching him like a hawk. "Toff seems to think he's ready to get back on his board once you take the stitches out."

Toff bit down hard on his lower lip as the doc prodded a particularly sore spot. He couldn't show pain or they'd never let him surf again. The doc wasn't fooled. She pressed the same spot again, and this time he swallowed a yelp. Her eyes narrowed behind her glasses, and she glanced at his dad.

"I looked at the X-rays from the ER." She returned her attention to Toff. "Good thing you didn't crack a rib, but the bruising is deep, and you need more time to heal. That was a deep laceration."

"*Doc*. Come on. I'm fine," he protested.

Ignoring him, she slowly peeled off the bandage. "Let's get these stitches out. If everything looks good, I can see you getting back in the water in two or three weeks."

"What?" His body vibrated, ready to explode off the table. "The Summer Spectacular is in two weeks! I can't miss that." He needed to get back on his board now to get ready.

"Toff. Settle down." Dad grimaced and exchanged a worried look with the doc. "I don't suppose you have a cage I can lock him in until then?"

"Ha-ha," Toff said sarcastically. He squeezed his eyes shut as the doctor removed the stitches. This was a nightmare. He was trapped in a crappy version of the *Groundhog Day* movie, waking up to find out he still couldn't get back in the water.

The doc covered his cut with some goopy stuff and a clean bandage, then glared at him like a crabby teacher. "Stay off your board and out of the ocean for two more weeks. Give your body a chance to heal *completely*. I recommend you skip the Spectacular."

He forced himself to sit up and not show how much it hurt. "Doc, I can't do it. I'll die. My skin will shrivel up from lack of water." He glanced at his dad. "I'll get so depressed,

I'll start watching soap operas. Gain fifty pounds." And he wasn't going to miss the Spectacular.

His dad shot Toff another warning look. "We'll follow doctor's orders."

"Excellent." Dr. Brooks removed her gloves with a *snap* and tossed them into a hazmat receptacle. "How many painkillers are you taking, Christopher?"

"Just ibuprofen, maybe three or four a day." After the Percocet incident, which Dallas still mocked him for, he was sticking with the over-the-counter stuff.

She regarded him closely. She'd known his family forever. When his mom died, he'd learned she wasn't always grumpy. She'd held him for a long time when he'd broken down in her office after a booster shot because his mom wasn't there anymore to take him for ice cream. She'd given his dad the name of a family therapist who'd helped. A lot.

"All right," she said, pinning his dad with a fierce glare. "I'm trusting you, Paul. You know him best, and I know you'll keep an eye on him. No more than six ibuprofen in twenty-four hours."

She turned back to Toff. "Christopher, if you plan to compete again, which I'm sure you do, please do as I say. Rest. Let your body heal. Then you can kick everyone's butt like you always have."

It took him a few seconds to process her words. He appreciated her compliment, but it didn't diminish the frustration building inside him. "I don't know how I'm going to survive." He groaned. "But I'll stay out of the water." *Maybe*.

"Excellent. Come back and see me in two weeks." She typed quickly on the computer, pausing to glance over her shoulder at his dad. "I hear congratulations are in order. I'm thrilled for you and Rose."

Toff grimaced, thinking of Amy's book again. He'd

skipped ahead to the ending, skimming a few middle chapters full of makeup/breakup drama. The couple finally got their act together, and in the last scene, they were in love again and everyone was all, *You two were always so perfect for each other, even in high school.*

Blech. Who fell in love in high school? Besides Dallas and Viv, but they were the exception. Exceptional weirdoes.

"Toff." His dad's voice was sharp. "Are you listening?"

Toff blinked, yanking himself out of book brain into the present. Was this why Amy always had that dreamy look in her eyes? Was she reliving those books she read nonstop? Was she thinking about the *non-gratuitous* scenes she got all defensive about? How experienced was she in that arena anyway?

"Toff!"

"Yeah, yeah. I'm listening."

"Dr. Brooks was saying how amusing it is that you're getting a sister at this age."

Toff met his dad's gaze, surprised by the anxiety etched on his dad's face. "Viv's been like my sister forever," he said. "This wedding thing just makes it official."

His dad's features relaxed, relief filling his eyes. *Crap.* Was his dad worried about him and Viv? Hell, that was the easiest part of this whole deal. Toff swung his legs around so they dangled off the table and grabbed his T-shirt, tugging it over his head.

"Thanks, Doc." He needed to get out of here. Flashing her his most charming smile, he said, "I promise I'll stay out of the water."

Her eyebrows rose over her glasses and she shook her head. "I'm sure you leave a trail of broken hearts everywhere you go, Christopher."

Trail of broken hearts? Hardly. He did casual, not relationships. And right now, the only girl he wanted to hang out with was Amy. It was strange for him, but he was going with it.

He slid off the table and shoved his feet into his flip-flops. Like he'd ever talk about girls with these two.

Dr. Brooks opened the examining room door and paused in the doorway. "I'll see you soon." She gave him a sympathetic smile. "In the meantime, please behave."

Toff shrugged. He didn't feel like behaving.

As they left the doctor's office, he struggled to get a grip on the anger slowly building inside him as the reality of his extended prison sentence sank in.

He felt so trapped by his own body, which was nuts. Doc had told him not to, but he wanted to run straight into the ocean. He craved the waves—ached for water and the wind and his board and the challenge of reading the swells and pushing himself to execute his most difficult maneuvers over and over, until his legs gave up.

Dammit all.

On the ride home, the anger continued to swirl inside his gut, his chest, clogging his throat. His body vibrated with it, coiling inside him like a snake ready to strike. Two more weeks landlocked. And miss the Summer Spectacular. Toff's jaw clenched as he stared out the window.

He was *so* done.

"I want to go pro."

"What? You think you're ready after how you behaved today?" Dad snapped. "No way in hell."

Toff's head whipped toward his dad. "What's that supposed to mean?"

Dad shot him a glare. "I know you. You're not going to

follow the doctor's orders. You're going to try to push yourself before you're ready."

"I am ready!" His hands fisted on his thighs, the coiled snake inside him rearing back, hissing. "Stop the van." Toff unbuckled his seat belt, his hand on the door handle.

"What are you doing?" Dad gaped at him, his glare replaced by panic.

"Stop the damn van!" Toff flung the door open. His dad swerved to the side of the road, slamming on the brakes, horns blaring behind them.

Toff jumped out and unleashed his fury. "It's my life, Dad. My decision to go pro, not yours. If I screw up, it's on me." His breathing was ragged. "Don't you want me out of the house anyway? So you and Rose can live happily ever after?"

Dad's head jerked back like Toff had slapped him.

Fuck it. Toff spun around and sprinted off, the searing pain of his injury only fueling his anger.

"Toff! Get back here!"

Dad's voice faded into the background as he ran…and ran…toward the welcoming cry of seagulls and crashing waves, ignoring the pain in his ribs.

And his heart.

*L*ater that night, Toff was dozing on the couch, his video game paused on the TV, when a knock sounded on the front door, startling him awake.

He'd come home hours after flipping out on his dad. He'd hung out on the beach with his surfer posse, indulging in self-pity and too many beers. He'd had a couple of offers of another type of consolation, but he hadn't been interested, especially when he thought about Amy's soft lips. Soft *everything*. He hadn't texted her, though. He didn't want to see her with a mood on.

"Just a minute!" Toff yelled, blinking away his sleepy haze.

Dad wasn't home. He'd texted Toff that he was at Rose's and to call him when he got home, but Toff hadn't. He felt sort of stupid about jumping out of the van. Okay, *really* stupid.

Maybe he should add a new hashtag to his and Amy's posts: #FlipperFlipsOut.

"Don't get up!" a familiar gruff voice called out. "I'll let myself in."

Coach Diggs. *Damn*. He was so busted. Toff sat up quickly, wincing as he swung his legs around to the floor. His ribs still ached from the run, but at least he'd pounded out the anger.

"Uh-huh," Coach said, leaning against the living room doorframe. "That's what I thought." He scowled as he crossed the room, pausing to switch on a lamp. "Stand up. Let me check you out."

Toff did as he was told, feeling like a kid caught cheating on a test. Coach huffed as he lifted Toff's T-shirt and examined his midsection, poking and prodding as much as Dr. Brooks had. Toff tried his best not to react or show pain.

Coach glanced up from under his bushy gray eyebrows. "You know you're supposed to call me immediately if you injure yourself." He grunted. "Good thing Dr. Brooks let me know. And your dad." He stepped back and glared at Toff, his dark-brown eyes turning almost black. "I just got back from vacation last night or I'd have busted your ass the day this happened."

Of course Dad had ratted him out.

"You need to do what Doc says." His eyes narrowed to slits. "And what I say. Stay out of the water. Don't ignore pain." He ran a hand across his stubbled chin. "Basically, don't be a dumb-ass."

Toff sighed heavily. Coach Diggs had been his mentor since he was seven years old. He'd been tough on him but also fair. He'd pushed Toff harder than he pushed anyone else, and Toff had risen to every challenge.

"You're not messing this up, Nichols. You're the best damn surfer I've seen in years. You need to stay on target if you want to go pro after your senior year."

Toff blinked, unsure he'd heard right. Coach had pushed hard for that, but Dad had shut it down. Where was this coming from?

Coach tilted his head toward the sliding door. "Go outside and sit. I'm grabbing myself a beer. You want anything?"

"Gatorade."

"You got it." Coach grabbed the remote from the footstool and turned off the TV. "These games rot your brain from the inside out."

Toff rolled his eyes as he headed for the deck. The man was as predictable as the tide. A few minutes later, Coach plopped down next to Toff and handed him his drink. The full moon reflected off the sliver of ocean visible from the deck.

"We both know your dad wants the best for you," Coach said. "Which in his mind is a college education."

Toff's shoulders tensed. "Can we not talk—"

"But he also wants you to be happy." Coach barreled right over him like a Banzai Pipeline wave. "And it's not like your dad didn't have a hell of a good time when he was on the circuit." He took a swig of beer, then leaned back in the deck chair, looking up at the stars.

What the...? Why was Coach...?

"Wait a minute." Toff tugged at his hair as the puzzle pieces slid into place. "Did Dad send you over here?"

Coach shrugged, taking another pull from his beer bottle.

Son of a…

"Are you telling me Dad's suddenly cool with me going pro?" He didn't believe that. Not after the way he'd smacked him down about the doctor visit.

"I'm saying you oughta have a civilized conversation about it." Coach side-eyed him. "You and your dad have always been tight. More like brothers."

"Not lately," Toff said. "He's riding my ass all the time." He missed his chill dad. The guy he laughed with, surfed with.

"Lots of changes ahead," Coach bit out. "Your dad getting married. You graduating, figuring out what's next." He took another swig of beer. "You scared the hell out of him with that wipeout. Parent's worst nightmare, getting called to the ER."

Toff glugged his Gatorade, wishing it was a beer. "Didn't know you were a therapist, too."

Coach side-eyed him again, and Toff laughed.

"Will you give me your word you won't do anything stupid until Doc clears you to surf?" Coach asked, appraising Toff through narrowed eyes.

"Can't do that. You know me. I do stupid at least once a week."

"I'm talking surfing stupidity. The other stuff is out of my jurisdiction."

"Aw, Coach. I love you, too." Toff grinned and tilted back in his chair, closing his eyes and inhaling the briny scent of the ocean floating on the night breeze.

"Christopher Nichols, I know God gave you a brain. For once in your life, use it."

Coach wasn't kidding around. He looked genuinely worried. Toff huffed out a frustrated sigh as he faced the guy who'd been like an uncle to him for the past ten years.

"Fine."

Relief flitted across Coach's features. "Fair enough," he

muttered. They sat in silence, staring out at the moonlit sliver of ocean that called to Toff like a lighthouse beacon in the darkness.

"Maybe your dad can keep you busy in the workshop," Coach said, breaking the silence.

Toff nodded. "Yeah, maybe, but I don't want to take away paid hours from Slammer. He needs the cash." Toff shifted in his chair and cleared his throat as Amy's red curls and flashing eyes came to mind. "I've got some other stuff to do that'll keep me busy."

"Do I want to know?"

Toff grinned. "Probably not."

Coach squinted. "Just remember what I tell you idiots every year: Don't make a life; don't take a life."

Toff laughed. He and the other incoming seniors on the surf team were going to get Coach's infamous slogan printed on T-shirts and wear them at graduation. "Not planning to do either."

"Good," Coach replied. "Just get through these next couple of weeks, and then your life can go back to normal."

"Trust me," Toff said, a deep sigh gusting out of him, "back to normal is what I want."

CHAPTER TWENTY

"I didn't love this one, sweetie. What else have you got for me?"

Amy smiled as the elderly Mrs. Sloane handed over a sci-fi romance to trade in for bookstore credit. She was a regular customer at Murder by the Sea and an active participant in the Lonely Hearts Book Club. She also loved books with lots of *those* scenes, the same ones Toff liked.

"What are you in the mood for?" Amy asked. "Cowboys? Billionaires? Scots in kilts?"

She knew exactly what, or who, she was in the mood for, but she hadn't heard from him since yesterday. She hoped his doctor appointment went okay. He'd probably spent all afternoon surfing and forgotten he'd said he'd text her.

Mrs. Sloane tapped her chin, studying Amy through her thick glasses. "I still need to read our book club choice. How about that one, and maybe a football player?" She patted her silver hair and cleared her throat. "None of those men who shift into grizzly bears or panthers. That doesn't do anything for me."

Amy nodded, trying to keep a straight face. "Have a seat. I'll be right back."

After Mrs. Sloane was settled, Amy disappeared into the

romance aisle. She grabbed the gothic for book club and perused the shelves for a good football hero, deciding on a popular series about a Chicago NFL team, an oldie but a goodie.

The bell on the door jingled. Returning to the front of the store, she put on her best "Welcome to the best bookstore ever" smile and came face-to-face with Toff and a couple of tourists.

"Welcome to Murder by the Sea," she said to the tourists. "Please make yourselves at home and look around."

"I'll be with you in a moment, *sir*," she said to Toff. "I'm with another customer right now."

Toff raised his eyebrows and sent her a delicious smirk. *No*. Not delicious. She could not let her mind go down that dangerous train of thought, even though the rest of her was totally on board for a train ride with Toff.

She handed the books to Mrs. Sloane, whose eyes lit up as she checked out the covers.

"These look wonderful." She leaned over and snuck a peek at Toff, who was repeatedly tossing a hacky sack up in the air and catching it. "That young man is very"—she lowered her voice and stage-whispered—"cover-worthy."

Amy blushed. "Cover-worthy" was a secret code used by the book club members to describe real-life people who were kissable. And, uh, beyond. Which he definitely was.

Mrs. Sloane put the books in her tote bag and stood up slowly, leaning on her cane, Amy helping her.

"You have enough credit for all of these," Amy said as they walked toward the door. "I'll update the system."

Toff rushed over, surprising Amy by extending his arm for Mrs. Sloane. "I'll walk you out," he said. He smiled at Amy. "You can go help the other customers. One of them's in your favorite section."

"Thank you, young man." Mrs. Sloane paused in the doorway to examine him. "My. You are handsome, aren't you?" She tilted her head. "You could do with a haircut, but I suppose girls like all that messy hair, don't they, Amy?"

Amy did her best not to look at Toff, but from the corner of her eye, she saw him toss his head like a horse tossing its mane. She bit back a laugh.

"Amy, dear, introduce me to your young man."

"Oh, um, sorry. Mrs. Sloane, this is Toff Nichols." *And he's not* mine.

"What kind of name is that?" Mrs. Sloane asked. "Isn't that used in historical novels? A toff is a dandy, isn't it? A pretty boy." She smiled up at him. "I suppose it fits."

Toff gaped at Amy, who laughed out loud. "I'll explain later." She smiled at Mrs. Sloane. "In this case, it's short for Christopher."

"Ah, much better." She patted Toff's arm and smiled at Amy, eyes twinkling behind her glasses. "You behave yourself with this young man. If you can."

Gah. Mrs. Sloane was the biggest troublemaker in the Lonely Hearts, hands down. "Bye," Amy said. "I'll see you at book club."

Toff escorted Mrs. Sloane to the senior center's minibus, smiling and leaning down to listen to her as they slowly made their way across the parking lot.

Nice to little old ladies. Her heart squeezed as she watched him help Mrs. Sloane onto the bus. Fortunately, the other customers had a stack of books to ring up to refocus her attention.

When Toff returned, he flopped into a chair and waited, scrolling through his phone and drinking a smoothie. He had an addiction. Maybe he needed Smoothies Anonymous.

After the customers left, she approached him slowly, like

he was a hungry predator and she was dinner.

"How was your doctor's appointment?"

He shot her a guilty look. "Sorry I didn't text yesterday." He shrugged. "It sucked. I can't surf for another two weeks. I'll probably miss the Spectacular."

"Oh no. That's awful." She sat down across from him.

"Yeah." He propped an ankle on his thigh, leg bouncing. This must be what bottled-up surfer energy looked like. He exhaled roughly, then forced a smile. "But the good news is I was asked on a date."

Amy blinked, her stomach twisting. "You were?"

"Yep. With Mrs. Sloane."

She laughed, ridiculously relieved. "She moves fast."

"Can you blame her?" He winked. "Jealous?"

"Why would I be jealous?" She leaned back in her chair, doing her best to look like she had no interest in him at all.

Toff grinned like he saw right through her. "I'm glad you're so open-minded, Ames, and willing to share me with other women."

"I— *What?*"

He stretched out his legs and cupped the back of his head with his hands. "You should keep an eye on her. Make sure she doesn't put the moves on your coach." He waggled his eyebrows suggestively.

She gave up faking disinterest. He made her laugh like no one else. "Where's she taking you on your date?"

"Book club."

"What?" Panicked, she sat bolt upright. "You— you— can't—" Book club was a sacred space. No boys allowed.

"Relax, Bonnie. I turned her down. I knew you'd never let me in your secret clubhouse." His lips puckered around his smoothie straw.

Lucky straw.

She cleared her throat. "I'm surprised you can joke around with the bad news."

He stared down at his feet. "Yeah, well. Good thing you didn't see me yesterday." He glanced up, his smile sheepish. "I was in extreme alphahole mode."

"Really?" She was impressed he remembered.

"Oh yeah. Rage-quit on my dad. Traumatized some tourists when I was running to the beach. Almost took them out." His tone was joking, but his eyes were troubled.

"I'm sure your dad understands. He's a surfer, too."

"Maybe." His answering smile was forced. "He wanted to talk, but I avoided him." His gaze darted around the store, then back to her. "What time are you off work? I could use some cheering up."

Her heart did a jump-rope skip. "Six o'clock."

His attention drifted to her mouth. "Want to go hang out at the pier?"

"Sure." Amy willed her heartbeat to slow down, but now it was double-dutch jump-roping.

"Cool. I'll pick you up here." He stood, sucked down the last of his smoothie, then swished the empty cup into the trash can. "I should get going."

Disappointed he was leaving, Amy walked him to the door, pausing to grab a bookmark from the new releases table.

"Here. You need to use this. Breaking book spines is like forgetting to clean your board."

His forehead wrinkled. "What are you talking about?"

"Just humor me and use a bookmark. Please."

He quirked a smile. "Yes, boss."

His eyes didn't look troubled anymore. His gaze darkened, full of heat, and she held her breath, hoping for a kiss. Instead, he took a step back, tossed her another pantie-melting grin, and was out the door in a flash.

CHAPTER TWENTY-ONE

*T*off handed a five dollar bill to the girl running the Whack-a-Quack booth on the boardwalk. "Show me what you've got, Bonnie."

Amy lifted the pellet gun and fired off a volley of shots, knocking over three metal ducks stuttering in a jerky conga line.

"Wow." Toff whistled. "You're a good shot."

Amy lowered her weapon and flashed him a cocky grin. "Pick your prize, Clyde."

"You can pick from the second row." The duck-booth girl hooked her thumb over her shoulder to three rows of stuffed animals tacked to the wall behind her.

"I'll take that one." He pointed to a penguin in the top row and flashed her his flirtiest smile. The booth girl blinked like she was in a daze, then retrieved a stuffed penguin from an overflowing bin.

"Cheater," Amy huffed, rolling her eyes and heading for the next game booth. "She said the second row, not the top one."

He caught up to her in a few quick strides. "I can't help it if that girl got distracted." He patted the penguin's head. "Thanks for the prize, Ames," he said, dipping his voice low as they left the booth. "I'm gonna sleep with it every night."

Amy practically growled next to him, making him laugh. "You couldn't rein it in for a million dollars."

"Rein what in?" He blinked innocently, giving his eyelashes an extra flutter just to rile her.

"You know exactly what I mean." Her gaze slid down to his bare chest peeking out from his half-zipped hoodie. "Why don't you ever wear a shirt?"

He tossed her a lazy smile. "I need to air out my wound."

Her coppery eyes flashed with frustration…or was that something else? Something way more intriguing?

She tried to storm off again, but he reached out and caught her by the belt loop on her shorts.

"Freeze, gunslinger."

She turned, her gaze darting to his pecs, then away, but he didn't miss how she blushed. Reluctantly, he let go of her belt loop.

"Here. Hold Rico." He tossed the penguin to her and shrugged out of his hoodie, tossing that her way, too. He snagged his T-shirt from the waistband of his shorts.

"Rico?" Her voice sounded far away as he tugged the shirt over his head.

He popped his head through the neck hole. "From the Madagascar movies. Remember?"

"Um…"

"You don't remember Rico?"

"Not really. I mean, I saw the movies, but I don't remember the specific penguins."

Pretending to be shocked, he snatched Rico from her arms. "Don't listen to her, buddy," he whispered where the ear would be hiding under a few feathers, if this were a legit replica. Which it was not.

Amy's lips parted slightly; then she laughed, a throaty

sound he felt all the way down to his toes. An electric jolt shot through his body, switching his focus to female anatomy instead of penguin anatomy.

"Do you want your hoodie back?" Amy asked, flicking his hoodie like she was a bull trainer and he was the bull.

"Keep it. You might get cold later."

She hesitated, then tied his hoodie around her waist, making his chest swell like a caveman who'd just clubbed a mastodon. *Weird.*

"What's next, Ames?"

She glanced up and down the boardwalk. "Come on."

Two minutes later, they stood in line at a painted wooden facade of a sailor dude holding a mermaid, with the faces cut out for photos ops.

"You look like that mermaid," he said, "with all that red hair." He grinned. "And the sparkles."

"Wrong." She unleashed that sassy-sweet smile he liked so much. "Today you're the mermaid. I'm the sailor."

He blinked, then laughed. "Maybe you *should* fire me. You've got plenty of swagger tonight, Bonnie."

A sunburned tourist took their picture as they posed behind the facade, faces peeking through the cutout holes. "You two are adorable," the woman gushed, handing Toff his phone. "How long have you been dating?"

"Uh…" Toff's mind went blank.

"We're not," Amy said quickly. "He's my coach."

"Oh? What sport?"

Amy smirked. "Running from the cops. Penguin stealing. You know, Bonnie and Clyde stuff."

"You made your coach proud, Bonnie," Toff said as the tourist scurried off. "Bringin' the swaggah."

He moved to the railing, leaning against it as he tweeted and Instagrammed their mermaid and sailor photo, tagging

@RedheadRecs and adding their shipping hashtag.

"What are you doing?" Amy asked, joining him at the railing and eyeing him suspiciously.

He glanced up. "We've been over this, Bonnie. Trust your coach."

The breeze kicked up, swirling Amy's hair around her face. She turned toward the ocean, a secretive smile curving her lips. Toff took a quick photo of her and posted it, too.

#BonnieandClyde

#MyMermaid

"You'd better not be stirring up our shippers," she warned. "The buzz has been fun, but I want the focus on books, my reviews."

Uh-oh.

She turned toward him, leaning against the railing. "It's hard for me to compete with…" She waved her hand at him again, like she had earlier. "All this."

"But I'm your coach, not your competition."

"I know, but you kind of suck up all the air in the room. Online, too." She flashed her new sweet and sassy smile.

Crap. Should he delete the posts? Or trust his gut?

He hadn't been wrong about anything Amy-related yet. And really, she was underselling herself. Maybe her book planet thought they were a cute ship, but they mostly engaged with Amy, talking about books. She was doing a great job keeping up with the comments, making jokes and references he didn't get.

She needed this, even if she didn't realize it yet.

After a Skee-Ball showdown, which she won, Toff leaned against an arcade machine, watching Amy turn the crank on one of those old-school machines that imprinted tourist scenes onto pennies. Hanging out with her was more fun than he'd had with a girl in a long time. Maybe ever.

When the stamped penny dropped into the slot, she squealed. He grinned, thinking about the hero in the *Redo* book, when he helped the chick plant a garden. Toff thought it was dorky when the guy said dirt on her nose was sexy or whatever, but watching Amy's smile light up her face playing silly games? He could see the guy's point.

"Look!" Amy practically skipped over to him, holding a stretched-out copper oval coin stamped with an image of the boardwalk.

As he examined the penny, a sudden, intense memory washed over him. He was eight years old again, standing right here with his mom, turning the crank for her. Mom was wrapped up in layers, even though the day was warm. A scarf was tied around her head because of the chemo, though he didn't know that word then.

"Oh, Toff," she'd teased, coughing as she spoke. "Look how strong you're getting, turning that crank by yourself." Mom dug more coins from her wallet with shaky hands. "Make another one, sweetie. Then we'll have matching pennies."

He'd known she was sick, but at the time he had no idea how ill she really was. His parents hadn't told him until the very end.

"Toff? Are you okay?"

He exhaled roughly and blinked, commanding himself to focus on the girl he was supposed to be coaching. His body was clenched tight, and his brain was fuzzy.

"Uh, yeah. I'm good." He tried to force conviction into his voice but failed.

"What's wrong?" Her eyebrows dipped.

Why'd she have to make worrying look cute?

"Nothing's wrong." He sounded like a jerk, even to himself. "Sorry," he said roughly. "I just remembered something about my mom. Something I'd forgotten." Somewhere at home were two stretched-out carousel pennies. He had to find them.

Amy held his gaze, then reached out for his hand. "Come on. It's *my* turn to coach *you*."

He let her tug him away from the penny machine. Her grip was warm and reassuring, like she was anchoring him, but to what he didn't know.

She led them to the Dippin' Dots line, where they waited behind a couple of bouncing little kids. "You want your own or do you share?"

He studied her, slowly emerging from his mom fog. He wondered what it would be like to kiss her with the freezing-cold ice-cream pebbles in his mouth. "I can share."

"That was a test," she teased. "I don't share my Dots with anybody." Grinning, she turned to the Dots scooper and ordered two servings.

His phone buzzed in his pocket. He tightened his grip on Amy's hand, just in case she thought her coaching duty was finished, and fished out his phone with his free hand.

Viv: Will you help me decorate for the engagement party? It'll be fun.

"Toff. *Toff*." Amy extricated her hand from his to take the Dippin' Dots from the server.

"Sorry." He shoved his phone in his pocket and followed her down the pier jutting out into the ocean.

"Thanks."

They ate silently, watching the gulls swoop and dive, people playing on the beach, and, out in the distance, surfers cresting the waves that should've been his. He squeezed his eyes shut.

His phone buzzed again. He knew it was Viv, but he wasn't ready to answer her.

"Are you busy next Friday?" The question popped out without his permission.

"Why do you ask?" Amy looked wary, not the reaction he was hoping for.

"Are you busy or not?" He sounded desperate, even to himself.

Her expression softened. "Um, I don't think so."

He dropped his gaze to the melting dots. "Good. I need you to do something with me," he said roughly, then shoved another spoonful of Dots into his mouth.

"What's going on?"

Toff sighed, his gaze tracking the surfers. He recognized a couple of them from his team.

"Toff," Amy prompted. "What's happening next Friday?"

"Engagement party," he muttered. "For my dad and Rose." He braced for impact. She would go apeshit over this party. Get all gooey and romantic or whatever. Still, he wanted her there.

"Of course I'll go," she said gently. Her mellow reaction surprised him, in a good way. Her fingertips brushed against his clenched fist like he was a wild animal and she was trying to calm him, which was sort of true. Slowly, he unclenched his fist, letting her lace her fingers through his.

"Thanks." He squeezed her hand, hoping the gesture said more than a single word could. It was time to answer the question she wasn't asking. He owed her that much. "Let's go."

They chucked their empty Dots containers and rejoined the noise and chaos of the boardwalk, holding hands.

"I was eight when my mom died," he said abruptly. "Almost ten years ago."

"I remember."

He glanced down at her, surprised. Of course she did. All the kids in his class had made him sympathy cards. He still had them. Somewhere.

"I guess I never…" He took a deep breath. He had to keep talking. If he didn't, he'd never be able to get through this story. "My mom's parents stayed with us for about three months afterwards." He swallowed. "They said it was the best way to honor my mom. They said taking care of my dad and me made it hurt less for them."

He remembered how his grandma read to him every night, even though he'd told her he was too old for that. After she and Gramps went back to Arizona, he'd tried to read himself to sleep, but he'd given up. It wasn't the same as snuggling up with someone else and being read to. Like his grandma. Or his mom. *Redo in the Rockies* was the first time he'd read himself to sleep since he was a kid.

Amy didn't know how big of a deal that was for him.

He swung their hands between them as they walked, gathering his thoughts. He liked how she waited instead of bugging him to keep talking. "My dad didn't date much, or if he did, he hid it from me."

There was one time, he was maybe eleven, when he'd gotten up in the middle of the night for a glass of water and had run into a half-naked woman in the kitchen doing the same. He wasn't sure who'd been more embarrassed. She'd been gone by the time he woke up the next morning.

Throngs of people swarmed them. Music blared from the performers lining the pier hustling for cash. It was dusk, and the Ferris wheel lit up like a spinning beacon in the sky. Amy tilted her head back to watch.

"Want to ride?" Toff squeezed her hand. He wouldn't mind stealing another kiss, maybe getting stuck at the top of the wheel, if they got lucky.

Amy turned to him, a hint of anxiety in her eyes. "Not really. I don't like heights."

"That's cool. We'll skip it."

"Really?" Relief filled her eyes. "You're not going to make me ride it as a 'swagger' lesson?"

He frowned, a flicker of karaoke guilt pinching his gut. "Not if you're scared."

"Thanks." She smiled, a warm, open smile that made him want to keep talking.

"No problem. Besides, if I don't finish telling you my tragic backstory, you won't get a chance to hear it again."

"Toff. Don't joke about that." Her tone was soft, sympathetic.

He didn't want pity.

"Anyway," he continued, tugging her along next to him. "Like I was saying, my dad didn't date for a long time. I don't know if he did secret Tinder hookups or what, but—"

"Toff! Stop it." Amy yanked at his hand, laughing but scowling at the same time. He held on tight, not wanting to let go of her hand. It was easier to joke about hard stuff. That's why class clown had been his default mode for so long.

He dragged her into a souvenir shop crowded with tourists. He'd never held a girl's hand this long in his life. At a spinning hat stand, he released her hand and grabbed a tie-dyed beanie hat embroidered with *Surf Naked* and tugged it on his head.

"Yes or no?" He pointed to himself, and she shook her head. "How about this?" He set Rico down, tossed her the hat, and held up a T-shirt. *Save a Wave, Ride a Surfer.* "Yes or no?"

Blushing, she shook her head again.

"You're right. You should wear this, not me." He tossed it to her, grinning wickedly.

She caught the shirt and put it back where it belonged. "Finish your story."

He held up another shirt. *Surfers Know How to Get Up and Stay Up.*

"Toff." She looked like she couldn't decide whether to laugh or smack him.

Being with her felt so good. Easy. Fun. Fiery.

Safe.

Right. Finish the story.

He grabbed a fidget spinner from a display, twirling it between his fingers. "Okay, so sometime during freshman year, Viv and I figured out our parents were getting together."

Amy's eyebrows shot up, and he laughed.

"Not like that, but doing stuff together. Movies, concerts, whatever." He shrugged. "Just the two of them. That went on for a while, but they never said they were dating."

Amy waited patiently, but he could tell she was hooked. She ate this stuff up just like she inhaled books.

"One night, Viv texted me freaking out because she'd woken up at three in the morning and her mom wasn't home yet. My dad wasn't home, either." He raised his eyebrows meaningfully. "I was the one to break it to Viv they were together in a motel in Huntington Beach." He waved his cell around. "Live 360. Kid stalker *and* parent stalker."

Amy blushed and spun the hat rack. Toff grabbed the rack to stop it from spinning. "This is the good part, Ames." He leaned down and whispered in her ear. "The stuff you live for."

She shot him another stink eye, which warmed his chest. It was like they had their own secret code. He blinked, forgetting where he'd left off.

"The stuff I live for," she prompted.

"Right." That smile, sweet with a dash of trouble, was dangerous. He cleared his throat and gave the fidget spinner another whack. "Anyway. I was cool with them dating. Happy for my dad. I mean, a guy has needs…" He slanted her a wicked grin.

"Whoa." Amy raised her hand in a stop gesture. "You did not just *dudes have needs* me!"

He was officially addicted to that fire in her eyes. "What? We do." He smirked as he pushed off the wall. "So do girls. Even penguins mate at least once a year. The luckier little guys get it on all year long."

She huffed out a frustrated laugh. "What is it with you and penguins?"

"I might be an expert. It was all those Madagascar movies. I was obsessed." He picked up Rico and tucking him under his arm. "And *Surf's Up.* Now that's a classic." He'd watched a million surf movies, but the animated penguin one was his favorite.

"Wasn't there a sequel to it? With wrestling stars—"

It was his turn to make the stop gesture with his hand. "We will not speak of this travesty."

"Come on, penguin freak." Laughing, Amy tugged his hand, dragging him out of the store to a faded metal bench facing the ocean. "Sit." She pointed.

He sat, hugging Rico to his chest, feeling like a little kid but okay with that.

"Now your dad and Rose are getting married," she said, sitting next to him. "And it's freaking you out. Do you think it's because this is permanent?" she asked, her voice gentle. "Not just dating?"

He shrugged. "Did you know most penguin species mate for life? Except those emperor dudes who switch it up every year. But most of them…" He stared at his hands. An ancient, faded friendship bracelet from Viv encircled his left wrist, along with a thin beaded leather one that was his mom's.

"Maybe you should talk to your dad about the wedding and how you're feeling." Amy took his hand in hers, her slender fingers entwining with his.

"My dad's busy at his shop and worried about my injury," he said gruffly. "We don't talk about that stuff."

"Are you going to be the best man?" Amy asked.

Where had that come from? "I don't know." He glanced at her, then away. "He hasn't asked me. He's got a bunch of friends. I'm sure he'll ask one of them."

"I bet he'll ask you. How sweet if you were his best man and Viv was maid of honor for her mom."

"I don't even know if they're doing a big wedding. They might just do the court thing."

Amy's lips twitched. "You mean justice of the peace?"

"Whatever. I don't know what it's called."

"Even if they do, you can still be a witness and stand up for them. You said most penguins mate for life, right?"

He frowned. "What does that have to do with my dad getting married?"

"How old were you when you became obsessed with penguins?"

He shrugged. "Kindergarten and up, I guess. I remember watching *Escape to Madagascar* not long after…my mom…"

Compassion filled her eyes.

Other than the therapist he saw as a kid, he'd never talked to anyone about this stuff. *Never.* Yet here he was, spilling his guts.

"If you were so into penguins," Amy said, "and you knew they mated for life, but then your mom died…" An embarrassed half smile tilted her lips. "Maybe in your little-boy mind, that meant your dad couldn't marry again."

He didn't know what to say. It was either the dumbest idea he'd ever heard or *not* the dumbest idea ever.

Amy ducked her head, blushing. "Sorry. That was stupid."

"It's not stupid," he said. "I don't know if it's true, but I like how your brain works."

She glanced up. "You do?"

"Yeah. I don't talk about my mom much. Or my dad's *love life*." He rolled his eyes as he said the words. "But I can talk to you." He locked eyes with her, and the way she looked at him?

Damn.

He set Rico on the bench, pulled Amy in close, and kissed her softly, gently, then drew back. He didn't want to talk about sad stuff anymore.

"We're having an official coaching meeting tomorrow, Bonnie. Time to plan your last challenge. Let's meet at the Bean at ten." He tried out a serious, not too scary coach face. "Make sure you bring the swagger you brought tonight."

He held out his phone to take a selfie with her, grabbing Rico to make sure he was in the shot, too.

"Swagger for the camera."

Amy laughed as he took a burst of photos, making goofy faces with his penguin.

He'd post one of these later, #PenguinsRuleSharksDrool. No shipping tags.

Well, maybe just one…

CHAPTER TWENTY-TWO

$\mathcal{D}$ ad was sitting in the dark living room when Toff got home from the pier, watching old videos of his own pro competitions on YouTube. When he was a kid, Toff had watched those clips over and over, idolizing his dad the same way Cody worshipped Big Z in the *Surf's Up* movie.

"Haven't seen you watch those in a long time," Toff said. He joined his dad on the couch, hoping he wasn't in for another lecture. That would kill his mellow buzz from spending time with Amy.

Dad shrugged. "Yeah. Tripping down memory lane." He exhaled a heavy sigh. "I'm sorry about yelling at you earlier." He locked eyes with Toff. "You scared me, kid, sprinting off. How are your ribs?"

A stab of guilt poked at Toff's gut. "I'm sorry, too. Like Coach Diggs always says, I'm kind of a dumb-ass." He lifted his shirt, rubbing the bandage. "I took a couple of ibuprofen earlier. I'm feeling okay."

"Good." Dad smiled wearily. "Some days I really miss your mom. Injuries never rattled her." He shook his head, his smile fading.

On the TV screen, his twenty-two-year-old dad pulled off an epic alley-oop, catching a ton of air, spinning in a backward aerial rotation high above the water. That was one of Toff's favorite tricks, too.

"Nice," he said.

"Right?" Dad smiled his chill-Dad smile, which Toff hadn't seen since his accident, and the tightness in his chest eased.

"You're coming to the engagement party, right?" Dad asked, glancing anxiously at Toff. "Rose asked Dallas to come, and of course Viv will be there."

Toff's gut twisted when he saw the worry in Dad's eyes. "Of course I'll be there."

"Good." Dad looked relieved.

Toff thought of what Amy had said, about penguins mating for life being somehow connected to his feelings about the wedding. Yeah, it sounded goofy, but also felt right.

"I'm bringing someone to the party, if that's okay."

Dad's eyebrows lifted in surprise. "A date?"

"No," Toff said. "A friend." *A friend I like kissing.*

"Fine with me." Dad yawned and stood up. "Now that you're home safe, I'm heading to bed."

"I'm gonna stay up for a while," Toff said. "Sorry to worry you."

"Gonna watch me smoke the Pipeline Masters?" Dad grinned at the TV, where another YouTube surfing highlights reel played. "Man, I loved competing in Oahu. What a rush."

Toff wanted to ask why his dad was so opposed to him chasing the same rush, but he didn't want to start another argument.

After Dad went to bed, Toff remembered he owed someone a text.

Toff: Yeah, I'll help decorate for the party, Wordworm.

Viv: Yay! I'll need all your hot air to blow up balloons.

Toff sent her a GIF of a little boy trying but failing to blow up a balloon, then texted Amy.

Toff: Thanks for the Dippin' Dots. And for Rico.

And for listening, he thought, *and making me laugh*, but he wasn't going to get all emo and weird.

*A*fter the conversation with Dad, Toff spent the night tossing and turning, dreaming about penguin weddings on the boardwalk, reading aloud with his mom, and struggling on his surfboard like a baby grommet, unable to catch a wave, slammed under the water over and over again.

As early-morning light filtered through his bedroom curtains, he gave up trying to sleep. He grabbed his phone, scrolling through Twitter and Instagram. Their goofy pier photo was a hit, especially with the book planet.

"Cutest real-life #OTP ever!"

"Omigod, just kiss already."

"Hellooo, sailor!"

Man, those bookworms liked shipping. The picture of Amy staring at the ocean with the #BonnieandClyde hashtag really got them going.

"True love for @SurferGodCA and @RedheadRecs?!"

"Surfer + Bookworm = #allthefeels."

Excellent. His plan was working to get her as much buzz as he could going into the final challenge. Pretending to be a real-life OTP for Amy's contest was easy. He liked hanging out with her, and kissing her, and talking to her.

If he had to fake it with somebody, she was the perfect choice.

A slither of guilt poked at him, remembering what she'd said about him taking up all the air in the room. He probably should've given her a heads-up last night after he posted their pics.

Checking the HeartRacer contest hashtags, he found a bunch of Twitter chatter about how tough the final challenge was. Some contestants were resorting to bribing their "reluctant romance readers," which he thought was funny, but that had set off a side drama about how everyone made fun of "the genre of hope."

How could reading a book give somebody hope?

He doubted it would do anything for him, but spending time with Amy on the pier? That had definitely helped. Spilling his guts and having fun all in one night was new for him. He'd liked it. A lot.

Toff glanced at *Redo in the Rockies*, still facedown on his desk. Amy would freak. Spine-breaker, that was him.

"I dunno, Rico. What do you think about these cheesy books?" He side-eyed the penguin who'd spent the night on his extra pillow. "Why'd I even ask you, mate-for-lifer?" he grumbled.

Yawning, he rolled over and grabbed the book. He'd try reading a few pages to get his head in the game before meeting Amy at the Bean. If he was lucky, the book would put him back to sleep for another couple of hours.

"How hard is it to hide a dead body?" Amy asked Viv's mom. "For real."

She leaned against the counter in the bookstore, spinning the rack of Shady Cove postcards. Rose sat at the desk, an assortment of pencils stuck in her messy hair bun, unmatched Crocs on her feet, wearing an inside-out T-shirt.

Rose was deep into drafting a new book—about halfway through, Amy guessed, based on her outfit. When Rose got close to the end, there was a good chance she'd come into the store in her jammies, wondering why customers gave her funny looks.

"Who do you want to kill, sweetie?" Rose asked.

"Your almost son," Amy said, scowling at a postcard of a surfer catching air above a cresting wave.

"Ah." Rose folded her hands and smiled indulgently. "What did he do this time?"

Despite her irritation, Amy's lips quirked. She really hoped Toff could get past his worries about the wedding. Rose loved him.

"He's helping me with the HeartRacer publisher contest," Amy said, "and he...um..." What could she say? *I asked him to stop pretending we're an OTP to ship, but he did it again last night? I hate it but also secretly love it? Each time he kisses me, I want more?*

"The truth about Toff," Rose said, "is that underneath all that chest-pounding swagger"—Amy snorted—"and the jokes and the pranks," Rose continued, her dark-brown eyes going soft, "is a sweet, kind...lost...little boy."

For a long moment, neither of them spoke, Rose getting all misty-eyed, Amy thinking about the ragged penguin stuffie on his desk. About the desperation underneath his gruff request for her to come to the engagement party.

She glanced at the surfer postcard again.

Stupid squishy alpha hero.

Amy sighed. "So you won't help me bury his body?"

Rose blinked away her thoughts, whatever they were, and shook her head.

"Nope." She grinned at Amy with the same gleam in her eye as Viv. "In fact, I'd turn you in and collect the reward."

"I'm thinking of suing you," Amy said, staring Toff down over her iced mocha.

"For what?"

"Coaching malpractice. Impersonating an OTP." She pointed an unwrapped straw at him. "Faking a ship is a high crime and misdemeanor."

He laughed, stretching his legs out under the table and bumping her foot with his. "It's all for a good cause, Bonnie. HeartRacer retweeted our funny pier picture. That's awesome, right?"

"It's cheating, Toff. We're not a real couple." She was practically breathing fire…which distracted him. He'd never kissed a dragon before.

"Yeah, but you said ships can be anybody people want to see together, right? It doesn't have to be real," he protested. "It's like when actors in a movie pretend they're together so everybody gets all hyped and goes to see the movie."

She looked surprised. "How do you even know about that?"

"I know lots of stuff."

"This is real life, Toff, not a movie. Romance isn't a joke. Not to me." Her eyes flashed, shining like the pennies he still needed to find. "I asked you not to post any more ship pics, but you did it anyway."

"I was gonna delete them after you said that on the pier, but…"

"But what?"

Damn. She'd incinerate him with X-ray eyes like Superman if she could. He cleared his throat and sat up straight. Time to get down to business.

"Look, let's focus on your final challenge." *Here goes nothing.* Maybe the idea he'd come up with would work as an apology, too. "I have good news. I found the perfect reluctant romance reader for you."

"*You* found me a reader?"

"Yep." He flashed her the grin that got him out of all sorts of trouble. "Me."

Amy opened her mouth to argue, but he held up his hand, putting on a coach face. Not a scary one but a don't-argue-till-you-hear-me-out face.

He held up a finger for each point. "One, I'm a reluctant romance reader. Very reluctant. Two, since people are shipping us, they'll watch our vlog interview—"

"Our *what*?"

He kept going. "Three, you're going to interview me about the book. Ask me all the stuff you talk about at book club. Bookworm/surfer throw-down." He grinned. "Make me look like an idiot, I don't care."

"But...but..."

He tossed *Redo in the Rockies* on the table. With a bookmark in the pages. He didn't have a death wish.

"Give me two days to finish it. I've kind of, um, skipped around, but I promise I'll read it straight through. Dallas can record us, or Viv. I don't care as long as Viv stays behind the scenes."

"Hold up! Let me talk for a minute!" Amy was blasting enough energy to fuel the whole town.

His chest expanded, full of pride, like it did when one of his teammates won. This wasn't the same girl he'd rescued from rabid raccoons three weeks ago. She tossed her hair over her shoulder, sticking her nose in the air, like Hermione about to rip into Harry and Ron.

"First"—she held up a finger, mimicking him—"*you* are not in charge. Second, *if* we do this, I run the whole thing. You have to do what I say."

He nodded, waiting, impressed with Swagger Amy.

"And third…" She took a deep breath. "Third…it's not a horrible idea. It might actually work."

"Sweet! I knew you'd—"

"Zip it, Flipper. I'm not finished." She held up the book like a shield. Or maybe a weapon. "You still owe me an apology for posting pics of us when I asked you not to. That wasn't cool."

He squirmed. "You're right." When he met her eyes, the realization hit him square in the chest. Even though he'd had good intentions, he'd overstepped. "I'm sorry, Ames. I really am."

She held his gaze for a long moment, then nodded. Why did he feel like the Mother of Dragons had just spared his life?

"Okay. I believe you." She sipped from her mocha, then folded her arms on the table. "Remember Dora the Explorer? Swiper no swiping?" She pointed a commanding finger. "That's you from now on—Flipper no Shipping, got it?"

"Got it." He grinned as something warm and tingly fizzed through his veins.

He couldn't wait to see Amy win this contest. She was finally stepping out of the shadows. Watching her light up like a rocket and take charge, he knew she'd win.

Not because of him.

Because of her.

CHAPTER TWENTY-THREE

*A*my reviewed her plan, happy with what she'd come up with, then texted it to Toff, one line at a time. Coaching her coach felt awesome.

HeartRacer Contest Final Challenge Plan

1. @SurferGodCA agrees to be interviewed LIVE on Instagram this Saturday as a reluctant romance reader.

2. @SurferGodCA finishes Redo in the Rockies. Reads. Every. Word.

3. @SurferGodCA preps for LIVE interview on Tuesday, using the Hunkalicious Heroes review template.

4. @RedheadRecs invites followers to view the live interview. @SurferGodCA can retweet or regram the posts but does not do any shipping of the #BonnieandClyde OTP. Swiper no Swiping!

. . .

1. Agreed.
2. I promise to read. Every. Word.
3. I don't do templates. I'll wing it.

4. Oh, man!

Amy laughed when she read number four, Swiper the Fox's standard response to Dora the Explorer, but she wasn't sure about number three.

Amy: Interview preparation is important.

Toff: Trust me, I know how to improvise. That's what surfing is.

Amy: I'm going to be very prepared. You'd better bring your best game, Clyde.

Toff: Challenge accepted, Bonnie.

CHAPTER TWENTY-FOUR

*T*oday was the day. Her on-screen debut. Well, not her debut, but the first time she'd actually be talking on camera instead of just holding up rating paddles while Viv did the talking.

And she'd chosen to do it live. Go big with the swagger or go home, right?

More like, she couldn't chicken out in the middle of the recording. They were doing this, and there was no escaping until they were done.

After the bookstore closed, Amy and Viv set up the reading nook, displaying several of their favorite HeartRacer romances on the table. Toff was in the employee kitchen with Rose, polishing off the pizza she'd ordered for them.

Dallas adjusted his phone on a tripod. Amy was no social media influencer, so the likelihood of many people actually watching it live was so low. They planned to save the video and upload it to the Hunkalicious blog for later viewing.

"I'm so excited you're doing this." Viv bounced around like a kid at a birthday party. "I can't wait to watch you give Flipper a smackdown."

Dallas glanced up from the tripod. "It's not a battle, *Galdi*," he said, drawling her last name.

"Yes it is, *Lang*," Viv said, "and Amy's going to win." She grinned. "Bet you a new *Star Trek Discovery* T-shirt."

"You're on." Dallas pointed to the love seat. "Have a seat, Amy, so I can frame the shot."

Amy sat. She wore jeans and her favorite *Life's Good* T-shirt, with a drawing of a girl drinking coffee and reading a book, and had doubled up on the hair sparkles.

"Come on, Flipper!" Viv hollered. "It's showtime!"

Toff emerged from the kitchen, laughing with Rose. Amy's heart lifted. Maybe he was going to be okay with the wedding after all.

He flopped on the love seat next to her, stretched his arm out behind her, giving her hair a gentle tug. "Ready to bring our OTP game, babe?"

"We talked about this," she warned. "We aren't doing any fake ship stuff. We're just being ourselves. No 'babe' business." She made air quotes and he grinned, his gaze drifting down to her mouth.

Last night, he'd stopped by her house unexpectedly with an AceWare rashguard shirt for Brayden, who'd reacted like Toff gave him one of his trophies. Dad had insisted Toff stay for dinner—and dessert, of course.

After dinner, she'd walked Toff out to his van. He'd scary-coach-faced Brayden back to the house and then pushed her up against his van, kissing her so deeply and thoroughly, she couldn't think. Couldn't breathe. Couldn't remember if they were fake or real or something in between.

"Let's roll," Dallas said, jarring her out of the kissing memory. Rose and Viv leaned against the counter to watch.

"You got this, Ames," Toff said. "Remember how great we were at karaoke."

She didn't feel nervous like she had that night, but the bookstore was her safe space. She nodded to Dallas, who gave them a 3-2-1 countdown with his fingers.

"Hi. I'm Amy McIntyre, but you know me as @Redhead-Recs. Today I'm here with my…friend Toff Nichols. You might have seen him in my #BookFaceFriday posts for HeartRacer Publishing's second contest challenge."

"Yo." Toff leaned in, flicking a shaka wave. "Call me Clyde." Amy slanted him a warning look, but he just grinned.

"Anyway," she continued, "we're here for HeartRacer's third contest challenge—convincing a reluctant romance reader."

"I'm very reluctant," Toff interjected, grinning at the camera. "The first time Amy tried to get me to read this book, I refused." He shot her a wink. "But she's very persuasive."

Amy elbowed him. They had a plan, for him to give a two-minute review, talking casually like he was chatting with readers, and she'd chime in and ask questions, then wrap it up. She really wished he'd written something like she'd asked.

"Toff read *Redo in the Rockies* by Millie Templeton." She held up the book, then gestured to Toff. "Tell us what you thought, SurferGodCA."

"You got it, babe."

She lifted an eyebrow at the "babe," and he blasted her with the double dimples. He was in full-on, flirtastic charmer mode. Distracting, but it would make good TV.

"So this book wasn't terrible," he said to the camera. "I can't compare it to any romances because this was the first one I read. *Reluctantly.*

"My favorite parts were these scenes *some* people call 'non-gratuitous,' which is code for…you know." He winked. Dallas ran his hand over his mouth, smothering a laugh. "At first I just skimmed the book and read *those* scenes," Toff said, "but then I got a big lecture"—he side-eyed Amy—"on those scenes being there for a reason."

"Because they are," she huffed. She didn't want him to go too far down that road. "How about the main characters? Did you like them?"

Toff smirked. "Not at first, but I guess they sort of grew on me." He turned to the camera. "So this couple hooks up in high school and are still together at graduation, and they figure they'll be together forever. Like that ever happens." He stared straight at Dallas, who narrowed his eyes. Toff grinned and continued.

"But the hero ghosts the girl after high school, without telling her why." He paused. "And I can't tell you why because it's a 'spoiler.'" He did air quotes and slanted Amy another smirk. "Amy's got a lot of bookworm rules. Like always use a bookmark. What is up with that?"

From across the room, Amy heard Rose and Viv laugh.

"Something to be aware of with reluctant readers," Amy said. "You have to be patient and explain everything." She rolled her eyes. "It's like getting a new puppy. They're cute but a lot of work."

Toff's eyebrows shot up. "You're comparing me to a *dog*, Bonnie?"

Amy gave him a saccharine smile. "A cute dog, like my golden retriever." She reached out to pat his head. "What a good boy."

Dallas squinted at the comments coming in on the live video. His eyes went wide, but as he scrolled, a grin spread across his face. Viv scurried across the room and gasped at whatever they were looking at. But then Dallas pointed at something on the screen and their shoulders shook with suppressed laughter.

Great.

Amy turned back to Toff. He held her gaze, his blue eyes sparking. She knew that look. It was his bring-it competitive face. After a long beat, during which her heart rate tripled as his eyes flared with heat, he turned back to the camera.

"Anyway," he said, "I didn't get why this chick—"

"Heroine," Amy interrupted, earning a side-eye with the tiniest hint of a smile.

"—was all freaked out when this jackass—"

"Hero," Amy corrected, giving the camera an I-know-he's-clueless shrug. Grinning, Viv waved the thumbs-up paddle.

"When the *alpha hero*"—Toff smirked at her—"showed up at their fifteen-year high school reunion."

Amy held up ten fingers and mouthed, *Ten years*.

Toff side-eyed her but kept talking. "I'm like, just kick his ass to the curb, right? He had his chance but he blew it. So they do this whole do-we-or-don't-we dance." Toff gestured with his hands, getting more animated. "The dude does dumb stuff like, he comes by to check on her after a big storm when her power goes out." He shook his head in disgust. "I mean, come on."

Amy's mouth dropped open. "What's wrong with you? That was sweet. Thoughtful."

Toff rolled his eyes. "Ames, really. What he actually wanted was to hook up with her, which, okay fine, just hook up if you both want to, but it was all *dramatic*."

He tossed his hair and spoke in a falsetto. "'Oh, thank you for checking on me in this big scary storm!'" He dropped his voice low. "'I guess we'll have to light candles and sit here in the dark and think about how we couldn't keep our hands off each other in high school.'"

Toff leaned back against the love seat, crossing his arms over his chest like he'd just made a great point. "Dumb stuff like that."

"*Stuff like that* is what keeps people reading, Toff." Amy was fired up, heat flashing through her like when she and Natasha argued at book club. "It's called adhesion. Reasons for a couple to spend time together." She glared. "So the reader keeps rooting for them, watching them fall for each other, hoping it will work out."

"Doesn't it always work out in these books?" Toff asked, his lips quirking. "Everybody gets their HEA, right? Or... what's the other one? HFN?" He winked at the camera. "That's Happy for Now, for you newbies."

Amy gaped at him. Viv hovered next to Dallas, beaming at them and the screen and waving the thumbs-up paddle.

"Why do you look surprised?" Toff tossed Amy a lazy grin. "I told you I'd be ready for this." He turned to the camera again. "Anyway, I can see why those non-*gratuitous* scenes are mixed in to keep people reading because I got tired of all the talking about feelings with her friends."

"Omigod," Amy said, "you read the chapters in order this time, right?"

"Yeah." He pouted. "I told you I would."

Rose wandered closer, her eyes as bright as Viv's.

"I told you before, Toff, those scenes aren't just mixed in. They change the relationship." Was he really that clueless? "Anyway, let's move away from *those* scenes." She smiled at the camera. "A lot of readers like to read sweet romances, with just kissing."

"Oh yeah?" Toff shifted on the couch to face her, his smile dangerously sexy. "I hope those kissing scenes are hot."

"Sometimes." Amy's cheeks burned, but she couldn't let him get the upper hand. "It depends on the book."

"I can guess what type of kissing scenes you like." He slanted a knowing grin at the camera. "Actually, it's not a guess. I *know*."

Viv gasped. Rose's face lit up. Dallas glanced at the comments again and gave them two thumbs-up.

Omigod. She didn't even want to think about what people

were saying. Toff was going to pay. *Big-time.* She sucked in a breath, reminding herself she was the boss.

"Any thoughts about the other characters?" Amy asked, avoiding Viv's what-have-you-been-hiding dagger eyes.

"Yeah," Toff said. "That dog was awesome, always getting in trouble, like when he dug up the nosy neighbor's flower garden."

He held up the book. "Hey, if anyone at HeartRacer is watching this, you might want to have whoever makes your covers actually read the books."

Amy's hand flew to her mouth, horrified. Why was she doing this live? Someone from HeartRacer might be watching *right now.*

"What?" Toff turned to Amy, looking all innocent and angelic, which he was *not.* "The dog in the book was a black Lab and this one is yellow."

"Yes but…" Amy struggled for words. She'd have to cut this whole part from the recording that she posted to Hunkalicious. Plus the kissing part.

"We need to wrap this interview up." She hoped she sounded calm. In control. She sure didn't feel like it. "One last question. Would you read another romance?"

He grinned. "With or without my favorite scenes?"

She wanted to throttle him. "You're winding me up on purpose, aren't you?"

"I like it when you get wound up, Bonnie. You know that." His gaze roved over her face.

Amy flung her hands in the air and turned to her small audience. "Can I hit him with a book?"

"Yes! A really big one!" Viv exclaimed. "Get us that latest Stephen King," she told her mom. "That one's huge."

Amy squeezed her eyes shut, then forced herself to talk to the camera. "So…this wasn't quite what I expected, but I think it's obvious this book inspired a lot of...*passion* in my reluctant reader. I'd call that a success."

"Something's inspiring passion," Toff drawled. "And it's not the book."

Crap. She'd walked right into that. "You are the *worst*, Clyde."

He laughed, then surprised her by leaning in close, going nose to nose just like they had for bookface.

"That's not what you said last night, *babe*."

Amy reared back and smacked him on the chest with the book, then pointed to Dallas. "Cut!"

CHAPTER TWENTY-FIVE

*R*ose and Dallas burst into applause, Toff stood up to take a bow, and Hiddles the cat streaked across the store, knocking over a display of graphic novels. Viv gaped at Amy, not moving. While the chaos continued, Amy slowly approached her.

"He's just messing around," she said. "Nothing happened last night." She cleared her throat. "Well, just kissing, but that's it." Super-*hot* kissing that had shut down her brain cells.

Viv studied her closely. "Last night wasn't the first time you kissed."

"Um, no." Amy blushed, glancing at Toff, who was grinning at Dallas's phone screen. They must be watching the recording.

"I guess I've been in denial," Viv said, surprising Amy with a grin instead of a glare. "But after watching you two just now...I can't deny it anymore."

"It's nothing serious. We're just having fun," Amy said.

"You're definitely having fun," Viv said. "But are you *sure* it's not more serious than that?"

Amy looked away, her gaze drifting down the romance aisle. She'd been telling herself they were just having fun, because what else could it be with Toff, the king of casual? Still, way deep down, underneath her own layers of denial, she was afraid her crush-with-kissing-benefits coaching deal was slowly turning into something more. At least for her.

She forced a laugh. "Serious with Toff? No way."

Viv held her gaze, then nodded, but she didn't look like she bought it. "Well, anyway, you were great on camera, Amy. No more silent paddle waving for you. From now on we take turns hosting the review shows."

A warm rush of pride swept over Amy. "I'd love that."

Toff appeared at her side, bright-eyed and grinning. "Damn. We killed that."

Amy gave him her sweetest, fakest smile. *Fun*, she told herself. That's what they did best. "You're confused, Clyde. *I'm* going to kill *you*."

Toff laughed and grabbed her hand. "Fine, but let's celebrate first. We earned it." Viv shrugged, grinning as Toff tugged her toward the door.

"I want to watch the v-video," Amy sputtered.

"It's awesome," Toff said. "Dallas showed me some of it. You should see the comments. Everyone loved it. We had more than three hundred viewers!"

Amy blanched. Three…*hundred*?

Toff grinned. "My tweet telling everyone to watch our #BonnieandClyde showdown must've worked."

"Don't hurt him too much, Amy," Dallas called as Rose unlocked the door. "He's injured."

"Remember what I said," Rose whispered to Amy as they brushed past her. Was Rose joking about turning Amy in if she tried to kill Toff? Or did she mean the stuff about him being a sweet, lost boy?

"I've got a surprise for you," Toff said as they headed for his van.

Amy's stomach pitched, wondering if he meant a troublemaker surprise or a sweet one. "After what you just did, Clyde, I don't know if I can handle any more surprises from you."

He squeezed her hand, slanting her a secretive smile. "You'll like this one, Bonnie. Promise."

"Where are we going?" Amy asked Toff as they drove up the coastal highway, the breeze blowing through the windows, the stars winking overhead through the sunroof.

"You'll see."

"Please tell me we aren't hopping the fence at The Lodge. I don't want another run-in with the sheriff."

The Lodge was a secret getaway outside of town that movie stars and other celebs stayed at when they needed a break from the paparazzi and Hollywood. From what Dallas told her, Toff liked to sneak in.

Toff grinned, accelerating as they rounded a curve. "I thought about it, but they have guard dogs. I didn't think you were ready for that."

Amy snorted. "You'd be right. I suppose you charmed the guard dogs."

"Didn't have to. All I needed was bacon."

The anticipation to watch the video was killing her. She dug her phone from her bag, then watched in stunned silence as what she'd worried might be a disaster instead played out as funny, smart, and…um…*wow*.

No wonder Viv had said she couldn't deny their chemistry. All the emojis and comments posted during their live session confirmed it.

"See?" Toff said, slanting her a smug and sexy grin. "Told you we killed it."

"Um, yeah." She scrolled through more of the comments, gasping when she saw the heart and applause emojis posted by @HeartRacer. "Omigod. HeartRacer watched it! And they liked it."

"Of course they did."

She ignored him, scanning more comments to see if the publisher had posted anything about Toff's clueless smackdown of their cover artists. They hadn't. She sighed with relief, closing her eyes and leaning back against the worn seat fabric.

"Time to chill, Ames," Toff said. He turned up the volume on the radio, and she let the music wash over her. Amy was getting used to spending time in his van. Spending time with *him*. She couldn't deny their chemistry, either, especially after watching it on-screen.

She snuck a glance at him, thinking of how she'd told Viv they were just having fun. Kissing Toff was epic, but he'd probably kissed a million girls. Or a hundred. At least fifty. She'd bet her UK edition of *Harry Potter and the Philosopher's Stone* that Toff had stronger feelings about her dad's cookies than he did for her.

After a while, Toff turned off the coastal highway, steering the van down a bumpy path that looked more like a hiking trail.

"Is this a legit road?" Amy asked, a bubble of anxiety forming in her chest.

"Nope." He shot her a quick grin. "It's a secret. I might have to blindfold you when we get closer."

A few minutes later, the road-not-road spilled them out onto a patch of dirt barely big enough for two vehicles. Amy caught her breath at the view. The tiny island of dirt was surrounded by cypress trees, the ocean glittering in the distance.

"You have a secret hideout," she breathed. Was this his hookup hideout? How many other girls had he brought here? She squeezed her eyes shut, pushing the thought away.

"Super secret." His voice dropped low, and he killed the engine. "You're the first person I've brought here."

"Really?" Her stomach cartwheeled.

"Yeah. It's my favorite place. I found it right after I got my driver's license." He opened his door. "Come on."

She waited a few moments, absorbing the fact that he'd never brought anyone else here; then she hopped out of the van, sending up a puff of dirt when she landed.

Exhaling a deep breath, she walked to the edge of the cliff to peer at the ocean sprawling below like a deep-blue velvet blanket. She closed her eyes, letting the breeze wash over her, inhaling the briny scent of the sea.

Toff's footsteps scuffed the ground, followed by the familiar squeak of the van's sliding door. She kept her eyes closed, listening to the waves rhythmically lapping the beach below.

Footsteps sounded again, moving closer. Toff's body heat enveloped her before he even touched her. Standing behind her, he wrapped his arms around her waist and rested his chin on top of her head. She leaned back against his chest, sighing happily as his familiar warmth seeped into her skin.

"Thanks for bringing me here. I love it."

His arms tightened around her waist, his touch sending electric jolts through her body. "I've always kept this place to myself, but I wanted to show it to you."

"Why?" Her question was almost drowned out by the breeze and the pounding waves below.

He didn't answer right away, but when he did, his lips brushed her ear, his breath warm on her neck. "I'm not sure. I just…wanted you to see it."

. . .

A shiver racked Amy's body, and he pulled her even closer. "Cold?"

She nodded against his chest, and he felt a weird caveman urge to find two sticks and build a fire.

"It's warmer in the van." He wasn't going to be the idiot who started another raging California wildfire. He relaxed his grip around her waist as she turned to face him. She brushed a few strands of windblown hair out of her eyes and smiled up at him, and something flipped over in his gut.

"Let's stay out here for a while. It's so beautiful."

"Okay. Be right back." He sprinted to the van to grab his hoodie and a hammock. He tugged the hoodie over her head, and she emerged like a turtle, a really cute turtle in a too-big shell. "Come on." He headed to the trees and quickly strung up the hammock.

"You do this a lot," she commented, moving next to him and pushing the rainbow-striped hammock like a swing.

"Like I said, it's my favorite place." He sat in the hammock, spreading his legs wide and planting his feet on the ground. "Sit right here." He patted the fabric, and she cast him a skeptical look.

"We're not going to flip over?"

He grinned, pointing to the space between his legs. She blushed, and he hoped her thoughts were headed the same direction his were. She bit her lip, then turned around and sank onto the hammock.

"Ready?" He lifted his legs and spun, holding her tight. They landed perfectly, sending the hammock swaying, and she laughed, making him really, really glad he'd brought her here.

He kept his arms around her, and she nestled into him.

It was a two-person hammock, perfect for tonight. He kissed her temple, once, twice, gently turning her toward him so he could get his mouth on hers.

Instead, she surprised him with a question. "What does it feel like to win all the time?"

So no kissing right now. Okay. He could wait.

"I don't *always* win. Just most of the time."

Her soft laughter was like a gust of wind, circling around him, then fading away. "Okay, what's it like to win *most* of the time? To know you're in the top tier?" Her foot bounced against his. "I can't imagine what that feels like, to be so talented that you know you're always going to knock it out of the park."

Her words landed like a punch. Why couldn't she see her own talent, especially after just watching their video? He wanted to watch her shoot across the sky. Ignite her light and let it shine, like in that old Katy Perry song the girls on the surf team sometimes sang on the beach at bonfire parties.

He ran a hand through her hair, entwining his legs with hers. He liked having her this close to him. Horizontal. His body was starting to get all sorts of interesting ideas, but he forced himself to focus on her question.

"You sell yourself short, Ames. Like you said, people like me, we suck up all the oxygen in a room. All the attention."

Most of the time, he reveled in being in the spotlight, but after spending time with her, he was starting to realize how people like him overshadowed the quiet people. It wasn't intentional, but it wasn't cool, either. He'd gambled tonight, pushing all her buttons during their book review, hoping she'd rise to the challenge, and she had. He loved how she came across in the video—sparky, funny, smart.

"Why are you worrying about this, Ames? We're supposed to be celebrating all the swagger you've been bringing."

"I know, but…so far it's all been online. Even tonight. The only real audience was our friends and Rose. If I actually win and get to meet Lucinda, I'll probably freeze up." She sighed, resting her head on his chest. "That's how the world works. Extroverts rule, introverts drool." She slanted him a resigned smile.

"That's bullshit."

Amy rolled her eyes. "Says the extroverted winner of all the things."

"I'm not winning much of anything this summer," he said, pointing to his ribs, hoping to distract her from talking crap about herself.

"Is that the worst part of your injury? Not competing?"

"Yeah." Everything else about it sucked, but not hanging with his friends at comps? Not smoking it? That was the worst.

Amy nodded, her eyes downcast, and it hit him that maybe there were worse things than not competing.

"What are you afraid of?" he asked. "I'm not talking about singing in front of an audience. I mean what scares you *here*." He moved his hand from her hair to her chest, right over her heart, locking eyes with her.

Toff's voice was sandpaper wrapped in velvet, the heat of his body making it hard to think. She was quiet for a beat, struggling for an answer as a jumble of emotions swirled through her.

What was she afraid of? She was afraid of losing the contest. Of losing out on the opportunity to meet Lucinda. Of her dad not finding another job soon. Of being mocked for loving romance, which was starting to happen on Twitter, now that she'd gained more of a following.

She could ignore Twitter, but she was afraid she'd backslide, lose the confidence she'd started to build, reverting to staying quiet instead of speaking up, or worse—letting someone else do the talking for her, like Viv or Toff. That wasn't her only Toff-related anxiety. There was also the I've-crushed-on-you-forever-and-now-I'm-actually-falling-for-you problem.

"Look at me, Ames," Toff said, his voice soft, his hand still on her heart. Cajoling. Seductive. And a whole bunch of other adjectives that made her skin tingle.

"Do you ever feel like you're…" She hesitated, then met his gaze. He didn't look like a tough coach ready to pump her up or like he was about to crack a joke.

"Feel like what?" he prompted. "Tell me." His hand moved from her chest, his fingertips reaching underneath her T-shirt, stroking her bare stomach, trailing hot sparks.

"Um." She swallowed. "Are you asking as my coach? So you can attack my fears?"

"I'm asking for a lot of reasons, not just coaching." His eyes darkened, and a muscle ticked in his jaw. "You don't have to tell me your deep, dark secrets. Just tell me one fear."

He shifted, making the hammock sway, his sunshiny Toff scent filling her nose. They'd never been horizontal before. *Do not freak out*, she commanded herself.

"Here's one of mine," he said. "I joke about shark attacks all the time, but honestly, sharks scare the shit out of me. Too many surfers have gotten chomped. I don't want to be one of them."

Amy giggled, and he reared back, eyes wide.

"You're not scared of sharks? You wouldn't care if Jaws showed up to terrorize Shady Cove? What if I'd gotten attacked by one instead of it just being a crazy rumor your brother started?"

He was joking, of course, but she realized he'd shared a real fear, and she should reciprocate.

"I'm not a fan of sharks, either," Amy said. "I'd hate to see you get chomped."

"Hmph." He pretended to be offended. "Not sure I believe you."

"You want to know what I'm afraid of here?" She took a breath, putting her hand over her heart. "I'm afraid of failing. Not just this contest but a lot of things. I want so much, but I always hold back." She glanced up, smiling. "I mean, I used to hold back. I'm getting better at it, thanks to my coach."

He propped himself up on his elbow, looking down at her. "I know what it's like to be afraid."

"Do you? To me, it seems like you're made of Teflon." She shrugged, half smiling. "Everything rolls right off you."

"No," he said sharply, surprising her. "Not true. When I was a kid, after my mom died, I was like a…an open wound. Everything upset me." He looked up through the trees to the sky, his gaze unfocused.

"One time my dad found me crying about some crappy stuff an older surfer said." He hesitated, then kept talking, like he had that night on the pier. "I cried a lot after Mom died. Dad and I both did."

He swallowed, then continued. "This probably sounds weird, but I used to smell her perfume after she died. It would happen out of nowhere, when I was riding my bike or digging for snacks in the pantry, just normal stuff." He glanced away. Amy could see his blush even in the dark. "I know it was just my imagination."

Her heart ached for that little boy. And the boy holding her. "It wasn't your imagination," she said firmly. She knew it, deep in her heart. "It was your mom checking in on you, letting you know she was still watching over you."

"You don't have to say that to make me feel better." He still wouldn't look at her.

"But I know it's true, Toff."

Slowly, he turned toward her. "How?"

"People who love us always find a way to show it while they're here, somehow. I think they still find a way, even when they've moved on to the stars." She pointed to the sky.

Toff watched her, his eyes full of hope, like he wanted to believe her. Like he *had* to believe her. His eventual smile was slow, hesitant. He nodded once, then tugged her in even closer. They lay together, swaying softly in the breeze, breathing in sync, watching the stars for a long time. Amy wondered if he could hear her thundering heart.

"So when Dad found me crying that day," Toff said eventually, picking up his original story, "he told me a story about a kid who drew himself an invisible bubble made of magic glass. It was unbreakable. Nothing could puncture it." His smile was boyish. Embarrassed. "Dad said no sticks or stones or words would hurt me, as long as I stayed in that bubble."

Amy held her breath, afraid if she breathed too loudly, he'd stop talking. Also, he was back to stroking her bare stomach underneath her shirt, leaving a trail of sparks with each rotation.

"It worked," he said. "Every day I drew that magic, imaginary bubble around myself in the morning before I left the house. Then at night, before I went to bed, I erased it."

Amy gasped. "*Harold and the Purple Crayon*!"

Toff frowned. "What's that?"

"Oh my gosh! You don't know? It's this amazing kids' book about a little boy who draws his world with a purple crayon, just like you drew your magic bubble. He draws a boat when he falls in the ocean and a hot air balloon when he falls off a mountain."

"I've never seen someone get so excited about books." Toff grinned. "You need to do more vlogs, Amy. People are gonna love how you get so excited." His eyes locked onto hers, and they softened. "You know, I think I still draw my magic bubble every morning."

"Really?"

He nodded. "It's second nature. I don't even realize I'm doing it." He flashed her a teasing grin. "I must've forgotten to draw it that day I saved you from the po-po and the raccoons."

"Or maybe you just didn't close it all the way," Amy said. "Maybe you left a tiny gap, and that's how I got through." She mimicked drawing a circle, her hand slicing through the top as she made a crashing sound.

Toff laughed as he smiled down at her. "Or maybe I made room in my bubble just for you." His legs moved against hers, warm and taut with muscle. "I like coaching you, Bonnie. Teasing you. You keep me on my toes. I never know what you're going to say. Or do."

Neither do I, she thought. *Especially when I'm with you.*

The energy between them pulsed like a beating heart. The air crackled as his gaze dipped to her mouth, and a muscle ticked in his jaw. She bit her bottom lip, and his eyes flared like Fourth of July sparklers.

"I can't stop thinking about you, Ames," he said, his voice rough as his hand continued to stroke her stomach, then drifted slowly upward, his thumb running along her bra line, and she stopped breathing, her pulse pounding in her ears, her throat. Everywhere. "I can't stop thinking about kissing you. About a lot more than kissing."

He leaned in, brushing a soft kiss across her lips, then kissed her jawline, his lips searing her like a sweet, hot fire as he worked his way to the soft skin behind her earlobe. He enfolded her body with his, like a sun god, warm and strong.

His mouth found hers again, their lips sliding against each other. She flattened a palm against his chest, right over his heart, feeling his heartbeat, fast and urgent. She wrapped her arms around his waist, pulling him closer, hoping she wasn't hurting his bruised ribs.

He didn't seem to mind.

Toff's lips coached hers, soft and gentle one minute, desperate and urgent the next, when his hand cupped her breast through her bra. Amy shivered, his touch igniting a fire she'd never felt before.

She wondered if anyone had ever died from the pure adrenaline rush of kissing. Her heart thudded against her rib cage and her stomach became a roller coaster that flew over its internal tracks, up and down and backward. At some point she'd need to breathe, to gulp in air, but not now.

"Hold on tight," he said, his voice ragged in her ear. In one swift move, they were out of the hammock, standing upright, never breaking the kiss. Their mouths crashed together as his hands cupped her bottom. She wrapped her legs around his waist and he staggered to the van, still kissing her fiercely. Before she realized what was happening, they tumbled into the van, landing on a nest of blankets.

"You could've put me down first," she said with a laugh, her body on fire with the need to touch him.

"Why would I do that?" He released his hold on her just long enough to yank his shirt over his head. "Can I take off your shirt?"

He was breathing hard, his eyes dark, hooded. She nodded. She didn't want to stop. He removed the hoodie and her T-shirt in one quick move.

Amy shivered as the cool air hit her bare skin. Toff's jaw went tight, his eyes darkening to blue-black as his gaze swept her up and down. He wrapped his arms around her, his biceps flexing as he lowered her to the blanket. Their gazes locked for a long, heated moment. Was she still breathing?

"God, Amy." He covered her body with his, kissing her like his life depended on it, his hands busy unhooking her bra.

She stopped thinking, giving in to the rush, the fiery heat of touch, of his hands and mouth. This was what she wanted, right now, in this moment. In a flurry of tugging, and kissing, and touching, the rest of their clothes came off, and Toff held a condom packet. Once they were naked together, skin to skin, she ducked her head against his chest, heart pounding, wanting to keep going but overcome by shyness.

"Hey," Toff whispered, tilting her chin up so she met his gaze. "Don't be shy, Ames. It's just me." He kissed her softly, sweetly. "We'll go slow. If you change your mind, just tell me. I want you, all of you, but I'll never force you. You're the coach tonight, okay?"

"Okay," she whispered.

"Show me what you want," he said, his voice rough and gravelly as he pulled them down to the blankets.

"What about your ribs? I don't want to hurt you."

He laughed softly against her neck. "Trust me, babe, I'm not feeling any pain right now."

True to his word, he went slow and gentle at first, but when she whispered that she wanted to keep going, he quickly handled the protection issue, then kissed her fiercely, his hands everywhere, and she kissed him back, and the energy between them rocketed to explosive.

She was a piece of paper and Toff was the match, both of them burning bright and hot, going up in flames.

Afterward, when their breathing returned to almost normal and the sweat had cooled on their skin, Toff tugged a blanket over their intertwined bodies, wrapping them up like an oversize burrito. Amy sighed as she snuggled against his chest.

First times were supposed to be flubs—awkward and embarrassing—but theirs had been sweet. Hot. Perfect.

"I don't suppose you brought cookies with you," Toff murmured against her ear as his hand cupped her hip, his fingers lazily stroking her thigh.

"Oh, so now you're hungry?" she teased, even though she was hungry, too. Ravenous, in fact.

"Hell yeah. We burned a lot of calories, Bonnie."

She heard the wicked grin in his voice and blushed.

"But as hungry as I am, I'm not leaving this van." He clamped his leg around hers like he didn't want her to even think of leaving.

"You have a one-track mind."

"Not true." He kissed the back of her neck and tightened his grip on her hip. "I want to do a lot of things with you, Ames. Not all of them naked."

Amy stared up at the stars through the sunroof as Toff drove her home. He'd put her in charge of music, so she'd queued up her secret playlist. No one knew about her customized Totally Toff playlist she'd created in the seventh grade and added to ever since, not even Viv.

"Great playlist," he said, slanting her a grin.

"Thanks." She swallowed a nervous laugh.

"What's so funny?"

"Nothing. Just…nothing." She had to hold on to some secrets, and his playlist was one of them. Had they really…? Yes, they had. And she had no regrets.

He pulled up to the curb in front of her house.

"Can we sneak in?" he asked. "I like it when we play criminals together."

She laughed. "Sure."

Toff held Amy's hand as they tiptoed up her driveway. It was *way* past curfew, but she wouldn't take back the last few hours for all the groundings in the world. She was drunk, not on booze, on him. On kissing. On life. On the stars, the moon, the breeze... She could write one hundred romance novels in one hundred days. She giggled as they snuck around to the back door.

"Shh," Toff whispered. "If we get busted, your parents won't let me see you again. And I will die."

His eyes glowed like blue planets. Planets she wanted to live on.

"Don't joke about dying!" She giggled again, then sobered up. "But I would, too, if I couldn't see you again."

"That's not going to happen." He raised his arm, drawing a huge, imaginary circle around them. "Now we have our own magic bubble. Just for us."

Amy sighed, leaning into him. "Who knew you were a romantic?"

"I'm not," he said. "I'm a penguin."

Her mouth dropped open. She knew how he felt about penguins. But he couldn't mean that...right?

He tilted her chin up, closing her shocked mouth. "Get inside." He opened the side gate slowly, quietly.

"I hope Brayden's not awake," she whispered, sliding through the gate.

"Don't worry about him. I'll take care of that situation."

"Ooh, you sound so alpha. You Tarzan. Me Jane."

He grinned and leaned over the gate to kiss her on her lips one last time. "Go to sleep, Bonnie. You sound like you're on crack."

She opened her mouth, ready to argue, but he spun her around by her shoulders and gave her a gentle push toward the house.

"Sleep tight, babe."

And then he was gone, slipping into the shadows, leaving her breathless. Dizzy. Smitten.

Ten thousand bonus points to the surfer with the magic bubble and the magic mouth.

CHAPTER TWENTY-SIX

*T*off lay in bed staring up at the ceiling as the early-morning light filtered through the window shades. He wanted to fall into a sleep coma, but he couldn't. He'd slept restlessly the last couple of nights, but not because of pain.

That night with Amy had rattled him.

He grunted in frustration. "Rattled" was the wrong word.

Since when did he even care about picking the right words?

Since Amy.

He laced his fingers behind his head and closed his eyes, letting memories wash over him. The night had been awesome, and not just what happened in the van. He couldn't stop thinking about when they'd laid in the hammock, talking and watching the stars. And after, when she'd snuggled into him and he'd laid there wondering if he'd ever been so happy in his life.

He'd been trying to rock her world. But he hadn't expected *his* world to be rocked, flipped upside down and inside out.

His hookups with other girls had been fun. Casual. No strings. He always made sure things were consensual, and he never made any false promises about sex meaning anything other than a good time. It was cotton-candy sex—a rush, yeah, but light as air.

But sex with Amy was…was…not cotton candy.

Damn. Why couldn't he think of the right words this morning? He stared at the ceiling as if the perfect description would magically write itself in the fading paint. Why had it been different with her? Not just different but better. Way, way better. This wasn't at all what he'd expected when he'd agreed to be her coach. Maybe sneak a few kisses when it was obvious they had an insane chemistry thing going, but not *this*. This constant desire to see her, to laugh with her, to watch her come alive. To touch her. It was a rush unlike anything he'd felt before, and he'd experienced plenty of rushes.

All the unexpected feelings had shaken him so much, he'd avoided Amy for two days— avoided everyone, really— turning off his phone and holing up and playing video games while he tried to sort out his head. He felt crappy about it, but he didn't know what to do with everything swirling inside him. Plus, he'd said some cheesy stuff to her in the driveway when he took her home, about them having their own magic bubble, about him being a penguin, which made him cringe now.

Still, he'd meant it at the time.

Hell, maybe he still meant it. That's what he needed to figure out.

Somehow during their coaching gig, this *whatever* between them became…more. More than he knew what to do with. Until he figured it out, he'd wanted to keep his distance, but he couldn't do that forever.

Tonight was the engagement party. He'd asked Amy to come with him for support. He wasn't going to un-invite her, but he wasn't sure how she'd react to seeing him. If Viv knew what had happened between them— which she probably did because girls told each other *everything*—

Shit.

He needed to get in the water, even though he technically wasn't supposed to yet. Time on his board would clear his head and release the coiled-up energy tying him in knots. After that, maybe he'd know what to do with the complicated, confusing emotions pinging around in his head.

And his heart.

*T*hirty minutes later, Toff stood on the beach. He'd snuck out of the house so his dad wouldn't try to stop him. Closing his eyes, he inhaled the briny scent of the ocean, the breeze blowing through his hair. Gulls cawed above him, and the rhythmic splashing of the surf on the sand matched his heart rate.

Finally.

He blew out a long, slow breath and opened his eyes. A few surfers were already out there, but the ocean was mostly all his.

He knelt to Velcro the surfboard leash to his ankle, then jumped up, grabbed his board, and jogged into the water. He dove onto his board and paddled fast. When a three-foot wave came at him, he duck-dived under the water and came out on the other side, grinning. This was the only medicine he'd ever need.

A vivid memory of kissing Amy in the back of his van, limbs entwined, sent a jolt of heat through his body, as if to remind him that the ocean didn't seem to be *all* he needed these days. Spending time with her had definitely helped the days pass. Not just the physical stuff but everything else, too.

He kept paddling, scanning the water for a rideable wave. The other surfers welcomed him back.

"Next one's yours!" Murph called out.

Nobody gave up their spot in the lineup willingly, but Murph was cool.

"Thanks, man!" Toff yelled. In the distance, he spotted a promising swell in the water. He straddled his board, shading his eyes from the sun. He twisted his torso, testing the pain in his abdomen. It was definitely still there, but he could work with this. He'd just take it easy.

"Mahalo." He whispered the prayer of thanks he sent up to the surfing gods every time he was in the water. "I got this," he told himself, then spun around, positioning himself with his back to the waves. He glanced over his shoulder and grinned. This was a good one. It was like Huie the surfing god had sent him a welcome-back gift.

He leaned right as he paddled perpendicular toward the beach, keeping his weight on the inside rail. As the wave began to lift his board, he popped up, leaning in and taking the drop like he'd been surfing every day instead of stuck on land. He rode the water as easily as a knife spreading melting butter on bread.

All the agitation and frustration of being landlocked melted away as his body did what he was born to do. He didn't need or want anything but this.

Everything else was just…gratuitous. A distraction.

Except, the moment the thought hit him, it felt wrong. Amy wasn't just a distraction.

He had to fix this.

*I*t had been two days since the big event. Two days since Toff had texted, Snapped, FaceTimed, or called. She'd texted him once, late last night when she couldn't take the silence anymore, asking if he was feeling okay, but he hadn't replied.

Her stomach was tied up in knots, and so was her heart.

"This stinks," Viv said. They sat in the bookstore kitchen, powering through snacks. Viv had put a RING BELL FOR SERVICE sign on the counter so they could have a private conversation. "You said you two were just having fun, but I knew it was more than that. I really saw it when you did the vlog."

"It started out as fun," Amy said, heaving a sigh. "But with me already crushing on him, and some of the conversations we had…" She crossed her arms over her chest, squeezing tight, like that would somehow protect her heart. "It felt like more than just fun, especially, um, that night." Her vision blurred, but she refused to cry.

She didn't regret that night. She'd wanted sex as much as he had, and he'd made her feel safe. He'd been sweet, and patient, and then…well…wow. That night was a magic bubble like Toff's protective one, where everything flowed and felt perfectly right in the heat of the moment.

But now she wondered if she had imagined, or exaggerated, the connection between them. She didn't think so. They'd spent a lot of time together outside of working on the contest. He'd pushed her out of her comfort zone, because he believed in her. He'd seen something in her she hadn't. She'd told him about her fears, and he'd told her about his mom and his anxiety about his dad marrying Rose. He'd taken her to his secret hideout—no one else—and shown her how he felt. Or how she *thought* he felt.

"I can ask Dallas to beat him up," Viv said, nibbling on a cracker. "Not too badly, since he's his bro-dude, but enough to knock some sense into him."

Amy shook her head. She didn't want to hurt Toff. She wanted to look into his eyes and ask him what the heck was going on, but she didn't have that much swagger. If he didn't want to see her, she wasn't going to throw herself in his path.

But if she went to the party tonight, she'd definitely be in his path.

"You're sure you want me to come to the engagement party?"

"Of course! I was going to ask you to come. Toff just beat me to it." Viv scowled. "You're my friend. That's more important than whatever that idiot Flipper does. I want you there, and so does my mom."

Amy gave Viv a wobbly smile. She loved Viv and Rose. She wanted to go. No matter how things were between Toff and her, she hoped he'd eventually be okay with the wedding, for his dad's sake. And his own.

"Yeah," she said, dropping her gaze. "I guess I have to see him sometime. Might as well be at a party where I can avoid him. Please tell me I'm not the TSTL heroine in my own stupid story."

"You are *not* too stupid to live," Viv said firmly.

Maybe not, but letting herself start to fall for Mr. No Strings Attached *was* stupid. She groaned. "Just imagine what Lucinda Amorrato would say. Her alpha heroines are always kicking butt and taking names. Romance is their side gig."

"Not always," Viv said. "She's written about beta girls and guys, too. They kick butt in different ways." Viv reached across the table to squeeze Amy's hand. "You've had an intense summer, and you've just hooked up with your dream guy, who's now being a jerk. If he doesn't talk to you tonight, I'm going to kick his surfer ass all the way to the moon."

Amy was quiet for a long beat. "It's a great ass," she finally said, darting Viv a half-embarrassed smile. "Don't damage it permanently."

Viv's mouth dropped open, and a few cracker crumbs fell out.

"Don't look so shocked. It is." Amy was proud of herself for making a joke, even as doubt swept over her again.

She might not be too stupid to live, but she was definitely in way over her head.

CHAPTER TWENTY-SEVEN

*T*he sound of ancient rock music and a whirring sander drew Toff to his dad's workshop.

He would've stayed out in the water longer, but he was tired, which sucked, and he had to go to Viv's to help with prepping for the engagement party.

He'd have to work on his endurance to be ready for the Summer Spectacular. That meant that his body was going to need to spend every spare hour out on the water, as opposed to where he craved to be—with Amy.

He'd accepted that much while spending wave after wave thinking about her and not what he was doing on his board. He needed to get out of his head, to stop worrying about whether or not he and Amy could make something out of whatever they had going, and make a damn decision. It was the best thing he'd ever had with a girl, and he wanted to keep it. Somehow. That's the part he wasn't sure of yet.

Toff leaned in the doorway, swigging Gatorade and watching his dad shape the nose of a six-four short board. Foam dust dotted his dad's beard like snow. Toff thought back to when his dad had made him his first custom board and how stoked he'd been. His dad made all his boards—his eggs, his big-wave guns, and his long boards.

Slammer, a surfer who somehow survived on the cash he made from Toff's dad and delivering pizza, was hyper-focused on glassing a board, smoothing down the thin sheet of fiberglass with a squeegee. Toff liked that job, too, finding just the right pressure to apply and getting into a Zen groove.

His dad powered off his sander and looked up, removing his protective mask. "You lasted longer than I thought you would."

Of course his dad knew he'd snuck out to the beach. He was surprised Dad wasn't mad, since he hadn't gotten final doc clearance yet. Maybe he was in a good mood because of the engagement party.

"Not long enough."

"Your endurance will bounce back." His dad wiped his sweaty brow and grinned. "You're young and full of piss and vinegar, like your grandma says."

Slammer glanced up, shooting Toff a quick grin. "Not lasting long enough? With waves or girls?"

Toff rolled his eyes and crossed the room to check out the board his dad was shaping.

"No pain?" his dad asked.

Toff shrugged. "Not much. I paced myself."

"Good, but I want you to stay off your board until your doc appointment next Friday. Coach will kill both of us if you don't."

"Yeah, yeah." Toff ran his hand along the board's edge, wondering how many hours Dad would spend on this one. Surfers from all over the world loved his custom boards. His dad assessed surfers quickly—their body shape, their skill level, how aggressively they attacked the water or not. Each board was unique, and the battered file cabinet was stuffed with hundreds of postcards, letters, and printed emails full of praise. His dad was an artist. Like Z in *Surf's Up*, carving boards out of trees.

"We'll hit the cove once Doc clears you," his dad said. "Bring Dallas with us."

Toff nodded. Hitting one of their favorite local surf spots sounded good.

"Aren't you heading to Rose's house to help decorate for tonight?" Dad asked.

"Yeah, but I wanted to talk to you first."

Dad studied Toff's face, then lowered the sander and tilted his head at Slammer. "Give us a few, Slam."

Slammer nodded, removing his face mask and ducking out the door.

"What's up?" Dad took a long drink from his water bottle, then wiped his mouth on the back of his work glove. "Everything okay?"

Toff shrugged. Now that he had Dad's full attention, he was having trouble finding the right words. Dad brushed sanding dust off the board, waiting patiently. He'd always been that way, ever since Toff was a kid, giving him time and space to figure out what to say and when. Especially after Mom died. Toff squeezed his eyes shut, sending up a quick prayer to Mom. She knew what he wanted to say.

"So…you've been in love. Twice," Toff said.

Dad tossed aside his work gloves. "Yes." He pointed to the beat-up chairs in the corner of the workshop. "Let's sit."

They sat, Dad's expression open and thoughtful. Still patient.

"I…" Toff began, then ducked his head, staring at his hands. He had lots of small scars, like most hard-core surfers, from coral, rocks, the board itself. A few on his legs, but nothing as big as what he'd have from his current injury.

His biggest scar was the one on his heart, from losing Mom. Dad's scar from losing Mom had to be bigger and deeper than his, but here he was, taking a risk and getting married again. Toff exhaled a shaky breath and looked into his dad's eyes.

"How do you know? If you're in love. If it's real."

Dad's eyes softened. "Do you think you are?"

Toff shrugged. "Just wondering what it's like."

Dad eyed him. "Fair enough," he said after a long beat. "The first time, with your mom, it was fast. Almost instant. Your mom and I…" His voice trailed off.

Wistful, thought Toff. One of those words he knew but never used. An Amy word.

Dad shifted in his chair and smiled. "She was a wild child. Not afraid of anything." His lips quirked. "A lot like you. Underneath all her fearlessness, the riskiness, the refusal to take no for an answer, she had a huge heart." Dad tilted his water bottle toward Toff. "Also like you."

Toff wasn't sure about that.

"It was impossible to resist her," Dad said. "Not that I wanted to. I never quite got over the fact that she chose me out of all the guys she knew."

Toff's body buzzed with restless energy. He and Dad had never talked about Mom like this before.

Dad propped his ankle on his thigh. "With Rose, it's been the opposite. Love crept up on us. We were friends since we were kids, like you and Viv."

That got Toff's attention. "Wordworm and I have *no*—"

Dad laughed. "I know, I know. Rose and I joke about it all the time, how we always thought you kids would get together, but instead *we* did." Dad slanted him a sly look. "Besides, you couldn't compete with Dallas."

"You wish he was your son instead of me." Toff was kidding, but his dad glared at him.

"Christopher. Don't joke about that."

Toff raised his hands and laughed. "Okay, okay. So you and Rose—the slow-burn thing, right? Friends to lovers."

Dad blinked. "What are you—"

Toff grinned. "Amy's teaching me a lot about all the different types of romances." He hesitated. "I even read one. Amy made me read it because she wanted me to... She was hoping I'd..." Toff sighed. "It was about this couple who'd been together in high school, then split, then hooked up again when they were old, like you and Rose."

"Old?" Dad cocked an eyebrow, but he was grinning.

"Old*er*," Toff amended, and Dad laughed. "Anyway. That's the other thing I wanted to talk to you about." Toff ducked his head. "I love Rose. I'm happy for you." He looked up, meeting his dad's eyes. "I'm sorry it took me so long to say this. But I'm okay with the wedding. Better than okay."

Dad blew out a long breath. "You know it doesn't change my feelings for Mom, right? I'll always love her."

Toff nodded. He'd never stop loving Mom, either.

"Can I, um." Toff squared his shoulders, remembering what Amy had said. *Who else would he ask?*

"Can I be your best man?" Toff asked, his heart thudding. "Please?"

Dad stared like he couldn't believe his ears. *Crap.* He shouldn't have asked. Dad had probably asked Burner or Crash or—

"Who the hell else did you think I'd ask?" Dad's eyes blazed. "Of course you're my best man."

The words settled around Toff like the cozy blanket his grandma had made him years ago, still on his bed.

"Thanks."

Dad stood up and slugged Toff on his shoulder. "Why are you so smart about some things and so clueless about others?" He smiled. "At least you're smart about Amy. I'm glad you're hanging out with her."

Toff averted his gaze, staring down at his feet. He hadn't been smart at all, not the past couple of days anyway. The way Dad had described falling in love with Rose, being friends and then love sneaking up on them…was that what was happening to him?

He couldn't believe he was even thinking about the L-word.

Whatever it was between them, he'd been an ass, ghosting her after they'd had a great night together. He needed to apologize. Exhaling roughly, Toff stood up and headed for the door.

Behind him, Dad fired up the sander, the whirring sound merging with Mick Jagger's voice blaring through the corner speaker. "Send Slammer back in here!" Dad yelled, reaching for his face mask. "We've got a board to finish before the party."

CHAPTER TWENTY-EIGHT

Viv: Can you pick up balloons from Party Palooza on your way?

Toff: I live to serve the Galdi ladies.

Viv: Also, you suck and I'm going to kill you if you don't talk to Amy today.

*T*off struggled to remove the balloons from his van. Viv had gone overboard, no surprise. There were at least one hundred red and pink heart balloons mixed in with shiny silver ones and plain white ones. Okay, maybe not one hundred, but a lot.

Dallas met Toff outside of Viv's house. "Need help?"

"I'm afraid to let go," Toff said. "If these fly away, Viv will murder me. She already wants to."

"Yeah, I know." He took some of the balloons and pinned Toff with a glare. "Ghosting Amy was shitty, dude."

Here we go, thought Toff. He deserved this. "I know. I suck."

"You ghosted me, too," Dallas said, still glaring. "You've ignored all my texts."

Toff tugged at his hair, frustrated and embarrassed, something he wasn't used to feeling. "I know, okay? I'm just…

trying to figure stuff out."

"Stuff?" Dallas's eyes narrowed suspiciously.

"Dude, cut me a break, okay?" He felt like an idiot arguing while they both held giant balloon bouquets. "I'm going to talk to her." He glanced at the house. "If she's here."

"She is."

Toff's gut twisted. This was gonna be weird. Hard. But he had to do it. "Good. Maybe you can call off your attack girlfriend so Amy and I can talk privately."

"Are you dumping her?" Dallas's eyes burned into him like lasers.

Great. Dallas was pulling his Superman act, with his nerdy glasses and dumb *Star Trek* T-shirt, looking like he wanted to tear Toff apart limb by limb. Which he could, if he wanted to.

"I'm apologizing," Toff said. "As for dumping her, we were never, like, official or whatever."

"You're such a moron." Dallas rolled his eyes, turning toward the house. "No promises on me stopping Viv from murdering you."

"Then say nice stuff about me at my funeral," Toff said. "Make something up."

Dallas shot him a sideways smirk. "*If* there's a funeral. Rose knows how to hide the evidence *and* the body. You might just…*disappear*," he said dramatically.

"You ever worry about that?" Toff asked, relieved Dallas was joking with him. "Dating a girl whose mom plots murders for a living?"

"Rose loves me. I'm good." He slanted a sly grin at Toff. "You, on the other hand…"

Toff couldn't help but laugh.

Dallas held the door open. "Brace yourself. It looks like a cheesy Hallmark store in there. Hearts and sparkly stuff everywhere."

Toff grinned. "I can handle it."

"Just don't offer any suggestions," Dallas whispered as they headed for the living room. "Basically, they have a plan and we don't know crap."

Toff almost tripped over a box overflowing with decorations. "Noted."

"Yay!" Viv ran across the room and snatched the balloons from Dallas, then shot Toff a glare. Toff handed her his balloons…

…and spotted Amy.

She stood on a chair across the room, taping a huge blown-up photo to the wall.

"Holy crap," breathed Toff. It was a picture of his dad and Rose dancing outside at a party under strings of lights. It reminded him of a romance novel cover. It made him twitchy. He wondered if his dad would feel the same way.

Amy bit her lip, glancing at him, then away. "What do you think?" She gestured to the poster, arms outstretched, glitter in her hair and falling from her hands. She looked beautiful. And freaked out, like she wanted to bolt. The apprehension on her face was a throat punch.

"It's, uh, great. My dad will love it," he lied. He glanced at Viv, then tilted his chin at Dallas.

"Come on, Spock," Dallas said, steering a protesting Viv out of the room. "I need food."

Toff waited until Viv's voice faded away, then approached the chair. "Hey," he said softly, looking up at her. "Can we talk?"

He offered his hand to help her down from the chair, but Amy crossed her arms over her chest, her cheeks pink. He couldn't tell if she was about cry or yell. She shrugged, glancing away from him. *Shit.* He lowered his outstretched hand, unsure what to do. He sucked at this.

His earlier conversation with his dad replayed in his mind, about going from friends to something more. He still wasn't sure about his own feelings, but he could see how much he'd hurt hers.

"I know I was an ass," he said. "The worst type of alphahole." She still wouldn't look at him. He sucked in a breath. His chest felt like a vise was squeezing it. "Please, Ames. Come down here and talk to me."

She side-eyed him, then hopped off the chair, ignoring his outstretched hand.

"I'm sorry about ghosting you. It was a crappy thing to do." He hesitated. "Especially because it was, you know, a good night. Really good."

Slowly, Amy looked up, her pretty eyes locking onto his, her expression unreadable. He swallowed, overwhelmed with the desire to hold her. To kiss her. But now wasn't the right time.

"Why did you, though? If it was so good."

Toff shook his head. "I was all up in my head. Trying to sort out some stuff. I didn't even touch my phone."

She nodded but didn't look convinced.

He sighed. "Remember how I said I'd find a big eraser to undo the stupid stuff I said about the sponge bath?"

Was that a hint of a smile?

Encouraged, he kept going. "I looked everywhere, but nobody makes erasers big enough to undo my ignoring you."

That was *definitely* an almost smile.

"Can we just… Will you please give your coach another chance? A redo?"

"Maybe," she said. But this time she smiled for real.

Relief swept through him as he grinned down at her. "Awesome."

They stared at each other for a long moment. Was this

a kissing moment? Or not? He'd better wait. "I, uh, caught up on social media before I came over. Looks like our book interview blew up."

Amy nodded, her cheeks going pink again. The book planet was shipping #BonnieandClyde harder than ever. From what he'd seen, Amy had stuck to her standard replies of "Just friends!" "LOL!" "Nope!" Which sort of bugged him.

But more important than the ship stuff, she had a lot of new followers hitting her up for her Redhead Recs. She'd suggested at least one title for every request. Her brain was a giant database of books. It was impressive. And weirdly hot.

"Now it's wait-and-see time, until they announce the winner on Monday," she said.

"Better pack your bags for LA, Bonnie." He grinned. "Time to meet your idol."

Amy shrugged. "I don't know. Even if…" She hesitated.

"What?" Toff asked. He wanted to know what she was thinking.

"Even if I don't win, I still want to celebrate. I'm proud of my new swagger."

There was that fire he loved, lighting her up.

"Great idea. How about if we have dinner on Monday? A celebration slash apology dinner?"

She glanced over her shoulder as Viv and Dallas entered the room, then turned back to him. "I already accepted your apology. Let's make it a celebration dinner." She smiled, but the look on her face…he'd never seen it before. "You can pay, though, if it'll make you feel better, Coach."

Fierce. That's what the look was. *Damn.*

"Everything okay in here?" Dallas asked, shooting Toff a flinty Clint Eastwood stare.

"Yeah, do I need to stab anyone?" Viv's suspicious gaze zinged between Amy and Toff.

Amy laughed. "Stabbing's my specialty, but I forgot my 'knitting stick.'" She smirked at Toff. "Lucky for you." She pointed to a box on the dining room table. "You need to unpack that and tape the decorations to the walls."

Toff opened the box and pulled out a Cupid cutout with creepy eyes. Wasn't Cupid supposed to be happy? This baby looked psychotic, plus he was armed with a crossbow.

"Looks like everything's under control," Dallas said. "I mean every*one*."

Toff hated that smug grin. Check that—*both* smug grins, because Viv was blasting him with one, too. He glanced at Amy.

She was smiling, too, a familiar flash of warmth and laughter in her eyes that he'd missed. A lot. The vise grip on his chest finally released.

Hell, he'd tape this ugly cardboard baby to his bare chest if she told him to.

"W ear something other than a T-shirt, Toff."

"It's not like tonight's the wedding." Toff was going for a joke, but Dad wasn't amused.

Dad, dressed in a Hawaiian shirt and khakis he'd actually ironed—Toff didn't even know they owned an iron—scowled. "Christopher. Don't argue."

Wow, busting out the full name. Dad must be nervous. That was too bad. Toff was looking forward to the party, now that he'd apologized to Amy.

"Don't stress, Dad. The party will be great. You should see the decorations." He smothered a laugh. "I mean, you should really see them, to prepare yourself." He pulled out his phone. "I took pictures."

Dad shook his head. "I'll wait and be surprised."

"You sure will." Toff grinned. He drained his Gatorade. "I'll see what I've got in my closet."

"You mean what's lying on your bedroom floor that's clean?"

"Nah. If I have anything that's not a T-shirt, it's on an actual hanger."

His dad laughed, relief flashing in his eyes, and Toff felt bad for giving him a hard time. "This party's gonna be cool, Dad. It's just your regular gang, right?"

"And a couple of friends of Rose's I haven't met. They flew down from San Francisco."

"Wow. No wonder you ironed." Toff grinned and shoulder-bumped his dad as he left the kitchen.

"You need to shower!" Dad called after him. "The iron's still set up in my bedroom if you need to use it!"

Like that would ever happen.

After he showered—and, yes, *ironed*—Toff sat on his bed. He picked up the photo on his desk. Mom and Dad grinned at the camera, while his laughing four-year-old self pointed to something in the ocean.

His conversations about his mom with Amy and today's talk with Dad—and maybe even some of that stuff in the book Amy made him read—all of it had come together today while he'd help decorate for the party.

He'd never seen so much glitter and so many hearts in his life. He used to make fun of that stuff, but by the time he left to come home and change, he was happy Viv and Amy had detonated a Valentine's bomb. He was even okay with that huge photo on the wall.

A memory suddenly struck him like a lightning bolt, and he jumped up. The pennies. He needed to find them. He dug through his sock and underwear drawer but came up empty-handed. *Crap*. Where could they be?

He leaned on his dresser, racking his memory. Where had his eight-year-old self hidden stuff? He stared at Rico lying on his bed. "Help me out, fish breath."

An image flickered at the edges of his memory.

He bent down and pulled out the shoebox he'd hidden underneath the bed years ago. When he removed the lid, a sigh gusted out of him. Inside the box were sympathy cards made by his third grade classmates. He dug through the pile. Amy's had to be in here somewhere.

Her card was in the middle of the stack, a piece of red construction paper cut into the shape of heart. Hearts seemed to be the theme of the day. She'd drawn a puppy and a kitten, flowers, and a surfboard with a boy riding it. A boy with blond hair and blue eyes.

Moms love their kids forever, she'd written in loopy cursive, *even from heaven.*

His throat went tight. Dammit. He could not cry. Not tonight. It would kill his dad and Rose. He set the card on his desk and dug through the box, searching for what he was really after.

His fingers closed around one coin, then the other. He glanced at Rico again. "Thanks, bro." The coins were tarnished, but he knew how to fix that. He rushed to the bathroom and scrubbed the pennies with toothpaste, returning their coppery shine. He shoved them in his pocket, then brushed his teeth, too, just in case kissing was back on the agenda.

As he left the house, the scent of his mom's perfume slammed into him, stopping him in his tracks. He reached into his pocket, rubbing the pennies together.

"Mom?" he whispered. "Are you here?" He walked slowly to his van, the perfume swirling around him. He leaned against the van and squeezed his eyes shut, thinking of Amy's card. *Moms love their kids forever, even from heaven.*

"I love you, too, Mom," he whispered, then jumped into his van. He had to make a quick stop before the party.

*T*off hesitated on the threshold of the dining room. The party was in full swing, old eighties and nineties music playing from speakers, clumps of people eating and drinking. Friends surrounded Dad and Rose. Dad draped his arm around Rose's shoulders and pulled her in close. She looked up at him with a dreamy expression, and Toff's chest squeezed, in a good way.

He took a deep breath and crossed the room, stopping to say hi to everyone he knew. Eventually he made it to his dad and Rose.

"There you are," Dad said, frowning slightly. "I wondered why—" Dad broke off when he saw what Toff was holding. Dad smiled, his eyes crinkling at the corners.

Rose turned from her friends, her dark eyes lighting up when she saw Toff.

"Here he is! My bonus kid."

Toff blinked, not sure what to say, the faint scent of Mom's perfume still lingering.

"I've been so lucky to have this boy—this young man—in my life for so long," Rose said, beaming at him.

Viv wandered over just in time. "I don't know if I'd call it *lucky*." She grinned, and her familiar teasing snapped Toff out of his daze. She waggled her eyebrows, looking at what he still held in his hands, sending him a silent message.

"Oh right," Toff said, heat creeping up his neck. He held up the bouquets from the florist. "These are for you."

He handed the bouquet of peach and cream roses to Rose. The florist had told him peach symbolized appreciation and gratitude, and cream was for charm and thoughtfulness. All of those fit Rose.

"Oh!" Rose gasped, tears springing to her eyes. "You are so sweet, Toff." Everyone murmured and cooed at him.

"Don't you dare say 'a rose for a Rose,'" Viv grumbled.

Toff grinned. "I don't have to, since you just did."

Rose handed the flowers to a friend, who rushed off to find a vase. She pulled Toff into a full-body hug. "I love you, you little rascal."

He hugged her back. "I love you, too." When they pulled apart, he reached into his pocket and pulled out the coins. He took a shaky breath. "I want you to have one of these."

Toff handed her one of the stamped carousel pennies. His dad leaned in, putting a hand to his heart when he saw what Toff held. Dad looked up, holding Toff's gaze, his eyes filling with tears. Wow. He hadn't seen Dad cry since…

Rose didn't move, her wide eyes flicking between Toff and his dad.

"My…my…mom and I made these together at the pier. Before she died." He swallowed hard. He wouldn't cry, not tonight. "I thought if I hid these, she'd…she'd…get better." He'd remembered that as he drove to the party, his little-boy wish on the pennies.

"You've always been there for me, Rose. For so long, you've been like a mom. I didn't realize…" He glanced at Dad, who was having a hard time keeping it together. "Anyway." He cleared his throat. "Obviously I'm not gonna give you a ring"—he smiled, trying to lighten the mood and help his dad get it together—"but I can give you this, and I'll always have the other one."

Rose clutched the penny to her chest and burst into tears. Dad wrapped her in a hug, then reached for Toff, pulling him into the hug, too.

"Way to go, Flipper. Way to go," Viv said when Dad released him. Her eyes shone with tears, but she was smiling. "I suppose those are for Amy," she said, gesturing to the small bouquet of yellow roses he still held.

"Nope." He presented them with a bow. "These, my most annoying sister, are for you."

Viv gasped, then launched herself at him. "I take back every bad thing I've ever said about you."

He laughed, stumbling backward, catching her in a hug.

Dallas and Amy joined them, Dallas giving him a thumbs-up when Viv finally let him go.

Amy smiled up at him, eyes shining.

"Damn," Toff grumbled, "did I make *everybody* cry?"

"Not me," Dallas said.

"I heard everything," Amy said. "That was amazing."

"Thanks." He handed her the single unicorn rose in a plastic cylinder he'd been clutching the whole time. "This is for you. I'm sorry they only had one, but I thought you'd like it."

The petals were a swirl of colors, like a rainbow. When he'd asked the florist what the colors symbolized, he'd shrugged and said, "They make people happy."

That worked for Toff, since he wanted to give Amy an apology rose but didn't want to choose other colors on the chart the florist showed him, like red for true love, yellow for friendship, or lavender for love at first sight.

Amy took the rose, blasting him with a brilliant smile that

made him feel…all sorts of feelings. Feelings he wasn't ready to name but that fit like a puzzle piece into his conversation with Dad.

Rose's friends from San Francisco herded everyone outside to the deck for a toast with champagne and sparkling cider.

"Here's to the sweetest Rose in the garden," Dad called out from the far end of the deck, everyone gathered around him. All the women *ooh*ed and *aah*ed, and some of the guys *Hell-yeah*ed.

"Wow," Toff said. "He's drunk." He shrugged. "I guess he's allowed, since it's his party."

"He's not," Amy whispered, "he's happy."

Surprised, he stared down at her.

"He's sweet, okay? Not drunk."

"I've been lucky in love," Dad continued. "Not once but twice. That's more than one man deserves."

Everyone *ooh*ed and *aah*ed again. Dad scanned the crowd, his gaze landing on Toff.

"I got that wrong," he said, lifting his glass toward Toff. "I've been lucky in love three times. I couldn't ask for a better son, even when he drives me crazy."

Relief and pride filled his dad's eyes, and Toff felt his neck grow warm as the crowd turned toward him. He hadn't felt this happy—this bone-deep happy—for a long, long time. He lifted his glass toward his dad and smiled.

Overhead, a shooting star arced across the sky like somewhere in heaven, Mom was celebrating, too.

CHAPTER TWENTY-NINE

*T*witter Thread:
@HeartRacerChallenge Winner Announced!

@HeartRacerPublishing thanks everyone who entered their contest! Check out this thread to see what Lucinda Amorrato has to say about the winner:

"Thank you to all who entered. You have my awe and admiration. I'm much too old to 'do' social media, and it has been an awakening to 'lurk' in the online book lover world. Your passion and creativity astound me. This was an incredibly difficult decision.

"I chose @RedheadRecs as the winner because of her terrific reviews (buried on that Hunkalicious blog that you should all check out) her thoughtful recommendations to other readers, and her passion for the romance genre...

"on full display in her interview with her reluctant reader. Many of you shipped #BonnieandClyde. I admit, I did as well. There's nothing a romance author enjoys more than seeing a real romance play out. Congratulations, Amy! I can't wait to meet you!"

• • •

*I*n the early-morning quiet, Amy screamed so loudly, her entire family came running. Her bedroom door flew open, Brayden brandishing her missing giant knitting needle like a weapon, her parents hovering behind him.

"Omigod! I won! I get to meet Lucinda! She picked me! Omigod!" She jumped out of bed, waving her phone around. "Hey!" She pointed at Brayden. "Stop stealing stuff from my room. That's a crafting tool, not a weapon."

"That's fantastic, honey! I'll make something special to celebrate. Maybe an apple tart." Dad rubbed his hands together. "French meringues? I haven't made those in a while."

Mom wrapped her in a hug. "I knew you'd win. Especially after I watched you interview Toff."

Amy gaped at her mom. "You saw that? But you don't do social media."

"You put the recording on the Hunkalicious blog, honey. I always check that for your book reviews."

Omigod. How had she forgotten her mom checked the blog? Amy blushed, thinking of her mom watching Toff being so extra.

"Make those chocolate crispy thingies," Brayden said to Dad, pointing the giant needle at his chest. "Meringues are gross."

Dad put a hand to his heart, pretending to stagger back. "You dare to insult the meringue?" He snatched the knitting needle from Brayden, crouched into a fencing position, then glanced at Amy. "I watched it, too. The Cupcake Kid and I need to talk."

Ohhhh no.

Dad turned back to Brayden. "My name is Quinn Declan

McIntyre. You insulted the French meringue. Prepare to die."

Brayden clutched his throat and theatrically collapsed to the ground. "No…meringues…" He gasped between gulps of air. "It's…my…dying…wish."

Amy laughed while Mom applauded *The Princess Bride* parody. Her family was so weird. She couldn't imagine them *not* weird.

But as much as she loved them, she needed to call Viv. And Toff.

*T*off was stoked for Amy. He'd panicked when she'd called instead of texted this morning, but then she'd screamed the good news in his ear. Now he was wandering Main Street, checking out shops to buy her a congratulations gift. He wasn't sure what to get.

He'd only seen Amy once since the engagement party. She'd picked up Brayden from the beach and they'd snuck off to steal a few kisses, but something felt off. She'd ended the kissing sooner than he'd wanted, leaving him wanting more. Not just more kissing but more time with her, too.

He wasn't sure what was wrong, but he hoped dinner would fix it somehow. He pushed open the door of a cheesy gift shop.

"Hello! Welcome to Seashells and More!"

Toff glanced toward the chipper voice, grinning when he saw his surfer friend Claire.

"What are you doing here?" She smirked as she approached him. "We don't get many locals."

Toff shrugged, his neck heating with embarrassment. "I need a present."

Claire tilted her head, eyeing him closely. "For Amy?"

"Yeah." How'd she know?

"Want some help?"

"Maybe." He reached out to examine a necklace hanging from a display rack.

"Hell to the no," Claire said, batting his hand away.

More heat crept up his neck. He didn't know how to do this. He'd never bought a girl a present before. Except the Swedish chick. He'd given her a California flag beach towel. Boring. He needed to do better for Amy.

Claire tapped her sandal on the floor. "Do you honestly think Amy would wear a necklace with a giant palm tree on it? With those stupid flashing lights?"

"No." Toff sighed and scanned the shop. "I don't even know what I'm looking for," he grumbled.

The shop door opened, and a group of sunburned tourists walked in. Claire squeezed his shoulder. "Just wander around. Don't think too hard, and something will call to you."

Toff snorted. "Call to me?"

"Just do it," Claire commanded; then she left to go help the other customers.

"Call to me," he muttered to himself as he slowly wandered the back of the store, crammed with cheesy souvenirs. *Come on*, he told himself, *you can do this.*

Shot glasses painted with the Hollywood sign. Inflatable Corona bottles. A whole bunch of tiki crap. Nope, nope, and nope. He kept wandering, even though he was pretty sure this was the wrong place to find her something special.

Then he stopped. Picked up the small replica VW van with the miniature surfboard strapped to the roof. The van had old 1960s-style flowers painted on it. He eyed the shelf. There was another van, this one decorated with hearts instead of flowers.

He wasn't sure why this called to him or whatever, but it did. He put the flowered van back and grabbed the heart van, glad no one he knew was in here, except Claire.

On his way to pay, a table of sparkly stuff caught his eye—a whole bunch of stuff that had been attacked with a glitter bomb, including a basket of hair things. He dug into it, like his hands knew what he was looking for before he did.

"Perfect." He clutched the hair pin decorated with sparkly starfish, then grabbed the one with unicorns. It went with the flower he'd gotten her the other night. Amy was a unicorn girl—he knew it deep in his bones.

As he waited behind the noisy tourists to pay, he scoped out the impulse buys on the counter, spotting a rack of wooden surfboard bookmarks hanging by yarn loops.

"Okay, fine," he grumbled, snatching three bookmarks off the rack. One for his dad, one for Viv, and one for him, so he wouldn't freak out Amy again. If he ever read another book.

When it was his turn to pay, he stared down Claire. "I was never here."

"Who are you, weirdo? I've never seen you before in my life." She shoved his items in a paper bag and handed it over, shooting him a wink.

"Uh." Toff hesitated. "Do you do gift wrapping?" He glanced behind him. The line was long, and Claire was the only employee. "Never mind. I'll figure it out." It couldn't be that hard.

"Hang on." Claire ducked down, popping up a minute later with a fancy bag covered in sparkles. She stuffed a bunch of tissue paper in it. "You can handle this, right? It's ninety percent done for you."

"Thanks, Claire."

"You're welcome." She flashed him a quick grin. "I like seeing you try, for once."

He opened his mouth to protest, but he wasn't sure what to say.

Back on the sidewalk, he breathed a sigh of relief. He had a gift for Amy. Dinner reservations were made. He had a clean shirt and knew where the iron was.

Now he just had to wait a few more hours until he could pick her up. Hopefully by the end of the night, they'd be all the way okay again.

CHAPTER THIRTY

*T*off checked himself out in the bathroom mirror. Hair washed and styled—check. All he did was run his fingers through it, but girls always loved it. Shaved—check. No disgusting pimples—check. Teeth brushed—twice. His shirt was clean and mostly wrinkle-free. He was still getting the hang of the iron.

He glanced at the fancy bottle of aftershave cologne on the sink. He'd had it since sophomore year—a gift from the Swedish girl—but hardly ever used it. Was it weird to wear a present from one girl when he took another girl out to dinner?

Probably.

He grabbed the bottle anyway, unscrewed the top, and sniffed. It smelled good. Manly. Alpha. He squinted, holding the bottle up to the mirror, wondering how much to use. Last time he'd worn it, his dad pretended to choke to death and told him "less is more."

He aimed the nozzle at his neck and squeezed, coughing as the spray filled his nose.

Good enough.

"Okay," he told his reflection. "Time to do this." He grabbed the gift bag and headed for the deck to tell his dad goodbye.

"Look at you," Dad said with a grin. He put a thumb in his book to hold his place.

"Oh, here," Toff said, handing Dad one of the surfboard bookmarks from the bag.

Dad's eyebrows lifted in surprise. "Thanks. Where are you off to?"

"Taking Amy to dinner. She won the publisher contest."

"That's great! Tell her congrats for me." He tapped his mouth with the bookmark, lips quirking. "I hear there's a book review video I need to watch."

Toff winced. Rose must've told him about it. "Uh…you don't need to. Really."

Dad grinned. "You want some cash for tonight?"

"Nah. I've got it covered. Don't wait up," Toff said.

"Make sure you get Amy home by curfew. It's a good way to win over her parents."

"They already love me."

Dad looked ready to make a smart-ass comeback, but instead he raised his glass in a salute. "What's not to love?"

*A*my was waiting in front of her house when Toff arrived. She practically ran to his van, glancing over her shoulder like she was being chased.

"What's up?" Toff asked as she climbed into the passenger seat. "I was going to come inside to say hi to your parents." He grinned. "And your monster brother."

Amy didn't laugh. "Let's go. Please." She buckled her seat belt.

His chest tightened. "What's wrong, Ames?"

She shrugged, glancing away. "Just family stuff. I don't

want to talk about it."

"Is it your brother?"

"No." Amy frowned. "Why do you ask?"

"Uh…he's the family troublemaker, right?" Toff joked.

Amy didn't smile. "Can we go to dinner? Please."

Toff studied her, hoping she'd say more. She didn't, so he put the van into gear and drove, hoping their dinner wasn't doomed before it even started.

Amy started a playlist.

"What's this?" asked Toff. It sounded like the sleepy music Natasha played in the herb shop.

"It's supposed to be calming music."

Their eyes met briefly; then Toff refocused on the road, troubled by the worry in her eyes and the way she kept looking away from him.

"It's, uh, money stuff," she said quietly. "Dad says it's time to take any job he can get, even at the hot dog shack, and Mom's upset. She says that's beneath him. And she feels guilty about not going back to work full-time once Brayden started school."

"Ouch." Toff cringed, imagining the argument.

"Today started out great, but then it all went down the tubes," Amy said, sighing heavily. "My family was so excited and happy for me this morning. Then after I called you, Viv and I celebrated with a pancake breakfast—"

"You should've invited me."

"—and I got a call from HeartRacer." She glanced at him. "But right before you picked me up, my parents just… exploded. Arguing about money and jobs. Mom was crying, and Brayden freaked, hiding out in his room."

"Damn. That sucks." He hated how helpless he felt. "Are you sure you want to do this tonight? We don't have to. We can go to a movie or the pier. Whatever you want."

"I want to go to dinner."

He glanced over. "You sure?"

Amy blew out a breath and smiled. "Yes. I want to end today the way it started—happy."

*A*my stared out the window as they drove up the coast. Her feelings for Toff were all over the place—still crushing on him, unsure of where they stood, starting to realize she might want more than a laid-back guy like Toff would be willing to give. It didn't help that she'd seen him only once since the engagement party on Friday.

When she saw him at the beach while picking up Brayden, she'd been so caught off guard when he kissed her that she'd awkwardly pulled away sooner than usual.

Other than that, he hadn't texted or Snapped her. Their #BonnieandClyde OTP was still going strong, especially because of the interview. Toff had liked some of the comments that made fun of him, posting laughing emojis, but he ignored all the questions asking if they were in an actual relationship.

Amy glanced at Toff, who was being unusually quiet, and sighed. She'd replayed his apology over and over in her mind. He'd said he was "up in his head" and had to "sort stuff out." What did that mean? She wished he'd open up to her.

Was he sorting out how he felt about her? About them? Were they back to coaching only, or did he want more? And what did *she* want?

She'd spent a lot of time thinking about that.

She hoped they could talk about this tonight. He'd opened up some at the pier and then again that night under the stars, but she worried those had been exceptions to his no-sharing-feelings rule. Never to happen again. She'd like to know where they stood, because she had other worries on her mind, too, like her family and the news from HeartRacer she couldn't wait to share with him.

Toff pulled off the road, turning into a small parking lot. The restaurant was fancier than she'd expected. A large deck covered in glittering lights overlooked the water.

"Wow," Amy said, impressed.

"I hope you like it." Toff looked anxious. He took her hand as they approached the restaurant. Her heart did a little flip, but she told it to simmer down.

Once inside, they were led to a cozy table in the far corner of the outside deck, half hidden by a huge plant. Had Toff arranged this? She glanced at the gift bag in his hand. He'd gone all out tonight. Maybe he *had* sorted out his feelings, and maybe, just maybe, he'd planned to spill them tonight.

As Toff sat across from her, she drank him in. Suntanned and smiling, blue eyes sparkling, he made her heart skip a beat. Confused or not, she was going to enjoy this. Enjoy him. Them. Turn around what had become a crappy day and focus on all the awesome that had happened, including some uninterrupted time with Toff.

"Do I get my present now or later?" she teased.

He lifted an eyebrow. "That's like eating dessert before dinner."

"Since when do you follow that rule?"

"Since now." He shoved the gift bag into the corner of the booth, and she laughed.

"I'm not going to jump over the table and steal it."

"You might, Bonnie. Let's not forget how we first met." He grinned, looking more relaxed as they joked. "Someone was running from the cops, and it wasn't me."

"We *met* in elementary school, Clyde." He might have forgotten who his second-grade reading buddy was, but she hadn't.

"Welcome to The Reef."

Their waiter arrived to take their drink orders and told them about the chef's special. Amy had a hard time concentrating because Toff started playing footsie under the table, looking at her like *she* was the chef's special, stirring up all sorts of conflicting emotions.

"I'll be back shortly with your drinks," the waiter said.

"Take your time," Toff said. "We're not in a hurry. It's a special night."

"Of course, sir." The waiter dipped his head and glided away.

"Smooth. Did you see that in a movie?" Amy teased.

He leaned back against the booth. "Read it in a book some girl recommended."

"Oh yeah? Which one?"

"The only one I've read."

Amy laughed; then her phone buzzed. She frowned when she saw Brayden's name on the screen.

Brayden: When will you be home?

Her stomach twisted.

Are Mom and Dad still arguing? she texted back.

Brayden: No.

Amy: Good. I'll be home later. I'm out with your idol.

Brayden sent a frowny-face emoji as his reply.

Toff's forehead pinched. "Everything okay?"

"It's just Brayden. I think he's bummed out about earlier and bored. He'll probably be waiting outside when we get back, hoping for a chance to see you." She couldn't think about that now, though. She had fun news. Nerve-racking news. "So…I have something to tell you."

"Yeah? Hit me with it." Toff stretched his arm across the booth. Amy wished she were next to him.

She leaned forward, a rush of excitement buzzing in her veins. "I'm not just meeting Lucinda—I get to interview her at the Sunset Bookstore! In front of a ton of people."

"Wow." Toff's eyes lit up. "That's awesome. You can nerd out with her." He hesitated. "Are you nervous about the interview?"

Amy nodded. "Yeah, but not like I would've been at the beginning of the challenge." She smiled. "So thanks, Coach. All that swagger stuff worked."

It was true. She'd already started making a list of questions for Lucinda.

"I'm glad." He fidgeted with the bread basket, not looking at her. Amy was surprised he wasn't acting cocky, taking all the credit. "When's the interview?"

"Friday in LA."

"The day before the Spectacular? Cool."

Amy frowned. "I didn't think you were cleared to compete yet."

"I'm not." He shrugged. His follow-up appointment was on Friday. "We'll see. If she clears me to surf, I might just go for it, even though I haven't been practicing."

"Have you talked to your dad about that?" She hoped so. She'd hate to see him reinjure himself.

"I already know his opinion." Toff grimaced. "And my coach's."

"But if you're not ready—"

"C'mon, Ames." His expression darkened. "Not you, too."

She gaped at him. "What do you want me to say? Go out there and hurt yourself?"

"Have we had time to decide on dinner?"

Amy frowned at the waiter who'd reappeared out of

nowhere. Weren't waiters supposed to know when to stay away?

"We have not," Amy said, glancing at Toff, who was scowling at his glass of water. "Give us another five minutes. Please."

"Very good, miss." The waiter turned away, but Amy caught his condescending smirk.

She turned back to Toff. "I'm not trying to tell you what to do. I'm just worried, same as your dad. But if you do compete, I hope you win." She hesitated, then decided to go for it. "Then we can have another celebration dinner. My treat?"

Toff shifted restlessly, looking everywhere but at her. "Yeah, maybe."

Amy's stomach twisted. Clearly the competition was a sore spot. Was that what he meant by having to "sort stuff out" and *not* her? But he'd shut down after their night together, so it couldn't be that. *Ugh.* She hated how little he was giving her. If he wasn't going to say anything, she was going to ask.

"Toff." She waited until he stopped fidgeting and looked her in the eye. "Will you please tell me what's going on?"

"What do you mean?" He ran his thumb along the handle of the butter knife, avoiding eye contact again. "Nothing's going on."

She sighed in frustration, chiding herself once again for not falling for a beta boy who *liked* to talk or a romantic who'd make hundreds of origami flowers as an apology, like in one of her favorite YA romances.

"I *mean*," she said, calling on the swagger that was becoming easier and easier to find, "what's going on with *us*?"

• • •

*T*off tried not to panic.

Us, us, us…

The word bounced around in his brain like double red flags warning surfers and swimmers to stay out of the water. There was no way he could answer Amy, not when he was still trying to figure out the answer for himself. He needed to be around her like he needed air, wanted to make her smile and laugh more than almost anything, but putting a label on those emotions was harder than he'd expected.

So he hadn't.

He forced a lopsided grin, hoping Amy couldn't read his face. "Nothing's going on. We're Bonnie and Clyde, the OTP everyone's shipping, and we're here to celebrate." He looked around. "Can we order now? I need to eat so my growling stomach doesn't scare everyone."

He spotted the waiter, who glided toward them like a penguin on ice skates. A *mean* penguin, like the chinstraps. Those little dudes were assholes.

"Toff…" Amy's eyes searched his. He squirmed, unsure how to react to all the emotion he saw there. All the *feelings*.

"Are we ready, sir?" the waiter asked.

We weren't, but Toff wasn't giving this guy any ammo. "You go first, Amy."

She frowned at him, then handed her menu to the waiter. "I'll have the grilled shrimp, please."

"Excellent choice."

The penguin took Amy's menu and raised his eyebrows expectantly at Toff. Was that a lip curl or was Toff hallucinating? Just because Toff was a teenager didn't mean he didn't know how to tip well. If this guy didn't drop the attitude, he'd end up with zilch.

"Sir?" the waiter prompted.

"The chef's special," Toff said. "The chicken one."

"*Coq au vin?*"

"*Oui,*" said Toff, drawing out the word sarcastically. The waiter flared his nostrils, took Toff's menu, and left.

"I don't like that guy," Toff grumbled.

"Just ignore him." Amy sighed. "Look, forget I asked that question. We don't have to talk about it."

She looked sad. Upset. He hated that, but he'd take her up on her offer and ignore the question he wasn't ready to answer.

Amy tugged at her hair, and a sparkly butterfly clip fell to the table. He watched her re-clip it into that crazy red hair he loved. He didn't know why he liked her sparkles so much, but he did. He hoped she liked the ones he'd bought for her.

His gaze drifted from her hair to her glossy lips down to her neck. Maybe they should forget about dinner and go to his van. Go back in time to that night at his hideout. Only this time he wouldn't screw it up by ghosting her afterward.

Amy's phone buzzed again. "Sorry." She flashed an apologetic smile. "I'd better check."

"No worries. I'll be right back."

Toff slid out of the booth. He needed to regroup. Calm his nerves. Snarky Waiter cocked a questioning eyebrow when Toff brushed past him on his way to the entrance, but Toff ignored him.

Once outside, he sat on a bench underneath a palm tree and closed his eyes, Amy's question echoing in his mind. As freaked out as labeling their…relationship…was making him, Amy deserved an answer. He'd never wanted to be part of an official "us" before, but he also couldn't imagine *not* having her around, not having all their teasing, laughing. Kissing.

And more.

Was that what it would be like if they were official?

"Nichols! I thought that was you."

Damn. He knew that voice. Toff opened his eyes slowly,

not thrilled to see one of his biggest surfing rivals looming over him. Mack was a bad-ass short boarder from San Francisco. They'd gone head-to-head in a lot of comps, often vying for first and second place in their categories.

"Hey, Mack. What are you doing here?" There weren't any comps this weekend.

Mack smiled like the Big Bad Wolf stumbling upon Little Red Riding Hood. He looked like a wolf, too, with sharp teeth and bristly hair.

"On my way south to get some runs in at Lowers." He glanced toward the front door, where a couple of other guys waited impatiently.

Toff nodded. Everyone loved to surf the Trestles. Mack had enough cash to eat dinner here the same way most people chose In-N-Out Burger. His family was loaded.

Mack gestured to Toff. "You're all dressed up. Grandma's birthday party?"

Bastard. Mack'd never let him forget the time he had to change into a suit and tie after a comp. His grandparents had flown in three summers ago to watch Toff compete and to celebrate Gram's seventieth birthday with Toff and his dad.

Toff stood up so he could stare this guy down, which was easy, since he had a good four inches on him.

"Not Grandma's dinner." He crossed his arms over his chest.

"Come on, Mack!" one of the guys by the entrance yelled. "We're hungry!"

Mack gave the guy the stop-sign hand signal, narrowing his gaze at Toff. "You on a date with that reader chick? I saw some of that Bonnie and Clyde crap on Twitter." He smirked. "She must be something to tie *you* down. Can't wait to meet her."

Shit. Could this night get any worse?

. . .

"Brayden, please stop texting," Amy whispered into her phone.

"I'm hungry," Brayden grumbled. "Are you at the hot dog shack? You guys should have brought me with you."

Amy sighed into the phone. "We aren't at the hot dog shack. Toff took me somewhere nice."

Where was Toff anyway? She scanned the restaurant, but he was nowhere in sight.

"Bring Toff inside when you get home. I want to show him something."

Amy rolled her eyes. Toff's blond hair caught her eye, and she exhaled a sigh of relief. "I need to go, Bray. I'm putting my phone on DND."

"Wha—"

Amy shoved her phone in her purse as Toff approached the table with some guy she didn't recognize. Toff didn't look happy.

"Amy, this is Mack, a surfer I know from up north." Toff stood next to her side of the booth, crossing his arms over his chest and widening his stance like he was her bodyguard. What the heck?

"So this is her?" Mack sneer-smiled just like Draco Malfoy did to Ron Weasley. "The girl who lassoed the biggest player in—"

"Shut it, Mack." Toff adjusted his stance to block her from Mack's view, his hands curling into fists. "You can leave now."

Amy tilted her head to peek around Toff. Mack scoped her up and down, his expression twisting like he found her… lacking. What a jerk.

"You're not at all what I expected," he said. "You're so—"

"Leave," Toff snarled. "Now."

Mack raised his hands innocently. "Chill, dude. I just wanted to say hi."

Unfortunately, they were attracting attention from the other diners.

"Never thought I'd see this." Mack aimed a smug grin at Toff. "You're a tub of Cool *Whipped*. Should be easy for me to beat your ass at the Spectacular."

She didn't know who this Mack guy was, but he needed to shut up and leave.

A burly man in a suit approached their table, his face a mask of cool authority. "Is there a problem, gentlemen?"

"No, sir." Mack stepped back, giving Toff a mock bow. "Just wanted this dude's autograph. I guess he's a big-deal surfer around here, but he doesn't have time for the riffraff."

Suit Guy's appraising gaze shifted between Toff and Mack, who stared each other down. Toff's hands bunched into fists. Amy groaned. Stupid boys and their stupid…measuring sticks.

"Is that true?" Suit Guy asked Toff. "We don't tolerate paparazzi or overzealous fans interrupting diners, but we don't want you taking things into your own hands."

Amy heaved a sigh. Time for her to pull off a get-out-of-trouble save for her coach. She put her hand on Toff's arm, moving him aside so she could stand up. Their waiter appeared behind Suit Guy, hovering in the aisle with their dinners.

Amy pivoted to face Suit Guy. "Yes, he's a *very* big deal," she said sweetly. "If you watch the Summer Spectacular next weekend, you'll see him smoke everyone." She waved a dismissive hand at Mack. "Including this poser, I bet."

Adrenaline lit up her nerve endings as she grinned at Toff, who blinked like he'd just emerged from a dark cave. "Let's eat, *babe*," she added. She snaked her arm around his waist. "Don't let this loser get under your skin." She fired a glare at Mack that would singe off his hair, if only she had superpowers. Mack shot her a glare, but he back-stepped away.

"My apologies, Mr....?" said Suit Guy.

"Nichols," Amy supplied, since Toff was still in daze. "Toff Nichols. He'll be as big as Kelly Slater someday. Just you watch."

Suit Guy cracked a barely perceptible smile, motioned for their waiter to serve them, then headed toward Mack's table.

Amy sat, tugging Toff down next to her. Yeah, her feelings for him were all tangled up, but her swagger and her swoony heart had won out. This time.

"Will there be anything else?" asked the waiter. He didn't look so superior now.

Amy smiled. "Not now. Check back later, please." The waiter nodded and glided away. She leaned into Toff. "Dig in, Clyde."

The waiter dropped off the leather bill holder, and Toff counted out enough cash to leave the guy a generous tip. He didn't want to add to his bad karma. He'd barely touched his own dinner, losing his appetite after the scene with Mack.

Amy had tried to pull him out of his funk, joking about Bonnie and Clyde and pretending to case the restaurant like a bank, but he hadn't played along. Eventually she'd given up, finishing her dinner in silence.

He glanced at the gift bag. Could he still salvage tonight? Maybe she'd like his presents enough to forgive him for ruining dinner. Then again, maybe not. They were dumb presents.

He heaved a resigned sigh. "Guess we should go."

"Toff. Tell me what's going on." Amy met his eyes from across the table.

He hated how the fire had gone out of her after he'd gone silent. She'd been awesome, telling off Mack even after how crappy Toff had treated her. He should've high-fived her. Kissed her into oblivion even though they were in a fancy restaurant.

But he hadn't done any of that. He was embarrassed he hadn't stood up for himself, that he'd let Mack insult her. That he'd let that jerk get inside his head.

His spinning thoughts tortured him like hamsters on a wheel. What if he wasn't 100 percent for the Spectacular and lost to this asshat? What if Dad was right and he wasn't ready to go pro? What if…what if all this time with Amy… *Hell.* Did he even deserve her?

"Let's go," he said abruptly, sliding out of the booth and grabbing the gift bag. He doubted she'd want any presents from him, not after tonight. After a beat, Amy followed him.

He could feel himself losing control, a monster wave of frustration and confusion and anger cresting inside him, about to slam him underwater.

CHAPTER THIRTY-ONE

*A*my hurried to catch up with Toff as he stalked to his van. She was frustrated, but mostly she was worried. She'd never seen him like this. It was like an alien pod person had taken over happy-go-lucky Toff.

She wished she could read his mind, since he wasn't willing to tell her what was going on.

"Sorry about tonight." He bit the words out like they cost him penalty points.

"At least the food was good," she said. "Thanks for treating."

Toff nodded and opened the sliding door, gesturing inside to the nest of pillows and blankets. "I'm too pissed off to drive," he said, crawling into the van and leaning against the pillows. "I need to chill before we head back."

"What do you mean by 'chill'?"

"Nothing. Can't we just hang out, Ames?" The look he gave her was mostly frustrated, but she spotted another emotion, too. One that made her crawl into the van next to him and take his hand in hers.

"I don't want our night to end like this," Toff said. "Maybe we can salvage what's left before I have to take you home."

A tiny flame of hope flickered in her chest. Maybe they could.

"I'd like that," she said, angling her body to face his. "Will you tell me what's going on with you? I mean, obviously that Mack guy was a jerk, but—"

He moved in close, wrapping his arms around her and swallowing her words with a kiss. It was another fast and furious kiss, shutting down her brain cells…but not for long. She couldn't do this with him…not yet. She pushed against his chest, breaking the kiss.

"What's wrong?" His arms were still wrapped around her, and he was looking at her like…the way he had that night in the hammock.

"Please tell me what's going on with you. Why you shut down on me tonight." She took a deep breath and went all in. "And why you shut me out before the party."

"God, Amy." He dropped his arms from her waist, leaning back against the pillows. "I don't want to *talk*. I just want to…" He sighed, closing his eyes. "Can't we just be with each other?"

Her heartbeat sped up, then slowed as her emotional roller-coaster ride of the past week came to a sudden stop, the answer to her own question crystal clear.

"What do you mean, 'be with each other'?" She swallowed, pushing forward when his eyes flew open and locked on hers. "Do you mean…sex?"

"Yeah." He rose up on his elbows, his gaze roving over her. "Let's just…you know…dinner sucked, but at least we can end the night with a bang."

Was he for real? With a *bang*?

Was that all sex was to him? She bit her lip. She knew the answer—he was the player, after all. Even though their night together had seemed to be a lot more than just fun, maybe it wasn't. Not for him.

"You won't talk to me, but you want me to hook up with you again." She shook her head, frustration and sadness warring within her. "That's not okay, Toff."

He dug his hands into his hair and groaned in frustration, throwing his head back against the pillows. "Why do you have to make such a big deal—"

Something inside her snapped. "Because it is a big deal, Toff. To me, if not to you." She scrambled back, feet tangling in the blankets. No more holding back on her feelings, her truth.

"Look, I never expected any type of relationship from you. I'm not an idiot." She took a deep breath, shaking her head. "Except…I am an idiot."

She held his gaze, a swirl of power and anxiety pulsing through her as she spoke. This wouldn't be easy, but she had to say it.

"We've joked about our ship for weeks, right? Bonnie and Clyde. Ha-ha. The bookworm and the surfer. We've teased and flirted…and kissed…and more. But the truth is…" She did a yoga breath. In. Out. Strong.

If she couldn't be honest, what was the point?

"The truth is, Toff, I've always liked you. As much more than a friend or a coach. And this summer, well…" She shrugged, tossing her hair over her shoulder. "This summer I fell for you, for real. Full stop."

His lips parted, those pretty blue eyes wide and shocked.

"I don't have any regrets about the time we've spent together." She did another yoga breath. "Or the sex. That was great." She was on a roll, an incredible one. "Except for the ghosting."

He opened his mouth like he wanted to say something, but she kept going. She had to finish before this crazy swagger evaporated.

"I know you're not a relationship guy. I'm not asking you for that. But I've figured out that I can't do this hookup thing.

It doesn't work for me." She took one last breath. "Especially with a guy I really…well…" She shrugged and smiled, an embarrassed but relieved smile. "I know it was never real to you, Toff. But for me…it's never been fake."

He was frozen, just like in the restaurant.

Amy scrambled across the floor of the van and jumped out, pulse pounding. She faced him, hands on her hips. She was a freaking rock star but she needed to get home, stat, and collapse on her bed.

"Until you figure out what I mean to you, I can't see you anymore, Toff. Please drive me home."

CHAPTER THIRTY-TWO

The next day, Amy and her mom drove to LA to spend time with her aunt and her cousins before the big Lucinda interview. The Lonely Hearts Book Club gave her a big send-off party, which had both hyped her up and distracted her from the whole Toff thing.

"Do you want to talk about what happened between you and Toff?" Mom asked as they idled in gridlocked traffic on the 405. The drive to LA from Shady Cove would take a couple of hours at least.

"No," Amy said. "I want to focus on the contest and spending time with my cousins."

"Fair enough," Mom said. "Let me know if you change your mind."

"I will."

Not only had Mom watched the *Redo in the Rockies* interview with Toff, she'd checked out Amy's social media, too. Now the whole family knew all about #BonnieandClyde, much to Amy's horror.

Toff had driven her home in silence after dinner, sneaking so many looks at her, she was afraid he'd crash the van. She'd been shocked yet relieved he could go that long without saying a word. She hadn't heard a peep from him since.

She was relieved…and crushed.

Amy stared out the window at the hazy sky. She hadn't cried, though. Hadn't fallen apart like a weepy heroine. Maybe she was still in shock from everything she'd said to him.

The best part about her speech to Toff was how even *more* ready she felt to interview Lucinda. Giving your unrequited crush that you'd fallen for—and hooked up with, and been ghosted by, and still, stubbornly, had all kinds of feelings for—a love-me-or-leave-me speech was empowering.

Mom honked at a muscle car that had forced its way into their lane. "We'll start with mani-pedis with your cousins tomorrow."

"Are you sure we can afford it?" They were staying with her aunt and cousins this week to save on hotel costs. The money argument was still fresh in her mind.

"Please don't worry about money, Amy. I want you to enjoy this week." Mom patted Amy's knee. "Dad and I are so proud of you, hon. You deserve to celebrate."

Amy was ready to celebrate, too. She'd vowed to make the most of her time with her cousins and not get dragged down by a broken heart. She didn't know how to delete the looping movie reel of highlights of the Bonnie-and-Clyde romance-that-never-was playing in her brain, but maybe she could minimize that screen and fill up the main screen with new memories, starting right now.

The rest of the week in LA passed in a blur, with Amy and her cousins playing tourist at the Griffith Observatory, Hollywood Boulevard, and Universal Studios. When she wasn't playing tourist, she was busy on social media with the fun outreach posts HeartRacer had given her.

Finally, she'd prepared a lot of questions for Lucinda, about everything from why she wanted to be a writer to why she wouldn't sell her books to Hollywood to why she never went on book tours anymore. She had a color-coded stack of index cards and was as ready as she'd ever be.

The HeartRacer publicist would be at the interview, too, and she'd told Amy not to worry. If she panicked, she'd step in. Amy figured they were the pros and knew what to do, but she hoped she wouldn't freeze up.

As for Toff…she still hadn't heard anything. Late at night, when she allowed herself ten minutes of wallow time, she'd look at their bookface photos, remembering how much fun they had, and all the kissing, and think about what she'd said to him.

Until you figure out what I mean to you, I can't see you anymore.

She hoped he figured it out soon.

*T*he Sunset Bookstore was enormous—three stories high, nearly every inch covered with shelves and shelves of books. Magazines, too, and some toys, and a café with treats and coffee. But mostly? Books.

Amy was in heaven.

She stood in the middle of the main floor of the store gaping up at the open floors above her, where she could see even more people browsing. Escalators ran up one side of the store. Everywhere she turned, she saw readers. Her people. Her planet.

"You must be Amy." A tall woman with short silver hair and a wide smile approached her and her family. "I recognize

that beautiful red hair. I'm Katrina, Lucinda's publicist."
Katrina greeted Mom and the rest of her family, then put a
hand on Amy's shoulder. "Ready to meet Lucinda?"

Tingles raced up and down Amy's spine, spreading out to
her fingertips and the top of her head. This was it.

"Yes."

She'd never been readier for anything in her life.

Katrina led Amy through the crowded store, past the rows
and rows of chairs set up for the signing. Posters of Lucinda's
book covers were on the walls, and tables full of her books
lined either side of the space. She followed Katrina down a
cluttered hallway. A few employees glanced up to say hi, a
girl with rainbow-dyed hair giving her a thumbs-up.

"Love those Redhead Recs!"

Katrina stopped outside a closed door. "We call it a green
room, but it's really just a break room." She grinned. "Ready?"
She bit her lip, looking as excited as Amy felt.

Katrina opened the door, and Amy stepped inside, coming
face-to-face with her idol.

"Hello, Amy." A tiny, birdlike woman, who looked more
like her author photo than a lot of the writers who visited
Rose's store, darted across the room and held out her hand.
"I'm so happy to meet you."

"I…I…" Amy's throat closed up. No, no, no. Not now.

C'mon, Bonnie. Bring that swagger. Toff's voice cut
through the fuzziness in her brain, clear as if he were standing
next to her, holding her hand.

The pressure in Amy's throat eased, and she sucked in
air. Squaring her shoulders, she took Lucinda's hand in hers.
"I've never been so excited to meet someone in my life!"

Lucinda blinked in surprise, then threw back her head and
laughed. "We're going to have fun," she said, "maybe even
as much fun as you had interviewing that cute surfer boy."

. . .

Half an hour later, Amy and Lucinda *were* having fun—so much fun that Amy forgot all about her color-coded index cards, and her stage fright, and how sometimes she snorted when she laughed.

They sat in two cushy chairs facing at least two hundred fans. Five minutes into the interview, Amy had stopped trembling. Ten minutes in, she started talking to Lucinda the person instead of "Lucinda the author," and twenty minutes in, they were having a raucous debate about the Harry/Hermione OTP, which Lucinda did not support.

"One hundred percent Team Ron," Lucinda said, banging her fist on the table to applause.

"I disagree!" Amy exclaimed. "Ron's cute but clueless. He could never keep up with Hermione. Team Harry for the win!"

Half the audience booed while the other half cheered, Amy egging on her Team Harry crowd and Lucinda winding up Team Ron. Laughing, Amy glanced at the HeartRacer publicist and the photographer filming the interview. They both grinned.

"As an author, I can see why readers love OTPs," Lucinda said. "Early in my career, I forced two characters to be together who clearly shouldn't have been."

Amy gasped as the audience exploded with questions and guesses. A ton of readers shipped two iconic characters from Lucinda's first series for teen readers. Was she admitting the ship should be canon?

Lucinda put up a hand, silencing the excited crowd. "I'll tell you who it was," she said, pausing dramatically and shooting Amy an impish smile, "if Amy will tell us if Bonnie and Clyde was a fake ship for the HeartRacer contest or the real thing."

Amy froze. Toff and her being a OTP had been a big part of the contest, after all. She shouldn't be surprised this came up. Still, she'd never expected to have so much riding on her personal life.

Lucinda leaned toward her, face crinkling with worry. "Honey, I'm sorry. I can tell by your face this is a painful question. You don't have to answer. I'll go ahead and give them the truth anyway."

"It's okay," Amy said. "I'll do it."

"You don't have to." Lucinda patted her hand sympathetically.

Amy took a deep breath and turned to the audience, forcing a big smile. "You know how it is with ships. I wish BonnieandClyde was real, but it's not."

Lucinda gave her a sad smile, then told the keyed-up audience that their speculation all these years was right. After all the excitement died down, the bookstore staff had people line up to get their books signed. Amy posed for photos with Lucinda, who gave her a big hug. "I love that big book brain of yours. You keep doing what you're doing."

"Fantastic job. You've got a great future ahead of you," the HeartRacer publicist added. She gave Amy her business card. "If you ever want an internship, give me a call."

Amy glowed with pride. She'd done it. All by herself. She'd brought her own swagger, asked great questions, and made people laugh.

But as her family swooped in to hug her, a stab of pain twisted in her heart.

She missed Toff.

Lucinda stepped away from the crowd and pulled Amy aside.

"Honey, don't give up on your own HEA. I know what I saw in that video." She smiled. "I assume he messed up, big-time. The thing is, we all do." She squeezed Amy's shoulder. "You need to decide if the good outweighs the bad, and if he's worth a second chance."

Lucinda glanced toward a bookshelf where a beautiful older woman watched them, smiling cryptically. "Somebody gave me one, once upon a time, and we're living our HEA today."

CHAPTER THIRTY-THREE

"**Y**ou're an asshole," Dallas said as Toff slammed his free weights back into the rack, earning glares from their fellow weightlifters at the gym.

"I know." Toff wiped his sweaty face with a towel.

Dallas was right. He was the biggest asshole on the planet, maybe the universe. Every time he closed his eyes, he saw Amy telling him that she had fallen for him. That she'd always liked him. And he'd let her go, not able to say a word. The memory tormented him, punching him in the gut over and over.

While Dallas finished his dumbbell raises, Toff studied his reflection in the mirror. Messy, unwashed hair. A stinky T-shirt he'd worn three days in a row. Dark circles under his bloodshot eyes. He'd barely slept since she'd left, and when he had, it was restless sleep haunted by dreams of a red-haired girl who ran so fast, he couldn't catch her.

He didn't know why he'd ruined the best relationship he'd ever had, but he knew he'd never forgive himself. Hoping Amy would forgive him—again—was stupid.

Dallas racked his weights and joined him, his penetrating gaze locking with Toff's in the mirror. "I don't know what she ever saw in you. You're a train wreck."

"Fuck off," Toff said, but his heart wasn't in it. His heart was in hiding, locked up in a tiny prison cell.

"Let's go, shithead." Dallas gripped Toff's shoulder and steered him across the gym floor.

"I liked you better when you stuck to your mom's no-swearing rule," Toff grumbled. Dallas laughed as they parked themselves on spinning stools at the smoothie bar.

After they placed their orders, Dallas tossed a twenty on the counter. "This one's on me."

Toff frowned. "Why?"

Dallas shrugged. "Because Viv wants me to hurt you. Because you're a sorry excuse for a human." He chewed on his compostable straw. "Because you're heartbroken and don't know how to fix the mess you made."

Deep inside his chest, Toff's heart peeked out of its cell. "Do you?"

"Do I what?" Dallas jammed his straw into his green smoothie and slurped.

"Know how I can fix things with Amy."

Dallas spun on his stool, deep in thought. Or at least that's what Toff assumed, since Dallas's brain was a computer, always processing input and output.

Short of cutting out his own heart and offering it to Amy on a platter, Toff couldn't think of anything he could do to prove he loved her. He hated that he'd never told her exactly how he felt, that he'd never said the L-word.

"I know what I'd do if I screwed up big with Viv," Dallas said, jolting Toff out of his thoughts.

"Tell me."

"I can't." Dallas shook his head. "I only know what I'd do for *my* girlfriend. You have to figure out what to do for Amy."

Toff's heart slammed the cell door shut. "So much for helping me."

"I *am* helping you, idiot." Dallas's green eyes narrowed behind his glasses. "You can't do a generic apology. You have to knock this out of the park. Do something that shows how well you know *her*." Dallas pointed to Toff's smoothie. "Aren't you going to drink that?"

"Not hungry." He hadn't eaten much at all the past few days. He knew he should sleep and eat healthy if he was going to compete, especially since he still wasn't 100 percent, but Toff couldn't find it in himself to give a crap.

Dallas's phone lit up with a text. "I'm due at Viv's in ten minutes." He glanced up. "Want to try out your groveling skills on her first?"

Toff shook his head. He needed to figure out a way to win back Amy, not face down his almost-sister, who'd rip him a new one.

Dallas hopped off his stool and grabbed Toff's smoothie. "I'll tell her this is a peace offering from you." He grinned. "Hope she doesn't throw it in my face."

Hours later, Toff unzipped his wet suit and flopped onto his towel. He was exhausted and in pain. He'd spent the afternoon channeling his frustration and cluelessness about how to apologize on his board. He'd pushed himself too far, much farther than Doc wanted when she'd cleared him to "ease back into surfing." Coach would be pissed if he saw him.

He lay on his back, one arm behind his head, the other holding his ribs.

Dad's words echoed in his head: *Why are you so smart about some things and so clueless about others?*

His legs shook and his stomach felt hollow. He really

should have drunk that smoothie earlier. He closed his eyes, listening to the gulls' cries overhead and shouts and laughter echoing down the beach. His stomach curdled. Nothing sounded appetizing…except one of Mr. McIntyre's cookies. He sighed. He'd never taste those epic cookies again.

Wait…

Buzzing tingles streaked through Toff's body, from the top of his head to the soles of his feet. He sat up abruptly, scrabbling for his phone in his backpack.

Was this what people meant by a light-bulb moment? Being zapped with a genius idea? His idea might be crazy, but somehow, it felt right.

It would take every ounce of swagger he had, but if he could pull this off…

He swiped open his phone and dialed.

Thirty minutes later, Toff met Brayden at the bottom of Monarch Lane. Brayden perched on the bus stop bench, holding a small box, wearing oversize sunglasses and a baseball cap pulled low over his eyes. A grin tugged at the corner of Toff's mouth as he approached his favorite troublemaker.

"What's the code word?" Brayden asked when Toff sat down.

"There isn't one."

Brayden clutched the box to his chest. "No code word, no merch."

Toff huffed a sharp laugh. "Brayden. Come on. I need your help, bro. You're the only person I called."

Brayden lowered his sunglasses, surveying Toff suspiciously. "What about your other friends?"

Toff shook his head. "You're my main man, dude. The

only guy who can help me."

Brayden removed his sunglasses and squinted at Toff. "I don't see how my dad's cookies are going to help you win back my sister. She can eat them whenever she wants."

"You've gotta trust me." Toff reached for the box, but Brayden clutched it tighter.

"I'm not sure I should help you." His face pinched into a glare. "You made Amy sad, Toff. I sort of want to punch you."

Toff nodded. "I want to punch me, too. You go first." He flexed a bicep. "Right here. Hard as you can."

Brayden's eyes lit up, and Toff clenched his muscles, ready to take a hit.

"Go on. Do it." Somebody needed to hit him. He deserved it. He'd half hoped Dallas would, because it would've hurt like hell and left a mark, but he hadn't. Stupid best friend.

"Nah." Brayden sighed. "I can't." He scowled at the box in his lap. "I'm probably supposed to hate you, but I don't." He swallowed and looked up, the hurt and confusion in his eyes making Toff flinch. "I've never liked somebody as much as I like you, then been so mad at them. It's confusing."

Toff wished Brayden would've punched him. It would've hurt less.

Brayden's eyebrows pinched together. "Why'd you stop liking her, Toff? I know she's weird, but she's great, too. I thought you *liked* that she was a weirdo. I mean, I saw you two kissing all the time, and you even read one of her stupid books and—"

"I *do* like her," Toff rasped, desperation threading his voice. "I like her so damn much, Brayden. I— I—love her."

He choked on the last words and turned away. How fucked up was this, spilling his guts to a kid? Finally saying the L-word but to Amy's brother instead of her? He didn't know whether to laugh or howl at the moon.

Brayden tugged on his sleeve, then handed him the pastry box. "I was kidding about a code word, but I think you just said it."

*T*off took the turnoff at the secret rock pile, his van bouncing up and down as he navigated the dirt road. Once he reached The Lodge, he headed to the employees' parking area, where Mark the security guard had said he'd meet him. As he approached the employees' entrance, the guard dog charged the fence.

"Yo, Buster. Don't you remember who brought you bacon?" Toff glanced up at the security camera mounted over the employees' door and waved.

Mark pushed through the door looking like a legit cop, except he didn't carry a gun.

"Christopher." He gave a curt nod, then motioned Toff inside. "Come on. I'll take you to the chef."

"You don't have to do that," Toff said, a spike of nervous adrenaline shooting through him. He didn't know how to talk to a chef. He hoped Mr. McIntyre's desserts would speak for themselves.

"It's not a problem," Mark said. "Lucky for you, Chef's a surfing fan."

Toff frowned, not sure what to think, but he followed Mark through the boring employees' wing into the main lodge.

"Don't stare," Mark murmured under his breath as they crossed the enormous lobby. Toff recognized several of the celebrities gathered around the huge fireplace.

Like all the locals, he knew the unwritten Shady Cove rule about ignoring celebrities, so he didn't gawk. They crossed the courtyard to the dining cabin. Well, it wasn't a cabin so much as another huge building that pretended to be a cabin.

Mark led Toff to the kitchen, which was in total chaos. People dressed in white uniforms shouted and gestured, pots boiled and sizzled on multiple burners, and the sounds of chopping and mixers assaulted them.

"Uh, maybe I should just leave this with you," Toff said, holding out the box.

Mark ignored him and caught the eye of a woman standing at a giant stove. She glanced at Toff, then hollered, "Chef! Mark and his guest are here!"

Toff's neck burned as everyone stared at him.

A petite woman dressed in chef garb that looked fancier than the others zipped down the line, pausing to snap in French at a couple of the cooks, who nodded and said, "Yes, Chef," the same way Toff imagined soldiers responded to generals.

Toff didn't speak French. A sheen of sweat slicked his skin. Was it because of the hot kitchen or his nerves? He glanced at Mark, who grinned as the chef bustled up to them, her blue eyes flashing with excitement. Her curly dark hair was cropped short, and she was pretty in the way old movie stars were. The ones who didn't mess up their faces with surgery like the ones in the main lodge.

"*Alors!*" she exclaimed. She beamed at Toff, then glanced at Mark. "This is *le surfeur*, no?"

Mark nodded. "Chef Marie, this is Christopher Nichols. Christopher, this is Chef Marie, one of the most renowned chefs in—"

"Pfft." Chef waved away Mark's compliments and clasped her hands under her chin. "*J'adore regarder les compétitions de surf. Tu es très talentueux.*"

"She loves watching local surf comps," Mark said. "She

says you're very talented."

"Oh." Toff blushed, surprised she knew who he was. "Um, *merci beaucoup*?" He hoped he pronounced it right.

Chef laughed, then pointed to the pastry box. "You want me to taste, no?"

"Go on." Mark nudged him. "She never gives outsiders the time of day. You're lucky."

Toff swallowed, reminding himself that he was here for the McIntryes, not himself. For Amy. So what if he was embarrassed? He opened the box.

"My g-girlfriend—" He stumbled over the word that he'd never said to the person he should've. "Her father is a pastry chef. He's really good." Toff's blush deepened. "I mean, I think he is." He glanced at Mark, who nodded encouragingly. "He used to work at a fancy restaurant." He blanked on the restaurant name but kept talking. "But he, um, needs a job, so I thought—"

Chef reached into the box and selected a madeleine. She examined it with narrowed eyes, held it to her nose, and sniffed, then nibbled a small bite. She raised a dark eyebrow, then nibbled another bite.

Toff held his breath. He glanced at the line cooks, who darted them curious glances.

"May I?" Chef asked, holding out her hands.

"Yeah. I mean, yes, Chef." He handed it over, hoping his hands hadn't sweated through the cardboard.

Chef smiled up at him, batting her eyelashes. "*T'es charmante*, Christopher. So charming." She closed the lid. "I will taste. I will consider." She tilted her head, studying him. "Ahh…young love. To be so young again."

Toff's stomach lurched. He had no idea if Amy still loved him or if she'd ever forgive him. But even if she didn't, he wanted this to work out for her dad. For their whole family.

Mark made a snorting noise, then turned it into a cough when Chef shot him a withering glance.

Toff's heart thudded. "Thank you, Chef. *Merci beaucoup.*"

"You are welcome." Chef laughed and patted his shoulder. "*Je suis exigent*…I am, how do you say, hard to please." She shrugged. "I do no favors, not even for *le surfeur.*"

Toff nodded, grateful she'd agreed to at least try the pastries. He pointed to the lid of the box, where he'd scrawled Mr. McIntyre's name and phone number. "This is the pastry chef."

Chef nodded and spun around. She snapped back into General mode, shouting orders in French and English as she stopped at each station to taste or scold.

"Let's go," Mark said, steering him out of the kitchen.

Once they were outside, Toff shook Mark's hand. "Thanks a lot, man. I owe you."

"Stop feeding my dogs bacon and we'll call it even." Mark crossed his arms over his chest, staring him down.

"Uh…" Toff swallowed. He thought he'd stayed out of the camera's line of sight. Guess not.

Mark gave a gruff laugh. "You're lucky I like your dad. Get outta here, *le surfeur.*"

CHAPTER THIRTY-FOUR

Viv: Book club meets tomorrow at 9:00. Amy's going to tell us all about her big interview.

Toff's heart raced like he'd just caught a barrel wave; then it stuttered and stalled. Was that an invitation? *Damn it.* If he won his heats and moved up to the finals tomorrow—which he would—he'd be surfing way past nine o'clock.

If he surfed. He was in more pain than he had been a week ago because he'd pushed it too far today.

But he didn't quit stuff. He needed to beat Mack, show him on the water what he hadn't been able to do in the restaurant. Anxious and hopeful in a way he really didn't deserve, he settled in for what he knew would be another sleepless night.

Toff's restless gaze took in the Summer Spectacular scene. Warm sand spread out in front of him. Sparkling waves rolled toward shore in perfect sets. Fans buzzed with excitement as they watched their favorite surfers get their boards ready. Photographers roamed through the crowds, catching every last detail. Groms chased one another while older local legends soaked up the attention. Judges perched on their tower for a decent view of the surf action. Sun glinted off the row of trophies waiting to be awarded.

Toff had wanted this so badly. Badly enough that he'd pushed himself too hard when he shouldn't have. He needed to beat Mack. Needed to prove he still had it. That an injury wasn't enough to take him out. That he was ready to go pro. He'd take that trophy and add it to the already huge collection in his room.

Yep. One more shiny dust collector.

For the first time in his life, winning felt…hollow. A high that would last a couple of days but fade. Then, he'd be on to the next rush. The next win.

What was wrong with him?

He'd gone out long before everyone else arrived this morning, surfing a few easy waves to see how he felt. Definitely not 100 percent.

Book club at 9:00.

"You gonna do it?" Murph asked, joining him at the registration booth.

Was he? Viv's text had given him hope that he still had a shot with Amy. His soon-to-be sister had ignored him all week, but this had to mean something. Last night, he'd Googled the book event and found pictures of Amy online. She freaking glowed with excitement. With happiness. He wished like hell he'd been there to celebrate with her.

Maybe he'd text her after the comp was over. Maybe even swing by her house if he was feeling brave enough to face her family.

*Or…*he could just go to the bookstore now.

He looked out at the waves. At the other surfers warming up. A few yards away, Mack was talking to a local reporter, grinning like he'd already won.

Was he seriously considering walking away from this?

Yes. Yes, he was.

"You know what," Toff said, "I'm out."

Murph's mouth dropped open. "You're kidding, right?"

"Nope."

"Dude. You're walking away from the chance to shove it in Mack's face."

Until you figure out what I mean to you, Toff, I can't see you anymore.

"First time for everything." Toff shot a cocky grin over his shoulder and started jogging up the beach, past Mack, who made chicken squawking sounds, past a group of girls in bikinis who called out for him to join them.

"You sure about this?" Murph yelled after him.

Toff didn't turn back. He'd never been surer about anything in his life.

"To Amy!" Viv raised her glass of sparkling cider. The Lonely Hearts Book Club cheered and toasted Amy. She was so happy to celebrate with her reader friends.

"It was incredible." Amy beamed, still floating on a cloud from her time with Lucinda. "I still can't believe I won."

"You won because of your talent, Amy. Give credit where credit is due," Rose said.

"Hell to the yeah!" Megan, their grad student member, chugged her cider, and everyone laughed. She was writing a thesis on the subversive power of the romance genre. "Hey, did HeartRacer give you any free books or swag?"

"They did." Amy jumped up to grab the box of books

she'd brought home, including a couple of gift bags from the Sunset Bookstore. As she handed one to Megan, she thought of the one Toff had brought to their dinner gone wrong. She still wondered what was in it.

Not like she'd ever find out. To her dismay, tears burned the backs of her eyes.

"Don't think about Flipper," Viv whispered, pulling her into a sideways hug. "I hope he didn't make it past his first heat."

Amy huffed a laugh, swallowing over the lump in her throat. She hoped he didn't reinjure himself by competing too soon. Even though he'd steamrolled her heart by not contacting her, she still hoped he'd surf well.

Not well enough to win another trophy, necessarily—she wasn't *that* big of a person—but not completely suck, either.

Viv released Amy from her hug and grinned, eyes shining with excitement. "Give us the full replay. Start at the beginning."

"Don't leave out anything," Rose said, grabbing one of the cupcakes Mrs. Sloane had made.

Amy laughed. What would she do without her book planet?

Toff's van chugged sluggishly up the coast, jerking erratically when he downshifted. "Come on, baby." He patted the dashboard. "Don't fail me now."

Most of the time, he loved his old beast, but today he wished for a Maserati that would hug the curving road at high speeds. At the rate he was going, he'd get to Murder by the Sea too late.

He rounded another curve. The van sputtered and groaned, then stalled.

Shit.

Toff pounded the steering wheel in frustration. He tried all his tricks to restart the engine, but his beast had rolled over to play dead. He glanced at his phone: 9:05. Book club was just starting. The meeting would last at least an hour, hopefully longer.

No way was he giving up. He could still make it in time if someone picked him up in twenty minutes or so, then drove straight to the bookstore. He tugged at his wet hair. All his surf buds were at the comp. Viv was with Amy, probably plotting his death, since he hadn't shown up yet.

Heart pounding, Toff texted a Batman signal to his ride-or-die friend who always came through, even when he screwed up massively. He hoped like hell Batman wasn't busy.

He jumped out of the van, pacing up and down. His cell rang.

Dad. *Crap.*

"I told you to turn your location services back on so I can see where the hell you are," Dad barked.

"Morning to you, too."

Dad huffed into the phone. "Are you at the Spectacular?"

"I'm not."

"You're not?" Dad sounded shocked.

"I was," Toff said, "but I left." He stopped pacing and leaned against the van. "I made a smart decision for once." Hopefully more than one. "I'm not one hundred percent. Wasn't worth it."

Dad didn't say anything for a long beat; then he chuckled into the phone. "I'll be damned. You do have a brain."

"Looks like it," Toff said, grinning.

"I'm proud of you. Sounds like it's time for a serious

conversation about you going pro"

A jolt of adrenaline surged through Toff's veins. "Awesome. Thanks, Dad."

"Love you, kid."

"Love you, too."

Toff ended the call, glanced down, and pulled at the wetsuit sticking to his skin. He'd blasted out of the comp, not wanting to waste time changing clothes. He checked his rearview mirror and grinned when he spotted the T-shirt he'd bought at Murder by the Sea after he'd given the cookies to the French chef. Rose hadn't asked any questions when he bought it, but her smile said plenty.

He'd never tried to win back a girl before, but at least he knew what to wear.

CHAPTER THIRTY-FIVE

Viv refilled the M&M's bowl with a noisy clatter. The Lonely Hearts were plowing through the snacks today. Amy chalked it up to her enthusiastic reenactment of the Lucinda event.

"So after the interview," she continued, "my aunt took us to dinner at this fancy hotel. Guess what famous celebrity I saw in the lobby?"

"Robert Redford," Mrs. Sloane guessed.

"Huh." Megan frowned. "Is he still alive?"

Rose gasped and put a hand to her heart. "Don't you dare curse him to an early grave, Megan."

Viv smirked. "He's *old*, Mom. He could bite it any day."

Rose glared. "Hush your mouth, child."

"So *anyway*," Amy continued, "my cousins and I were posing for selfies when this extremely talented, incredibly gorgeous celebrity"—she clutched her chest and pretended to swoon—"photobombed us." She dropped her voice dramatically. "Then he...he kissed me!"

Gasps filled the room. She winked at Viv, who already knew the story but was sworn to secrecy. Amy flung out her arms with a flourish. "It was—"

Crash! The door flew open, banging against the wall. Toff

rushed into the room, followed by Dallas. Amy stared, not sure whether to believe her own eyes.

"So *that's* where you snuck off to," Viv said to Dallas, who shot her a wink and put a finger to his lips.

"I'm sorry to interrupt," Toff said, his nervous gaze darting around the table, then settling on Amy, "but I need to talk to Amy. Now."

The group stared at him, stunned—except for Rose, who beamed at Toff like an indulgent mom.

Amy couldn't tear her eyes from Toff's face. He looked deranged, his blond hair a wild, tangled mess, his nose and cheeks covered in a T-shape of white sunscreen. Deranged but still annoyingly hot.

"I—um—just need to talk to her for a minute." Toff swallowed and shot a desperate glance at Viv, who pointed to Dallas.

"Guard the door, McNerd."

"Wait, what?" Toff said, his eyes wide and panicked. "I... We need a private conversation."

"You can't expect us to leave after that entrance," Mrs. Sloane said. "It's been ages since I saw a good show."

Toff grimaced, and his neck blotched red. Her gaze drifted down his neck to his shirt... *Wait.* Amy blinked, reading his shirt three times to make sure she wasn't hallucinating.

Talk Darcy to Me.

"Okay, then." Toff took a deep breath and gestured to the table. He clutched a gift bag in one hand, the same one he'd brought to dinner. "I guess you all get to hear this."

He cleared his throat and locked eyes with her. "Congratulations on your interview. I checked out social media. You did great."

He ducked his head, his cheeks coloring underneath the sunblock. "I, um"—he heaved a shaky breath—"I've done some stuff I'm not proud of. Stuff I wish I could undo." He glanced at her. "I'm sorry, Amy. So, so sorry." Desperation cracked his voice. His glorious blue eyes never left her face. "I'm an idiot, but you already know that."

Amy's heart jackhammered when he took a step toward her. Though her brain was making a case that she shouldn't give him another chance, her heart had opinions, too—very loud opinions that pounded at her rib cage. Plus, the Darcy shirt earned him about one thousand bonus points.

Toff took another deep breath. She'd never seen him this nervous.

"My whole life has been about competing," he began. "I have so many trophies and medals, I've lost count—"

"Twenty-one," Dallas stage-whispered. "I have twenty-four."

Viv grinned and swished an imaginary three-pointer.

"As I was saying," Toff continued, clearly ready to throttle both Viv and Dallas, "I'd give up all my trophies to undo what I said and did." His eyes softened. "I'd burn them into a pile of...of...metal goop or whatever, if I could have a do-over."

Amy sighed, and her heart cracked open even more, allowing Toff to step inside.

Natasha sniffed dismissively. Rose scowled and passed her the bowl of candy. "You need sugar, Natasha," Rose whispered. "A person can't live on kale and seeds."

Toff looked ready to lose it. "Maybe everyone could, um, save their comments until I'm done." He cleared his throat, taking a step toward her. "All my life, surfing was all I cared about. Winning is—was—*everything*."

The intensity pouring out of him almost knocked Amy over.

"I still want to win, but I figured something out. All the

wins in the world don't mean anything if you can't share them with the person you love." He tugged at his shirt. His ridiculous, perfect shirt. "Or celebrate with the person you love when she wins."

Amy's scalp tingled. Had he just said he loved her?

"Are you okay?" she asked. Had he reinjured himself? Or not made it past his first heats? She'd fangirled him at enough comps to know that he should still be there if he was in top form.

Toff's cheeks reddened again. Was he embarrassed? A wave of sympathy rushed through Amy, and she realized she hadn't wanted him to lose after all. She'd wanted him to win, just like she did.

"He bailed," Dallas piped up, slashing a finger across his throat. Toff launched a death ray from his eyeballs.

"Bailed?" Amy couldn't believe it. "I thought you wanted to beat Mack. Show him who's the real Surfer God."

He met her gaze, but this time his were lit with something new. Something bright and hopeful.

"Do you wish I had?"

Amy nodded, and a hint of a smile curved his lips.

"I bailed because I had something more important to do."

Hope filled her lungs, and she breathed it in deep. Her clenched heart slowly unfurled.

Toff closed the gap between them.

"Telling you I love you was a hell of a lot more important than winning." He sucked in his bottom lip. "Also I needed to apologize for being a jackass." He rolled his eyes. "Again."

His sincerity washed away any lingering doubts she had. She reached up, wrapping her arms around his neck, pulling him down for a kiss. God, she'd missed kissing him.

Somebody wolf-whistled, followed by applause…and Mrs. Sloane's surprisingly loud voice.

"Is he a better kisser than that movie star?"

Toff broke their kiss, panic flashing in his eyes. "You... you...kissed a...?"

Amy held him tight and faced their rapt audience. "This is the part where the story fades to black." She pointed to Mrs. Sloane. "Sorry, Mrs. S., but I'm putting you on probation."

She grabbed Toff's hand and dragged him out of the employee kitchen and through the crowded bookstore to the sound of laughter and more applause.

Outside, she headed straight for her kniffitied bench. The yarn had faded from all the time in the sun, but it still looked great, making her fizz with happiness when she thought back to the night Toff had rescued her.

"Did you know there are three different species of rockhopper penguins?" Amy asked, pulling him down to sit next to her.

His answering grin warmed her like sunshine blasting out from behind a cloud, lighting her up inside. "Depends on who you ask." He laced his fingers through hers. "Some experts say there are two rockhopper species, others say just one." He brushed a lock of hair behind her ear. "Are you trying to impress me?"

"Maybe."

"It's working."

"Good." Amy scooted closer and smiled up at him. "It must've been tough for you, walking away from a comp."

"Nope," he said. "It was the smart choice for my body, too. I can't keep doing dumb stuff when I go pro." He wrapped his arms around her waist and bent his head toward hers, touching his nose to hers. "After we graduate. After I take you to the Surfer Ball."

"Mm. No hot dog shack for dinner. You'll have to take me back to The Reef," she whispered. "For a redo."

"Redo at the Reef. Got a good ring to it." He smiled against her lips, then pulled back. "Did you really kiss a movie star?" he whispered, his eyes clouded with worry. Or was that jealousy?

"Yes."

His eye twitched, and he smashed his lips together.

"He was so sweet." Amy batted her eyelashes and gave him an impish smile. "Every girl in the hotel lobby wanted to snuggle with him."

Toff's shoulders drooped, and he looked away. "I guess it's none of my business what you did in LA, especially after the way I treated you."

She almost put him out of his misery, but she was having too much fun. "Want to see who it was? My cousin took pictures." She exhaled an exaggerated, dreamy sigh. "He was so…mm…*enthusiastic*. We even fell off the couch." She giggled.

His face went pale. "I—I—don't need to see pics," he said faintly.

She shoved her phone in his line of vision. "Don't be a chicken, Clyde."

He side-eyed her phone, barely peeking at the screen; then he yanked it from her hands, his grin widening as he thumbed through the photos until he threw back his head and laughed.

"Nice one, Bonnie. You had me going. Guess I deserved it." He returned her phone. "I want to be there when you tell Mrs. Sloane you kissed a dog, not a real movie star."

"Not just *any* dog," Amy corrected. "Brownie's more famous than Clifford the Big Red Dog. I had to fight off a pack of wild children to get those puppy kisses." She side-eyed Toff. "Too much tongue, though."

Toff wrapped his arms around her, pulling her in close.

His lips brushed hers. "Maybe you should show me just how much tongue you like."

"Maybe I should."

She closed her eyes, ready for the kiss, but he stopped, jumping up from the bench.

"Be right back!"

"Where are you—"

He ran toward the bookstore, weaving in and out of the crowd.

"—going?" she whispered. What the heck?

He returned in record time, out of breath, and handed her the slightly crumpled gift bag. "Here." He grinned. "Better late than never, right?"

"Finally!" Amy snatched the bag from his hands, giddy with anticipation.

"Um, I'm not great at presents—"

Amy squealed as she tore open the small package of hair clips. "I love them! Thank you!" She beamed up at him, and he rubbed the back of his neck, smiling sheepishly.

"Sit," she commanded, and he did. She leaned over and kissed him on the cheek, then removed an oddly shaped package, haphazardly wrapped and taped in tissue paper.

"Um, the next one is—" he began, then stopped when she sucked in a breath.

She stared at the heart-covered van replica, putting the pieces together. "Was this in the bag the night of our horrible dinner?"

Blushing, Toff nodded. Every swoony, squishy, starry-eyed feeling Amy had for him bubbled up and burst like a bottle of champagne, unleashing a torrent of happiness.

"What?" he asked, his eyebrows knotting.

"You said you were still trying to figure stuff out that night." She tapped the roof of the little van. "But I think you already had." She held it up, examining it closely. "*Ohh*, look. It even has a love nest." She grinned at him. "Just like yours."

Toff cleared his throat, blushing again. "I, um, just picked something that called to me, like Claire said."

Amy gave him another kiss on the cheek. "I love it. Thank you."

"You're welcome." He rubbed the back of his neck again, glancing down and fidgeting with one of her knitted flowers. "I, uh..." He looked up, his eyes searching hers. "Will you..." He winced like he was in pain. "I suck at this," he muttered.

"You don't," Amy said, her heart doing the samba in her chest. "Just say it."

"Okay." He swallowed, reaching for her hand. "I quit as your coach. You don't need one anymore. Maybe you never did." He shrugged. "But I'm glad you thought you did, because otherwise we never would've...you know." He shrugged again, neck reddening, and her heart ramped up its samba.

"Get to the point, Clyde," she whispered, leaning in and cupping his face in her hands. "Don't make me do everything."

He laughed. "Okay, Bonnie. Will you be the other half of our real, not fake, OTP?"

"Are you asking me—"

"To be my official girlfriend? Yes." He rested his forehead on hers, grazing her lips with his. "Please."

"Yes," Amy whispered as her heart leaped and twirled, making up its own dance moves. "A thousand times yes."

"One last thing," he said, pulling out his phone. "Selfie time. Kiss me like you mean it, babe."

Amy laughed, kissing him with all the feelings she didn't have to hide anymore, not at all worried about PDA in the middle of Main Street. She heard Toff's phone clatter to the ground, but he didn't stop kissing her for a long time.

When they finally stopped to catch their breath, Toff

grabbed his phone.

"Damn, this is hotter than our #BookFaceFriday photos. Prepare for our ship to explode." He blasted her with the double dimples. "Hashtag BonnieandClydeForever. Hashtag BonnieandClydeTheRealOTP."

"Hashtag SurfersAreTrouble. But worth it."

Still grinning, Toff set his phone aside and wrapped his arms around her. Amy sighed against him as they melted into another deliciously steamy, book-worthy kiss.

Happily Ever After, Happy for Now, whatever this was, Amy was embracing it.

No regrets.

EPILOGUE

*A*my, Toff, and Brayden sat on the couch in her family room eating popcorn and watching *Surf's Up*. Amy snuggled up next to Toff, who wore his *Talk Darcy to Me* shirt again. She wished her parents had taken Brayden with them to run errands.

"Pay attention, dude," Toff warned Brayden, who was playing *Cranky Cows* on his phone. Brayden ignored him, until he reached out and snatched the phone from his hands.

"Hey!" Brayden yelped, gaping at Toff.

"This movie is a classic. No distractions. No talking." He pinned Brayden with his scary coach glare, making Amy laugh.

"Whatever," her brother grumbled, grabbing a handful of popcorn from the bowl on Amy's lap.

Toff flicked an M&M at Brayden's head, then winked at Amy. "Kissing *is* allowed."

"Gross." Brayden side-eyed them, scooted to the other end of the couch, and called Goldi up to be his blockade from the potential kissers.

Halfway through the movie, even though kissing was allowed, they hadn't. Amy was okay with that, because Toff was completely, adorably sucked into the story he'd probably watched one hundred times. Brayden was, too, making Amy's heart squeeze.

"Guess what?"

Dad's booming voice startled them from their daze. Amy grabbed the remote to pause the movie as her parents rushed into the room.

"You!" Dad exclaimed, grinning and pointing at Toff. "Come 'ere, Cupcake Kid!"

Mom clasped her hands under her chin, beaming at Toff.

"What's going on?" Amy asked, baffled. Toff looked as confused as she felt.

"Is Toff in trouble?" Brayden asked. Amy shot him a stink eye.

Toff eased himself out of Amy's embrace and stood up, his gaze darting nervously between her parents. "Um, what's up?"

"What's up?" Dad echoed. "What's *up* is that thanks to you, Cupcake Kid, I have a new job! A great one. Get over here." Dad pulled Toff into a giant bear hug.

"He got a job at The Lodge," Mom told them, practically bouncing up and down. "He's the new pastry chef!"

"Wow! That's great news, Dad." Amy frowned at Toff, who Dad had released from his hug. "But what did you have to do with—"

"He gave the head chef a sample box of my pastries." Dad clapped Toff on the shoulder. "I had an interview last week after she called me out of the blue." He cocked an eyebrow at Toff. "At least, I *thought* it was out of the blue until fifteen minutes ago when she called to offer me the job and told me about my daughter's *boyfriend* visiting her in person."

Toff was blushing as red as she'd ever seen him. He glanced at her and shrugged, smiling.

"Hey!" Brayden jumped up from the couch, his eyes dancing with excitement. "Was that the box I gave you, Toff?"

Amy stood, her mind racing to connect the dots. She crossed the room, stopping inches from Toff, staring up at him with wide eyes. "You went to The Lodge? With a box of Dad's pastries for the chef to taste?"

He nodded, glancing at her parents, who looked completely enraptured.

"That *I* gave him," Brayden announced proudly. "When he called and said he needed to fix how he messed up with you."

She spun to her brother. "When was that?"

"When you were in LA with Mom for your book thing."

Heart pounding, Amy's attention bounced between her brother and Toff. She swallowed, glancing down at Toff's T-shirt.

Talk Darcy to Me.

Darcy.

Her heart shimmied and spun.

Darcy…racing off to force Wickham to marry Lydia…

…and not telling anyone he'd done it.

She put a hand on her chest, staring up at Toff. "You… you…pulled a Darcy."

He bit the corner of his lip, frowning. "I did?"

She laughed. "Yes, you idiot. Omigod!" She launched herself at him, flinging her arms around his neck. He stumbled, then wrapped her in a hug, laughing against her hair.

"Close your eyes, Mom," Brayden said ominously, "they're going to kiss."

Mom laughed, and so did Dad. Amy realized she was starting to shake. Starting to cry. She didn't care. "We need to, um, go talk," she said, releasing her grip on Toff's neck and dragging him from the room.

"Be back in an hour!" Dad called after them. "I'm whipping up a special dessert, just for the Cupcake Kid."

"I'm coming with you!" Brayden yelled, chasing after them.

"Sorry, Bray. Not this time." Amy slammed the front door in his face.

Once outside, she ran for Toff's van, clutching his hand.

"Where are we going?" he asked, opening the passenger door.

"Somewhere no one will bother us." She hopped in, pulled him toward her, and kissed him.

He groaned against her mouth, then dragged his lips from hers. "I can do that."

Five minutes later, he'd driven down the hill and pulled into a dark, abandoned parking lot full of weeds. "No one will bother us here."

"Good. Come on, Darcy."

Twenty seconds later, after closing the curtains on the van's windows, since it was still light outside, they were a half-naked tangle of arms and legs, kissing each other fiercely. Amy tugged at the waistband of Toff's shorts—

A sharp rap on the back window startled them apart. Amy sat up and peeked through the curtains.

"Oh no," she breathed. "It's the sheriff."

Toff struggled to sit up, but she pushed him back down. "Don't worry, babe," she said. "I've got this."

"You sure, Bonnie?" Toff asked, his mouth curving in a proud grin.

"Oh yeah. Don't freak out, okay? It's all cool. Just pretend you're my boyfriend and he'll *skedaddle* right out of here."

Toff was still laughing when Amy tugged on his Darcy shirt and cracked open the sliding door, peeking out.

"Yo, Officer," Toff called, waving. "It's nap time."

Officer Hernandez frowned. "You two again." He cocked an eyebrow at Amy. "Sneaking in some quality couple time, I see."

Amy stifled a giggle. "Yeah. We're, um, celebrating."

The sheriff crossed his arms over his chest. "Technically you're trespassing. This is a private lot." He pinned her with his interrogating gaze. "Humor me. Tell me what you're celebrating."

Amy glanced over her shoulder at Toff, who gave her an encouraging thumbs-up.

"My dad got a new job, and, um, it's our two-week anniversary." She flashed Toff a grin. "Officially. Unofficially, it's almost eight weeks."

The sheriff sighed, shaking his head. Did his lips quirk up?

"It's your lucky day," he said. "Today's my twenty-fifth anniversary, which I'm celebrating with my wife as soon as I'm done with you two and off the clock." He peered over Amy's shoulder at Toff. "I'm cutting you another break, Nichols."

Officer Hernandez surprised Amy by flashing her a quick grin. "I'm cutting you *two* breaks. No ticket, and I won't tweet that I just busted hashtag BonnieandClyde in action."

"Wh-what?" Amy gaped at him, stunned.

"My daughter's a fan." He shook his head. "I'm getting too old for this job. All I've heard about this summer is books, books, books." He rolled his eyes. "And how cute Bonnie and Clyde are."

He stepped back, hand on the door. "You two need to skedaddle," he said.

"Yes, sir!" Toff piped up as the door slammed shut.

Amy turned back to Toff, collapsing on top of him, shaking with laughter. He grabbed her hips, moving her right where he wanted her.

"We have to skedaddle," she said as Toff started to tug off her shirt. "Plus my dad's making dessert."

"You heard him, babe. It's his anniversary. He's not coming back to check on us." Her shirt came off. "And your dad said dessert would be ready in an hour. We've only been gone about fifteen minutes."

He gave her a ridiculous, over-the-top alpha leer, making her laugh, then swallowing her laugh with a kiss.

A sweet, hot, fade-to-black kiss.

ACKNOWLEDGMENTS

Some books take a cadre of magicians to transform them into what they are meant to be, and this was one of those books. I am tremendously grateful for the magicians who brought this book to fruition. I've wanted to tell Toff and Amy's story ever since I wrote *The Replacement Crush*, in which Toff stole every scene he was in, and Amy advocated for true love, secretly crushing on Toff.

First, thank you to Entangled Publishing, a fiercely independent publisher of HEAs and HFNs. I'm thrilled to be part of your family. This book would not exist without Liz Pelletier, who read multiple versions of this story, pushing me to dig deeper; Lydia Sharp, whose brilliant ability to separate the wheat from the chaff found the essence of this book; and Heather Howland, editorial goddess who can spin straw into gold. Heather, six years ago you pulled my first book from the slush pile. It was a joy to work on my sixth book with you.

Thank you to everyone else at Entangled, including Stacy Abrams, whose eagle eye always catches things I miss, and the dedicated marketing and production teams who give 110 percent and worked extra hard on this one. Hugs to Heather Riccio for juggling a million plates and making it look easy. Tremendous thanks to Elizabeth Turner Stokes for the gorgeous cover.

Much appreciation to all the professionals and friends who contributed their expertise: Lindsey Steinriede, professional surfer; author Claire Petri Martin for introducing me to Lindsey; the California beach lifeguards and EMTs who answered questions and let me check out their gear and cool trucks; Jeremy Howland for additional injury and recovery expertise; author Robin Bielman for reading my first draft and providing great feedback; and my dear friend, "the fabulous Dr. D." for medical expertise.

Nicole Resciniti, agent extraordinaire — I heart you. Full stop.

I have so many wonderful writer friends and wish I could list you all, but that would be a novella. For this book, a special tribe of author peeps saved my sanity: David Slayton, steady rock, always ready with a hug and a lemon drop martini, I treasure your friendship. Jenna Lincoln, cheerleader, neighbor, and naughty texter who always sees the wineglass half full, I heart you. Amalie Howard, even naughtier texter, tear-catcher, fantastic advice-giver, you are a gift.

To my family. It's been another tough year, but we've made it. Without your love and support, I never would have seen my writing dreams come true. Erik, my rock and my Puck, thank you for always being there, always making me laugh, and being the reason I write about love. Ethan…my one and only treasured child…you're ready to rock the world. Our talks about pursuing a creative life fuel my soul and make me so proud to be your mom. Carpe diem, sweetheart, every damn day. Mom, I believe in the butterflies and the perfume and know that love goes on, long after we join the stars. I love you.

Finally, dear readers, I hope you never give up on your dreams. I hope you find your swagger. I hope you find your HFNs and HEAs with partners who love and respect you. Thank you for your support. I write for you, and I love hearing from you.

New York Times bestselling author Rachel Harris delivers a passionate, emotional romance perfect for fans of Sarah Dessen or Huntley Fitzpatrick

eyes on me

BY RACHEL HARRIS

Look up the word "nerd" and you'll find Lily Bailey's picture. She's got one goal: first stop valedictorian, next stop Harvard. Until a stint in the hospital from too much stress lands her in the last place a klutz like her ever expected to be: salsa dance lessons.

Look up the word "popular" and you'll find Stone Torres's picture. His life seems perfect—star of the football team, small-town hero, lots of friends. But his family is struggling to make ends meet, so if pitching in at his mom's dance studio helps, he'll do it.

When Lily's dad offers Stone extra cash to volunteer as Lily's permanent dance partner, he can't refuse. But with each dip and turn, each moment her hand is in his, his side job starts to feel all too real. Lily shows Stone he's more than his impressive football stats, and he introduces her to a world outside of studying. But with the lines blurred, can their relationship survive the secret he's been hiding?

ASK
ME
ANYTHING

BY MOLLY E. LEE

I should've kept my mouth shut.

But Wilmot Academy's been living in the Dark Ages when it
comes to sex ed, and someone had to take matters into their own
hands. So maybe I told Dean, the smartest person in my coding
class—and the hottest guy I've ever seen—that I was starting
an innocent fashion blog. And maybe instead, I had him help
me create a totally anonymous, totally untraceable blog where
teens can come to get real, honest, nothing-is-off-limits sex advice.

The only problem? I totally don't know what I'm talking about.

Now not only is the school administration trying to shut me down,
they've forced Dean to try to uncover who I am. If he discovers
my secret, I'll lose him forever. And thousands of teens who
need real advice won't have anyone to turn to.

Ask me anything...except how to make things right.

Don't miss the next book in the fast-paced, sexy hockey series
from *New York Times* bestselling author Julie Cross

ON THIN ICE

BY JULIE CROSS

Brooke Parker never expected to find herself in the tiny town
of Juniper Falls, Minnesota. Of course, she also never expected
to lose her dad. Or for her mom to lose herself. Brooke feels
like she's losing it…until she finds Juniper Falls hockey. Juniper
Falls girls' hockey, that is.

Jake Hammond, current prince of Juniper Falls, captain of the
hockey team, and player with the best chance of scoring it big,
is on top of the world. Until one hazing ritual gone wrong lands
him injured, sitting on the sidelines, and—shocking even to
him—finding himself enjoying his "punishment" as assistant
coach for the girls' team.

As Jake and Brooke grow closer, he finds the quiet new girl is
hiding a persona full of life, ideas, and experiences bigger and
broader than anything he's ever known. But to Jake, hockey's
never just been a game. It's his whole life. And leveraging the
game for a shot at their future might be more than he can give.

Let's be friends!

 @EntangledTeen

 @EntangledTeen

 @EntangledTeen

 bit.ly/TeenNewsletter

entangled teen

an imprint of Entangled Publishing LLC